# ROMEO & JULIET

Translated

SJ Hills

and

William Shakespeare

Faithfully Translated
into Performable Modern English
Side by Side with Original Text

Includes Stage Directions

## THE TRAGEDY OF ROMEO & JULIET

Book 8 in a series of 42

This Work First Published In 2019
by DTC Publishing, London.
www.InteractiveShakespeare.com

This paperback edition first published in 2019

Typeset by DTC Publishing.

Translated from Romeo & Juliet by Shakespeare, circa 1591-1595.

Second Edition, 2019.  A-VIII

ISBN 978-1-702-53309-6

Interactive Shakespeare
Making the past accessible

**SJ Hills Writing Credits:** Dramatic Works.

Shakespeare Translated Series. Modern English With Original Text.
  Faithfully translated line by line for students, actors and fans of Shakespeare.
  ***Macbeth Translated***
  ***Romeo & Juliet Translated***
  ***Hamlet Translated***
  ***A Midsummer Night's Dream Translated***
  ***Othello Translated***

Dramatised Classic Works.
  Twenty-two dramatised works written and produced by SJ Hills for Encyclopaedia
Britannica, based on classic stories including Shakespeare, for audiences of all ages
around the world.
  ***Greatest Tales of the World. Vol 1.***
  ***Greatest Tales of the World. Vol 2.***

New Works Inspired By Classic Restoration Comedy Plays.
  ***Scarborough Fair*** - inspired by *The Relapse*
  ***To Take A Wife*** - inspired by *The Country Wife*
  ***Wishing Well*** - inspired by *Epsom Wells*
  ***Love In A Nunnery*** - inspired by *The Assignation.*

Modernised English Classic Works.
  ***The Faerie Queene***
  ***Beowulf***
  ***The Virtuous Wife***
  ***Love's Last Shift***
  ***Wild Oats***
  ***The Way of the World***

Dedicated to my four little terrors;
Melody
Eve
James
Hamilton


*"From an ardent love of literature, a profound admiration of the men who have left us legacies of thought and beauty, and, I suppose, from that feature in man that induces us to strive to follow those we most admire, and looking upon the pursuit of literature as one of the noblest in which no labour should be deemed too great, I have sought to add a few thoughts to the store already bequeathed to the world. If they are approved, I shall have gained my desire; if not, I shall hope to receive any hints in the spirit of one who loves his work and desires to progress."*

R. Hilton. 1869

# PREFACE

When we studied Shakespeare at school we had to flick back and forth to the notes at the back of the book to understand a confusing line, words we were not familiar with, expressions lost in time, or even current or political references of Shakespeare's time.

What if the text was rewritten to make each line clear without looking up anything?

There are plenty of modern translations just for this. But they are cumbersome to read, no flow, matter of fact translations (and most this author has found are of varying inaccuracy, despite being approved by exam boards).

As a writer and producer of drama, I wanted not only to translate the play faithfully line by line, but also to include the innuendos, the political satire, the puns and the bawdy humour in a way which would flow and bring the work to life for students, actors prepping for a performance or lovers of the work to enjoy today, faithful to the feel and meaning of the original script and language without going into lengthy explanations for a modern day audience.

A faithful line-by-line translation into modern phrasing that flows, along with additional staging directions making the play interesting to read, easy to understand, and very importantly, an invaluable study aid.

For me it all started at about eight or nine years of age. I was reading a comic which contained the story of Macbeth serialized in simple comic strip form. I could not wait to see what happened next so I rushed out to the public library to get a copy of the book. Of course, when I got it home I didn't even recognise it as being the same story. It made no sense to me, being written in 'Olde English' and often using 'flowery' language. I remember thinking at the time that one day I should write my version of the story for others to understand.

Years went by and I had pretty much forgotten my idea. Then quite by chance I was approached by Encyclopaedia Britannica to produce a series of dramatised classic dramas as educational aids for children learning English as a second language. Included in the selection was Romeo And Juliet which I was to condense down to fifty minutes using modern English.

This brought flooding back the memories of being eight years old again, reading my comic and planning my modern version of Shakespeare. In turn it also led me to the realisation that even if a reader could understand English well, this did not mean they could fully understand and enjoy Shakespeare. I could understand English, yet I did not fully understand some of Shakespeare's text without serious research. So what hope did a person whose first language was not English have?

After some investigation, I discovered there was a great desire around the world to understand the text fully without the inconvenience of referring to footnotes or sidelines, or worse still, the internet. How can one enjoy the wonderful drama with constant interruption? I was also surprised to discover the desire was equally as great in English speaking countries as ones whose first language was not English.

The final kick to get me started was meeting fans of Shakespeare's works who knew scripts off by heart but secretly admitted to me that they did have trouble fully understanding the meaning of some lines. Although they knew the storyline well they could miss some of the subtlety and innuendo Shakespeare was renowned for. It is hardly surprising in this day and age as many of the influences, trends, rumours, beliefs and current affairs of Shakespeare's time are not valid today.

I do not pretend my work is any match for the great master, but I do believe in the greater enjoyment for all. These great works deserve to be understood by all, Shakespeare himself wrote for all levels of audience, he would even aim his work to suit a particular audience at times – for example changing historical facts if he knew a member of royalty would be seeing his play and it would cause them any embarrassment, or of course to curry favour with a monarch by the use of flattery.

I have been as faithful as possible with my version, but the original, iambic pentameter, (the tempo and pace the lines were written for), and other Elizabethan tricks of the trade that Shakespeare was so brilliant at are not included unless vital to the text and meaning. For example, rhyming couplets to signify the end of a scene, for in Shakespeare's day there were no curtains, no lights and mostly static scenery, so scene changes were not so obvious, these couplets, though not strictly necessary, are included to maintain the feel of the original.

This makes for a play that sounds fresh to today's listening audience. It is also a valuable educational tool; English Literature courses often include a section on translating Shakespeare. I am often asked the meaning of a particular line, sometimes scholars argue over the meaning of particular lines. I have taken the most widely agreed version and the one which flows best with the story line where there is dispute, and if you read this translation before reading the original work or going to see a stage version, you will find the play takes on a whole new meaning, making it infinitely more enjoyable.

SJ Hills. London. 2018

Author's Note: This version contains stage directions. These are included purely as a guide to help understand the script better. Any director staging the play would have their own interpretation of the play and decide their own directions. These directions are my own personal interpretation and not those of Shakespeare. You may change these directions to your own choosing or ignore them completely. For exam purposes these should be only regarded as guidance to the dialogue and for accuracy should not be quoted in any studies or examinations.

*Romeo and Juliet* is a love story and a tragedy combined. Shakespeare would symbolize the words of love or a lover by using rhyme, sometimes in the form of a sonnet. The rhymes have been included in the translation in order for the reader to understand that Shakespeare had meant these lines to be poetic. As the story starts as a love story and ends in a tragedy the rhymes are concentrated near the beginning of the play.

To aid in understanding speeches and for learning lines, where possible, speeches by any character are not broken over two pages unless they have a natural break. As a result of this, gaps will be noticeable at the bottom of pages where the next speech will not fully fit onto the page. This was intentional. A speech can not be fully appreciated if one has to turn the page back and forth when studying or learning lines.

The joy of having a highly accurate English translation is that it can be translated into other languages more readily, foreign language versions of the modern text will be published later this year.

Coming soon, *Romeo and Juliet for All Ages* by SJ Hills, for the script in modern English with study note stickies, illustrations and simplified text running alongside the main text for younger readers to share with students, actors and fans of the great work.

And also available soon, a wonderful, innovative app, a huge undertaking and the very first of its kind, which will include full, new interactive filmed versions of Shakespeare's plays in both original and modern English.

For further info

www.InteractiveShakespeare.com

www.facebook.com/InteractiveShakespeare

@iShakes1 on Twitter

# DRAMATIS PERSONAE

**Ruling Classes**

| | |
|---|---|
| PRINCE ESCALUS | Prince and Governor of Verona |
| MERCUTIO | Relative of the Prince and friend of Romeo |
| COUNT PARIS | Relative of the Prince, suitor of Juliet |
| PAGE | Errand boy to Count Paris |

**The Montagues**

| | |
|---|---|
| OLD MONTAGUE | Head of the Montague family, Romeo's father |
| LADY MONTAGUE | Montague's wife, Romeo's mother |
| ROMEO | Montague's only son and heir |
| BENVOLIO | Montague's Nephew, cousin to Romeo |
| BALTHASAR | Errand boy to Romeo |
| ABRAHAM | Montague's servant |

**The Capulets**

| | |
|---|---|
| OLD CAPULET | Head of the Capulet family, Juliet's father |
| LADY CAPULET | Capulet's wife, Juliet's mother |
| JULIET | Capulet's only daughter |
| TYBALT | Nephew of Capulet, cousin to Juliet |
| NURSEMAID | Nursemaid and nanny to Juliet |
| PETRUCCIO | Errand boy to Tybalt |
| CAPULET'S COUSIN | A guest at the feast |
| SAMPSON | Capulet servant |
| GREGORY | Capulet servant |
| 1ST SERVANT | Capulet servant – (Peter, head servant, a comic role) |
| 2ND SERVANT | Capulet servant - |
| 3RD SERVANT | Capulet servant - Anthony |
| 4TH SERVANT | Capulet servant - Potpan |

**Others**

| | |
|---|---|
| FRIAR LAURENCE | A Franciscan Monk |
| FRIAR JOHN | A Franciscan Monk |
| CHEMIST | Owner of an apothecary |
| MUSICIANS | Three musicians for the wedding party |
| GUARDS | The city police |
| CITIZENS | Townsfolk of Verona |
| MISC | Maskers, Torchbearer, Pages, etc. |

# Historical Notes

The story of Romeo and Juliet was first introduced to the English language by *Arthur Brooke* in 1562, whose long rambling poem, *The Tragical Historie of Romeus and Juliet,* was itself an adaptation of a French translation by *Pierre Boaistuau* of an old story retold by the Italian Monk *Matteo Bandello*. Bandello had fled to France to escape persecution, bringing with him stories he had collected together. In 1694 when Shakespeare's version of the tale was first performed in Elizabethan England the basic story was already well known and many different versions had been written. Many details of Shakespeare's plot are taken directly from Brooke's poem, such as Romeo and Juliet meeting at a ball, their secret marriage, Romeo's fight with Tybalt, the sleeping potion, and the timing of the lovers' suicides. *Brooke* mentions a stage performance of the story which predates Shakespeare but no copies or records of it exist.

Shakespeare would go on to base more of his plays on stories originally collected and retold by *Bandello*, from translations he obtained by various English authors.

Various rumours exist of the story being based on real life events, one stating it is based on two 3$^{rd}$ Century warring families; the *Capeletti* and the *Montecci*, others claiming it happened much closer to Shakespeare's time, though one thing is for sure, if it was originally a true story, it had gone through many translations, variations and embellishments as it was passed along, and saying something is based on a true story captures the imagination and helps sales.

Shakespeare's use of pre-existing material was not considered a lack of originality. In Elizabethan times copyright law did not exist, copying whole passages of text was frequently practiced and not considered theft as it is today. Nowadays, stage and movie productions are frequently 'adaptations' from other sources, the only difference being the need to obtain permission or rights to do so, unless the work is out of copyright.

The real skill Shakespeare displays is in how he adapts his sources in new ways, displaying a remarkable understanding of human psyche and emotion, and including a talent at building characters, adding characters for effect, dramatic pacing, tension building, interspersed by short bouts of relief before building the tension even further, and in the case of *Romeo and Juliet* condensing the action down from the original nine months of the source material to four intense action packed days, and, above all of course, his extraordinary ability to use and miss-use language to his and dramatic, bawdy or playful advantage.

It has been said Shakespeare almost wrote screenplays, predating modern cinema by over 400 years. However you view it, he wrote a powerful story and understood how to play on human emotions and weaknesses.

# CONTENTS

# PROLOGUE

THE CHORUS COMES ON STAGE AND RECITES A VERSE

*Note: The 'Chorus' was a single person acting as a narrator to introduce the story, or it could be the entire cast together, there were no hard and fast rules. This was common practice in tragedies of the time, and would prepare the audience. However, as Romeo and Juliet is also a romance the prologue is written in the format of a sonnet, which Shakespeare was rather adept at.*

*Similar to us reading a preview of a film before we go to see it so we have an idea of the story beforehand, this intro/prologue prepares the audience for the action that is to come, rather than throw them in at the start with no clear idea of what is happening until the plot unfolds. The audience will have some idea of why the two families are warring at the start of the play because the prologue explains the story is about two lovers from two warring households.*

### CHORUS

*Two households, both alike in dignity*
*In fair Verona, where we set our scene,*
*Their ancient grudge sparks new hostility,*
*Where noble blood leaves noble hands unclean.*

*And from the fated loins of these two foes*
*A pair of doomed young lovers get their life,*
*Whose tragic and ill-fated loving throes*
*Do with their death resolve their parents' strife.*

*The fearful passage of their death-cursed love,*
*And endless seething of their parents' rage,*
*Which till their children's end nowt could remove,*
*Is now the two hours' action on our stage.*

*Therefore, if you with patient ears attend,*
*What I miss here, our toil shall strive to mend.*

### CHORUS

*Two households, both alike in dignity*
*In fair Verona, where we lay our scene,*
*From ancient grudge break to new mutiny,*
*Where civil blood makes civil hands unclean.*

*From forth the fatal loins of these two foes*
*A pair of star-crossed lovers take their life;*
*Whose misadventured piteous overthrows*
*Doth with their death bury their parents' strife.*

*The fearful passage of their death-marked love,*
*And the continuance of their parents' rage,*
*Which, but their children's end, naught could remove,*
*Is now the two hours' traffic of our stage;*

*The which if you with patient ears attend,*
*What here shall miss, our toil shall strive to mend.*

*Note: Although the Chorus claims two hours of action, the play cannot be performed in full within two hours.*

# ACT I

## ITALY

VERONA, WHERE OUR TALE IS SET

SIXTEENTH CENTURY A.D.

# ACT I

## ACT I SCENE I

### THE STREETS OF VERONA. EARLY SUNDAY MORNING.

THE SCENE STARTS WITH TWO MALE STAFF FROM THE CAPULET HOUSEHOLD WALKING ALONG AN ITALIAN COBBLED 16TH CENTURY STREET EARLY SUNDAY MORNING SPOILING FOR A FIGHT.

THEY SEEM TO BE UPSET AT TREATMENT BY MEMBERS OF THE RIVAL MONTAGUE HOUSEHOLD WHO HAVE NO AUTHORITY OVER THEM.

SAMPSON IS FULL OF BRAVADO BUT NOT ACTUALLY VERY BRAVE, GREGORY CONSTANTLY TAUNTS SAMPSON'S BRAVADO WITH JOKING WORDPLAY.

THEY BOTH CARRY SHEATHED SWORDS AND SMALL SHIELDS KNOWN AS BUCKLERS, WHICH WOULD BE ADORNED WITH THE EMBLEM OF THE HOUSEHOLD THEY WORKED FOR - THE CAPULET FAMILY.

IT IS JULY, A SWELTERING HOT MONTH, IN THIS OPPRESSIVE HEAT TEMPERS ARE EASILY FRAYED.

---

*Note: To show the two characters are comedic, Shakespeare writes their lines in prose rather than the usual blank verse – a form of poetry which doesn't rhyme except for dramatic effect.*

*Deliberate bawdy words are <u>underlined</u>, rhymed lines are in italics.*

---

| | |
|---|---|
| **SAMPSON**<br>(*angry*) We'll not carry coal for them, I promise you, Gregory! | SAMPSON<br>Gregory, on my word, we'll not carry coals. |

*Note: 'Carriers of coals' was a common term for the lowliest of menials.*

| | |
|---|---|
| **GREGORY**<br>(*sarcastic*) No, Sampson. We're not colliers. | GREGORY<br>No, for then we should be colliers. |
| **SAMPSON**<br>They make me so hot under the 'collar' I'd draw. | SAMPSON<br>I mean, an we be in choler, we'll draw. |

*Note: 'Choler' meant angry, since it is not in use today, but is used in the wordplay, a familiar modern equivalent is used in the translation.*

*'Draw' – draw his sword, remove it from it's sheath ready to use.*

SAMPSON PUTS HIS HAND ON HIS SWORD TO SHOW HE IS READY TO USE IT.

**GREGORY**
Draw your sword an' you'll be drawing your neck from the hangman's 'collar'.

GREGORY
Ay, while you live, draw your neck out of collar.

*Note: The hangman's "collar" is slang for the rope noose used to hang a man.*

**SAMPSON**
I strike quickly, when I'm so moved.

SAMPSON
I strike quickly, being moved.

SAMPSON IMITATES A PRETEND THRUST OF HIS SWORD.

*Note: 'Moved' here means riled or angered into action.*

**GREGORY**
But you're not quickly *'moved'* to strike.

GREGORY
But thou art not quickly moved to strike.

GREGORY IMITATES A LESS ENTHUSIASTIC PRETEND THRUST.

**SAMPSON**
I am when moved by a dog of the Montague family.

SAMPSON
A dog of the house of Montague moves me.

SAMPSON SPITS ON THE GROUND IN BRAVADO.

*Note: Gregory now deliberately takes the alternative meaning of 'moved'.*

**GREGORY**
But to move, you take a step. To show courage, you stand your ground. So, if you're moved, it means you run away.

GREGORY
To move is to stir, and to be valiant is to stand; therefore, if thou art moved, thou runnest away.

**SAMPSON**
Then a dog of the Montague family moves me to stand still! I'll keep to the wall and force any Montague man or woman to step in the road.

SAMPSON
A dog of that house shall move me to stand. I will take the wall of any man or maid of Montague's.

*Note: The road was full of sewage (Elizabethan properties in England had overhanging upper floors so waste could be ejected from windows directly into the road). Menial workers would be expected to step into the road to let their masters 'keep to the wall' as they pass. Shakespeare, not being familiar with Italy, was writing from his experience in England, and writing for an English audience.*

GREGORY

That shows you're a coward; they say, 'the weakest goes to the wall'.

GREGORY

That shows thee a weak slave, for the weakest goes to the wall.

*Note: 'Goes to the wall', a common saying for being weaker, backing up until you can back up no further – 'backs against the wall'.*

SAMPSON

That's true. Then women, being the weaker sex, should all be <u>thrust</u> against the wall. Therefore I'll push Montague's men from the wall, and <u>thrust</u> his maids against the wall.

SAMPSON

'Tis true; and therefore women, being the weaker vessels, are ever thrust to the wall; therefore I will push Montague's men from the wall, and thrust his maids to the wall.

SAMPSON THRUSTS HIS PELVIS FORWARD IN BAWDY EMPHASIS.

*Note: In Shakespeare's time women were regarded as 'the weaker sex', having little or no rights. They were the property of their father until married, at which point they and everything they owned became the property of their husband. From this we have the father 'giving away the bride' at weddings.*

*'Weaker vessel' is a term lifted from the Bible, where the disciple Peter urges husbands to respect and protect their wives, being the weaker vessels.*

GREGORY

But our squabble is with his men, not his women.

GREGORY

The quarrel is between our masters and us their men.

GREGORY THRUSTS HIS PELVIS FORWARD TO MOCK SAMPSON.

SAMPSON

It's all the same to me. I'll be a tyrant. When I've fought with the men, I'll be <u>civil</u> with the maidens...

SAMPSON

'Tis all one. I will show myself a tyrant: when I have fought with the men, I will be civil with the maids -

SAMPSON MIMICS CARESSING A WOMAN.

SAMPSON (CONT'D)

...And then cut off their heads!

SAMPSON

...I will cut off their heads.

GREGORY FEIGNS SHOCK.

**GREGORY**
The heads of the maidens?

**GREGORY**
The heads of the maids?

**SAMPSON**
Yes, the heads of the maidens, or their maidenheads. Take it in whatever sense you like.

**SAMPSON**
Ay, the heads of the maids, or their maidenheads; take it in what sense thou wilt.

*Note: Maidenhead means female virginity.*

**GREGORY**
(*bawdy*) They can take the sense from how it feels.

**GREGORY**
They must take it in sense that feel it.

**SAMPSON**
(*bawdy*) They'll feel me while I'm able to stand erect, and I am well known as a good bit of flesh.

**SAMPSON**
Me they shall feel while I am able to stand; and 'tis known I am a pretty piece of flesh.

**GREGORY**
Are you sure it's not a good 'bit of fish', and you're not a limp pilchard?

**GREGORY**
'Tis well thou art not fish; if thou hadst, thou hadst been poor-john.

GREGORY WAGGLES HIS LITTLE FINGER MOCKINGLY.

*Note: 'Poor John' was cheap, dried, hake fish. Due to over fishing it is not common anymore.*

ENTER ABRAHAM AND BALTHAZAR
BOTH SERVANTS OF THE RIVAL MONTAGUE FAMILY.

GREGORY INDICATES HIS SWORD EXPECTING TROUBLE.

**GREGORY (CONT'D)**
Get your tool out now. Here come two of Montague's men.

**GREGORY**
Draw thy tool; here comes of the house of Montagues.

SAMSON IN TURN INDICATES HIS SWORD.

**SAMPSON**
My naked weapon is exposed. Start a fight, I'll back you.

**SAMPSON**
My naked weapon is out; quarrel, I will back thee.

*Note: Despite his previous words of bravado, Sampson has now asked Gregory to start the fight. But Gregory doesn't have much confidence in Sampson.*

GREGORY
How? Turn your back and run?

GREGORY
How? Turn thy back and run?

SAMPSON
(*full of pretend bravado*) Don't worry about me, Gregory!

SAMPSON
Fear me not.

GREGORY
(*scathing*) No, by God, I do worry about you!

GREGORY
No, marry; I fear thee!

*Note: 'Marry' is a light curse, a corruption of 'by Mary' (biblical mother of Jesus). Profanities and swearing were strictly forbidden, the audience knew it would have meant a bigger curse.*

SAMPSON
Let's get the law on our side. Let them start the fight.

SAMPSON
Let us take the law of our sides; let them begin.

*Note: Sampson has now descended from himself starting a fight with any Montague on sight, to Gregory starting the fight, to the enemy starting it.*

GREGORY
I will sneer at them as they pass, let them react if they wish.

GREGORY
I will frown as I pass by, and let them take it as they list.

SAMPSON
If they dare. No, I'll stick my finger up at them. They'd be disgraced if they ignored that.

SAMPSON
Nay, as they dare. I will bite my thumb at them, which is disgrace to them if they bear it.

SAMPSON DEMONSTRATES TO GREGORY WITH HIS FINGER, THEN REALISES HIS RIVALS ARE LOOKING RIGHT AT HIM ACCUSINGLY.

*Note: Originally biting the thumb was an insult, performed by placing the thumb in the mouth and catching the nail on the upper teeth while flicking it forward causing it to click. A modern equivalent was used here instead.*

ABRAHAM
Are you sticking your finger up at us, sir?

ABRAHAM
Do you bite your thumb at us, sir?

SAMPSON HOLDS HIS FINGER THERE, NOT SURE WHAT TO DO NOW.

**SAMPSON**

I am sticking my finger up, sir.

**ABRAHAM**

Are you sticking your finger up at *us*, sir?

**SAMPSON**

I do bite my thumb, sir.

**ABRAHAM**

Do you bite your thumb at us, sir?

SAMPSON NEEDS A WAY OUT OF THIS PREDICAMENT.

**SAMPSON**

(*aside to Gregory*) Is the law on our side if I say 'yes'?

**GREGORY**

(*aside to Sampson*) No.

**SAMPSON**

(*aside to Gregory*) Is the law of our side if I say 'Ay'?

**GREGORY**

(*aside to Sampson*) No.

GREGORY IS AMUSED AT SAMPSON'S SQUIRMING.

**SAMPSON**

No, Sir. I am not sticking my finger up at *you*, sir. (*pauses*) But I am sticking my finger up, sir.

**SAMPSON**

No, sir, I do not bite my thumb at you, sir; but I bite my thumb, sir.

GREGORY, WHO IS BRAVER THAN SAMPSON, STEPS IN.

**GREGORY**

Are you picking a fight, sir?

**ABRAHAM**

A fight, sir? No, sir.

**GREGORY**

Do you quarrel, sir?

**ABRAHAM**

Quarrel, sir? No, sir.

SAMPSON BECOMES BRAVER AT THEIR APPARENT UNWILLINGNESS TO FIGHT
AND NOW PUTS HIS FINGER DOWN.

**SAMPSON**

If you are, sir, I'm ready for you. The household we serve is as good as yours.

**SAMPSON**

But if you do, sir, I am for you. I serve as good a man as you.

ABRAHAM BAITS SAMPSON.

**ABRAHAM**

Not better than ours.

**ABRAHAM**

No better.

SAMPSON STRUGGLES WITH BRAVADO, REALISING HE IS BEING SET UP.

| | |
|---|---|
| **SAMPSON**<br>Well, sir... | SAMPSON<br>Well, sir. |

---

ENTER BENVOLIO, A MEMBER OF THE MONTAGUE FAMILY.

> *Note: As Benvolio enters at this point the next line is highly confusing to readers, they will assume Gregory means Benvolio. But Benvolio is not from the Capulet household which Gregory and Samson work for.*

| | |
|---|---|
| **GREGORY**<br>(*aside to Sampson*) Say 'better', here comes one of our master's family. | GREGORY<br>[*Aside to Sampson.*] Say `better'; here comes one of my master's kinsmen. |

> *Note: Gregory has obviously spotted a member of the Capulet family (probably Tybalt who enters shortly) and so is newly filled with bravado.*

| | |
|---|---|
| **SAMPSON**<br>(*brave now*) Yes, I would say ours is better, sir. | SAMPSON<br>Yes, better, sir. |
| **ABRAHAM**<br>You lie! | ABRAHAM<br>You lie. |
| **SAMPSON**<br>Draw your swords, if you are real men. | SAMPSON<br>Draw, if you be men. |

---

SAMPSON STEPS INTO THE ROAD DRAWING HIS SWORD, WAVING IT
THREATENINGLY AND CALLING TO HIS FRIEND BEHIND HIM BAWDILY.

| | |
|---|---|
| **SAMPSON (CONT'D)**<br>Gregory, remember your <u>thrusting</u> blow. | SAMPSON<br>Gregory, remember thy washing blow. |

> *Note: 'Washing' is the effect something has moving through air or water creating a wash. It is also used as bawdy innuendo as the wash repeatedly pounding a beach. In a time when censorship was very strict and a strict code of conduct was mandatory in plays, how the line was delivered by the actor determined the bawdy (or not) meaning.*

---

ABRAHAM, BALTHAZAR AND GREGORY DRAW THEIR SWORDS.

BENVOLIO SEES THE TROUBLE STARTING
AND DRAWS HIS OWN SWORD TO INTERVENE.

| | |
|---|---|
| **BENVOLIO**<br>Stop you fools! Put away your swords! Use your heads! | BENVOLIO<br>Part, fools!<br>Put up your swords; you know not what you do. |

ENTER TYBALT, OF THE CAPULET FAMILY. (WE ASSUME HE'D BEEN IN THE BACKGROUND WATCHING, ITCHING FOR AN EXCUSE TO JOIN IN THE AFFRAY)

TYBALT DRAWS HIS SWORD, SINGLING OUT HIS RIVAL, BENVOLIO.

**TYBALT**

(*to Benvolio*) What! You are preparing to fight with these lowly scoundrels? Turn around, Benvolio, (*indicates his sword*) and look death in the face!

**TYBALT**

What, art thou drawn among these heartless hinds?

Turn thee, Benvolio, look upon thy death

*Note: 'Heartless hinds' is clever wordplay, a hart is a male deer and a hind is a female deer. Calling them female without their male to protect them.*

**BENVOLIO**

I am trying to keep the peace. Put away your sword, Tybalt, or use it to help me part these men.

**BENVOLIO**

I do but keep the peace. Put up thy sword, Or manage it to part these men with me.

**TYBALT**

What! Your sword drawn and you talk of peace? I hate that word, as I hate hell, all Montagues, and you. Have this, coward!

**TYBALT**

What, drawn, and talk of peace? I hate the word As I hate hell, all Montagues, and thee. Have at thee, coward!

TYBALT ATTACKS BENVOLIO. THEY ALL FIGHT WITH SWORDS. AS THEY DO, CONCERNED MEMBERS OF THE PUBLIC COME RUNNING OUT.

**TOWNSFOLK**

Grab weapons, they're fighting again!
– Go men! - Beat them down!
- Stop the Capulets!
- Stop the Montagues!

**CITIZENS**

Clubs, bills, and partisans!
Strike! Beat them down!
Down with the Capulets!
Down with the Montagues!

*Note: 'Clubs, bills and partisans' (names of weapons) was a street cry in Elizabethan times to call the public out if a riot broke out.*

THE TOWNSFOLK GRAB WEAPONS AND RUN INTO A FIGHT WHICH SWIFTLY ESCALATES INTO A BIG BATTLE.

AN ALARM BELL RINGS OUT.

OLD CAPULET (THE HEAD OF THE CAPULET FAMILY) ARRIVES IN HIS NIGHTGOWN TO INVESTIGATE THE NOISE, LADY CAPULET (HIS WIFE) FOLLOWS BEHIND HIM.

| | |
|---|---|
| **OLD CAPULET**<br>What is all this noise? | **CAPULET**<br>What noise is this? |

OLD MONTAGUE (THE HEAD OF THE MONTAGUE FAMILY) ARRIVES FROM THE OPPOSITE DIRECTION, ALSO IN NIGHT ATTIRE, BRANDISHING A SWORD TOWARDS OLD CAPULET.

LADY MONTAGUE (HIS WIFE) HOLDS HIM BACK.

> Note: This melee makes better sense if you imagine the fight breaking out in a large town square where the Capulet household is one side and the Montague another. How else would the elders hear it and arrive so quickly? It was the Italian tradition from Roman times to base a drama around a town square, so it seems Shakespeare was following tradition.

| | |
|---|---|
| **OLD CAPULET**<br>(*Seeing Old Montague*) Get me my long sword now! | **CAPULET**<br>Give me my long sword, ho! |
| **LADY CAPULET**<br>A crutch more like at your age! Why call for your sword? | **LADY CAPULET**<br>A crutch, a crutch! Why call you for a sword? |
| **OLD CAPULET**<br>My sword, wife, I say! Old Montague has arrived and brandishes his sword at me! | **CAPULET**<br>My sword, I say! Old Montague is come,<br>And flourishes his blade in spite of me. |
| **OLD MONTAGUE**<br>(*a distance from Capulet*) You foul villain, Capulet!<br>(*to Lady Montague*) Let me at him, wife, let go of me! | **MONTAGUE**<br>Thou villain Capulet!<br>[*to Lady Montague*]   Hold me not; let me go |

LADY MONTAGUE STILL HOLDS HER HUSBAND BACK.

| | |
|---|---|
| **LADY MONTAGUE**<br>(*holding Montague*) You'll not move one foot to pick a fight. | **LADY MONTAGUE**<br>Thou shalt not stir one foot to seek a foe. |

ENTER PRINCE ESCALUS, THE RULER OF VERONA, WITH HIS ENTOURAGE.
A TRUMPET HERALDS HIS ARRIVAL.

**PRINCE ESCALUS**

(*loud over the din*) Rebellious subjects! Enemies of peace! Defiling your swords with your neighbour's blood. Are they deaf?
(*shouting*) Hear me! You men, you beasts! Quenching the fire of your destructive rage with the purple fountains spurting from your veins!

**PRINCE**

Rebellious subjects, enemies to peace, Profaners of this neighbour-stained steel - Will they not hear? What ho! You men, you beasts, That quench the fire of your pernicious rage With purple fountains issuing from your veins!

THE FIGHTING CONTINUES.

THE PRINCE SHOUTS DIRECTLY AT CAPULET AND MONTAGUE.

**PRINCE ESCALUS (CONT'D)**

On pain of torture, throw down your bloody weapons from your bloody hands and hear the judgement of I, your angry Prince and Ruler!

**PRINCE**

On pain of torture, from those bloody hands Throw your mistempered weapons to the ground, And hear the sentence of your moved prince.

MONTAGUE AND CAPULET LOWER THEIR SWORDS, FOLLOWED BY THEIR SERVANTS, ALL MUTTERING QUIET DEFIANCE. SILENCE RETURNS.

**PRINCE ESCALUS (CONT'D)**

(*angry*) Three street brawls because of a chance word by your men, old Capulet and you, Montague. Three times the peace and quiet of our streets has been disturbed, forcing the elders of Verona to cast aside walking sticks to take up old weapons, long since rotten from disuse, in peaceful old rotted hands, to part your rotten hate. If you ever disturb our streets again you will pay the price for peace with your lives! Now the rest of you leave. You, Capulet, will come with me now, and Montague, you will come at noon to receive my judgement at the old Freetown Magistrates Court.
(*angrier*) I won't tell you again, the rest of you leave now or pay with your lives!

**PRINCE**

Three civil brawls bred of an airy word By thee, old Capulet and Montague, Have thrice disturbed the quiet of our streets And made Verona's ancient citizens Cast by their grave-beseeming ornaments To wield old partisans, in hands as old, Cankered with peace, to part your cankered hate.
If ever you disturb our streets again, Your lives shall pay the forfeit of the peace. For this time all the rest depart away. You, Capulet, shall go along with me; And, Montague, come you this afternoon To know our further pleasure in this case, To old Freetown, our common judgement-place.

Once more, on pain of death, all men depart.

27

THE THRONG DISPERSES IN ALL DIRECTIONS. OLD MONTAGUE, LADY
MONTAGUE AND BENVOLIO TALK AS THEY WALK FROM THE BATTLE SCENE.

Note: Freetown is a translation of Villa Franca, the town in the original Italian tale
upon which Brooks' poem and subsequently this play was based.

### OLD MONTAGUE

Who restarted this old quarrel, Benvolio?
Tell me, nephew, were you here when it
began?

### BENVOLIO

(*panting from fighting*) When I arrived
servants of your old adversary, Capulet,
were fighting with your own. I drew my
sword to separate them when suddenly the
fiery Tybalt appeared, his sword already
drawn. He came at me in a threatening
manner, swearing oaths, cutting the wind
with wild swings, making the air hiss in
rage. Then while we were exchanging
thrusts and blows more and more joined
the fighting until finally the Prince arrived
and parted both parties.

### LADY MONTAGUE

*And where's Romeo? Have you seen him today?*
*I'm right glad that he was not part of this fray.*

### BENVOLIO

Madam, an hour before the golden sun
peered above the Eastern horizon, a
troubled mind drove me to take a walk,
where, beneath the sycamore grove on the
west side of the city I saw your son taking
an early stroll. I made towards him, but
when he saw me he stole into the cover of
the wood.
I assumed he felt as I did, seeking to be
where others were not - even my own
weary self being one too many. So I walked
on alone pursuing my thoughts, gladly
avoiding the one so glad to avoid me.

### MONTAGUE

Who set this ancient quarrel new abroach?
Speak, nephew; were you by when it began?

### BENVOLIO

Here were the servants of your adversary
And yours, close fighting ere I did approach.
I drew to part them; in the instant came
The fiery Tybalt with his sword prepared,
Which, as he breathed defiance to my ears,
He swung about his head and cut the winds,
Who, nothing hurt withal, hissed him in scorn.
While we were interchanging thrusts and blows,
Came more and more, and fought on part and
 part,
Till the prince came, who parted either part.

### LADY MONTAGUE

*O where is Romeo? Saw you him today?*
*Right glad I am he was not at this fray.*

### BENVOLIO

Madam, an hour before the worshipped sun
Peered forth the golden window of the east,
A troubled mind drive me to walk abroad,
Where, underneath the grove of sycamore
That westward rooteth from this city side,
So early walking did I see your son.
Towards him I made, but he was ware of me
And stole into the covert of the wood.
I, measuring his affections by my own,
Which then most sought where most might not
 be found,
Being one too many by my weary self,
Pursued my humour not pursuing his,
And gladly shunned who gladly fled from me.

| | |
|---|---|
| **OLD MONTAGUE** | **MONTAGUE** |
| He's been seen there on many mornings, his tears adding to the fresh morning dew, and his deep sighs adding to the clouds in the cool morning air. But as the cheerful sun rises in the east throwing open the bed curtains of the dawn goddess, Aurora, my heavy hearted son steals home away from the light. There he locks himself in his bedroom, shutting out daylight, creating his own artificial night. | Many a morning hath he there been seen, With tears augmenting the fresh morning's dew, Adding to clouds more clouds with his deep sighs; But all so soon as the all-cheering sun Should in the furthest east begin to draw The shady curtains from Aurora's bed, Away from light steals home my heavy son, And private in his chamber pens himself, Shuts up his windows, locks fair daylight out, And makes himself an artificial night. |
| *This doom and gloom of his bodes not well,* *Good counsel is needed to break the spell.* | *Black and portentous must this humour prove* *Unless good counsel may the cause remove.* |
| **BENVOLIO** | **BENVOLIO** |
| My dear Uncle, do you know the cause? | My noble uncle, do you know the cause? |
| **OLD MONTAGUE** | **MONTAGUE** |
| I neither know it, and nor will he tell me. | I neither know it nor can learn of him. |
| **BENVOLIO** | **BENVOLIO** |
| You have questioned him about this? | Have you importuned him by any means? |
| **OLD MONTAGUE** | **MONTAGUE** |
| I have, and so have many others, but he confides only in himself. So, truthfully I cannot say, as he keeps it so secretive and private. As hidden from the world as the rosebud eaten inside by an envious worm before it can spread its sweet petals to the air and reveal its beauty to the sun. | Both by myself and many other friends; But he, his own affections counsellor, Is to himself - I will not say how true - But to himself so secret and so close, So far from sounding and discovery, As is the bud bit with an envious worm Ere he can spread his sweet leaves to the air Or dedicate his beauty to the sun. |
| *If we could learn what makes his sorrow grow,* *We'd willingly give treatment for his woe.* | *Could we but learn from whence his sorrows grow,* *We would as willingly give cure as know.* |

---

ENTER ROMEO IN THE DISTANCE, DEEP IN THOUGHT.

---

| | |
|---|---|
| **BENVOLIO** | **BENVOLIO** |
| *Look, here he comes. So please, do step aside* *I'll find his grievance, and not be denied.* | *See where he comes. So please you, step aside;* *I'll know his grievance or be much denied.* |
| **OLD MONTAGUE** | **MONTAGUE** |
| *I wish you the luck, that here by your stay* *You find the truth. Dear wife, come let's away.* | *I would thou wert so happy by thy stay* *To hear true shrift. Come, madam, let's away.* |

OLD MONTAGUE AND LADY MONTAGUE LEAVE.

> Note: Shakespeare often uses the word 'shrift' to confess something, although its common use is only in the religious sense.

ROMEO APPROACHES BENVOLIO SEEMINGLY NOT NOTICING HIM.

BENVOLIO JOINS HIM, SLOWLY WALKING BACK TOWARDS THE SCENE OF THE EARLIER TROUBLE, TALKING AS THEY GO.

| BENVOLIO | BENVOLIO |
|---|---|
| Good morning, cousin Romeo. | Good morrow, cousin. |

> Note: 'Cousin' used to mean a relative of any kind, though they are cousins.

BENVOLIO STARTS WALKING ALONGSIDE ROMEO, BACK TOWARDS THE SCENE OF THE EARLIER TROUBLE, TALKING AS THEY GO.

| ROMEO | ROMEO |
|---|---|
| Is the day still so young? | Is the day so young? |
| **BENVOLIO** | **BENVOLIO** |
| The clock's just struck nine. | But new struck nine. |
| **ROMEO** | **ROMEO** |
| Dear me! (*sighs*) Sad hours seem longer. Was that my father I saw leaving so quickly? | Ay me! Sad hours seem long. Was that my father that went hence so fast? |
| **BENVOLIO** | **BENVOLIO** |
| It was. So, what sadness lengthens Romeo's hours? | It was. What sadness lengthens Romeo's hours? |
| **ROMEO** | **ROMEO** |
| I don't have that which shortens them. | Not having that which, having, makes them short. |
| **BENVOLIO** | **BENVOLIO** |
| You're in love? | In love? |
| **ROMEO** | **ROMEO** |
| Out. | Out. |
| **BENVOLIO** | **BENVOLIO** |
| Of love? | Of love? |

**ROMEO**

Out of favour, Benvolio, with the one I love.

**BENVOLIO**

Alas, that love, outwardly seeming so gentle, should inwardly prove to be such rough torment.

**ROMEO**

*Alas, love is blind, but then even still,*
*Though without eyes, steers my course by his will.*

**ROMEO**

Out of her favour, where I am in love.

**BENVOLIO**

Alas that love, so gentle in his view,
Should be so tyrannous and rough in proof.

**ROMEO**

*Alas that love, whose view is muffled still,*
*Should without eyes see pathways to his will.*

Note: 'Muffled' means blindfold. 'Love' (or Cupid), the mythical little boy with the bow whose arrows struck people making them fall in love, was blind.

ROMEO'S STOMACH RUMBLES.

**ROMEO (CONT'D)**

Anyway, where shall we eat?

**ROMEO**

Where shall we dine?

THEY HAVE ARRIVED BACK AT THE SCENE OF THE EARLIER RIOT.
ROMEO SEES BLOOD AND WEAPONS ON THE GROUND FROM THE FIGHT.

**ROMEO (CONT'D)**

Oh my! - Was there a riot here?

**ROMEO**

O me! - what fray was here?

Note: Romeo now compares the turmoil of his love with the turmoil of the fight. We find out later that his secret love is Rosaline, a Capulet and therefore comes from the family at war with his.

**ROMEO (CONT'D)**

No, don't tell me. I've heard it all before. It's a lot about hate, but more about love.
*This love of brawling, this love of hatred,*
*Out of nothing in the first place created!*
This heavy lightness, sensible foolishness, this twisted turmoil of normality. Like a heavy feather, clear fog, cold fire, ill health or waking sleep, this is anything but what it seems!

**ROMEO**

Yet tell me not, for I have heard it all.
Here's much to do with hate, but more with love.
*Why then, O brawling love, O loving hate,*
*O anything, of nothing first create!*
O heavy lightness, serious vanity,
Misshapen chaos of well-seeming forms,
Feather of lead, bright smoke, cold fire, sick health,
Still-waking sleep, that is not what it is!

ROMEO SIGHS DEEPLY.

ROMEO (CONT'D)

I feel love, but I don't love this feeling. Do I make you laugh?

BENVOLIO

No, cousin, you make me weep.

---

ROMEO

This love feel I, that feel no love in this. Dost thou not laugh?

BENVOLIO

No, coz, I rather weep.

---

Note: Coz was a friendly term for cousin. Then, cousin meant any relative, but Benvolio was an actual cousin of Romeo.

---

ROMEO

My dear man, why?

BENVOLIO

At the sadness in your good heart.

ROMEO

Such is the effect of love.

*My own grief it lies heavy in my heart,*
*More so with the addition on your part,*
*Of more of yours. The love that you have shown*
*Just adds more grief to my much burdened own.*
*Love is a mist made with the breath of sighs.*
*When pure, fire sparkling in a lover's eyes,*
*When troubled, a sea fed with lovers' tears.*
*What else? A silent madness, bitter treat,*
*A choking sour wrapped in a soothing sweet.*
*Farewell, my cousin...*

---

ROMEO

Good heart, at what?

BENVOLIO

At thy good heart's oppression.

ROMEO

Why, such is love's transgression.

*Griefs of mine own lie heavy in my breast,*
*Which thou wilt propagate, to have it pressed*
*With more of thine. This love that thou hast shown*
*Doth add more grief to too much of mine own.*
*Love is a smoke made with the fume of sighs;*
*Being purged, a fire sparkling in lovers' eyes;*
*Being vexed, a sea nourished with lovers' tears;*
*What is it else? A madness most discreet,*
*A choking gall, and a preserving sweet.*
*Farewell, my coz.*

---

ROMEO TURNS TO LEAVE.

BENVOLIO RESTRAINS HIM BY HIS ARM.

---

BENVOLIO

*...Wait, I'll come along;*
*You leave me not knowing, you do me wrong.*

---

BENVOLIO

*Soft, I will go along;*
*And if you leave me so, you do me wrong.*

---

THEY START WALKING SLOWLY.

---

ROMEO

*Tut, I'm lost in thought, I am not here.*
*This is not Romeo, he is elsewhere.*

BENVOLIO

From the depths of your sadness, tell me who it is you love?

---

ROMEO

*Tut, I have lost myself; I am not here.*
*This is not Romeo, he's some other where.*

BENVOLIO

Tell me in sadness, who is that you love?

| ROMEO | ROMEO |
|---|---|
| You want me to cry out loud and tell you? | What, shall I groan and tell thee? |

| BENVOLIO | BENVOLIO |
|---|---|
| Not cry, no, just tell me sadly who? | Groan? Why no; but sadly tell me who. |

Note: Romeo suggests that even saying her name would be too painful.

| ROMEO | ROMEO |
|---|---|
| *Ask a sick man to sadly make his will?* | *Bid a sick man in sadness make his will?* |
| *A word ill-advised for one that's so ill.* | *A word ill urged to one that is so ill.* |
| But *sadly*, cousin, the one I love is a woman. | In sadness, cousin, I do love a woman. |

| BENVOLIO | BENVOLIO |
|---|---|
| (*Sarcastic*) I was so close then, when I guessed who you loved. | I aimed so near when I supposed you loved. |

| ROMEO | ROMEO |
|---|---|
| You must be a marksman! And the one I love is pretty. | A right good markman! And she's fair I love. |

| BENVOLIO | BENVOLIO |
|---|---|
| And pretty targets are the fastest hit, cousin. | A right fair mark, fair coz, is soonest hit. |

| ROMEO | ROMEO |
|---|---|
| *Well, with that shot you miss: she'll not be hit* | *Well, in that hit you miss: she'll not be hit* |
| *By Cupid's arrow. She has Diane's wit,* | *With Cupid's arrow. She hath Dian's wit,* |
| *Likewise in chastity she is well armed,* | *And, in strong proof of chastity well armed,* |
| *From Cupid's childish bow she lives unharmed.* | *From love's weak childish bow she lives unharmed.* |
| She'll not submit to sweet words of love, | She will not stay the siege of loving terms, |
| nor yield to a lover's smouldering gaze, | Nor bide th' encounter of assailing eyes, |
| (*bawdy*) nor open her legs for gold enough | Nor ope her lap to saint-seducing gold. |
| to seduce a Saint! | *O she is rich in beauty, only poor* |
| *Oh, she is rich in beauty, but she's poor* | *That when she dies, with beauty dies her store.* |
| *For when she dies, her beauty ends right there.* | |

Note: By remaining chaste her beauty will not be passed onto her children. This was a theme Shakespeare also used in his sonnets.

| BENVOLIO | BENVOLIO |
|---|---|
| *Then she has sworn that she will live life* | *Then she hath sworn that she will still live chaste?* |
|    *chaste?* | |

ROMEO

*She has. And in that choice there lies such waste.*
*Her beauty, by keeping her chastity,*
*Is ended here for all eternity*
*Her beauty, and her virtue, so unfair,*
*Earns her place in Heaven, but my despair.*
*She's sworn to bar all love, and in that vow*
*A living death, I live to tell you now.*

BENVOLIO

Take my advice, forget her. Stop thinking about her.

ROMEO

Oh, teach me how I can forget to think!

BENVOLIO

By giving freedom to your eyes to view other beauties.

ROMEO

It would only remind me more, how exquisite she is in comparison. These dark masks ladies wear at parties just remind us they hide the light of beauty beneath. A man suddenly struck blind cannot forget the precious memories of his lost eyesight. You show me a surpassingly beautiful girl, all her beauty does is remind me of the one whose beauty surpasses all else.
*Farewell, you cannot teach me to forget.*

BENVOLIO

*I'll pay you that lesson, or die in your debt.*

ROMEO

*She hath, and in that sparing makes huge waste;*
*For beauty, starved with her severity,*
*Cuts beauty off from all posterity.*
*She is too fair, too wise, wisely too fair,*
*To merit bliss by making me despair.*
*She hath forsworn to love, and in that vow*
*Do I live dead, that live to tell it now.*

BENVOLIO

Be ruled by me; forget to think of her.

ROMEO

O, teach me how I should forget to think!

BENVOLIO

By giving liberty unto thine eyes;
Examine other beauties.

ROMEO

'Tis the way
To call hers, exquisite, in question more.
These happy masks that kiss fair ladies' brows,
Being black, puts us in mind they hide the fair.
He that is strucken blind cannot forget
The precious treasure of his eyesight lost.
Show me a mistress that is passing fair,
What doth her beauty serve but as a note
Where I may read who passed that passing fair?
*Farewell; thou canst not teach me to forget.*

BENVOLIO

*I'll pay that doctrine, or else die in debt.*

> Note: Rhyming couplets here signify the end of a scene. In Shakespeare's day there were no curtains, no lights and mostly static scenery – so scene changes were not so obvious. The rhyming lines, though not strictly necessary, are included to maintain the feel of the original.
>
> Audiences were conditioned to hear the rhyme and knew the significance. The remainder of the play would be mostly written in blank verse, which is not rhymed, so the contrast was apparent. Shakespeare also used rhyme for certain characters, most often mad, evil or supernatural characters, or in the case of lovers, the rhyme was in the format of a sonnet.

# ACT I SCENE II

## THE STREETS OF VERONA. SUNDAY AFTERNOON.

OLD CAPULET AND COUNT PARIS ARE TALKING TOGETHER WHILE
A SERVANT OF THE CAPULET HOUSEHOLD STANDS IN ATTENDANCE.

### OLD CAPULET

So Montague has been fined the same as me. You'd think that men as old as us could learn to keep the peace.

### COUNT PARIS

You are both honourable men, Mr. Capulet, it's a pity you've lived at odds with each other for so long.
But anyway, my Lord, what about my proposal?

### OLD CAPULET

As I have said before, Count Paris, my daughter is still not wise to the ways of the world. She has yet to reach her fourteenth year.
*Let two more summers pass us in their pride*
*Before she'll be ready to be a bride.*

### COUNT PARIS

There are happy mothers younger than she is.

### CAPULET

But Montague is bound as well as I,
In penalty alike; and 'tis not hard, I think,
For men so old as we to keep the peace.

### PARIS

Of honourable reckoning are you both,
And pity 'tis you lived at odds so long.
But now, my lord, what say you to my suit?

### CAPULET

But saying o'er what I have said before:
My child is yet a stranger in the world;
She hath not seen the change of fourteen years.
*Let two more summers wither in their pride*
*Ere we may think her ripe to be a bride.*

### PARIS

Younger than she are happy mothers made.

Note: In Shakespeare's day, 18-20 was the average age women married, not 13. Shakespeare married at 18, his already pregnant bride was 26. Juliet's mother apparently married at 13 and was 14 when she gave birth to Juliet. Perhaps Shakespeare made Juliet 13 to emphasise her defiance against her parents, or simply because his own daughter, Susanna, was 13 at the time and he had experience of the stubbornness at this age. In Brooke's poem, which Shakespeare borrowed heavily from, Juliet was 16. There is belief that Susanna could read in an age where only boys were educated at school, she wouldn't have seen the play performed in London, so perhaps she was able to read it.

If a woman was unmarried at 26 it was difficult to find a husband, especially when she was a lowly milk maid, so it's possible Shakespeare was seduced into marriage with the encouragement of Anne Hathaway's parents to further their interests and hers, it was an unlikely match.

| OLD CAPULET | CAPULET |
|---|---|
| And they are marred by having children so young. She is my only child still living, so she is my world, my future. | And too soon marred are those so early made. Earth hath swallowed all my hopes but she; She is the hopeful lady of my earth. |

> Note: Old Capulet's words suggest he has lost other children and therefore Juliet is special to him and his last hope to further the family line. We will discover later that Romeo is also the only child of the rival Montagues – which adds extra dimension to the story. Before vaccines and penicillin It was common for children to die before they reached eleven, Shakespeare lost his own son Hamnet at the age of eleven.

| OLD CAPULET | CAPULET |
|---|---|
| So woo her, noble Paris, win her heart. | But woo her, gentle Paris, get her heart; |
| My giving her consent is just a part; | My will to her consent is but a part; |
| I did agree that when she makes her choice | And, she agreed, within her scope of choice |
| I'd give consent with fair and ruling voice. | Lies my consent and fair according voice. |
| Tonight I hold my customary feast. | This night I hold an old accustomed feast, |
| To which I did invite many a guest, | Whereto I have invited many a guest, |
| All dear to me, and you are one as well, | Such as I love, and you among the store, |
| One more most welcome, makes my numbers swell. | One more most welcome, makes my number more. |
| To look on at my humble house tonight, | At my poor house look to behold this night |
| Heavenly bodies radiating light. | Earth-treading stars that make dark heaven light. |
| Some comfort for young lusty men to bring | Such comfort as do lusty young men feel |
| Now we've left the soft delights of Spring. | When well-apparelled April on the heel |
| Though winter nears you still can find delight | Of limping winter treads, even such delight |
| Among fresh female buds you'll see tonight. | Among fresh female buds shall you this night |
| So see and hear them all, then choose the best, | Inherit at my house. Hear all, all see, |
| The one whose merits stand out from the rest. | And like her most whose merit most shall be; |
| And mine is one among many on view, | Which on more view of many, mine, being one, |
| But as your number one? That's up to you. | May stand in number, though in reckoning none. |
| Come, walk with me... | Come, go with me. |

OLD CAPULET HANDS THE WAITING SERVANT A PIECE OF PAPER.

| OLD CAPULET (CONT'D) | CAPULET |
|---|---|
| (to Servant)      ...Now go, boy, walk about | Go, sirrah, trudge about |
| Through fine Verona, seek the good folk out | Through fair Verona; find those persons out |
| Named upon this list, and at their leisure, | Whose names are written there, and to them say |
| Invite 'em to my house for evening's pleasure. | My house and welcome on their pleasure stay. |

OLD CAPULET AND COUNT PARIS EXIT, LEAVING THE SERVANT PETER,
(COMMONLY REFERRED TO AS 'CLOWN') STANDING ALONE, LOOKING AT THE
PAPER AND SCRATCHING HIS HEAD.

HE TURNS THE PAPER IN HIS HAND, OBVIOUSLY UNABLE TO READ, AND
JOKINGLY MAKES UP NAMES THAT ARE WRITTEN DOWN AND MIXES UP THE
ITEMS OF THEIR TRADE. A 'LAST' BEING A SHOEMAKER'S SHOE HOLDER.

Note: The part of Peter would be played by a comic actor, who would often add
additional topical jokes of their own into the performance. He speaks in prose.
Will Kemp, a famous comic actor, played the part originally.

PETER

Huh - find the people whose names are written on this list!
It says the shoemaker should fiddle with his measure, and the tailor with his last, the fisher with his pencil, and the painter with his nets, but I am sent to find the people whose names are written here, when I can't find the names of the people the writing person has written down. I must find me an educated man.

1ST SERVANT

Find them out whose names are written here! It is written that the shoemaker should meddle with his yard and the tailor with his last, the fisher with his pencil and the painter with his nets; but I am sent to find those persons whose names are here writ, and can never find what names the writing person hath here writ. I must to the learned.

RIGHT ON CUE, BENVOLIO AND ROMEO APPEAR, WALKING AND TALKING.

Note: Peter has mixed up the tools of the trades to emphasise his confusion. A
tailor woud use a 'yard', a stick to measure cloth. By law cloth was sold by the
yard, which was three feet by English standards. Around the world the length of a
yard differed and it was not until 1959 that countries who used the yard
measurement agreed to a standard length of 36 inches. (0.9144 metres). Football,
cricket and golf still officially use yards, but most other sports had converted to
metres by the end of the 20th Century. A 'Last' is the foot shaped wooden block a
shoemaker uses.

PETER (CONT'D)

Perfect timing!

BENVOLIO

Tut, Romeo,
One fire burns out another fire's burning,
One pain is lessened by more agony.
Turning giddy's cured by backward turning.
Desperate grief quells a lesser tragedy.
So take a new infection in your eye,
And then the bitter sting of old will die.

1ST SERVANT

In good time!

BENVOLIO

Tut man, one fire burns out another's burning,
One pain is lessened by another's anguish.
Turn giddy, and be holp by backward turning;
One desperate grief cures with another's languish.
Take thou some new infection to thy eye,
And the rank poison of the old will die.

| | |
|---|---|
| ROMEO | ROMEO |
| The leaf of the plantain plant is good for that, Benvolio. | Your plantain leaf is excellent for that. |
| BENVOLIO | BENVOLIO |
| Good for what? | For what, I pray thee? |
| ROMEO | ROMEO |
| For your broken shin! | For your broken shin. |

ROMEO PRETENDS TO KICK BENVOLIO IN THE SHIN.

| | |
|---|---|
| BENVOLIO | BENVOLIO |
| Have you gone mad, Romeo? | Why, Romeo, art thou mad? |
| ROMEO | ROMEO |
| Not mad, but bound like a madman in a straitjacket. Shut up in prison, deprived of food, whipped and tormented and.... | Not mad, but bound more than a madman is; Shut up in prison, kept without my food, Whipped and tormented and... |

THEY STOP WALKING AS THEY REACH THE SERVANT (CLOWN), WHO IS LOOKING AT THEM HOPEFULLY AS IF TO CATCH THEIR ATTENTION.

| | |
|---|---|
| ROMEO | ROMEO |
| (to Servant) Good afternoon, good fellow. | Good e'en, good fellow. |
| PETER | 1ST SERVANT |
| Good afternoon to you. If you please, sir, can you read? | God gi' good e'en. I pray, sir, can you read? |
| ROMEO | ROMEO |
| Yes, my misfortune in my misery. | Ay, mine own fortune in my misery. |
| PETER | 1ST SERVANT |
| Perhaps you have learned to do that without a book, but, if you please, can you read anything you see? | Perhaps you have learned it without book. But, I pray, can you read anything you see? |
| ROMEO | ROMEO |
| Only if I recognise the letters and the language. | Ay, if I know the letters and the language. |

THE SERVANT WRONGLY BELIEVES THIS MEANS ROMEO CANNOT RECOGNISE WORDS AND LETTERS, JUST LIKE HIMSELF.

| | |
|---|---|
| PETER | 1ST SERVANT |
| Well that is honest of you, sir. I bid you good day then. | Ye say honestly. Rest you merry! |

---

THE SERVANT TURNS TO LEAVE.

ROMEO
No, stay fellow. I can read.

ROMEO
Stay, fellow, I can read.

ROMEO TAKES THE PAPER FROM THE SERVANT AND READS IT ALOUD,
REACTING WITH FACIAL EXPRESSIONS OF APPROVAL, DISAPPROVAL AND
SARCASM THROUGHOUT.

ROMEO
*(reads)*
*"Signor Martino, his wife and daughters.*
*Count Anselme and his beautiful sisters.*
*The lady widow of Utruvio.*
*Signor Placento and his lovely nieces.*
*Mercutio and his brother Valentine.*
*My cousin Capulet, his wife and daughters..."*

ROMEO
*(reads)*
*"Signor Martino and his wife and daughters.*
*County Anselme and his beauteous sisters.*
*The lady widow of Utruvio.*
*Signor Placentio and his lovely nieces.*
*Mercutio and his brother Valentine.*
*Mine uncle Capulet, his wife and daughters..."*

ROMEO EMPHASISES THE NAME 'ROSALINE' IN THE NEXT LINE,
SHE IS HIS CURRENT INFATUATION.

ROMEO
*"My fair niece 'Rosaline', and her friend Livia!*
*Signor Valentio and his cousin Tybalt.*
*Lucio and the feisty Helena."*

ROMEO
*"My fair niece Rosaline, and Livia.*
*Signor Valentio and his cousin Tybalt.*
*Lucio and the lively Helena."*

ROMEO FOLDS THE PAPER AND HANDS IT BACK TO THE SERVANT, NOW
INTERESTED IN THE GATHERING.

ROMEO
A tempting gathering. Where are they meeting?

ROMEO
A fair assembly. Whither should they come?

PETER
Up there.

1ST SERVANT
Up.

THE SERVANT NODS OVER HIS SHOULDER AS IF INDICATING SOMEWHERE.

ROMEO
Up where?

ROMEO
Whither?

PETER
For supper at our household.

1ST SERVANT
To supper. To our house.

| | |
|---|---|
| **ROMEO** | ROMEO |
| Whose household? | Whose house? |
| **PETER** | 1ST SERVANT |
| My master's. | My master's. |
| **ROMEO** | ROMEO |
| Indeed, I should have asked you that in the first place. | Indeed, I should have asked you that before. |
| **PETER** | 1ST SERVANT |
| Now, before you ask I'll tell you. My master is the great, wealthy Capulet, and as long as you are not from the house of Montague, I invite you to come and enjoy a glass of wine. Good day to you! | Now I'll tell you without asking. My master is the great rich Capulet; and if you be not of the house of Montagues, I pray come and crush a cup of wine. Rest you merry! |

---

Note: To crush a cup of wine is to empty it by drinking it all.

---

THE SERVANT TURNS AND LEAVES.

---

| | |
|---|---|
| **BENVOLIO** | BENVOLIO |
| So, the beautiful Rosaline, the girl you love so much, will be at Capulet's feast together with all the desirable beauties of Verona. You can go to the feast with an open mind. | At this same ancient feast of Capulet's Sups the fair Rosaline, whom thou so loves, With all the admired beauties of Verona. Go thither, and with unattainted eye |
| *Compare her face with other girls on show,* | *Compare her face with some that I shall show,* |
| *You'll think your swan is no more than a crow.* | *And I will make thee think thy swan a crow.* |
| **ROMEO** | ROMEO |
| *Should the idol of devotion in my eye* | *When the devout religion of mine eye* |
| *Appear so false, then turn my tears to fires,* | *Maintains such falsehood, then turn tears to fires;* |
| *These eyes, though often drowned they never die,* | *And these, who often drowned could never die,* |
| *Like witches who won't drown, burn them as liars.* | *Transparent heretics be burnt for liars.* |
| *One fairer than my love? The all-seeing sun* | *One fairer than my love? The all-seeing sun* |
| *Ne'er saw her match since all the world begun* | *Ne'er saw her match since first the world begun.* |

*Note: Heretics, or more commonly witches, were ducked in water on a ducking stool. If they survived the immersion in water they were deemed to be proven heretics and burned alive. The theory being that if they didn't drown, God had rejected their soul.*

*Though women were burnt at the stake in England, it was typically for treason (which included counterfeiting money), despite popular belief, women found guilty of witchcraft were all hanged in England, it was other countries that burnt witches. Public burnings were popular events, (men were not burnt for treason, they were hung, drawn and quartered), the burning of Phoebe Harris in 1786 for counterfeiting a single coin attracted an estimated 20,000 spectators in London. The last public burning in England was in 1789 after which legal changes banned its practice.*

BENVOLIO

Tut.

*She looked so good with no one else close by,*

*Alone you weighed her beauty in your eye.*

*But in those glassy scales let there be weighed*

*Your lady's love against some other maid*

*That I will show you shining at this feast,*

*She'll scarce seem fine, the one you now think best.*

ROMEO

*I'll go along, not to see such a sight,*

*But to take pleasure in my love's delight.*

BENVOLIO

*Tut, you saw her fair, none else being by,*

*Herself poised with herself in either eye;*

*But in that crystal scales let there be weighed*

*Your lady's love against some other maid*

*That I will show you shining at this feast,*

*And she shall scant show well that now seems best.*

ROMEO

*I'll go along, no such sight to be shown,*

*But to rejoice in splendour of mine own.*

*Note: The final rhyming couplet is not so obvious here as the previous lines had lso been rhymed. However, Romeo would have delivered the line as if a final statement and then left the stage, which the audience would understand.*

*Important Note: The stage directions (between main text in capital letters) are included purely as the author's guide to understand the script better. Any director staging the play would have their own interpretation of the play and decide their own directions. These directions are not those of Shakespeare. You can change these directions to your own choosing or ignore them completely. For exam purposes these should be only regarded as guidance to the dialogue and should not be quoted in any studies or examinations.*

# ACT I SCENE III

## A Room In Capulet's House. Sunday Afternoon

Lady Capulet and Juliet's Nursemaid are talking.

Juliet is the only child of the Capulets.

Romeo is the only child of the Montagues.

> Note: In the time the play is set, a Nurse (or Nursemaid) was a woman who breastfed the child so the mother did not have to, and who would then be a nanny to the child once she was weaned. The nurse is a comic role.

| | |
|---|---|
| **LADY CAPULET**<br>Nurse, where is my daughter? Call her for me. | LADY CAPULET<br>Nurse, where's my daughter? Call her forth to me. |
| **NURSE**<br>I swear by my innocence as a twelve year old I called her.<br>(*calling*) Come lamb! Come sweetheart!<br>(*to no one*) God forbid! Where is that girl?<br>(*shouts loudly*) J u l i e t ! | NURSE<br>Now, by my maidenhead at twelve year old,<br>I bade her come. What, lamb! What, ladybird!<br>God forbid! Where's this girl? What, Juliet! |

> Note: If she swears by her virginity (innocence) when she was last a virgin, then twelve is a very young age even in those days.

| | |
|---|---|
| **JULIET**<br>(*off*) Goodness me! Who is calling? | JULIET<br>How now! Who calls? |
| **NURSE**<br>Your mother. | NURSE<br>Your mother. |

Juliet enters the room.

| | |
|---|---|
| **JULIET**<br>Mother, I am here. What is it you want? | JULIET<br>Madam, I am here. What is your will? |
| **LADY CAPULET**<br>I have something to say. Nurse, leave us a while, we must talk in private. | LADY CAPULET<br>This is the matter. Nurse, give leave awhile,<br>We must talk in secret... |

As Nurse turns to leave Lady Capulet changes her mind
and calls her back.

**LADY CAPULET (CONT'D)**
No wait, Nurse, come back, I have remembered, you should hear our conversation. You know my daughter is at a delicate age.

**NURSE**
Indeed ma'am, I can tell her age to the hour.

**LADY CAPULET**
She's not yet fourteen...

**NURSE**
I'll bet fourteen of my teeth - though I lost the teen and have only the four left - she's not fourteen. How long is it till the Lammastide festival?

---

**LADY CAPULET**
Nurse, come back again,
I have remembered me, thou's hear our counsel.
Thou knowest my daughter's of a pretty age.

**NURSE**
Faith, I can tell her age unto an hour.

**LADY CAPULET**
She's not fourteen.

**NURSE**
I'll lay fourteen of my teeth -
And yet, to my teen be it spoken, I have but four -
She's not fourteen. How long is it now
To Lammas-tide?

> Note: Lammastide is 1ˢᵗ August, a harvest festival. 'Tide' was a Puritan term replacing the Catholic 'mass'. e.g. Christ-tide. This should have said Lamb-tide, was the mistake deliberate? Probably as he next writes 'Lammas Eve'.
>
> 'Teen' means sorrow, but used here to pun with fourteen.
>
> This is the second mention of Juliet's age being almost fourteen. In Brooke's poem, which Shakespeare borrowed from, Juliet was almost sixteen, and in Paynter's novel (translated from Bardello's French) she was almost eighteen.

**LADY CAPULET**
A fortnight and the odd day or two.

**NURSE**
Even or odd, of all the days in the year, come the night of Lammas Eve she will be fourteen. Susan and her - God rest her soul! - were the same age. Well, Susan is with God now, she was too good for this world. But as I said, on Lammas Eve, that night she will be fourteen, that she will. Oh Lord, I remember it well. It is eleven years since the earthquake when she was weaned - I shall never forget it, of all the days of the year - because on that day I had rubbed a wormwood leaf on my tit to wean her. I was sitting in the sun under the dove-house wall. The master and yourself were then away at Mantua. Yes, my memory hasn't failed me yet!...

---

**LADY CAPULET**
A fortnight and odd days.

**NURSE**
Even or odd, of all days in the year,
Come Lammas Eve at night shall she be fourteen.
Susan and she - God rest all Christian souls! -
Were of an age. Well, Susan is with God;
She was too good for me. But, as I said,
On Lammas Eve at night shall she be fourteen;
That shall she; marry, I remember it well.
'Tis since the earthquake now eleven years,
And she was weaned, I never shall forget it,
Of all the days of the year, upon that day;
For I had then laid wormwood to my dug,
Sitting in the sun under the dovehouse wall;
My lord and you were then at Mantua.
Nay, I do bear a brain! -

NURSE PAUSES, FORGETTING WHAT SHE WAS SAYING.

| NURSE (CONT'D) | NURSE |
|---|---|
| ...But as I was saying, the youngster tasted the wormwood on my nipple and found it bitter. Pretty little fool, you should have seen her tantrum at my tit! | - but, as I said, When it did taste the wormwood on the nipple Of my dug and felt it bitter, pretty fool, To see it tetchy and fall out with the dug. |
| Shake! went the dovehouse. There was no need telling me to shake a leg and hie out of there... | `Shake!' quoth the dovehouse. 'Twas no need, I trow, To bid me trudge. |
| That was eleven years ago, for she could stand on her own then. - No, by heavens, she could run and waddle about, because just the day before, she cut her forehead. Then my husband - God rest his soul, he was a jolly man! - he picked up the child and said 'Why do you fall on your face? (*bawdy*) You will <u>fall on your back</u> when you have more sense, won't you Jule?' And by all that's holy, the pretty wretch stopped her crying and said 'Aye'. | And since that time it is eleven years; For then she could stand high-lone. Nay, by th' rood, She could have run and waddled all about; For even the day before she broke her brow, And then my husband - God be with his soul! A' was a merry man -took up the child. `Yea' quoth he `dost thou fall upon thy face? Thou wilt fall backward when thou hast more wit, Wilt thou not, Jule?' And, by my holidam, The pretty wretch left crying and said `Ay'. |
| To see now the jest about to come true. I tell you, if I live to be a thousand years I shall never forget it. | To see now how a jest shall come about! I warrant, an I should live a thousand years I never should forget it. `Wilt thou not, Jule?' quoth he, |
| (*laughing*) 'Won't you Jule?' he said, and the pretty little fool stopped crying and said 'Aye'. | And, pretty fool, it stinted and said `Ay'. |

> Note: The earthquake most likely refers to one in England in 1580, suggesting the play was being written in 1591. There was a much larger one in Italy in 1570.

| LADY CAPULET | LADY CAPULET |
|---|---|
| Enough of this. Please be quiet, Nurse. | Enough of this; I pray thee hold thy peace. |

| NURSE | NURSE |
|---|---|
| (*laughing too much*) Yes ma'am, yet I cannot help but laugh, to think she should stop crying and say 'Aye'. Yet, I tell you she had upon her forehead, a bump as big as a young cockerel's testicle. A terrible knock, she cried bitterly. 'You', said my husband, 'Fall on your face? You will <u>fall on your back</u> when you come of age, won't you Jule?' She just shut up and said 'Aye'. | Yes, madam. Yet I cannot choose but laugh To think it should leave crying and say `Ay'. And yet, I warrant it had upon it brow A bump as big as a young cockerel's stone, A perilous knock; and it cried bitterly. `Yea' quoth my husband `fall'st upon thy face? Thou wilt fall backward when thou com'st to age, Wilt thou not, Jule?' It stinted and said `Ay' |

JULIET
And you will shut up too, I beg you, Nurse, says 'I'.

JULIET
And stint thou too, I pray thee, Nurse, say I.

> Note: Juliet puns on nurse's repetition of the word 'Aye' (old word for yes)

NURSE
(*stopping herself laughing*) I will, I'm done. God marked you with his grace! You were the prettiest baby that I ever nursed, and that I might live to see you married has always been my wish.

NURSE
Peace, I have done. God mark thee to his grace! Thou wast the prettiest babe that e'er I nursed. An I might live to see thee married once, I have my wish.

LADY CAPULET
Yes, marrying is the very subject I came to talk about. So tell me, Juliet, what are your thoughts about getting married?

LADY CAPULET
Marry, that ` marry' is the very theme I came to talk of. Tell me, daughter Juliet, How stands your dispositions to be married?

JULIET
(*surprised*) It is an honour that I have no thoughts of as yet.

JULIET
It is an honour that I dream not of.

NURSE
'An hon-our'!. Had I not been your only nurse I would have said you sucked wisdom from my teat.

NURSE
An honour! Were not I thine only nurse I would say thou hadst sucked wisdom from thy teat.

NURSE PRONOUNCES 'HONOUR' AS A BAWDY, 'ON HER'

> Note: More humour from Nurse, she is saying in effect, she would like to say that Juliet sucked wisdom from her breast, but Nurse knows she is a foolish woman who talks a lot about nothing in her flights of bawdy fancy. She often gets words wrong to comedic effect, trying to sound educated when she clearly is not, uses old fashioned curses, and is surprisingly bawdy for one whose job is to raise a child.

LADY CAPULET
Well start thinking about marriage now. There are ladies here in Verona younger than you, ladies of high esteem, who are already mothers. By my reckoning, I was your mother pretty much when I was the age you are now, and you are still unmarried. Anyway, in short, the valiant Count Paris seeks you for his bride.

LADY CAPULET
Well, think of marriage now. Younger than you - Here in Verona, ladies of esteem - Are made already mothers. By my count I was your mother much upon these years That you are now a maid. Thus, then, in brief: The valiant Paris seeks you for his love.

**NURSE**

(*excited*) What a man, young lady! Such a man in all the world, why he is... (*struggles to find words*) a man above men.

**NURSE**

A man, young lady! Lady, such a man
As all the world - why, he's a man of wax.

**LADY CAPULET**

He is the pick of the bunch in Verona this summer.

**LADY CAPULET**

Verona's summer hath not such a flower.

**NURSE**

Aye, he's a flower, a fine flower indeed.

**NURSE**

Nay, he's a flower; in faith, a very flower.

**LADY CAPULET**

What do you say? Can you love this gentleman?

**LADY CAPULET**

What say you, can you love the gentleman?

WITHOUT PAUSING FOR AN ANSWER LADY CAPULET FOLLOWS ON WITH AN ELABORATE FANTASY AS IF SHE HAD PREPARED A SPEECH FOR THIS MOMENT.

**LADY CAPULET (CONT'D)**

Tonight you shall see him at our feast. Study the face of young Paris like you would a fine book, read what great delights are written there with beauty's pen.

*Examine every feature written there,*
*See how each one compliments the other,*
*And anything found missing in this prize*
*Find written in the footnote of his eyes.*
*This precious book of love, this unbound lover,*
*To make complete he only lacks a cover.*
*Plain fish within the sea, to gain much pride*
*Among the pretty fish they choose to hide.*
*That book in many's eyes does share the glory*
*That with gold rings completes the golden*
  *story.*
*Together you'll share all he does possess*
*And having him, better yourself no less.*

**LADY CAPULET**

This night you shall behold him at our feast;
Read o'er the volume of young Paris' face,
And find delight writ there with beauty's pen.

*Examine every married lineament,*
*And see how one another lends content;*
*And what obscured in this fair volume lies*
*Find written in the margent of his eyes.*
*This precious book of love, this unbound lover,*
*To beautify him only lacks a cover.*
*The fish lives in the sea, and 'tis much pride*
*For fair without the fair within to hide.*
*That book in many's eyes doth share the glory*
*That in gold clasps locks in the golden story;*
*So shall you share all that he doth possess*
*By having him, making yourself no less.*

| | |
|---|---|
| **NURSE** | **NURSE** |
| No less indeed, bigger in fact. | No less; nay, bigger:... |

NURSE MIMES A PREGNANT STOMACH.

| | |
|---|---|
| **NURSE (CONT'D)** | **NURSE** |
| Women grow by men. | ...women grow by men |

LADY CAPULET IGNORES NURSE AND CARRIES ON.

| | |
|---|---|
| **LADY CAPULET** | **LADY CAPULET** |
| (*to Juliet*) Now quickly. | *Speak briefly, can you like of Paris' love?* |
| *On liking Paris's love, what do you see?* | |
| **JULIET** | **JULIET** |
| *I'll see if looking sets a liking in me,* | *I'll look to like, if looking liking move;* |
| *But my eye no further I would consent* | *But no more deep will I endart mine eye* |
| *Be smitten, than you give it your assent.* | *Than your consent gives strength to make it fly.* |

Note: This is prophetic as she will do just the opposite.

A KNOCK ON THE DOOR INTERRUPTS THE CONVERSATION.

DOOR OPENS AND PETER, THE COMIC SERVANT, ENTERS LOOKING STRESSED.

| | |
|---|---|
| **PETER** | PETER |
| (*stressed, dramatic*) Ma'am. The guests have arrived and supper is served. You are called for, my young lady is asked for, the Nurse is being cursed in the kitchen, and everywhere is madness. I have to serve dinner, please come right away. | Madam, the guests are come, supper served up, you called, my young lady asked for, the Nurse cursed in the pantry, and everything in extremity. I must hence to wait; I beseech you follow straight. |

LADY CAPULET DISMISSES HIM.

| | |
|---|---|
| **LADY CAPULET** | **LADY CAPULET** |
| *We'll follow you...* | *We follow thee.* |

PETER EXITS, SHE TURNS TO JULIET.

| | |
|---|---|
| **LADY CAPULET (CONT'D)** | **LADY CAPULET** |
| *Juliet, the Count awaits.* | *Juliet, the County stays.* |

NURSE

*Go, girl, (bawdy) for happy days, seek happy nights!*

NURSE

*Go, girl, seek happy nights to happy days.*

---

Note: For reasons which are never explained, Paris does not make an appearance at the Capulet's feast, and nor does Rosaline, paving the way for Romeo to meet Juliet.

# ACT I SCENE IV

## THE ROAD TO CAPULET'S HOUSE. SUNDAY EVENING.

ENTER ROMEO, MERCUTIO AND BENVOLIO CARRYING MASKS WITH OTHER
YOUNG MEN BEARING TORCHES AND A DRUM.

THEY WALK TO THE BEAT OF THE DRUM.

**ROMEO**

How shall we announce our arrival, Benvolio? With the customary speech, or straight in without apology?

**ROMEO**

What, shall this speech be spoke for our excuse, Or shall we on without apology?

Note: They are wearing masks to disguise themselves as this is the house of their enemy. The customary speech when uninvited involved sending a messenger in advance to make an apology on their behalf. A pre-prepared speech would praise the beauty of the ladies present and compliment the generosity of the host. In the play 'Henry VIII', the King goes uninvited to Wolsey's party in a mask and sends a messenger in advance to make an apology for his intrusion.

**BENVOLIO**

Speeches are so out of fashion these days, Romeo. We'll not have a pretend Cupid, blindfold and carrying a toy bow, to announce us, scaring the ladies away like a scarecrow. Nor any timid, half remembered speeches. A brief prompt at our entrance, let them measure us by what they see. We'll take our measure of the girls with the measure of a dance, and then be gone.

**BENVOLIO**

The date is out of such prolixity. We'll have no Cupid hoodwinked with a scarf, Bearing a Tartar's painted bow of lath, Scaring the ladies like a crowkeeper; Nor no without-book prologue, faintly spoke After the prompter, for our entrance. But let them measure us by what they will, We'll measure them a measure, and be gone.

Note: 'Hoodwink', from falconry, a hawk has a hood over its head to calm it. Shakespeare uses falconry terms frequently in his plays.

**ROMEO**

Give me a torch, Mercutio, I do not feel up to dancing tonight. Being of heavy heart, I will carry the light.

**ROMEO**

Give me a torch. I am not for this ambling; Being but heavy, I will bear the light.

**MERCUTIO**

No, dear Romeo, we'll see to it that you dance.

**MERCUTIO**

Nay, gentle Romeo, we must have you dance.

49

| ROMEO | ROMEO |
|---|---|
| Not I, believe me. You have dancing shoes with light soles, my soul feels like lead, it binds me to the ground so I cannot move. | Not I, believe me. You have dancing shoes With nimble soles; I have a soul of lead So stakes me to the ground I cannot move. |

| MERCUTIO | MERCUTIO |
|---|---|
| You are a lover, borrow Cupid's wings and with them soar above your bounds. | You are a lover; borrow Cupid's wings And soar with them above a common bound. |

Note: A common bound was a leap in a dance common in Elizabethan times, it is also where we get the 'lords a-leaping' in the song, 'Twelve Days Of Christmas'. Wordplay on 'bound' meaning two opposites; leaping and being tied down.

| ROMEO | ROMEO |
|---|---|
| I am too sore from his arrow's piercing to soar with his light feathers, and so bound, I could not bound even an inch above my dull misery. I sink under love's heavy burden. | I am too sore empierced with his shaft To soar with his light feathers, and so bound I cannot bound a pitch above dull woe. Under love's heavy burden do I sink. |

| MERCUTIO | MERCUTIO |
|---|---|
| (*bawdily*) You burden love by <u>sinking in it</u>; too much weight for such a <u>tender thing</u>. | And to sink in it should you burden love; Too great oppression for a tender thing. |

| ROMEO | ROMEO |
|---|---|
| Is love a tender thing, Mercutio? It is rough, rude and wild, and it pricks like a thorn. | Is love a tender thing? It is too rough, Too rude, too boist'rous, and it pricks like thorn. |

THEY ARRIVE AT THE GATEWAY TO CAPULET'S HOUSE. THE DRUM STOPS.

| MERCUTIO | MERCUTIO |
|---|---|
| If love is rough with you, be rough with love. (*bawdy*) <u>Prick</u> love for <u>pricking</u> you, and you'll <u>beat love down</u>. Give me a cover for my face. | If love be rough with you, be rough with love; Prick love for pricking, and you beat love down. Give me a case to put my visage in. |

HE PUTS ON THE MASK SOMEONE PASSES TO HIM.

| MERCUTIO (CONT'D) | MERCUTIO |
|---|---|
| An ugly mask for my ugly face. What do I care if curious eyes find this unattractive? The mask's stupid eyebrows can blush for me. | A visor for a visor. What care I What curious eye doth quote deformities? Here are the beetle brows shall blush for me. |

THEY ALL PUT ON MASKS FOR MASQUERADING.

BENVOLIO

Come on, knock and enter. As soon as we're inside every man take to the floor, find a lady and dance.

BENVOLIO

Come, knock and enter; and no sooner in
But every man betake him to his legs.

ROMEO

Just give me a torch, Benvolio. Let wanton ladies with roaming eyes tickle the unfeeling carpet with their heels, for I am befitting of the old proverb –
*I'll be the candle holder and look on.*
*There is no better game, so I'm all done.*

ROMEO

A torch for me. Let wantons light of heart
Tickle the senseless rushes with their heels,
For I am proverbed with a grandsire phrase;
*I'll be a candle-holder and look on.*
*The game was ne'er so fair, and I am done.*

> Note: 'Game' means party or Rosaline, and 'fair' either good, beautiful or pure. The saying was probably corrupted from two proverbs; "A good candle-holder proves a good gamester," meaning an onlooker cannot lose a game, and, 'He is wise who gives over when the game is fairest', which means quit while you're ahead. He is saying in a round-about way that no other is as fair (beautiful) as the game (Rosaline) so he is 'done' – finished. This is game in the sense of hunted prey, such as game hunting of wild animals for food or sport.

MERCUTIO

Tut. So the dark horse is as timid as a mouse. If you are a stick-in-the-mud dark horse, then we'll drag you from the mire of - God help us - your love, where you stick up to your ears. Come, we are burning up the daylight. Let's go!

MERCUTIO

Tut, dun's the mouse, the constable's own word;
If thou art Dun, we'll draw thee from the mire
Of - save your reverence - love, wherein thou
 stickest
Up to the ears. Come, we burn daylight, ho!

> Note: Dun's the mouse meant 'quiet or timid is the mouse'. Constables (private security guards for estates) were famed for sitting around doing nothing either through laziness or they were timid. Dun was a dull brown colour often used to describe horses, cows or mice. Dun was also punned with the word 'done' which Romeo used in the line before. A modern alternative expression is used here, dropping any mention of constable or dun.

ROMEO

*That makes no sense.*

ROMEO

*Nay, that's not so.*

MERCUTIO

*I mean, sir, by delay,*
*We waste our torches, using lights by day.*
*Use all five senses when you gauge the sense,*
*Not make five senses of what I pronounce.*

MERCUTIO

*I mean, sir, in delay*
*We waste our lights in vain, light lights by day.*
*Take our good meaning, for our judgement sits*
*Five times in that ere once in our five wits.*

| | |
|---|---|
| ROMEO | ROMEO |
| *We mean no harm in going to this masque,* | *And we mean well in going to this masque;* |
| *But it's not 'sens'-ible to go.* | *But 'tis no wit to go.* |

> *Note: 'Masque', here short for masquerade, or masked ball. In Shakespeare's day a 'Masque' was a performance of dancing and acting by masked players.*

| | |
|---|---|
| MERCUTIO | MERCUTIO |
| *Why, may one ask ?* | *Why, may one ask?* |
| ROMEO | ROMEO |
| *I had a dream last night.* | *I dreamed a dream tonight.* |
| MERCUTIO | MERCUTIO |
| *And so did I.* | *And so did I.* |
| ROMEO | ROMEO |
| *Well, what was yours?* | *Well, what was yours?* |
| MERCUTIO | MERCUTIO |
| *That dreamers often lie.* | *That dreamers often lie.* |
| ROMEO | ROMEO |
| *(as if finishing the sentence)* | *In bed asleep, while they do dream things true.* |
| *...in bed asleep, while dreaming of things true.* | |
| MERCUTIO | MERCUTIO |
| *Oh, then I see Queen Mab has been with you.* | *O, then I see Queen Mab hath been with you.* |
| She's the fairy who gives dreams their birth. She's no bigger than the agate stone in the ring on a town principal's finger, and she's drawn by a team of miniature creatures across dreamers noses as they sleep. | *She is the fairies' midwife, and she comes In shape no bigger than an agate-stone On the forefinger of an alderman, Drawn with a team of little atomi Athwart men's noses as they lie asleep.* |

> *Note: Queen Mab meant a sloppily dressed harlot in Shakespeare's day and in Irish folklore Queen Medb was the Fairy Queen who intoxicated or seduced men. 'Queen' was also slang for a prostitute, so to the audience of the time it would have suggested a woman of low morals.*
>
> *Though Queen Mab had been famous in Irish folklore for hundreds of years, this is the first reference to her in English literature. She subsequently became popular material among poets and authors, including Ben Jonson (who told the tale of Queen Mab in rhyme to the wife of James I as she journeyed from Scotland to England), and most famously the poet, Shelley.*
>
> *Agate is not a precious gem, it is pretentious, cheap and trashy, further suggesting the fairy is lowlife. Worn on the forefinger suggests a jibe at aldermen, pointing accusing fingers while guilty of low morals themselves.*

THE OTHERS GROAN, THEY KNOW WHAT IS TO COME, ONE OF MERCUTIO'S
FLIGHTS OF FANCY – AND A LONG SPEECH OF NONSENSE.

### MERCUTIO (CONT'D)
Her chariot is a hazelnut shell crafted by squirrels and old grubs, coach-builders to the fairies since time began. The spokes of her carriage wheels are made of long spiders' legs, and the cover from grasshoppers' wings.

### MERCUTIO
Her chariot is an empty hazelnut,
Made by the joiner squirrel or old grub,
Time out o'mind the fairies' coachmakers.
Her waggon-spokes made of long spinners' legs;
The cover, of the wings of grasshoppers;

*Note: Squirrels crack hazel nuts open and grubs bore into them, both to devour the contents leaving the empty shell. Spinners are crane flies, commonly called 'daddy long legs'.*

### MERCUTIO (CONT'D)
Her reins are the smallest spider's web, her bridles, the moonshine's watery beams. Her whip, a crickets leg bone with a gossamer lash, the coachman, a small grey coated gnat, less than half as big as a round little worm pricked from under the fingernail of a lazy maid.

In this state she gallops night by night through lovers' brains and makes them dream of love. Over courtiers' knees so they dream of bowing and scraping. Over lawyers' fingers so they dream of fat fees. Over ladies' lips, so they dream of kisses, which often the angry Queen Mab will plague with sores because their breath is foul with rich food. Sometimes she gallops over a barrister's nose, and he'll dream of sniffing out a new lawsuit, and sometimes she comes with a tithe-pig's tail tickling the parson's nose as he sleeps, he then dreams of a richer parish.

### MERCUTIO
Her traces, of the smallest spider web;
Her collars, of the moonshine's wat'ry beams;
Her whip, of cricket's bone; the lash, of film;
Her waggoner, a small grey-coated gnat,
Not half so big as a round little worm
Pricked from the lazy finger of a maid.
And in this state she gallops night by night
Through lovers' brains, and then they dream of love.
O'er courtiers' knees, that dream on curtsies straight;
O'er lawyers' fingers, who straight dream on fees;
O'er ladies' lips, who straight on kisses dream,
Which oft the angry Mab with blisters plagues
Because their breaths with sweetmeats tainted are.
Sometime she gallops o'er a courtier's nose,
And then dreams he of smelling out a suit;
And sometime comes she with a tithe-pig's tail,
Tickling a parson's nose as a' lies asleep,
Then dreams he of another benefice.

*Note: A Tithe-Pig was given as part payment of a parson's wages. It was believed worms grew under the dirty fingernails of lazy maids who did little or no work, and Gossamer is a spider's web.*

THE GROUP LAUGH DURING MERCUTIO'S RAMBLINGS,
ALL EXCEPT ROMEO WHO REMAINS SULLEN FACED AND DOWN.

| MERCUTIO (CONT'D) | MERCUTIO |
|---|---|
| Sometimes she drives over a soldier's neck and he'll dream of cutting foreign throats, of battles, ambushes, the flash of a Spanish blade, of drinks five fathoms deep, and then she'll drum in his ear so he wakes with a start, and frightened, mutter a prayer or two before sleeping again. It is the very same Queen Mab who knots the manes of horses in the night, and mats tangled curls in foul sluttish hair, which bodes much misfortune when untangled. (*bawdy*) And this is the hag who teaches maidens how to <u>move</u> the first time they <u>lie on their backs</u>, making them more <u>enjoyable to ride</u>. That's who she is... | Sometime she driveth o'er a soldier's neck, And then dreams he of cutting foreign throats, Of breaches, ambuscados, Spanish blades, Of healths five fathom deep; and then anon Drums in his ear, at which he starts and wakes, And being thus frighted swears a prayer or two, And sleeps again. This is that very Mab That plaits the manes of horses in the night, And bakes the elf-locks in foul sluttish hairs, Which once untangled much misfortune bodes. This is the hag, when maids lie on their backs, That presses them and learns them first to bear, Making them women of good carriage. This is she - |

> Note: 'Spanish sword' refers to swords make in Toledo, supposedly the finest swords and the finest steel. A 'fathom' is six feet (1.8 m), used for water depth.

| ROMEO | ROMEO |
|---|---|
| Shut up, Mercutio, please! You talk a lot of nothing. | Peace, peace, Mercutio, peace! Thou talk'st of nothing. |

> Note: 'Nothing' was a common euphemism for female genitalia. Derived from the fact it is a round 'O' and also from a man having a 'something' between his legs, and a woman having a 'nothing'. Back then it was pronounced 'note-ing' (or nuttin' or nottin', depending on regional accent) with a hard 'T', the way it is still pronounced in Ireland as nuttin'.

| MERCUTIO | MERCUTIO |
|---|---|
| How true Romeo. I talk of dreams, which are the children of an idle brain, born of 'nothing' but vain fantasy, as lacking in substance as the air, and more changeable than the wind who sometimes woos the frozen bosom of the north, and then becoming angry, turns and blows his icy wind towards the mild dew-dropping south. | True, I talk of dreams, Which are the children of an idle brain, Begot of nothing but vain fantasy, Which is as thin of substance as the air, And more inconstant than the wind, who woos Even now the frozen bosom of the north, And, being angered, puffs away from thence, Turning his side to the dew-dropping south. |

*Note: A lot of suggestion and innuendo here. The wind warms up the cold north bosom, then turns his attentions to the 'dew dropping' south, both allusions to female bodies and also hinting at how the wind woos one lover then being unsuccessful, woos another.*

**BENVOLIO**

This wind you talk of blows us from our purpose, the feast will be finished, and we will be too late.

**ROMEO**

Too early I fear, Benvolio. I have a gut feeling that something written in the stars is destined to begin with tonight's revels, something I may end up paying for with my own wretched life in untimely death. But I cannot alter the course of my events, so lusty gentlemen, like my guiding star, lead on!

**BENVOLIO**

Strike up the drum!

---

BENVOLIO

This wind you talk of blows us from ourselves;
Supper is done, and we shall come too late.

ROMEO

I fear too early, for my mind misgives
Some consequence yet hanging in the stars
Shall bitterly begin his fearful date
With this night's revels, and expire the term
Of a despised life closed in my breast
By some vile forfeit of untimely death.
But He that hath the steerage of my course
Direct my sail! On, lusty gentlemen.

BENVOLIO

Strike, drum!

---

THEY MARCH OFF DOWN THE DRIVEWAY TO
CAPULET'S HOUSE IN TIME TO THE DRUM.

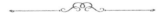

# ACT I SCENE V

## A Ball At Capulet's House. Sunday Evening.

PETER AND OTHER SERVANTS ARE HURRIEDLY CLEARING THE REMAINS OF A FEAST WHILE MUSICIANS SET UP FOR THE DANCING THAT FOLLOWS.

> *Note: The servants are comical so speak in prose. Potpan is a comic name related to his lowly job.*
>
> *There is a problem with the scenes at this point. Editors have added a scene change here, but originally Romeo and friends marched around the stage while the servants prepared for the ball with no scene change. The Capulets then enter as the servants leave, meeting Romeo's group. However, that makes little sense with modern stages. To make more sense of it, the first part of this scene is in the kitchen area with the servants, as they refer to the 'great chamber' as being elsewhere. The scullery is where the dishes are washed and cleaning is done.*

## The Scullery In Capulet's House. Sunday Evening.

| PETER | 1ST SERVANT |
|---|---|
| Where is Potpan, why isn't he helping clear away? (*sarcastic*) Him take a serving dish! Him scrape it clean! | Where's Potpan, that he helps not to take away? He shift trencher! He scrape a trencher! |

> *Note: A trencher was a wooden platter used to serve and carve meat.*

| SERVANT 2 | 2ND SERVANT |
|---|---|
| When it comes down to just one or two men getting their hands dirty, 'tis shameful. | When good manners shall lie all in one or two men's hands, and they unwashed too, 'tis a foul thing. |

| PETER | 1ST SERVANT |
|---|---|
| (*giving orders to one*) Fold the chairs away, take out the display cabinet, and be careful of the silverware.<br>(*ordering another*) Be a good fellow, save me a piece of marzipan, and do me a favour, tell the porter to let in (*with a suggestive wink*) Susan Grindstone and Nell. | Away with the joint-stools, remove the court-cupboard, look to the plate. Good thou, save me a piece of marchpane, and, as thou loves me, let the porter let in Susan Grindstone and Nell. |

56

*Note: Peter has plans for his own party later, but who were Susan Grindstone and Nell? We don't know. Nell (short for Eleanor) was not the famous Nell Gwyn as she was not born till 1650. It is interesting that Susan has a surname and not Nell. It is possible that 'grindstone' was a sexual reference which would suggest they were both 'party' women.*

2ND SERVANT LEAVES. PETER ANGRILY CALLS OUT FOR ASSISTANCE.

| PETER (CONT'D) | 1ST SERVANT |
|---|---|
| (*calls*) Anthony and Potpan! | Anthony and Potpan! |

ANTHONY AND POTPAN, TWO SERVANTS, ENTER. THEY SALUTE MOCKINGLY.

| ANTHONY | 3RD SERVANT |
|---|---|
| Aye aye, boy, ready. | Ay, boy, ready. |

*Note: 'Boy' is a sarcastic reply, suggesting the hired staff didn't like being talked down to by a fellow serving man.*

| PETER | 1ST SERVANT |
|---|---|
| We've been looking for you, calling for you, and shouting for you! You're required in the Great Hall. | You are looked for and called for, asked for and sought for, in the great chamber. |
| **POTPAN** | **4TH SERVANT** |
| We can't be here and there at the same time. Relax, boys! We'll do this in no time, enjoy life while you still can. | We cannot be here and there too. Cheerly, boys! Be brisk awhile, and the longer liver take all. |

*Note: 'The longer liver take all' is an old proverb about enjoying life and avoiding stress as the one who lives longest gets all that's left behind by everyone else.*

THE SERVANTS FINISH CLEARING AND EXIT.

## THE GREAT HALL IN CAPULET'S HOUSE. SUNDAY EVENING.

THE MUSICIANS SET UP, READY TO PLAY DANCING MUSIC.

ENTER OLD CAPULET, LADY CAPULET, JULIET AND HER NURSE, CAPULET'S COUSIN, TYBALT AND HIS PAGE AND INVITED GUESTS WEARING MASQUES.

Note: Rosaline and Count Paris are not mentioned as being present.

AS THE GUESTS SPREAD OUT, ROMEO, BENVOLIO AND MERCUTIO, ARRIVE AT THE ENTRANCE WEARING MASKS.

OLD CAPULET, SEEING THE MASKERS AT THE DOOR, BECKONS THEM IN.

**OLD CAPULET**
Welcome, gentlemen! The ladies that are unplagued with corns on their feet, will escort you about the floor.
(*loudly to the ladies*) Aha, my mistresses, now which of you will refuse to dance? She that's shy coming forward, I swear she has corns. Am I not near the truth?

**CAPULET**
Welcome, gentlemen! Ladies that have their toes
Unplagued with corns will walk a bout with you.
Ah, my mistresses, which of you all
Will now deny to dance? She that makes dainty,
She, I'll swear, hath corns. Am I come near ye
now?

Note: Corns on the feet are caused by wearing shoes too small, to make feet look dainty. He is shaming those who don't dance by suggesting they are vain.

THE YOUNG LADIES GIGGLE SHYLY.

THE MASKERS HAVE REACHED OLD CAPULET WHO GREETS THEM.

**OLD CAPULET (CONT'D)**
Welcome. Gentlemen! The days I wore a mask and would whisper a tale in a young ladies ear to please her, are long gone, long gone. (*sighs*) You are welcome, gentlemen!
(*calls*) Come musicians, play!

**CAPULET**
Welcome, gentlemen! I have seen the day
That I have worn a visor and could tell
A whispering tale in a fair lady's ear,
Such as would please: 'tis gone, 'tis gone, 'tis gone.
You are welcome, gentlemen! Come, musicians,
play.

THE MUSICIANS START PLAYING.

**OLD CAPULET (CONT'D)**
(*to everyone*) This is a dancing hall! Make some room. And girls take to the floor!
(*to servants*) More light, you wastrels, and move the tables out the way. And douse the fire, the room is too hot.

**CAPULET**
A hall, a hall! Give room; and foot it, girls!

More light, you knaves; and turn the tables up;
And quench the fire, the room is grown too hot.

Note: It would seem Shakespeare had never visited Italy in the summer. There would be no need for a fire, even at night, and Capulet is not impressed with the serving staff.

THE GUESTS AND THE MASKERS DANCE.

ROMEO STANDS TO THE SIDE NOT JOINING IN.

OLD CAPULET REMINISCES WITH HIS COUSIN.

| OLD CAPULET (CONT'D) | CAPULET |
|---|---|
| (*to Cousin*) Ah sirrah, it is just as well these masked men turned up. Sit yourself down, dear cousin Capulet, for you and I are past our dancing days. | Ah sirrah, this unlooked-for sport comes well. Nay sit, nay sit, good cousin Capulet, For you and I are past our dancing days. |

THE TWO MEN SIT DOWN, WITH SOME RELIEF.

| OLD CAPULET (CONT'D) | CAPULET |
|---|---|
| (*sitting*) How long is it since you and I were last in a mask? | How long is't now since last yourself and I Were in a masque? |
| **COUSIN CAPULET** | **COUSIN** |
| Goodness me, it must be thirty years. | By'r Lady, thirty years. |
| **OLD CAPULET** | **CAPULET** |
| What! No, it's not that long. It's not that long since the wedding of Lucentio. Come Whitsun, which is soon now, it will be some twenty-five years since we masqueraded. | What, man? 'tis not so much, 'tis not so much. 'Tis since the nuptial of Lucentio, Come Pentecost as quickly as it will, Some five-and-twenty years; and then we masqued. |

*Note: Pentecost is a Christian festival held on Whit Sunday, the seventh Sunday after Easter, to celebrate the Holy Spirit visiting the disciples of Jesus*

| COUSIN CAPULET | COUSIN |
|---|---|
| No, it's longer, it's longer. His son is older than that, sir. He's thirty now. | 'Tis more, 'tis more. His son is elder, sir; His son is thirty. |
| **OLD CAPULET** | **CAPULET** |
| Are you sure? His son was still living at home only two years ago. | Will you tell me that? His son was but a ward two years ago. |

*Note: If it was thirty years ago, this makes Old Capulet fifty years old or older. His wife we know is twenty-eight years old. If Old Montague is around the same age this makes Romeo up to thirty years in age. Nowhere in the text does Shakespeare tell us Romeo's age.*

ROMEO PULLS ASIDE A PASSING SERVANT. TYBALT OVERHEARS.

ROMEO

(*to Server 2*) My man, who is that lady gracing the hand of that gentleman over there?

ROMEO

What lady's that which doth enrich the hand Of yonder knight?

ROMEO POINTS OUT JULIET. IT APPEARS HE DOES NOT RECOGNISE HER, ALTHOUGH THE TWO FAMILIES ARE FAMILIAR WITH EACH OTHER, UNLESS THE LADIES WERE MASKED TOO. TYBALT SEES WHO ROMEO INDICATES.

SERVANT 2

I don't know, sir.

2ND SERVANT

I know not, sir.

THE FIERY TYBALT (A CAPULET), STORMS OFF TO FIND HIS SERVING BOY.

ROMEO GAZES AT JULIET, TRANSFIXED BY HER BEAUTY, LOST IN HIS DREAMS.

ROMEO

(*aside*)

*Oh, her radiance outshines the torches' light!*
*It seems she hangs on the cheek of the night*
*Like sparkling jewels in a dark woman's ear -*
*Beauty too rich, and for this world too dear!*
*Like a snowy white dove in a flock of black*
  *crows.*
*Over all other ladies her beauty it shows.*
*When this dance does end I'll watch where she*
  *stands,*
*And by touching hers, I'll bless my rude hands.*
*Did I love before now? I swear by my sight,*
*Beauty so true, I ne'er saw till this night.*

ROMEO

*O, she doth teach the torches to burn bright!*
*It seems she hangs upon the cheek of night*
*As a rich jewel in an Ethiop's ear -*
*Beauty too rich for use, for earth too dear!*
*So shows a snowy dove trooping with crows*
*As yonder lady o'er her fellows shows.*
*The measure done, I'll watch her place of stand,*
*And, touching hers, make blessed my rude hand.*
*Did my heart love till now? Forswear it, sight;*
*For I ne'er saw true beauty till this night.*

Note: A troop describes a group of any animals, here it has the double meaning of being in a group of crows and walking with them (which troop also means).

TYBALT FINDS HIS SERVING BOY.

TYBALT

(*to his page*) By the sound of his voice he must be a Montague. Fetch my sword boy!

TYBALT

This, by his voice, should be a Montague. Fetch me my rapier, boy.

TYBALT'S PAGE RUNS OFF TO GET HIS SWORD.

> Note: A page was a young attendant to a man or woman of note. The title is still used today in weddings and the hotel trade.

**TYBALT (CONT'D)**

(*aside angrily*) How dare the lowlife come here hiding behind a comic face to sneer and scorn our celebrations!
*Now, for the honour and pride of my kin,*
*To strike him down dead would not be a sin.*

**TYBALT**

What, dares the slave
Come hither, covered with an antic face,
To fleer and scorn at our solemnity?
*Now, by the stock and honour of my kin,*
*To strike him dead I hold it not a sin.*

OLD CAPULET SEES THAT TYBALT IS AGITATED.
HE STANDS UP TO QUESTION HIM.

**OLD CAPULET**

*What is it, Tybalt? What upsets you so?*

**CAPULET**

*Why, how now, kinsman; wherefore storm you so?*

**TYBALT**

*Uncle, this is a Montague – our foe!*
*A villain that comes to our house in spite*
*To scorn at our celebrations tonight.*

**TYBALT**

*Uncle, this is a Montague, our foe;*
*A villain that is hither come in spite*
*To scorn at our solemnity this night.*

**OLD CAPULET**

It's young Romeo is it?

**CAPULET**

Young Romeo is it?

**TYBALT**

It is. That villain, Romeo!

**TYBALT**

'Tis he, that villain Romeo.

**OLD CAPULET**

Calm down, Tybalt, and leave him be. He is behaving like a dignified gentleman, and in truth, all Verona boasts of him to be a virtuous and well bought up youth. For all the wealth in this town I would not allow such discourtesy to be shown in my house. So be patient, ignore him. It is my order, which I trust you to respect. Be courteous and stop these frowns, this is not the conduct befitting of a feast.

**CAPULET**

Content thee, gentle coz, let him alone.
A' bears him like a portly gentleman,
And, to say truth, Verona brags of him
To be a virtuous and well-governed youth.
I would not for the wealth of all this town
Here in my house do him disparagement.
Therefore be patient, take no note of him;
It is my will, the which if thou respect,
Show a fair presence and put off these frowns,
An ill-beseeming semblance for a feast.

**TYBALT**

It fits when such a villain is a guest. I'll not endure his presence.

**TYBALT**

It fits when such a villain is a guest.
I'll not endure him.

OLD CAPULET

(*getting angry*) He will be endured, boy, because I say so! Am I the master here or you? For heaven's sake.
(*mocking*) You'll not endure him! God save my soul! You'll start a mutiny amongst my guests to show off? You'll be the big man?

CAPULET

He shall be endured.
What, goodman boy! I say he shall. Go to,
Am I the master here or you? Go to.
You'll not endure him! God shall mend my soul!
You'll make a mutiny among my guests,
You will set cock-a-hoop, you'll be the man!

---

Note: Cock-a-hoop, an expression that means full of exuberance, swaggering, but is an expression that no one knows for sure how it came about. The theory that it is a tap in a barrel which cannot be turned off, so the barrel must be drunk in full in one session, is purely speculative and based on a single theory put forward in the 17$^{th}$ century with no evidence and continued by repetition. We may never know the source but the meaning is universally agreed.

---

TYBALT

It is a shame on us, Uncle.

TYBALT

Why, uncle, 'tis a shame.

OLD CAPULET

(*very angry*) Get away with you. You are an impudent boy! It's a shame indeed, is it? This will be your downfall boy. That much I know. You'll do as I say. Indeed, it is time...

CAPULET

Go to, go to;
You are a saucy boy. Is't so indeed?
This trick may chance to scathe you. I know what:
You must contrary me. Marry, 'tis time -

---

THE DANCE MUSIC ENDS ABRUPTLY.

JULIET RETURNS TO HER PLACE WHERE ROMEO AWAITS HER.

OLD CAPULET BREAKS FROM HIS TIRADE AGAINST TYBALT
AND CALLS TO HIS GUESTS CHEERFULLY.

---

OLD CAPULET (CONT'D)

(*to guests*) Well done my loved ones!
(*to Tybalt*) You are an impertinent youth, Tybalt - Now go! And keep quiet or...
(*to serving men*) More light, more light men!
(*to Tybalt*) ...to your shame I will make you keep quiet.
(*to guests*) I am glad to see you all enjoying yourselves my friends.

CAPULET

Well said, my hearts! - You are a princox; go,
Be quiet, or - More light, more light! - for shame,
I'll make you quiet. - What, cheerly, my hearts!

---

Note: Princox is an alernative word for 'Coxcomb'; a preening, insolent youth. Archaic in usage but still worth a useful eighteen points in Scrabble.

A NEW PERIOD DANCE BEGINS. THE GUESTS DANCE.

TYBALT

(aside angrily) Me show restraint with such
    forced provocation,
Makes my flesh tremble with rage and
    frustration,
I will withdraw, but this intrusion now,
We 'sweetly' bear, will turn bitterest sour.

TYBALT

*Patience perforce with wilful choler meeting*
*Makes my flesh tremble in their different greeting.*
*I will withdraw; but this intrusion shall,*
*Now seeming sweet, convert to bitt'rest gall.*

TYBALT STORMS OUT.

ROMEO, OBLIVIOUS TO WHAT IS HAPPENING, APPROACHES JULIET.

JULIET MAKES A QUIET EXCLAMATION OF SURPRISE AS
ROMEO TOUCHES HER HAND.

> Note: The lovers exchange words in sonnets, (fourteen line poems). A device
> Shakespeare used for the speech of lovers.

ROMEO

(to Juliet, touching her hand)
If by touching yours, my unworthy hand
Defiles all that's holy, the less sin is this:
My lips, two coy pilgrims, in readiness stand
To smooth that rough touch with a tender
    kiss.

ROMEO

(to Juliet, touching her hand)
*If I profane with my unworthiest hand*
*This holy shrine, the gentle sin is this:*
*My lips, two blushing pilgrims, ready stand*
*To smooth that rough touch with a tender kiss.*

> Note: The original texts said 'gentle sin', some later texts replace sin with 'fine', as
> in a penalty payment. Arguments are made by both sides. Here, the more common
> 'sin' is used as they discuss the sin in their actions shortly.

JULIET

Good pilgrim, you accuse your hand too much,
Good manners and devotion shows in this.
Saint's statues have hands pilgrims' hands do
    touch,
So hand to hand's the pilgrim's holy kiss.

JULIET

*Good pilgrim, you do wrong your hand too much,*
*Which mannerly devotion shows in this;*
*For saints have hands that pilgrims' hands do touch,*
*And palm to palm is holy palmers' kiss.*

> Note: Palmer is an archaic term for a pilgrim to the Holy Land who returned with
> palm tree fronds as proof, used here to pun with hands. Pilgrims would also visit
> statues of Saints and touch the hand to show reverence. Pilgrims to Rome were
> called "Romei", perhaps the reason this imagery was used.

| | |
|---|---|
| ROMEO | ROMEO |
| *Don't saints have lips, and holy pilgrims too?* | *Have not saints lips, and holy palmers too?* |
| JULIET | JULIET |
| *Yes, pilgrim, lips that they must use in prayer.* | *Ay, pilgrim, lips that they must use in prayer.* |
| ROMEO | ROMEO |
| *Oh then, dear saint, let lips do what hands do:* | *O then, dear saint, let lips do what hands do:* |
| *Grant their prayer, lest faith turns to despair.* | *They pray. Grant thou, lest faith turn to despair.* |
| JULIET | JULIET |
| *Saints do not move, while prayer's granting they make.* | *Saints do not move, though grant for prayer's sake.* |
| ROMEO | ROMEO |
| *Then do not move while prayer's effect I take.* | *Then move not while my prayer's effect I take.* |

HE KISSES HER.

| | |
|---|---|
| ROMEO | ROMEO |
| *So from my lips, to yours my sin is purged.* | *Thus from my lips, by thine my sin is purged.* |
| JULIET | JULIET |
| *Then now my lips have your sin which they took.* | *Then have my lips the sin that they have took.* |
| ROMEO | ROMEO |
| *Sin from my lips? Temptation sweetly urged!* | *Sin from my lips? O trespass sweetly urged!* |
| *Give me my sin again...* | *Give me my sin again.* |

HE KISSES HER.

| | |
|---|---|
| JULIET | JULIET |
| *...You kiss by the book.* | *You kiss by th' book.* |

> Note: Juliet's statement is three way wordplay – kissing expertly, abiding by the rules, and 'the book' being the Bible – and it rhymes with her previous line.

NURSE APPEARS, ALMOST CATCHING THEM KISSING.

| | |
|---|---|
| NURSE | NURSE |
| Madam, your mother wishes a word with you. | Madam, your mother craves a word with you. |

AS JULIET WALKS OFF BLUSHING, ROMEO PULLS NURSE ASIDE.

ROMEO

Who is her mother?

NURSE

My goodness, young man, her mother is the lady of the house, and a good, virtuous and wise lady. I nursed her daughter that you were just talking to. I tell you, the man who can lay hold of her will, 'Hit the jackpot'.

ROMEO

What is her mother?

NURSE

Marry, bachelor,
Her mother is the lady of the house,
And a good lady, and a wise and virtuous.
I nursed her daughter that you talked withal.
I tell you, he that can lay hold of her
Shall have the chinks.

> Note: The nurse's comment is a bawdy pun on sex and money. To lie or lay with someone meant to have sex with them as well as lay hold or claim them in marriage. 'Shall have the chinks' meant she was a good catch (bawdy) and worth money.

ROMEO IS SHOCKED AT THE NEWS.

ROMEO

(aside)                    She's a Capulet?
What price to pay! My life in my foes debt.

ROMEO

                    Is she a Capulet?
O dear account! My life is my foe's debt.

> Note: Quite why Romeo is surprised is confusing. The two families know and recognise each other well. Tybalt knew Romeo by voice alone, and he was at a Capulet party. One could argue that Juliet was wearing a mask, but if she was, how did Romeo fall so in love with her beauty?

BENVOLIO APPROACHES ROMEO TO TELL HIM THEY ARE LEAVING.

BENVOLIO

Come on, let's go.  The sport has passed its best.

BENVOLIO

Away, be gone; the sport is at the best.

> Note: Benvolio means they've seen all there is to see, there's nothing better to see by staying, Romeo agrees, as he has found what he believes is the best, but what he has found is not what he can have.

ROMEO IS STILLED STUNNED AT THE REVELATION.

ROMEO

You're right, I fear, and much to my unrest.

OLD CAPULET

Wait, do not leave now, gentlemen. We have a light supper still to come.

ROMEO

Ay, so I fear; the more is my unrest.

CAPULET

Nay, gentlemen, prepare not to be gone;
We have a trifling foolish banquet towards.

BENVOLIO LEANS IN AND WHISPERS SOMETHING IN
OLD CAPULET'S EAR IN CONFIDENCE.

| OLD CAPULET | CAPULET |
|---|---|
| Is that so? Well then, I thank you all for coming. I thank you, honourable gentlemen. Good night. | Is it e'en so? Why then, I thank you all; I thank you, honest gentlemen. Good night. More torches here! Come on then, let's to bed. |
| (*to servants*) More lights here, men! | Ah, sirrah, by my fay, it waxes late; |
| (*to all*) Come on everyone, it's time to retire for the evening. | I'll to my rest. |
| (*yawning*) Oh, my, upon my soul it is late. I'm off to bed. | |

OLD CAPULET LEAVES WITH HIS WIFE, FOLLOWED BY HIS COUSIN.

THE GUESTS BEGIN TO LEAVE.

JULIET REMAINS, WATCHING THEM LEAVE.

| JULIET | JULIET |
|---|---|
| Come here, Nurse. Who is that gentleman over there? | Come hither, Nurse. What is yond gentleman? |
| **NURSE** | **NURSE** |
| The son and heir of old Tiberio. | The son and heir of old Tiberio. |
| **JULIET** | **JULIET** |
| Who's that going out of the door now? | What's he that now is going out of door? |
| **NURSE** | **NURSE** |
| Goodness, that's young Petruccio I think. | Marry, that, I think, be young Petruchio. |

Note: Juliet deliberately picks out two people before asking after Romeo so that her Nurse does not suspect her true intention

| JULIET | JULIET |
|---|---|
| Who's that following behind that would not dance? | What's he that follows here, that would not dance? |
| **NURSE** | **NURSE** |
| I don't know. | I know not. |
| **JULIET** | **JULIET** |
| *Go, ask him his name...* | *Go, ask his name.* |

NURSE CHASES AFTER ROMEO AND QUESTIONS HIM.

| | |
|---|---|
| **JULIET (CONT'D)** | **JULIET** |
| *(aside)*　　　　　*and if he is wed,* | *If he be married* |
| *My grave will likely be my wedding bed.* | *My grave is like to be my wedding bed.* |

> Note: Married has three syllables here – marry-ed.

PROPHETIC WORDS FROM JULIET. SHE ANXIOUSLY AWAITS NURSE'S RETURN.

NURSE FINALLY RETURNS WITH THE ANSWER.

| | |
|---|---|
| **NURSE** | **NURSE** |
| His name is Romeo, and he's a Montague, | His name is Romeo, and a Montague; |
| the only son of your great enemy. | The only son of your great enemy. |

UPSET, JULIET RECITES A RHYME TO HERSELF AS THE GUESTS FILE OUT.

| | |
|---|---|
| **JULIET** | **JULIET** |
| *My only love, born of my only hate!* | *My only love sprung from my only hate!* |
| *Unknown when first seen, and now known too* | *Too early seen unknown, and known too late!* |
| 　　*late!* | *Prodigious birth of love it is to me* |
| *What fateful start of love it is for me* | *That I must love a loathed enemy.* |
| *That I should love my hated enemy.* | |

> Note: Loathed has two syllables here – loathe-ed.

| | |
|---|---|
| **NURSE** | **NURSE** |
| What? What was that? | What's this, what's this? |
| **JULIET** | **JULIET** |
| Only a rhyme I just learned from someone | A rhyme I learned even now |
| I danced with. | Of one I danced withal. |

LADY CAPULET CALLS FROM INSIDE THE HOUSE.

| | |
|---|---|
| **LADY CAPULET** | **LADY CAPULET** |
| *(off)* Juliet! | *(off)* Juliet! |
| **NURSE** | **NURSE** |
| *(calling)* Coming, Coming! | Anon, anon! |
| *(to Juliet)* Come on, Juliet, let's go. The | Come, let's away; the strangers all are gone. |
| guests have all left. | |

# PROLOGUE

THE CHORUS COMES ON STAGE AND RECITES A VERSE.

*Note: The Chorus could either be a single person acting as a narrator to introduce the story or the entire cast together. This was common practise in tragedies of the time so would prepare the audience. However, as Romeo and Juliet is also a romance the prologue is written in the format of a sonnet.*

CHORUS

Now old desire does die a death once more,
And new affection craves to be its heir.
Love which Romeo once groaned and died for,
When matched with Juliet, is now not there.

Now Romeo is loved and loves again,
Together bewitched by the charms of looks.
But from his foe, his love he hoped to gain,
And she takes love's sweet bait from frightful hooks.

But as a foe he may not have the means
To breathe such vows as lovers oft' do swear,
And she, as much in love, but with less means
To meet her new beloved anywhere.

But passion lends them strength, time the means to meet,
Beating down adversity makes it all more sweet.

CHORUS

*Now old desire doth in his deathbed lie,
And young affection gapes to be his heir;
That fair for which love groaned for and would die,
With tender Juliet matched, is now not fair.*

*Now Romeo is beloved and loves again,
Alike bewitched by the charm of looks;
But to his foe supposed he must complain,
And she steal love's sweet bait from fearful hooks.*

*Being held a foe, he may not have access
To breathe such vows as lovers use to swear;
And she as much in love, her means much less
To meet her new beloved anywhere.*

*But passion lends them power, time means, to meet,
Temp'ring extremities with extreme sweet.*

*Note: "Sweet bait from fearful hooks" is a fishing reference. The first 'beloved' is two syllables (he is loved), the second is three syllables (his loved one).*

# ACT II

A LOVERS' MEETING

# ACT II

## ACT II SCENE I

### THE ROAD TO CAPULET'S HOUSE. SUNDAY NIGHT.

PLAYFUL BANTER AND DRUM BEAT OF THE MASKERS AS THEY
WALK DOWN A LANE BY THE WALL OF CAPULET'S ORCHARD.

| ROMEO | ROMEO |
|---|---|
| (*aside*) How can I leave when my heart's desire is here? I must turn my cold body back, in search of the warm centre of my world. | Can I go forward when my heart is here? Turn back, dull earth, and find thy centre out. |

ROMEO DASHES OFF AND JUMPS THE WALL INTO CAPULET'S ORCHARD. THE
DRUM BEAT STOPS.

BENVOLIO MOCKS HIM FROM HIS SIDE OF THE WALL.

*Note: An orchard back then was a garden growing anything; herbs, vegetables, flowers, trees. It was in later times an orchard meant fruit trees.*

| BENVOLIO | BENVOLIO |
|---|---|
| (*calling mockingly*) Romeo... Cousin Romeo... Oh, Romeo! | Romeo! My cousin Romeo! Romeo! |

| MERCUTIO | MERCUTIO |
|---|---|
| He's not stupid, Benvolio, I'll bet he's slipped off home to his bed. | He is wise, And, on my life, hath stol'n him home to bed. |

| BENVOLIO | BENVOLIO |
|---|---|
| He ran that way, and leapt over Capulet's orchard wall. You call him, Mercutio. | He ran this way and leapt this orchard wall. Call, good Mercutio. |

| MERCUTIO | MERCUTIO |
|---|---|
| No, I'll summon him here with a spell. Romeo! Moody! Madman! Broody! | Nay, I'll conjure too. Romeo! Humours! Madman! Passion! Lover! |

MERCUTIO MOCKS ROMEO WITH A RHYME HE MAKES UP AS HE GOES ALONG
WHILE THE OTHERS GIGGLE AND BANG A DRUM IN ENCOURAGEMENT.

| MERCUTIO (CONT'D) | MERCUTIO |
|---|---|
| *Appear before us like a lover's sigh,* | Appear thou in the likeness of a sigh: |
| *Speak just one rhyme and I'm satisfied.* | Speak but one rhyme and I am satisfied; |
| *Cry out 'Oh my!', use the words 'love' and* | Cry but `Ay me!' pronounce but `love' and |
| *'dove'.* | `dove'. |
| *Speak one sweet word to the Goddess of love,* | Speak to my gossip Venus one fair word, |
| *Find a new name for her blind son and heir,* | One nickname for her purblind son and heir, |
| *Young Abram Cupid, whose aim is so fair* | Young Abram Cupid, he that shot so trim |
| *He charmed King Cophetua with a peasant* | When King Cophetua loved the beggar maid. |
| *maid's love,* | He heareth not, he stirreth not, he moveth not; |
| *(he cups his hand to his ear)* | |
| *But Romeo can't hear, can't see, can't move.* | |

MERCUTIO PAUSES, CUPPING HIS HAND TO HIS EAR, LISTENING.

THERE IS NO REPLY FROM ROMEO.

---

*Note: Some modern versions prefer 'Adam Cupid', which refers to Adam Bell, a famous archer, who is quoted as saying, "Hang me in a bottle and shoot at me; and he that hits me let him be clapped on the shoulder, and called Adam". Old versions say Abraham Cupid or Abram, which could refer to biblical Abraham, or to Abram men - as cheats and conmen were called - Cupid being deceptive in the love matches he made.*

*'He that shot so trim' is from the ballad of 'King Cophetua (pronounced koff-fet-chew-ah) and the beggar maid', which was popular at the time –*

> *"The blinded boy that shoots so trim,*
>
> *From heaven down did hie,*
>
> *And drew a dart and shot at him,*
>
> *In place where he did lie."*

*'Trim' meaning true or accurate. In short Shakespeare is saying that Cupid is blind where he shoots his arrow (dart) or a mischievous and deceptive rogue who can make a mockery of matches, such as a King with a maid, and Romeo with his enemy.*

---

| MERCUTIO (CONT'D) | MERCUTIO |
|---|---|
| The fool is dead, I must summon him back to life again. | The ape is dead, and I must conjure him. |

THEY ALL LAUGH AS MERCUTIO DRAWS A 'MAGIC' CIRCLE ON THE GROUND
AROUND HIM WITH HIS SWORD TIP.

MERCUTIO (CONT'D)

I summon thee by Rosaline's bright eyes,

By her high forehead and her scarlet lips,

*By her delicate feet, long legs and quivering thighs,*

*(bawdily) And the bushy domain that inbetween lies...*

That in likeness you appear before us again.

---

MERCUTIO

I conjure thee by Rosaline's bright eyes,

By her high forehead and her scarlet lip,

*By her fine foot, straight leg, and quivering thigh,*

*And the demesnes that there adjacent lie,*

That in thy likeness thou appear to us.

---

Note: A high forehead was considered a sign of beauty and good breeding.

The two bawdy lines which rhyme were omitted from some early texts due to their suggestive content.

Demesne (pronounced de- main) is the land, typically around a manor house, reserved for the sole use of the lord of the manor, often allowed to grow naturally, rather than cultivated, hence being bushy.

---

BENVOLIO

*(laughing)* Mercutio, if he hears you he'll be angry.

---

BENVOLIO

And if he hear thee, thou wilt anger him.

---

MERCUTIO

That wouldn't upset him. It would upset him if I cast a spell to raise another spirit in his beloved's 'magic circle', of some strange nature, letting it stand there erect until she had 'laid it' and magicked it back down. That would be spiteful. My spell is fair and honest. I used his beloved's name in the spell only to help him "rise up' to the occasion.

---

MERCUTIO

This cannot anger him. 'Twould anger him

To raise a spirit in his mistress' circle

Of some strange nature, letting it there stand

Till she had laid it and conjured it down.

That were some spite -my invocation

Is fair and honest. In his mistress' name

I conjure only but to raise up him.

---

THEY LAUGH AT MERCUTIO'S BAWDINESS.

---

Note: A 'circle' or anything referring to the number zero, such as nothing, O, naught, etc, were bawdy euphemisms for a vagina. The term 'nothing' in particular was well known as a euphemism for two reasons, one, it formed a circle when written, and two, a gentleman has something obvious between his legs, a lady has nothing, so it was referred to as her 'nothing'.

'Laid' was a euphemism for sex then as it is today, to 'lie with someone' had the same meaning then as 'to sleep with' means today.

> *It was believed that to conjure (raise) up a spirit one needed to stand in a circle drawn on the ground and recite incantations. To be rid of the spirit one needed to 'lay it down' again by reciting a different cantation to return it to where it had come from. The picture shown here is from Marlowe's Dr. Faustus and shows the raising of a spirit by standing in a magic circle.*

**BENVOLIO**

Let's go, Mercutio. He hides in the trees seeking the gloomy company of the night. His love is blind and best suited to the dark.

**MERCUTIO**

If love is blind, love cannot find its way. Now Romeo will sit under the Medlar tree, with its soft, erotic fruit that young girls giggle at because of its likeness to their <u>parts</u>, and wish his mistress were the kind of fruit he could <u>meddle with</u>. Oh Romeo, that she were,  oh that she were that soft, <u>yielding</u> medlar fruit and you the '<u>prick</u>'-ly pear!

Goodnight Romeo, (*he blows a kiss*) I'm off to my warm bed, this field-bed is too cold for me to sleep.

Come, Benvolio, shall we go?

BENVOLIO

Come, he hath hid himself among these trees
To be consorted with the humorous night.
Blind is his love, and best befits the dark.

MERCUTIO

If love be blind, love cannot hit the mark.
Now will he sit under a medlar tree,
And wish his mistress were that kind of fruit
As maids call medlars when they laugh alone.
O Romeo, that she were, O that she were
An open-arse, and thou a poperin pear!
Romeo, good night. I'll to my truckle-bed;
This field-bed is too cold for me to sleep.
Come, shall we go?

> *Note: An 'open-arse' was an Elizabethan slang term for the fruit of the medlar tree which had a gaping opening at the end of the fruit - a euphemism for a vagina.  A 'Poperin Pear' was a euphemism for a penis and a pun on 'pop 'er in' (put it in).*
>
> *In the earliest text the term "open et caetera" was used which was a subtle way of hinting at the name "open-arse" which later editions adopted probably to make the meaning clear to readers.*

**BENVOLIO**

Go on then. It's pointless looking for him here if he doesn't wish to be found.

BENVOLIO

Go then, for 'tis in vain
To seek him here that means not to be found.

DRUM BEAT STARTS UP AGAIN. THEY WALK OFF LEAVING ROMEO BEHIND.

# ACT II SCENE II

## CAPULET'S GARDEN. SUNDAY NIGHT.

ROMEO IS ALONE WITH HIS THOUGHTS IN CAPULET'S GARDEN. HE HEARS
THE TEASING FROM THE OTHER SIDE OF THE WALL BUT DOESN'T REPLY.

> *Note: This scene is more commonly referred to as 'The Balcony Scene".*
>
> *Shakespeare originally had no scene break here, as can be seen from the last line of the previous scene rhyming with the first line of this scene. Presumably Romeo would have been crouched, hiding one side of the stage while the others taunted him from the other side. As they walked off he would have stood up and started talking.*

| ROMEO | ROMEO |
|---|---|
| (*aside*) He that mocks love's scars has yet to feel a wound. | He jests at scars, that never felt a wound. |

> *Note: He refers to both Cupid's arrow and the pain of heartbreak.*

FROM ABOVE A LIGHT APPEARS AT A WINDOW. JULIET'S FACE APPEARS IN
THE WINDOW. AS ROMEO TALKS SHE OPENS THE DOOR AND WALKS OUT
ONTO HER BALCONY. SHE DOESN'T SEE ROMEO IN THE DARKNESS, BUT
ROMEO SEES HER SILHOUETTED AGAINST THE LIGHT SPILLING OUT FROM
HER ROOM.

| ROMEO | ROMEO |
|---|---|
| (*aside*) But hush, a light, shining from the window. | But soft, what light through yonder window breaks? |
| (*recognising Juliet*) It is the Eastern horizon, and Juliet is the sun! Rise, radiant sun, and kill the jealous moon, sickly and pale with grief that you, her servant, are far more beautiful. Don't be her servant, she is jealous since her dress is that sickly green only worn by fools and old maids. Cast it off. | It is the east, and Juliet is the sun. Arise, fair sun, and kill the envious moon, Who is already sick and pale with grief That thou, her maid, art far more fair than she. Be not her maid, since she is envious. Her vestal livery is but sick and green, And none but fools do wear it; cast it off. |

> *Note: He is saying 'don't remain an umarried virgin' (like his last infatuation, Rosaline), by following Diana, the goddess of the moon and virginity, because Diana would want Juliet to stay single as she is jealous of her beauty.*

*Note: 'Vestal livery' meaning virginal attire, referring to the vestal virgins who dedicated their lives to keeping the sacred fire burning at the alter of the Goddess, Vesta. It was said that if this flame ever went out Rome would fall. For over one thousand years, six women aged between six and ten from noble Italian families were chosen by the head priest of Rome. They served a minimum of thirty years and swore to remain chaste.*

*Sick and green is from the Renaissance belief that women who maintained their virginity were subject to green-sickness, named after a form of anaemia that could affect women, known medically as chlorosis, in which the skin actually takes on a greenish hue due to an iron (haemoglobin) deficiency. Although the condition had virtually nothing to do with virginity, the "cure" was believed to be in the lovemaking expected in marriage.*

JULIET MOVES TO THE EDGE OF THE BALCONY.

ROMEO NOW SEES HER CLEARLY, BATHED IN THE MOONLIGHT.

### ROMEO (CONT'D)

(*aside*) It is my Lady. Oh, it is my love! Oh, if only she knew she were! She speaks, yet she says nothing. No matter, her eyes speak for her, I will answer them... I am too bold. 'Tis not to me she speaks. Two of the brightest stars in the heavens, having some business elsewhere, plead with her eyes to sparkle in their place till they return. What if her eyes were up there, and the stars were shining in her head? The brightness of her cheek would put those stars to shame, like daylight to a lamp. Her eyes in heaven would stream so brightly through the sky, the birds would sing thinking it was no longer night. See how she leans her cheek upon her hand. Oh, how I wish I were a glove upon that hand so I might touch her cheek!

### ROMEO

It is my lady; O, it is my love!
O that she knew she were!
She speaks, yet she says nothing. What of that?
Her eye discourses; I will answer it.
I am too bold, 'tis not to me she speaks;
Two of the fairest stars in all the heaven,
Having some business, do entreat her eyes
To twinkle in their spheres till they return.
What if her eyes were there, they in her head?
The brightness of her cheek would shame those
   stars
As daylight doth a lamp. Her eyes in heaven
Would through the airy region stream so bright
That birds would sing and think it were not
   night.
See how she leans her cheek upon her hand.
O! that I were a glove upon that hand
That I might touch that cheek.

*Note: 'Twinkle in their spheres' –thanks to Ptolemy, people then believed the seven visible planets (including the Moon and the Sun) were carried around the Earth in invisible spheres, with an outer eighth sphere containing the seven planet spheres and all the stars (the firmament). The whole system was contained in a ninth sphere, the Primum Mobile, itself contained within the Empyrean, the fastest moving sphere, revolving around the earth (the centre of the system) in twenty-four hours, carrying the inner spheres with it. However, Copernicus had proved by 1543 that the earth revolved around the Sun, but the Church considered this heresy.*

JULIET

(*sighing*) Oh my!

JULIET

Ah me!

ROMEO

(*aside*) She speaks! Oh, speak again, bright angel high above me. For you are as glorious to this night as a winged messenger from heaven riding the slow passing clouds across the sky, as we mortals fall back to gaze up at you with white, upturned, wondrous eyes.

ROMEO

She speaks.

O speak again, bright angel, for thou art
As glorious to this night, being o'er my head,
As is a winged messenger of heaven
Unto the white-upturned wond'ring eyes
Of mortals that fall back to gaze on him
When he bestrides the lazy-puffing clouds
And sails upon the bosom of the air.

Note: The use of 'glorious' is intentional, one meaning of 'glory' is the circle of light believed to glow above saints and particularly the Virgin Mary.

JULIET

(*to self aloud*) Oh, Romeo, Romeo, why are you a Montague? Disown your family and renounce your name, or better still, be my sworn love, for then I'll no longer be a Capulet.

JULIET

O Romeo, Romeo, wherefore art thou Romeo?
Deny thy father and refuse thy name;
Or, if thou wilt not, be but sworn my love
And I'll no longer be a Capulet.

Note: This line is famously confusing for two reasons – it sounds like she is calling out to Romeo (she's not) and she really means 'Montague' rather than Romeo, as the modern translation explains.

ROMEO

(*aside*) Should I carry on listening, or should I answer this?

ROMEO

Shall I hear more, or shall I speak at this?

JULIET

(*aside*) 'Tis only your name that is my enemy, you'd be yourself even if you were not called Montague. What is 'Montague' anyway? It's not a hand, or a foot, or an arm, or a face, or any other part of a body. Oh, take some other name! What's in a name anyway? A rose would smell just as sweet whichever name we gave it. Romeo too would still be as sweet were he no longer named Romeo. Give up your name, Romeo, which is no part of you anyway, and in return, take all of me.

JULIET

Tis but thy name that is my enemy;
Thou art thyself, though not a Montague.
What's 'Montague'? It is nor hand, nor foot,
Nor arm, nor face, nor any other part
Belonging to a man. O, be some other name!
What's in a name? That which we call a rose
By any other word would smell as sweet;
So Romeo would, were he not Romeo called,
Retain that dear perfection which he owes
Without that title. Romeo, doff thy name;
And for thy name, which is no part of thee,
Take all myself.

*Note: 'Which he owes'. Owes = owns. The earlier sense of 'owe' was not to be in debt but 'to have', the final 'n' being dropped from the original 'owens'.*

ROMEO

(*aloud to Juliet*) I will take you at your word. Just call me love and I'll be newly baptised. From this moment I will never again be Romeo.

ROMEO

I take thee at thy word.
Call me but love, and I'll be new baptized;
Henceforth I never will be Romeo.

*Note: Babies were officially named at their baptism, also called, Christening, where the dated term 'Christian name' for a first name derived from, though again, Romeo really needs to change his surname, not his first name.*

JULIET

Who is that, hidden in the darkness, listening to my private thoughts?

JULIET

What man art thou that thus bescreened in night
So stumblest on my counsel?

*Note: Romeo had just said his name in the line above, did Juliet not hear him?*

ROMEO

I don't know how to tell you who I am. My name, dear saint, I find hateful because it is an enemy to you. If it were written down I would tear the word into pieces.

ROMEO

By a name
I know not how to tell thee who I am:
My name, dear saint, is hateful to myself
Because it is an enemy to thee.
Had I it written, I would tear the word.

JULIET REACTS AS SHE RECOGNISES ROMEO'S VOICE, AND HIS CALLING HER, 'SAINT', AS PER THEIR FIRST CONVERSATION TOGETHER EARLIER.

JULIET

My ears have not yet drunk a hundred words uttered by your sweet tongue, yet I recognise the sound. You are Romeo aren't you, and a Montague?

JULIET

My ears have yet not drunk a hundred words
Of thy tongue's uttering, yet I know the sound.
Art thou not Romeo, and a Montague?

ROMEO

Neither, sweet lady, if either displeases you.

ROMEO

Neither, fair maid, if either thee dislike.

JULIET

How did you get here, tell me, and why? The garden walls are high and hard to climb, and considering who you are this place will be the death of you if any of my family find you here.

JULIET

How cam'st thou hither, tell me, and wherefore?
The orchard walls are high and hard to climb,
And the place death, considering who thou art,
If any of my kinsmen find thee here.

ROMEO

With the light wings of love I leapt over these walls, their stony heights cannot hold back my love, and love will dare attempt whatever love desires, so the threat of your family is no barrier to me.

JULIET

If they see you, they will kill you.

ROMEO

Alas, there is more danger in one unfavourable look of your eye than from twenty of their swords. Look lovingly upon me and I am shielded from their loathing.

JULIET

For all the world I would not wish them to see you here.

ROMEO

I have the dark cloak of night to hide me from their eyes, but should you not love me, let them find me here. My life would be better ended by their hate than a long drawn out death waiting for your love.

JULIET

Who told you where to find me?

ROMEO

My love for you led me here. It gave me direction, I gave it eyes. I am no navigator, yet even if you were as far away as that vast shore washed by the farthest sea, I would venture my life in search of such merchandise.

ROMEO

With love's light wings did I o'erperch these walls,
For stony limits cannot hold love out;
And what love can do, that dares love attempt.
Therefore thy kinsmen are no stop to me.

JULIET

If they do see thee they will murder thee.

ROMEO

Alack, there lies more peril in thine eye
Than twenty of their swords. Look thou but sweet,
And I am proof against their enmity.

JULIET

I would not for the world they saw thee here.

ROMEO

I have night's cloak to hide me from their eyes;
And but thou love me, let them find me here;
My life were better ended by their hate
Than death prorogued, wanting of thy love.

JULIET

By whose direction found'st thou out this place?

ROMEO

By love, that first did prompt me to enquire;
He lent me counsel, and I lent him eyes.
I am no pilot, yet wert thou as far
As that vast shore washed with the furthest sea,
I should adventure for such merchandise.

Note: By 'love' he also means 'Cupid', and being blind he lent Cupid his eyes.

JULIET

If the mask of night were not upon my face, you would see the maiden-like blush painting my cheeks at the words you have heard me speak tonight. Gladly would I follow the customary behaviour, gladly, gladly withhold my love till you had wooed me, but now it's too late for formality. Do you love me?

JULIET

Thou knowest the mask of night is on my face,
Else would a maiden blush bepaint my cheek
For that which thou hast heard me speak tonight.
Fain would I dwell on form, fain, fain deny
What I have spoke; but farewell, compliment.
Dost thou love me?

JULIET DOES NOT WAIT FOR AN ANSWER, SHE ANSWERS HER OWN QUESTION BEFORE ROMEO CAN.

JULIET (CONT'D)

I know you will say yes anyway, and I will take you at your word, yet I know you could swear your love and it proves to be false. They say Jove laughs at lover's false promises. Oh, sweet Romeo, if you do love me, say it faithfully. Or if you think I am too easily won, I'll pout and frown and turn you down so you can woo me, but, for the world, I wouldn't behave that way otherwise.

JULIET

I know thou wilt say `Ay',
And I will take thy word. Yet, if thou swear'st,
Thou mayst prove false: at lovers' perjuries
They say Jove laughs. O gentle Romeo,
If thou dost love, pronounce it faithfully;
Or if thou think'st I am too quickly won,
I'll frown and be perverse and say thee nay,
So thou wilt woo; but else, not for the world.

ROMEO AGAIN GOES TO ANSWER BUT JULIET CARRIES ON.

JULIET (CONT'D)

In truth, my dear Montague, I am foolishly love-struck, and therefore you may think my behaviour frivolous. But trust me, sir, and I will prove to be truer than those with the sense to be less familiar. I should not have been so forward, I must confess, but I was unaware you could overhear my confessions of true love. Therefore, forgive me, and do not assume my yielding so readily, which this dark night has revealed, means my love is light.

JULIET

In truth, fair Montague, I am too fond,
And therefore thou mayst think my haviour light;
But trust me, gentleman, I'll prove more true
Than those that have more cunning to be
    strange.
I should have been more strange, I must confess,
But that thou overheard'st, ere I was ware,
My true-love passion; therefore pardon me,
And not impute this yielding to light love,
Which the dark night hath so discovered.

Note: Light love, meaning not serious, used here to pun with dark night.

ROMEO FINALLY TAKES THE OPPORTUNITY TO MAKE HIS VOW OF LOVE.

ROMEO

Lady, I swear by the blessed moon above, which lights the tips of the fruit trees with silver...

ROMEO

Lady, by yonder blessed moon I vow,
That tips with silver all these fruit-tree tops -

JULIET INTERRUPTS HIM.

JULIET

Oh, don't swear by the moon, the inconsistent moon, which changes monthly in her circular orbit, lest your love proves equally inconsistent.

JULIET

O swear not by the moon, th' inconstant moon,
That monthly changes in her circled orb,
Lest that thy love prove likewise variable.

ROMEO

What shall I swear by then?

ROMEO

What shall I swear by?

JULIET

Do not swear at all. Or if you must, swear by your gracious self, which is the god I idolise, then I'll believe you.

JULIET

Do not swear at all;
Or if thou wilt, swear by thy gracious self,
Which is the god of my idolatry,
And I'll believe thee.

Note: 'Gracious' has the double meaning of behaving in a goodly, 'saintly' manner as well as kind and courteous.

ROMEO

If my heart's dear love...

ROMEO

If my heart's dear love -

JULIET INTERRUPTS HIM AGAIN.

JULIET

No, do not swear. Although I am happy with your words, I am not happy to make this vow tonight. It is too rash, too sudden to be wise. It is too like the lightning in the sky which is gone before one can say it lightens the sky. My sweet, goodnight! This bud of love, ripening with the breath of summer, may have bloomed into a beautiful flower when we next meet.
*Goodnight, goodnight! May sweet dreams and good rest*
*Come to your heart, like I feel in my breast.*

JULIET

Well, do not swear. Although I joy in thee,
I have no joy of this contract tonight.
It is too rash, too unadvised, too sudden,
Too like the lightning, which doth cease to be
Ere one can say it lightens. Sweet, good night.
This bud of love, by summer's ripening breath,
May prove a beauteous flower when next we
  meet.
*Good night, good night! As sweet repose and rest*
*Come to thy heart as that within my breast!*

ROMEO

Oh, would you leave me so unsatisfied?

ROMEO

O wilt thou leave me so unsatisfied?

JULIET

What satisfaction could you have tonight?

JULIET

What satisfaction canst thou have tonight?

Note: 'Satisfaction' is a bawdy innuendo.

ROMEO

The exchange of your faithful vow of love with mine.

ROMEO

Th' exchange of thy love's faithful vow for mine.

JULIET

I gave you mine before you had asked for it, though I wish I had it back to give again.

JULIET

I gave thee mine before thou didst request it;
And yet I would it were to give again.

ROMEO

You wish to withdraw it? Why, my love?

ROMEO

Wouldst thou withdraw it? For what purpose, love?

JULIET

Only to be generous and give it to you again. And yet I wish for what I already have. My generosity is as vast as the ocean, my love as deep. The more I give to you, the more I have, there is no limit to our love... shhhh... I hear a noise within...

JULIET

But to be frank and give it thee again.
And yet I wish but for the thing I have.
My bounty is as boundless as the sea,
My love as deep; the more I give to thee,
The more I have, for both are infinite.
I hear some noise within.

A VOICE CALLS FROM INSIDE THE HOUSE.

NURSE

(off, calling) Madam.

NURSE

(off, calling)

JULIET

(to Romeo, low) Dear love, adieu.
(to Nurse, calling) I'm coming, dearest Nurse!
(to Romeo) Sweet Montague, be true.
Wait a moment, I will return.

JULIET

Dear love, adieu.
Anon, good Nurse! - Sweet Montague, be true.
Stay but a little, I will come again.

JULIET GOES BACK INTO THE HOUSE, LEAVING THE BALCONY DOOR OPEN.

ROMEO

(aside) Oh, blessed, blessed night! I am afraid that being night this is all a dream, it's all too perfect to be true.

ROMEO

O blessed, blessed night! I am afeard,
Being in night, all this is but a dream,
Too flattering-sweet to be substantial.

Note: 'Flattering' will be revisited in Act V Scene I. See note there.

---

JULIET REAPPEARS ON THE BALCONY.

---

**JULIET**
(*hurriedly*) Three words, dear Romeo, then it must be goodnight. If your love is honourable and your intention marriage, send me word tomorrow by the messenger I will send you, where and at what time the ceremony will be performed, and my life I will lay at your feet, to follow you, my lord, anywhere in the world.

JULIET
Three words, dear Romeo, and good night indeed.
If that thy bent of love be honourable,
Thy purpose marriage, send me word tomorrow
By one that I'll procure to come to thee,
Where and what time thou wilt perform the rite;
And all my fortunes at thy foot I'll lay,
And follow thee, my lord, throughout the world.

---

NURSE CALLS FROM INSIDE THE HOUSE AGAIN, MORE INSISTENT THIS TIME.

---

**NURSE**
(*off, calling*) Madam!

NURSE
[*Within*] Madam!

**JULIET**
(*to Nurse*) I'm just coming!
(*to Romeo*) But if your intentions are not honourable, I beg of you...

JULIET
I come, anon! - But if thou mean'st not well,
I do beseech thee -

**NURSE**
(*off, calling*) Madam!

NURSE
[*Within*] Madam!

**JULIET**
(*to Nurse*) Goodness me, I'm coming!
(*to Romeo*) ...to cease your efforts and leave me to my grief. Tomorrow I will send someone.

JULIET
By and by, I come! -
To cease thy strife and leave me to my grief.
Tomorrow will I send.

---

Note: 'Strife' – some editions say 'suit' which is the more likely original word as this is lifted straight from Brooke's poem - "and now your Juliet you beseekes To cease your <u>sute</u>, and suffer her to live emong her likes."

---

**ROMEO**
*By my soul I...*

ROMEO
*So thrive my soul -*

---

JULIET INTERRUPTS HIM AS HE TRIES TO ASSURE HER OF HIS INTENTIONS. SHE TURNS TO GO BACK INSIDE.

---

**JULIET**
*...A thousand times, good night.*

JULIET
*- A thousand times good night.*

JULIET GOES BACK INSIDE.

ROMEO

*(aside) A thousand times worse for want of your light.*

ROMEO

*A thousand times the worse to want thy light.*

ROMEO STARTS SLOWLY WALKING HAPPILY AWAY,
TALKING TO HIMSELF IN RHYME.

ROMEO (CONT'D)

*Like lovers seeking lovers happy schoolboys leave their books.*
*But like lover leaving lover, back to school with heavy looks.*

ROMEO

*Love goes toward love as schoolboys from their books;*
*But love from love, toward school with heavy looks.*

JULIET APPEARS BACK ON THE BALCONY AGAIN AND TRIES TO GAIN ROMEO'S
ATTENTION WITHOUT MAKING TOO MUCH NOISE.

JULIET

*(calls softly)* Psst, Romeo! Psst!
*(aside)* Oh, for the voice of a falconer to lure this hawk of a man back again. Restraint makes me hoarse, and I cannot call aloud, or I would free the mighty Echo from the cave where she lies, and make her airy voice more hoarse than mine repeating my *(hissing his name again)* 'Romeo's' name.

JULIET

Hist! Romeo, hist! O for a falconer's voice
To lure this tassel-gentle back again.
Bondage is hoarse and may not speak aloud,
Else would I tear the cave where Echo lies
And make her airy tongue more hoarse than
  mine
With repetition of my Romeo's name.

ROMEO CONTINUES WALKING, TALKING TO HIMSELF DREAMILY.

Note: Shakespeare often refers to falconry and hawks, this was a common sport in the countryside where he grew up. The 'tassel' or tiercel is a male hawk, called gentle because it was easy to tame, a favourite of princes.

Echo was a nymph in Greek mythology. Zeus loved entertaining the beautiful young nymphs on Earth. Zeus' wife, Hera became suspicious and descended from Mt. Olympus to catch Zeus with the nymphs. Echo, in trying to defend Zeus, angered Hera. She put a spell on Echo making her able to speak only the last few words spoken to her, like an echo. Subsequently, when Echo met Narcissus and fell in love with him, she was unable to tell him how she felt, and was forced to watch him fall in love with himself.

ROMEO

(*aside dreamily*) It is my soul that calls out my name. How sweet the sound of lovers' tongues are by night, like the softest music of silver bells to the ears!

JULIET

(*hissed louder*) Romeo!

ROMEO

It is my soul that calls upon my name.
How silver-sweet sound lovers' tongues by night,
Like softest music to attending ears!

JULIET

Romeo!

ROMEO REALISING THE VOICE IS NOT HIS IMAGINATION, STOPS AND TURNS.

ROMEO

(*turning*) My dearest?

ROMEO

My nyas?

> Note: 'Nyas' (or niess, or eyas) is again a term from falconry, a young hawk, especially an unfledged nestling taken from the nest for training. Linked to the word 'naïve' and also 'nidus', latin for nest. Used as a term of endearment.

JULIET

What time tomorrow shall I send my messenger?

ROMEO

By nine o'clock.

JULIET

I will not fail, it will seem like twenty years till then...
I have forgotten why I called you back.

ROMEO

Let me stand here till you remember.

JULIET

I will forget, so I keep you standing there, remembering how I love your company.

ROMEO

And I shall stay here, while you still forget, forgetting I have any other home than this.

JULIET

What o'clock tomorrow
Shall I send to thee?

ROMEO

By the hour of nine.

JULIET

I will not fail - 'tis twenty year till then.
I have forgot why I did call thee back.

ROMEO

Let me stand here till thou remember it.

JULIET

I shall forget, to have thee still stand there,
Rememb'ring how I love thy company.

ROMEO

And I'll still stay, to have thee still forget,
Forgetting any other home but this.

| | |
|---|---|
| JULIET | JULIET |
| It is almost morning. I should send you away, but no further than a spoilt child's bird, tied to his hand like a shackled prisoner, which he lets hop a little way, and then with a silken thread plucks back again, jealous of its desire for freedom. | 'Tis almost morning; I would have thee gone; And yet no further than a wanton's bird, That lets it hop a little from his hand, Like a poor prisoner in his twisted gyves, And with a silk thread plucks it back again, So loving-jealous of his liberty. |

> Note: Gyves - leg shackles attached to prisoners to prevent their escape.
>
> Wanton - a spoiled child, one who teases their pets, in this case a bird.

| | |
|---|---|
| ROMEO | ROMEO |
| I wish I were your bird. | I would I were thy bird. |
| JULIET | JULIET |
| My darling, so do I, but I would kill you with too much cherishing. | Sweet, so would I; Yet I should kill thee with much cherishing. |
| *Goodnight, goodnight. Parting is such sweet sorrow,* | *Good night, good night. Parting is such sweet sorrow* |
| *That I could say goodnight till it's tomorrow.* | *That I shall say good night till it be morrow.* |
| ROMEO | ROMEO |
| *Sleep dwell in your eyes, peace be in your breast!* | *Sleep dwell upon thine eyes, peace in thy breast!* |

---

JULIET GOES INSIDE THE HOUSE AND CLOSES THE DOOR.

---

| | |
|---|---|
| ROMEO (CONT'D) | ROMEO |
| *(aside)* | *Would I were sleep and peace, so sweet to rest!* |
| *Oh, to have sleep and peace. So sweet to rest!* | *Hence will I to my ghostly sire's close cell,* |
| *I'll head for my spiritual father's cell,* | *His help to crave, and my dear hap to tell.* |
| *To seek his help, and my good news to tell.* | |

---

ROMEO LEAVES ON THE LIGHT FEET OF LOVE.

---

> Note: A 'cell' is the friar's residence. It is a small monastery which is a dependant of a larger one. Not to be confused with a prisoner's cell.
>
> A 'ghostly sire' was a Catholic term for a priest.
>
> 'Hap' means luck or fortune.

# ACT II  SCENE III

## MONASTERY GROUNDS.  MONDAY AT DAWN.

FRIAR LAURENCE, A FRANCISCAN MONK, IS TENDING THE GARDEN AND
COLLECTING HERBS IN A BASKET WHILE CHURCH BELLS TOLL AND BIRDS
TWITTER THE DAWN CHORUS.

THE FRIAR RECITES A RHYME AS HE PICKS HERBS FOR MEDICINAL PURPOSES.

Note: A long soliloquy introducing the friar's knowledge of poisons.

**FRIAR LAURENCE**

The grey-eyed morn smiles at the frowning
   night,
Chequ'ring the eastern clouds with streaks of
   light,
And dappled darkness like a drunkard reels,
From day's path forged by Titan's fiery wheels.

Before the sun opens his burning eye,
The day to cheer and night's damp dew to dry,
I must fill this wicker basket of ours
With poisonous weeds and medicinal flowers.

Earth; nature's mother, and also her tomb;
For what is her grave is also her womb;
From where her children of various kind,
We, suckling on nature's bosom, do find.

Many with virtues, all quite excellent,
None have no use, and yet all different.
Oh, great is the power and goodness that
   flowers,
In plants, herbs and stones; their medicinal
   powers.

But none so vile, on mother earth do live,
That no special goodness to this Earth do give.
Nor any so good that, if put to bad use,
They take on new power, with deadly abuse.
Their goodness turns bad, when wrongly
   applied,
But bad turns to good, if its use dignified.

**FRIAR LAURENCE**

The grey-eyed morn smiles on the frowning night,
Chequ'ring the eastern clouds with streaks of light,
And fleckled darkness like a drunkard reels
From forth day's path and Titan's fiery wheels.

Now, ere the sun advance his burning eye
The day to cheer and night's dank dew to dry,
I must up-fill this osier cage of ours
With baleful weeds and precious-juiced flowers.

The earth that's nature's mother is her tomb;
What is her burying grave, that is her womb;
And from her womb children of divers kind
We sucking on her natural bosom find,

Many for many virtues excellent,
None but for some, and yet all different.
O, mickle is the powerful grace that lies
In plants, herbs, stones, and their true qualities;

For nought so vile that on the earth doth live
But to the earth some special good doth give;
Nor aught so good but, strained from that fair use,
Revolts from true birth, stumbling on abuse.
Virtue itself turns vice, being misapplied,
And vice sometime's by action dignified.

UNSEEN BY THE FRIAR, ROMEO ARRIVES, STILL DREAMILY THINKING ABOUT
HIS MEETING WITH JULIET EARLIER THAT NIGHT. HE HAS OBVIOUSLY NOT
BEEN TO BED THAT NIGHT BUT HAS BEEN WALKING DEEP IN THOUGHT.

**FRIAR LAURENCE (CONT'D)**

*Within the infant rind of this small flower,*
*Poison does reside, and medicinal power.*
*For this, if smelt, revives each body part,*
*But tasted, alas, brings a stop to the heart.*

*Two such opposed actions, live in them still,*
*In man as in herbs - bad and good will.*
*And where the badness is predominant,*
*The rot soon sets in, and eats up that plant.*

**FRIAR LAURENCE**

*Within the infant rind of this weak flower*
*Poison hath residence, and medicine power;*
*For this, being smelt, with that part cheers each part;*
*Being tasted, slays all senses with the heart.*

*Two such opposed kings encamp them still*
*In man as well as herbs - grace and rude will;*
*And where the worser is predominant,*
*Full soon the canker death eats up that plant.*

Note: Rind is the outer skin of fruit or a plant, or the bark of a tree.

'Slays' – in later texts this word was replaced with 'stays', (stops), though both versions have the same meaning overall.

**ROMEO**

*Good morning, Father.*

**ROMEO**

*Good morrow, father.*

**FRIAR LAURENCE**

*(in surprise)*  Benedicte!
*What sweet sounding tongue so early greets me?*

**FRIAR LAURENCE**

Benedicite!
*What early tongue so sweet saluteth me?*

Note: Benedicite is a Latin religious term, meaning 'bless you', here used as an exclamation as much as a blessing. Five syllables, ben-eh-dissi-tee.

THE FRIAR LOOKS ROMEO UP AND DOWN SUSPICIOUSLY.

**FRIAR LAURENCE (CONT'D)**

*Young man it suggests an unsettled head,*
*To bid me good morning so soon out of bed.*
*Worry is company, we old men do keep,*
*And when worry lodges, we old men can't sleep.*

*But when careless youth with untroubled brain*
*Relaxes his limbs, gold sleep there does reign.*
*Therefore your earliness does me suggest,*
*You are aroused with some kind of unrest.*
*If that is not so, then here I'll be right,*
*Romeo has not been to bed yet tonight.*

**FRIAR LAURENCE**

*Young son, it argues a distempered head*
*So soon to bid good morrow to thy bed.*
*Care keeps his watch in every old man's eye,*
*And where care lodges, sleep will never lie;*

*But where unbruised youth with unstuffed brain*
*Doth couch his limbs, there golden sleep doth reign.*
*Therefore thy earliness doth me assure*
*Thou art uproused with some distemperature;*
*Or if not so, then here I hit it right:*
*Our Romeo hath not been in bed tonight.*

ROMEO

*The last bit's true; a sweeter rest was mine.*

ROMEO

*That last is true; the sweeter rest was mine.*

FRIAR LAURENCE

*God pardon his sin! Were you with Rosaline?*

FRIAR LAURENCE

*God pardon sin! Wast thou with Rosaline?*

ROMEO

*With Rosaline, my holy Father? No.*
*I'd forgotten that name and all its woe.*

ROMEO

*With Rosaline, my ghostly father? No;*
*I have forgot that name, and that name's woe.*

FRIAR LAURENCE

*(relief) That's good, my son; so where have you*
*been then?*

FRIAR LAURENCE

*That's my good son; but where hast thou been then?*

---

ROMEO ANSWERS PLAYFULLY USING MISLEADING WORDS.

---

ROMEO

*I'll tell you before you ask me again.*
*I was out feasting with my enemy,*
*When, all of a sudden, one wounded me*
*And was wounded by me. The cure of ours*
*Lies in your help and in your holy powers.*
*I bear no hate, blessed Father, for lo,*
*My needs of you also benefits my foe.*

ROMEO

*I'll tell thee ere thou ask it me again.*
*I have been feasting with mine enemy,*
*Where, on a sudden, one hath wounded me*
*That's by me wounded. Both our remedies*
*Within thy help and holy physic lies.*
*I bear no hatred, blessed man, for, lo,*
*My intercession likewise steads my foe.*

> Note: 'Lo' is an exclamation to draw attention to something, still used in the
> expression, 'Lo and behold'.

FRIAR LAURENCE

*Talk plainly, my son, making effort to shorten,*
*Confessional riddles find riddling absolution.*

FRIAR LAURENCE

*Be plain, good son, and homely in thy drift;*
*Riddling confession finds but riddling shrift.*

> Note: 'Shrift' is the forgiveness of your sins given after confessing your sins to a
> priest (absolution) who stands as a representative of God. It is a Catholic religious
> service which Shakespeare refers to in a number of plays – fuelling the speculation
> he may have been a secret Catholic, or a Catholic sympathiser in a time when the
> practise of Catholicism was banned and punishable by death.

ROMEO

*Then plainly said, my heart's love is now set*
*On the fair daughter of rich Capulet.*
*My heart's set on hers, as hers is on mine,*
*They are as one, 'cept what you must combine*
*In Holy wedlock. When and where and how*
*We met, fell in love, and exchanged our vow,*
*I'll explain as we walk, but this I pray,*
*That you consent to marry us today.*

ROMEO

*Then plainly know my heart's dear love is set*
*On the fair daughter of rich Capulet.*
*As mine on hers, so hers is set on mine;*
*And all combined save what thou must combine*
*By holy marriage. When and where and how*
*We met, we wooed, and made exchange of vow,*
*I'll tell thee as we pass; but this I pray,*
*That thou consent to marry us today.*

#### FRIAR LAURENCE

*Holy Saint Francis! What a change of heart!*
*Rosaline, you loved so dear, so soon forgot?*
*So young men's love then not truly lies*
*Within their hearts, but within their eyes.*
*Mother Mary! How many seas of brine*
*Have washed your pale cheeks over Rosaline?*
*How much salt water thrown away in waste*
*Seasoning a love you'll never get to taste?*
*Your lingering sighs still hang in the air,*
*Your old groans still ringing in my aged ear.*

#### FRIAR LAURENCE

*Holy Saint Francis, what a change is here!*
*Is Rosaline, that thou didst love so dear,*
*So soon forsaken? Young men's love then lies*
*Not truly in their hearts but in their eyes.*
*Jesu Maria, what a deal of brine*
*Hath washed thy sallow cheeks for Rosaline!*
*How much salt water thrown away in waste*
*To season love, that of it doth not taste!*
*The sun not yet thy sighs from heaven clears,*
*Thy old groans yet ring in mine ancient ears.*

> Note: Saint Francis of Assisi was the founder of the first order of Franciscan Friars – monks based in monasteries. The word monastery derives from the Greek to 'live alone' and early monks were hermits. Franciscans were a religious order within the Catholic Church founded in 1209.

THE FRIAR GRASPS ROMEO'S CHIN, TURNING HIS CHEEK TO THE LIGHT.

#### FRIAR LAURENCE

*Look, here upon your cheek, a stain does sit*
*Of an old tear that is not washed off yet.*
*If you were true, and these tears genuine,*
*You and all these tears were for Rosaline.*
*Now you have changed? Remember these*
*  words then;*
*Women will stray when there's no strength in*
*  men.*

#### FRIAR LAURENCE

*Lo, here upon thy cheek the stain doth sit*
*Of an old tear that is not washed off yet.*
*If ere thou wast thyself, and these woes thine,*
*Thou and these woes were all for Rosaline.*
*And art thou changed? Pronounce this sentence then:*
*Women may fall when there's no strength in men.*

#### ROMEO

*You chastised me often for loving Rosaline.*

#### ROMEO

*Thou chidd'st me oft for loving Rosaline.*

#### FRIAR LAURENCE

*For doting, not loving, pupil of mine.*

#### FRIAR LAURENCE

*For doting, not for loving, pupil mine.*

#### ROMEO

*You said 'bury my love'.*

#### ROMEO

*And bad'st me bury love.*

#### FRIAR LAURENCE

                    *Not in a grave*
*To lay in one lover, then dig up another.*

#### FRIAR LAURENCE

                    *Not in a grave*
*To lay one in, another out to have.*

#### ROMEO

*I beg you, don't lecture me, the one I love now,*
*Grants what the other banned; exchange of*
*  love's vow.*

#### ROMEO

*I pray thee, chide me not; her I love now*
*Doth grace for grace and love for love allow;*
*The other did not so.*

### FRIAR LAURENCE

*She well knew your words were of some poet.*
*Spoken from memory, not from the heart.*
*Enough, young waverer, here, come with me,*
*In one respect your assistant I'll be,*
*For this alliance may happily move*
*Your families' hatred to one of pure love.*

### FRIAR LAURENCE

*O, she knew well*
*Thy love did read by rote that could not spell.*
*But come, young waverer, come, go with me,*
*In one respect I'll thy assistant be;*
*For this alliance may so happy prove*
*To turn your households' rancour to pure love.*

> Note: In Shakespeare's time, 'love' and 'prove' rhymed, they don't today.

### ROMEO

*Then let's go at once, with great haste withal.*

### FRIAR LAURENCE

*Wise and slow, run fast you stumble and fall.*

### ROMEO

*O let us hence; I stand on sudden haste.*

### FRIAR LAURENCE

*Wisely and slow; they stumble that run fast.*

> Note: This line is based on the latin phrase 'festina lente'. Literal translation is 'make haste slowly". From this we get the expression today of 'more haste, less speed'.
>
> Later on the Friar makes quite a thing of stumbling and it bringing about bad luck and slowing him down, preventing him from saving the lovers.

# ACT II  SCENE IV

## THE STREETS OF VERONA.  MIDDAY MONDAY.

ENTER MERCUTIO AND BENVOLIO WALKING ALONG A HOT DUSTY STREET.

*Note: This scene is predominantly in prose rather than the usual blank verse as it is playful and quite bawdy in places. Mercutio's bawdy lines were once ommited from some texts, but are restored in current versions.*

**MERCUTIO**
Where the devil is Romeo, Benvolio? Didn't he come home last night?

**BENVOLIO**
Not to his father's house, Mercutio, I spoke to his servant.

**MERCUTIO**
Why, that pale, hard-hearted wretch, that Rosaline. She torments him so, I'm sure he'll go mad.

**BENVOLIO**
Tybalt, the nephew of old Capulet, has sent a letter to Romeo's father's house.

**MERCUTIO**
A challenge to a dual, I'll wager.

**BENVOLIO**
Romeo will answer it.

**MERCUTIO**
(*deliberate misunderstanding*) Any man that can write may answer a letter.

**BENVOLIO**
No, Mercutio, he will answer the challenge, he is man enough to accept the dare.

**MERCUTIO**
Where the devil should this Romeo be? Came he not home tonight?

**BENVOLIO**
Not to his father's; I spoke with his man.

**MERCUTIO**
Why, that same pale hard-hearted wench, that Rosaline,
Torments him so that he will sure run mad.

**BENVOLIO**
Tybalt, the kinsman to old Capulet,
Hath sent a letter to his father's house.

**MERCUTIO**
A challenge, on my life.

**BENVOLIO**
Romeo will answer it.

**MERCUTIO**
Any man that can write may answer a letter.

**BENVOLIO**
Nay, he will answer the letter's master, how he dares, being dared.

MERCUTIO

Alas, poor Romeo, he is already dead. Stabbed with one look from that pale wench's dark eye; shot through the ear with a love song, the very heart of him pierced by Cupid's arrow - and is he man enough to meet Tybalt?

MERCUTIO

Alas poor Romeo, he is already dead; stabbed with a white wench's black eye, run through the ear with a love song, the very pin of his heart cleft with the blind bow-boy's butt-shaft - and is he a man to encounter Tybalt?

Note: A series of archery references, linked to Cupid's arrow.

'Butt-shaft' was an arrow used for shooting targets. It had no barb on the tip (the triangle metal end), having only a metal point so it could easily be pulled from the target and reused. 'Butts' were mounds upon which a target was stood. 'Pin' was the bulls-eye (centre) of a target, being an actual metal stud. 'Blind bow-boy' is Cupid with his arrow aimed at lovers' hearts.

BENVOLIO

(scornful) Why, what's so special about Tybalt?

BENVOLIO

Why, what is Tybalt?

MERCUTIO

(mocking) Why, he is the Prince of Cats, Benvolio. Oh, he is the courageous captain of duelling etiquette. He fights the way you would sing close harmony, keeping time, distance and rhythm. He pauses two beats - one, two - and on the third...

MERCUTIO

More than Prince of Cats. O, he's the courageous captain of compliments. He fights as you sing prick-song: keeps time, distance, and proportion; he rests his minim rests, one, two, and the third...

Note: Tibalt was a common name for a cat, named after Tibert or Tibalt the cat in the twelfth century animal folk tales, 'Reynard The Fox'.

'Prick-song' is a song written down, so it is only played to the correct time and accompaniment, as opposed to one played freely from memory.

'Minim' is two beats in music, and a 'rest' is a silent pause in music.

HE PRETENDS TO LUNGE WITH A SWORD.

MERCUTIO

...through your chest, through whichever shirt button he cares to choose. A duellist first, a duellist second, a gentleman of the top school, and an expert in the rules.

MERCUTIO

...in your bosom; the very butcher of a silk button. A duellist, a duellist; a gentleman of the very first house, of the first and second cause.

Note: It was said champions could pierce a shirt button of their choosing, and were said to be experts in the official rules for when a man is justified to fight a duel.

HE DEMONSTRATES THE VARIOUS FENCING STROKES USING THE ITALIAN
TERMS FOR VARIOUS FENCING MOVES.

FIRST, A THRUST WITH ONE FOOT FORWARD.

| MERCUTIO | MERCUTIO |
|---|---|
| Ah, the immortal passado! | Ah, the immortal passado! |

SECOND, A SPINNING BLOW TO THE REAR MIDRIFF OF THE OPPONENT.

| MERCUTIO | MERCUTIO |
|---|---|
| The punto reverso! | the punto reverse! |

FINALLY, A LUNGE WHICH RUNS RIGHT THROUGH THE OPPONENT.

| MERCUTIO | MERCUTIO |
|---|---|
| The hay! | The hay! |
| **BENVOLIO** | **BENVOLIO** |
| The what? | The what? |
| **MERCUTIO** | **MERCUTIO** |
| The crap spoken by all those pretentious, stuck-up, 'fantasticoes', and their nouveau sayings. | The pox of such antic, lisping, affecting fantasticoes, these new tuners of accent. |

> *Note: The duelling dialogue of Mercutio was a reference by Shakespeare to Gerard Thibault D'Anvers, who had published the work entitled 'Academy Of The Sword: The Mystery of the Spanish Circle in Swordsmanship and Esoteric Arts.' In Italian, the terms are 'passata' not passado, and 'Hai' not Hay.*
>
> *Gerard Thibault was the basis for Tybalt's character - a poet, physician, architect, painter, occultist, and master swordsman, a true renaissance man whose book was of a new system of swordsmanship based on the principles of sacred geometry and Renaissance occult philosophy.*
>
> *'Academy of the Sword' is reputedly still the most comprehensive manual of swordsmanship ever published. Perhaps Shakespeare found the system or the author pretentious.*

HE AFFECTS A MOCKING, PRETENTIOUS ACCENT, POINTING OUT PEOPLE.

| MERCUTIO (CONT'D) | MERCUTIO |
|---|---|
| (*pretentious*) By Jove, a jolly good blade, an exceptionally lusty man, a rather smashing whore! | By Jesu, a very good blade, a very tall man, a very good whore! |

MERCUTIO NOW MIMICS A STOOPED, GRUMBLING OLD MAN.

MERCUTIO (CONT'D)

(*old man's voice*) Why, is this not a lamentable thing, old chap, that we should be afflicted with these foreign terms, these fashion trends, from these bowing and scraping 'pardonez-moi's', who stand so much on ceremony they can't sit down without extra padding? Oh, their poor bones, their bones! Riddled with the pox.

MERCUTIO

Why, is not this a lamentable thing, grandsire, that we should be thus afflicted with these strange flies, these fashion-mongers, these ' pardon-me's', who stand so much on the new form that they cannot sit at ease the old bench? O their bones, their bones!

Note: Some publications use 'pardonnez-moys' instead of 'pardon-me's'. Some also use 'bon' (French for good, a word pretentious men would constantly say to each other) instead of 'bone'. It could have been a pun on both words or a printing error, but these pretentious people were famed for loose morals, and 'bone-ache' was a symptom and term for the pox (syphilis).

'Stand so much on the new form' – Stand on pretentious ceremony with the new trends. 'Form' is also another word for a bench. 'So they cannot sit at ease at the old bench', would be the opposite wording, appropriate because syphilis made sitting down difficult, following on from the earlier line, 'a pox of such antic'. A complicated wordplay difficult to translate into modern English.

ROMEO APPEARS. MERCUTIO CHANTS MOCKINGLY.

BENVOLIO

Here comes Romeo, here comes Romeo!

BENVOLIO

Here comes Romeo, here comes Romeo!

MERCUTIO MOCKS ROMEO LIKE AN OVERLY DRAMATIC ACTOR.

MERCUTIO

Like a dried herring; without his 'roe' and 'saline'. Oh flesh, flesh, like a limp fish!

MERCUTIO

Without his roe, like a dried herring. O flesh, flesh, how art thou fishified!

Note: 'Roe' being the first syllable of 'Rosaline', and 'Romeo'. He suggests Romeo is dried up and exhausted having spent his eggs (slept with Rosaline). Flesh fishified is limp and lifeless. Again bawdy.

MERCUTIO (CONT'D)

(*sarcastic*) Now, we are in for the sonnets of Petrach's love. How Laura was just a kitchen wench compared to his lady - she just had a better poet love her - Dido a dowdy, Cleopatra a gypsy, Helen and Hera, sluts and whores. Thisbe? Pretty blue eyes but not much else.

MERCUTIO

Now is he for the numbers that Petrarch flowed in. Laura to his lady was a kitchen wench - marry, she had a better love to berhyme her - Dido a dowdy; Cleopatra a gypsy; Helen and Hero hildings and harlots; Thisbe a grey eye or so, but not to the purpose.

---

Note: Gypsy's were incorrectly thought to originate from Egypt.

Romeo and Juliet, based on an established and at the time well know story, was also similar in plot, theme, and dramatic ending to the story of 'Pyramus and Thisbe', told by the great Roman poet, Ovid, in his 'Metamorphoses', and Shakespeare shows here he is aware of this similarity.

Petrarch (1304-1374) wrote poetry about his hopeless love for Laura. By putting down the romantic heroines mentioned, Mercutio is saying Romeo thinks his beloved is better than any of them.

---

ROMEO IS NOW LEVEL WITH THEM.

---

MERCUTIO

Signor Romeo, bonjour!

MERCUTIO

Signor Romeo, bonjour!

---

MERCUTIO MAKES AN EXAGGERATED BOW.

---

MERCUTIO (CONT'D)

That's a French greeting for the French slop you are wearing. You gave us the French slip well and truly last night.

MERCUTIO

There's a French salutation to your French slop. You gave us the counterfeit fairly last night.

---

Note: This passage of dialogue between Romeo and Mercutio is complicated and full of puns. 'Slops' were popular leg wear, especially for dancing, French style particularly. He is still wearing them from the previous night as he didn't go home. French slip is where you leave secretly. Interestingly the French call it the "Partir à l'anglais", meaning to leave the English way.

Counterfeit coins were also known as 'slips'. This passage is wordplay around deception, and Mercutio wants to know if Romeo stayed the night with a woman (though he suspects it would be Rosaline).

---

ROMEO

Good morning to you both. What slip did I give you?

ROMEO

Good morrow to you both. What counterfeit did I give you?

---

MERCUTIO

'The slip', sir, 'The slip'. Can you not conceive?

MERCUTIO

The slip, sir, the slip; can you not conceive?

---

95

---

> *Note: 'Conceive' has the double meaning of sex and understanding.*

**ROMEO**

Forgive me, good Mercutio. My business was important, in such a case a man may skip the constraints of courtesy.

**MERCUTIO**

So you are saying, such a <u>case</u> as you <u>had</u> constrains a man to <u>bowing his buttocks.</u>

**ROMEO**

Pardon, good Mercutio; my business was great, and in such a case as mine a man may strain courtesy.

**MERCUTIO**

That's as much as to say, such a case as yours constrains a man to bow in the hams.

> *Note: Mercutio puns on words here. Bowing in the hams - to bow at the waist - was a symptom of the disease, syphilis, which caused a man to stoop from the discomfort of the illness. 'Hams' meaning buttocks. He also suggests bent over for sexual reasons, apparent if he had accompanied the words with a pelvic thrust. To use this pun he deliberately pretends mishearing the word 'courtesy' as 'curtsy'. He also uses the word 'case' to refer to female genitalia.*

ROMEO PRETENDS TO MISUNDERSTAND MERCUTIO TO FOIL HIS MOCKING.

**ROMEO**

You mean to curtsy.

**MERCUTIO**

You have most kindly <u>hit it.</u>

**ROMEO**

Meaning to curtsy.

**MERCUTIO**

Thou hast most kindly hit it.

> *Note: 'Hit it' is again a sexual reference.*

**ROMEO**

A most courteous interpretation.

**MERCUTIO**

I am the very pink perfection of courtesy.

**ROMEO**

A fine pink flower.

**ROMEO**

A most courteous exposition.

**MERCUTIO**

Nay, I am the very pink of courtesy.

**ROMEO**

Pink for flower.

> *Note: Pink here has a triple meaning; 1, being the ornamental trimming with pinking shears of patterned shoe leather, 2, the pink flower (usually a carnation) worn by a gentleman, and 3, in the 'Pink', being in the best of condition, although Mercutio was really suggestng female genitalia.*
>
> *A little later they refer to a 'Wild Goose Chase', which originally involved hunting down a rider who could go in any direction to put off the pack of chasing riders. A bit like a fox hunt in which they wear a red jacket known as a pink. However, that form of fox hunting did not exist in Shakespeare's day so there is no connection between the hunt jacket and the Goose Chase.*

MERCUTIO
Exactly.

MERCUTIO
Right.

ROMEO
(*bawdy*) Well, then my <u>pump</u> is well <u>flowered</u>.

ROMEO
Why, then is my pump well flowered.

*Note: Romeo puns on 'pump' – double meaning of a shoe and a penis. The flowering is the perforated pattern in a leather shoe. But here he is also bawdily saying his penis has been enjoying a vagina.*

MERCUTIO
Such wit! Follow this wit through until you have worn out your <u>pump</u>. Then when the single sole of it is worn out, the joke will remain, after the wearing out, solely singular on its own.

MERCUTIO
Sure wit; follow me this jest now, till thou hast worn out thy pump, that, when the single sole of it is worn, the jest may remain, after the wearing, solely singular.

*Note: 'Single souled' was a term for a simple, silly person and also threadbare.*

ROMEO
Oh single soled joke, solely singular in its silliness.

ROMEO
O single-soled jest, solely singular for the singleness.

MERCUTIO
Separate us, Benvolio, my wit is fading.

MERCUTIO
Come between us, good Benvolio; my wit faints.

*Note: Some editions say 'my wits fail' rather than 'wit faints'.*

ROMEO
Use your whip and spurs, Mercutio, or I'll win the race.

ROMEO
Switch and spurs, switch and spurs, or I'll cry a match.

*Note: 'Cry a match', similar to the modern term, 'call it a match', or call it over. Match being the winning of the game, as in tennis, 'game, set and match'.*

MERCUTIO
Nay, if our wits are running a wild-goose chase, then I am out. You have more wild goose in one of your wits than I have in all five of mine. Did I keep up with your goose?

MERCUTIO
Nay, if our wits run the wild-goose chase, I am done; for thou hast more of the wild-goose in one of thy wits than I am sure I have in my whole five. Was I with you there for the goose?

> Note: 'Nay' is an old term for 'no', it is also the sound a horse makes.
>
> 'Was I with you there' – double meaning of 'was I right in my guess' (about him being with a woman last night), and did I keep up with your wild goose chase.
>
> As well as being a mad horse chase, 'Wild goose chase' is also a fruitless chase after something unattainable, or to search for something with no direction.

**ROMEO**
(*bawdily*) The only time you were with me was when you were there for the <u>goosing.</u> (*from a whore*)

**ROMEO**
Thou wast never with me for anything when thou wast not there for the goose.

> Note: Goose also meant 'whore'.

**MERCUTIO**
I will bite your ear for that jest.

**MERCUTIO**
I will bite thee by the ear for that jest.

> Note: A modern equivalent would be 'bite me'. It was not meant literally.

**ROMEO**
(*bawdily*) No, a good <u>goose</u> does not bite.

**ROMEO**
Nay, good goose, bite not.

**MERCUTIO**
Your biting wit is saucy, a most bitter sweet sauce.

**MERCUTIO**
Thy wit is a very bitter sweeting; it is a most sharp sauce.

**ROMEO**
And is it not then, best used to <u>stuff</u> a sweet <u>goose</u>?

**ROMEO**
And is it not then well served in to a sweet goose?

> Note: 'Sweeting' was a type of apple known for its sweetness, common at the time but rare now, and was also an archaic term for 'sweetheart'. Apple sauce was commonly served with roast goose, and apples could be used to 'stuff' a goose; to pack the insides of the goose as it was roasted, though Romeo suggests a bitter sauce served into a sweet whore, a sexual reference.

**MERCUTIO**
Oh, this wit is like elastic, stretching from an inch narrow to a mile wide!

**MERCUTIO**
O, here's a wit of cheveril, that stretches from an inch narrow to an ell broad.

**ROMEO**
I stretch it out for that word 'wide', which, added to the goose, proves far and wide you are a fat <u>gooser</u>.

**ROMEO**
I stretch it out for that word `broad', which, added to the goose, proves thee far and wide a broad goose.

> Note: This may have been a play on the term 'brood-goose'. A breeding goose, making yet further sexual innuendo. An 'ell' is an old unit of measure used by tailors of six hand lengths (roughly 45 inches or 1.15 metres). 'Mile wide' was used in the translation as mile is a common expression refering to exagerated length, such as when a footballer misses a shot on goal, 'he missed it by a mile'.

#### MERCUTIO

See, is this not better than pining for love? Now you are sociable, now you are Romeo again. Now you are here in mind as well as body. This drivelling love is like a village idiot running up and down, tongue hanging out, looking to hide his <u>stick</u> in a <u>hole</u>.

#### MERCUTIO

Why, is not this better now than groaning for love? Now art thou sociable, now art thou Romeo, now art thou what thou art, by art as well as by nature; for this drivelling love is like a great natural that runs lolling up and down to hide his bauble in a hole.

> Note: A 'great natural' was an idiot or a fool, often professionally, such as a court jester. A bauble is the stick jesters carry with a false jester's head on the end or an inflated bladder (like a balloon) to hit people on the head with for laughs. Jesters were hired by royal courts to play the fool and tell jokes.

#### BENVOLIO

Enough, Mercutio. Stop right there.

#### BENVOLIO

Stop there, stop there.

#### MERCUTIO

You want me to stop, Benvolio, with my <u>tale</u> so close to the <u>best part?</u>

#### MERCUTIO

Thou desirest me to stop in my tale against the hair.

> Note: 'Against the hair' means rubbing against the grain, going the wrong way about something, such as in wood where to rub the wrong way gets splinters.
>
> 'Tale' punning with 'tail', (story, or euphemism for penis), and 'hair' being a euphemism for female genitalia.

#### BENVOLIO

Yes, your <u>tale</u> would have <u>got longer</u> otherwise.

#### BENVOLIO

Thou wouldst else have made thy tale large.

#### MERCUTIO

No, you are mistaken. I would have made it short, for I was just coming to the <u>depth of my tale</u> and would have needed to <u>fill in</u> the subject no longer.

#### MERCUTIO

O, thou art deceived; I would have made it short; for I was come to the whole depth of my tale and meant, indeed, to occupy the argument no longer.

JULIET'S NURSE AND THE SERVANT, PETER, COME INTO VIEW.

#### ROMEO

Here's good material for mockery.

#### ROMEO

Here's goodly gear.

BENVOLIO PUTS HIS HAND ABOVE HIS EYES AS IF LOOK-OUT ON A BOAT.

| | |
|---|---|
| BENVOLIO | BENVOLIO |
| A sail! A sail! | A sail! A sail! |
| MERCUTIO | MERCUTIO |
| Two sails, his shirt and her dress. | Two, two; a shirt and a smock. |

NURSE CALLS TO PETER WHO IS LAGGING BEHIND HER.
SHE PUTS ON PRETENTIOUS AIRS.

| | |
|---|---|
| NURSE | NURSE |
| (*calling*) Peter! | Peter! |
| PETER | PETER |
| Coming. | Anon. |
| NURSE | NURSE |
| Pass me my fan, Peter. | My fan, Peter. |
| MERCUTIO | MERCUTIO |
| (*to his friends, mocking*) Yes Peter, to hide her face, for her fan's the better looking. | Good Peter, to hide her face, for her fan's the fairer face. |

THE MEN LAUGH. NURSE DRAWS LEVEL WITH THE MEN.

| | |
|---|---|
| NURSE | NURSE |
| Good morning to you, gentlemen. | God ye good morrow, gentlemen. |

MERCUTIO GREETS HER WITH OVER EXAGGERATED BOWING AND SCRAPING.

| | |
|---|---|
| MERCUTIO | MERCUTIO |
| Good afternoon to you, gentlewoman. | God ye good e'en, fair gentlewoman. |
| NURSE | NURSE |
| Is it afternoon? | Is it good e'en? |
| MERCUTIO | MERCUTIO |
| It certainly is. For the rude <u>hand</u> of the clock is now <u>pricking</u> up at noon. | 'Tis no less, I tell ye; for the bawdy hand of the dial is now upon the prick of noon. |

MERCUTIO MAKES A RUDE GESTURE WITH HIS ARM. THE MEN ALL LAUGH.

| | |
|---|---|
| NURSE | NURSE |
| Away with you! What kind of man are you! | Out upon you! What a man are you! |

ROMEO

One, madam, that God has made for himself to mock.

ROMEO

One, gentlewoman, that God hath made for himself to mar.

NURSE

Well said, young man. "For himself to mock"...
(*looks at Mercutio with scorn*) ...he says. Gentlemen, can you tell me where I may find the young Romeo?

NURSE

By my troth, it is well said. `For himself to mar' quoth a'? Gentlemen, can any of you tell me where I may find the young Romeo?

ROMEO

I can tell you, but 'young' Romeo will not be as young when you find him as he was when you started looking for him. I'm the youngest by that name, for want of a worse. (*instead of better*)

ROMEO

I can tell you; but young Romeo will be older when you have found him than he was when you sought him. I am the youngest of that name, for fault of a worse.

NURSE

(*grateful to have found him at last*) Welcome words, sir.

NURSE

You say well.

MERCUTIO

(*mocking*) So 'worse' is welcome? Very welcome words indeed, very wise, very clever!

MERCUTIO

Yea, is the worst well? Very well took, i'faith; wisely, wisely.

NURSE

(*ignoring him*) If you are Romeo, I need to have a 'confidence' with you.

NURSE

If you be he, sir, I desire some confidence with you.

> Note: Nurse has said 'confidence' instead of 'conference'.

BENVOLIO

(*laughing at miss-wording*) Confidence? She will 'indite' him to supper next.

BENVOLIO

She will endite him to some supper.

> Note: 'Endite' is a malapropism for 'invite'. However, 'endite' did not exist as a word in Shakespeare's time, despite Shakespeare using it in other plays. It seems he spelled 'indite' with an 'e'. In the 16th Century there were many variations in the spelling of words. The word 'indite' did exist, meaning to write. Editors often use 'indite' which is much closer in sound and spelling to 'invite'.

MERCUTIO

A whore, a whore, a whore! Tally ho! - after it! (*punning on the word 'hare'*)

MERCUTIO

A bawd, a bawd, a bawd! So ho!

Note: *A bawd was a regional name for a hare, because hare sounds like whore.*

ROMEO
You've seen a hare, Mercutio?

MERCUTIO
Not a hare sir, unless it is a hare, sir, wrapped in a crusty pie, stale and well past its best.
*(he walks by and sings bawdily)*
*"An old hairy whore*
*And an old hoary hare*
*Are very good meat for Lent.*
*But a worn out old whore*
*Is not worth a score,*
*When its whoring days are all spent".*
*(over his shoulder)* Romeo, are you coming with us to your father's for dinner?

ROMEO
What hast thou found?

MERCUTIO
No hare, sir, unless a hare, sir, in a lenten pie, that is something stale and hoar ere it be spent.
[*Sings.*]
*An old hare hoar,*
*And an old hare hoar,*
*Is very good meat in Lent.*
*But a hare that is hoar*
*Is too much for a score,*
*When it hoars ere it be spent.*
Romeo, will you come to your father's? We'll to dinner thither.

Note: *A Lenten Pie is a pie with no meat made during lent; a religious period when people eat no meat for forty days.*

*'Hoar' means stale or mouldy, and also puns with whore. He is saying she is a whore well past her best and only to be used if nothing else is available.*

*'Score' is a pun, it means rating, it also means twenty and to score something is to buy illegal goods. She is not worthy of a rating nor worth paying for.*

*'Dinner' was a midday meal, more commonly called 'lunch' now, though still in use in England for traditional midday meals such as school dinner.*

ROMEO
Go on, I'll follow you.

MERCUTIO
Farewell, old lady, farewell.
*(exaggerated bow walking backwards singing)*
*"Lady, lady, lady."*

ROMEO
I will follow you.

MERCUTIO
Farewell, ancient lady; farewell,
[Sings.]
*Lady, lady, lady.*

Note: *'Lady, lady' was a repeated line from a popular ballad called 'The Ballad of Constant Susanna' by Pepys, about a virtuous woman who is falsely accused of laying with a man after turning down two upstanding men who try to have their way with her. Justice prevails in the end, a tale of morality. It was also the name of Shakespeare's daughter. The ballad has no relevance to the storyline here, he is sarcastically saying she is no lady.*

MERCUTIO AND BENVOLIO MAKE OFF DOWN THE ROAD, LAUGHING.

NURSE

I ask you sir, who was that rude person so full of himself?

NURSE

I pray you, sir, what saucy merchant was this that was so full of his ropery?

Note: 'Ropery' was a common term for roguery, trickery and mischief with reference to the hangman's rope, the penalty for rogues. An alternative translation could be, 'with enough cheek to hang himself'.

ROMEO

A gentleman, Nurse, that loves to hear himself talk, and who will say more in a minute than could be endured in a month.

ROMEO

A gentleman, Nurse, that loves to hear himself talk, and will speak more in a minute than he will stand to in a month.

Note: The Nurse's following words can be misconstrued as double meaning.

NURSE

And if he speaks against me again I will have him, as I have those ruder than him - and twenty or so other scoundrels! And if I cannot, I'll find those who can. Insolent man! I am not one of his young flirts, I am not one of his wild friends.

(to Peter) And Peter, you stand by and allow every man to abuse me at his pleasure.

NURSE

An a' speak anything against me I'll take him down, and a' were lustier than he is - and twenty such Jacks!. And if I cannot, I'll find those that shall. Scurvy knave! I am none of his flirt-gills; I am none of his skaines-mates.

[To Peter.] And thou must stand by too, and suffer every knave to use me at his pleasure!

Note: Jack was a derogatory name for a man. See note at end of Act 4 Scene 5

PETER

(bawdily) I saw no man use you at his pleasure. If I had, my weapon would have quickly been out I promise you. I'm as quick as any man at getting it out if I see the chance of a good confrontation... and the law is on my side.

PETER

I saw no man use you at his pleasure; if I had, my weapon should quickly have been out, I warrant you. I dare draw as soon as another man if I see occasion in a good quarrel, and the law on my side.

NURSE

Before god, I am so worked up that every part of me quivers.

(about Mercutio) Stupid boy!

(to Romeo) Pray sir, a word.

NURSE

Now, afore God, I am so vexed that every part about me quivers. Scurvy knave!

Pray you, sir, a word;

NURSE TAKES ROMEO ASIDE.

NURSE

(*quieter, in confidence*) As I told you, my young lady sent me to find you. What she asked me to say I will keep to myself for the moment, but let me tell you first, if you are leading her a merry dance to a fool's paradise - as they say - it would be the very worst kind of behaviour - as they say. For the good lady is young, and if you should be deceiving her, truly it would be a terrible trick to be offered to any good lady, and a sign of very poor character.

NURSE

and, as I told you, my young lady bid me enquire you out. What she bid me say, I will keep to myself; but first let me tell ye, if ye should lead her in a fool's paradise, as they say, it were a very gross kind of behaviour, as they say, for the gentlewoman is young; and therefore, if you should deal double with her, truly it were an ill thing to be offered to any gentlewoman, and very weak dealing.

> Note: 'Double dealing' is deceiving someone by pretending one thing when intending another. From the practise of dealing an extra card to yourself in order to cheat.

ROMEO

Nurse, send my greetings to your lady and mistress, I swear upon my soul...

ROMEO

Nurse, commend me to thy lady and mistress. I protest unto thee -

> Note: 'Protest' here means solemnly state or swear something, as opposed to the objecting/disapproving meaning. Most famously used in Hamlet (and used today still but with the incorrect meaning of protest applied) "The lady doth protest too much".

NURSE

(*interrupting*) Thank goodness, I will tell her. Lord, she will be a happy woman.

NURSE

Good heart, and, i'faith, I will tell her as much. Lord, Lord, she will be a joyful woman.

ROMEO

What will you tell her, Nurse? You didn't hear me out.

ROMEO

What wilt thou tell her, Nurse? Thou dost not mark me.

NURSE

I will tell her, sir, that you swear, which, as I understand, is a gentlemanly vow.

NURSE

I will tell her, sir, that you do protest; which, as I take it, is a gentlemanlike offer.

ROMEO

(*deciding it best to use straight talk*)
Tell her to find some way to come to confession this afternoon at Friar Laurence's quarters, to be given absolution, and to be married.

ROMEO

Bid her devise
Some means to come to shrift this afternoon;
And there she shall at Friar Laurence' cell
Be shrived and married...

> *Note: Shrived is to receive Shrift or Absolution, which is the religious act of confessing one's sins to a priest and receiving forgivness from God. A Catholic practise often referred to by Shakespeare in a time when Catholicism was banned in England. Italy was predominantly Roman Catholic though so it makes sense in this play.*

ROMEO OFFERS NURSE SOME MONEY.

| | |
|---|---|
| **ROMEO** | ROMEO |
| Here is something for your trouble. | Here is for thy pains. |
| **NURSE** | NURSE |
| No, truly, sir, I could not take a penny. | No; truly, sir, not a penny. |
| **ROMEO** | ROMEO |
| Take it, I insist. | Go to, I say you shall. |

NURSE TAKES THE MONEY.

| | |
|---|---|
| **NURSE** | NURSE |
| This afternoon, sir? She'll be there. | This afternoon, sir? Well, she shall be there. |
| **ROMEO** | ROMEO |
| Oh, and, Nurse, wait behind the abbey wall. Within the hour my man will bring you a rope ladder which will be the secret passage to the heights of my desire tonight. Farewell. Stay true to me, and I will reward you for your troubles. Farewell. Give my love to your mistress. | And stay, good nurse – behind the abbey wall Within this hour my man shall be with thee, And bring thee cords made like a tackled stair, Which to the high top-gallant of my joy Must be my convoy in the secret night. Farewell. Be trusty, and I'll quit thy pains. Farewell. Commend me to thy mistress. |

> *Note: 'Top-gallant' was the highest sail on a ship reached by a 'tackled stair'.*
>
> *It is not clear why Romeo should say farewell twice to Nurse.*

| | |
|---|---|
| **NURSE** | NURSE |
| May God in heaven bless you! But listen, sir... | Now God in heaven bless thee! Hark you, sir. |

NURSE BECKONS ROMEO CLOSER.

| | |
|---|---|
| **ROMEO** | ROMEO |
| *(quietly)* What is it, my dear Nurse? | What sayst thou, my dear Nurse? |

**NURSE**

(*quietly*) Can your man be trusted? Have you not heard the saying, 'one may keep a secret, two will give it away'?

**NURSE**

Is your man secret? Did you ne'er hear say Two may keep counsel, putting one away?

> Note: 'Putting one away' - the literal translation would be: two may share a secret, sending one to jail or, providing the other is away where he can't hear. It means a secret is best kept if it is not shared.

**ROMEO**

I assure you my man's as true as steel.

**ROMEO**

I warrant thee my man's as true as steel.

**NURSE**

Well, sir, my mistress is the sweetest lady – Lord, Lord, and such a chatter-box... Oh! There is a nobleman in town, Count Paris, who would happily lay claim to her, but she, good soul, looks upon him as dearly as she would a toad, an actual toad. I make her angry sometimes, and tell her that Paris is the best man for her, but I can assure you that when I say this she looks as white as any sheet you've ever seen. Doesn't rosemary and Romeo begin with the same letter?

**NURSE**

Well, sir, my mistress is the sweetest lady - Lord, Lord, when 'twas a little prating thing - O! there is a nobleman in town, one Paris, that would fain lay knife aboard; but she, good soul, had as lief see a toad, a very toad, as see him. I anger her sometimes and tell her that Paris is the properer man; but, I'll warrant you, when I say so she looks as pale as any clout in the versal world. Doth not rosemary and Romeo begin both with a letter?

**ROMEO**

Yes, Nurse, but what of it? Both beginning with 'Rrrrrr'. (*sound like low growl*)

**ROMEO**

Ay, Nurse, what of that? Both with an R.

**NURSE**

Ah, you mock me. That's the sound dogs make. 'R' is for ar... no, I think that begins with some other letter, but she does have the prettiest saying about it, and of you and rosemary. You should hear it.

**NURSE**

Ah, mocker! - that's the dog's name. ` R' is for the - no, I know it begins with some other letter; and she hath the prettiest sententious of it, of you and rosemary, that it would do you good to hear it.

> Note: The Romans called the letter 'R' the dog's letter. Jonson wrote a familiar adage of the time which Nurse refers to, 'R is the dog's letter, and hurreth in the sound'. R is for... - the audience usually assumes nurse meant 'arse'.
>
> 'Rosemary' is the sea plant, Ros Marinus, not the girl's name or the herb, a plant washed by sea spray, representing salty tears.

ROMEO WAVES HER AWAY.

ROMEO

Send my love to your lady.

NURSE

Yes, a thousand times I will.
(*calling*) Peter!

PETER

Coming.

NURSE

Lead the way, and be quick about it.

ROMEO

Commend me to thy lady.

NURSE

Ay, a thousand times. Peter!

PETER

Anon.

NURSE

Before, and apace.

THEY ALL EXIT.

# ACT II SCENE V

## CAPULET'S GARDEN. MONDAY AFTERNOON.

JULIET IS ALONE IN THE GARDEN IMPATIENTLY WAITING FOR NEWS.

**JULIET**

(*aside*) The clock struck nine when I sent the Nurse and she promised to return in half an hour. Perhaps she cannot find him. No, that's not it, it's because she is so slow! Love's messengers should be thoughts, travelling ten times faster than the sunbeams driving the shadows from the dark hills. That's why nimble winged doves draw Venus' chariot, and why Cupid has swift wings. The Sun stands on the highest hill of this day's journey, and from nine to twelve is three long hours, and still she is not back.

Had she my affections and warm youthful blood she would be as swift as a struck tennis ball. My words would serve her to my sweet love, and his return her to me.

*But old folks act as if they are half dead,*
*Unwieldy, slow, pale, and heavy as lead.*

**JULIET**

The clock struck nine when I did send the Nurse;
In half an hour she promised to return.
Perchance she cannot meet him. That's not so.
O, she is lame. Love's heralds should be thoughts,
Which ten times faster glides than the sun's beams
Driving back shadows over louring hills.
Therefore do nimble-pinioned doves draw Love,
And therefore hath the wind-swift Cupid wings.
Now is the sun upon the highmost hill
Of this day's journey, and from nine till twelve
Is three long hours, yet she is not come.
Had she affections and warm youthful blood
She would be as swift in motion as a ball;
My words would bandy her to my sweet love,
And his to me.
*But old folks, many feign as they were dead -*
*Unwieldy, slow, heavy, and pale as lead.*

> Note: 'Bandy' was a popular word of the time, derived from tennis. To bandy a ball back and forth. The French word 'bander' means 'to take sides at tennis' so it may come from the French word, as do many tennis terms, though interestingly the French do not use the same French terms in tennis as English speakers.

NURSE AND PETER RETURN FROM THEIR MEETING WITH ROMEO.

**JULIET (CONT'D)**

Oh God, here she comes!

– Oh, dear Nurse, what happened? Did you meet him? Send your man away.

**NURSE**

(*breathing heavily from exertions*)
Peter, wait by the gate.

**JULIET**

O God, she comes! O honey Nurse, what news?
Hast thou met with him? Send thy man away.

**NURSE**

Peter, stay at the gate.

PETER RETIRES TO THE GATE. JULIET WAITS IMPATIENTLY
UNTIL HE IS OUT OF EARSHOT.

JULIET

Now, good sweet Nurse - oh Lord, why do you look so sad? If the news is sad, at least tell it with a smile, if it is good, you shame the music of sweet news by playing it to me with such a sour face.

NURSE

I am weary! Let me rest a while. My, how my bones ache! What a trudge I've had!

JULIET

I would gladly trade my bones for your news. Now come, I beg you, good, good Nurse, tell me!

NURSE

Jesus, what impatience! Can you not wait a moment? Can't you see I'm out of breath.

JULIET

Now, good sweet Nurse - O Lord, why look'st thou sad?

Though news be sad, yet tell them merrily;
If good, thou sham'st the music of sweet news
By playing it to me with so sour a face.

NURSE

I am aweary, give me leave awhile.
Fie, how my bones ache! What a jaunce have I!

JULIET

I would thou hadst my bones and I thy news.
Nay, come, I pray thee speak. Good, good Nurse, speak.

NURSE

Jesu, what haste! Can you not stay awhile?
Do you not see that I am out of breath?

> Note: Nurse is deliberately making Juliet wait for the answer, as penalty perhaps for not sympathising with her pains.

JULIET

How can you be out of breath when you have the breath to say you are out of breath? The excuse you make for this delay is longer than the answer you could have given me. Is the news good or bad? Answer that at least. Say one or the other, I can wait for the details. I have to know, is it good or bad?

JULIET

How art thou out of breath when thou hast breath
To say to me that thou art out of breath?
The excuse that thou dost make in this delay
Is longer than the tale thou dost excuse.
Is thy news good or bad? Answer to that.
Say either, and I'll stay the circumstance.
Let me be satisfied, is't good or bad?

NURSE

(sarcasm) Well, that's a foolish choice you've made. You know how to pick a man all right! Romeo? - no, not him. He may be better looking than any man, with legs above other men, and as for his hands, feet, and body, they're not so much to talk about, yet still beyond compare, but he's not the most courteous of men, though I believe him to be as gentle as a lamb. Anyway, off you go, girl, serve God. -- What, have you eaten already?

NURSE

Well, you have made a simple choice; you know not how to choose a man. Romeo? - no, not he; though his face be better than any man's, yet his leg excels all men's, and for a hand and a foot and a body, though they be not to be talked on, yet they are past compare. He is not the flower of courtesy, but I'll warrant him as gentle as a lamb. Go thy ways, wench; serve God. What, have you dined at home?

> Note: Nurse has tried to talk Romeo down to Juliet, but has inadvertantly sung his praises. She thinks she's finished the conversation and is hungry.
>
> "Flower of courtesy' – earlier Mercutio had said, 'pink of courtesy'.

JULIET

No, no. But I knew all this before. What does he say about our marriage? What of that?

JULIET

No, no. But all this did I know before. What says he of our marriage? What of that?

> Note: Nurse is not really listening to Juliet, she's finished her story and is making a drama out of the suffering she has endured on her errand, making a frustrated Juliet wait for the answer she so dearly needs to hear.

NURSE

Lord, how my head hurts! What a head I have! It pounds as if it were about to split into twenty pieces, and my back....

NURSE

Lord, how my head aches! What a head have I; It beats as it would fall in twenty pieces. My back! –

---

JULIET RUBS NURSE'S ACHING BACK.

---

NURSE (CONT'D)

Ah! No, the other side. Ah, my back, my back! Confound your heart for sending me out to catch my death of cold trudging up and down.

NURSE

A t'other side. Ah, my back, my back! Beshrew your heart for sending me about To catch my death with jauncing up and down!

> Note: 'Beshrew' is a mild curse, said without malice here, 'a curse on your heart' or 'damn your heart' and in place of a harder expletive which wasn't permitted back then. A bad tempered woman was known as a 'shrew'.

JULIET

I am truly sorry that you are not well.
Sweet, sweet, sweet Nurse, please tell me
what my love says.

NURSE

Your love says, like an honourable
gentleman, and a polite, kind, handsome,
and I'll even wager virtuous too...
- Where is your mother?

JULIET

(*angry*) Where is my mother? Somewhere
in the house, where do you think she
would be? What kind of reply is that?
(*sarcastic*) "Your love says like an
honourable gentleman, where is your
mother?"

NURSE

Oh, Mary, mother of God! You are so
impatient! Dear me, calm down, I don't
know. Is this the thanks I get for my
aching bones? Next time deliver your
messages yourself.

JULIET

What a drama you make! Come on, what
did Romeo say?

NURSE

Will you be permitted to go to confession
today?

JULIET

I'faith, I am sorry that thou art not well.
Sweet, sweet, sweet Nurse, tell me what says my
love?

NURSE

Your love says like an honest gentleman, and a
courteous, and a kind, and a handsome, and, I
warrant, a virtuous -
Where is your mother?

JULIET

Where is my mother? Why, she is within.
Where should she be? How oddly thou repliest:
"Your love says like an honest gentleman
Where is your mother?"

NURSE

O God's lady dear!
Are you so hot? Marry, come up, I trow;
Is this the poultice for my aching bones?
Henceforward do your messages yourself.

JULIET

Here's such a coil! Come, what says Romeo?

NURSE

Have you got leave to go to shrift today?

---

Note: Shrift was the process of going to church to confess your sins to God
through a holy person and to receive 'absolution' - to be pardoned by God. If you
were free of sins when you died you would go to Heaven. It is repeatedly mentioned
in this play and many of Shakespeare's other plays.

---

JULIET

Yes, why?

JULIET

I have.

NURSE

(*now serious*) Then get yourself to Father Laurence's lodgings right away. There awaits a husband, to make you a wife.
Now I see the wanton blood of desire flood to your cheeks, they'll be bright scarlet if I say any more. Hurry to the church. I must go the other way to fetch a ladder for your love to climb to your <u>love-nest</u> when it is dark.
*I am the slave, and work for your pleasure,*
*But (bawdy) you'll bear <u>the burden</u> tonight at*
    *your leisure.*
*Go, I'm off to dinner. Quickly, to the cell.*

JULIET

*Off to good fortune! My good Nurse, farewell.*

NURSE

Then hie you hence to Friar Laurence' cell;
There stays a husband to make you a wife.
Now comes the wanton blood up in your cheeks;
They'll be in scarlet straight at any news.
Hie you to church; I must another way
To fetch a ladder, by the which your love
Must climb a bird's nest soon when it is dark.
*I am the drudge, and toil in your delight;*
*But you shall bear the burden soon at night.*
*Go; I'll to dinner. Hie you to the cell.*

JULIET

*Hie to high fortune! Honest Nurse, farewell.*

> Note: 'Bird's nest' was a euphemism for female genitalia.
>
> A 'cell' is a small monastery, linked to a larger one.

# ACT II SCENE VI

## A Room In A Monastery. Monday Afternoon.

**FRIAR LAURENCE**

May the heavens smile upon this holy act, and not punish us afterwards with sorrow.

**ROMEO**

Amen, amen, Father. Let whatever sorrow lies in store come, it could never outweigh the joy one short minute in her sight brings me. Join our hands in marriage with your holy words, then let love-devouring death do whatever it dares, it is enough just to call her mine.

FRIAR LAURENCE

So smile the heavens upon this holy act
That after-hours with sorrow chide us not!

ROMEO

Amen, amen. But come what sorrow can,
It cannot countervail the exchange of joy
That one short minute gives me in her sight.
Do thou but close our hands with holy words,
Then love-devouring death do what he dare;
It is enough I may but call her mine.

> *Note: 'Amen' is used in prayer, from Hebrew meaning 'so be it', (I agree).*
>
> *Another prophetic speech, 'love-devouring death do what he dare', as is the following Friar's speech.*

**FRIAR LAURENCE**

These intense passions often have intense ends, which at their peak die, consumed like fire and gunpowder as they kiss. Even the sweetest honey is sickly if too much is consumed; the taste contradicting the desire. Therefore love in moderation, and your love will last. Too rushed arrives no sooner than too slow.

FRIAR LAURENCE

These violent delights have violent ends,
And in their triumph die, like fire and powder
Which, as they kiss, consume. The sweetest honey
Is loathsome in his own deliciousness,
And in the taste confounds the appetite.
Therefore love moderately – long love doth so;
Too swift arrives as tardy as too slow.

| FRIAR LAURENCE (CONT'D) | FRIAR LAURENCE |
|---|---|
| Here comes the lady now, oh, so light of foot she hardly touches the ground. A lover may step upon the fine webs that float on the summer breeze, and yet not break them, so light is fleeting joy. | Here comes the lady O, so light a foot Will ne'er wear out the everlasting flint. A lover may bestride the gossamers That idles in the wanton summer air, And yet not fall, so light is vanity. |

*Note: 'Vanity' here means the temporary joy felt when first in love.*

| JULIET | JULIET |
|---|---|
| Good afternoon to you, Father. | Good even to my ghostly confessor. |

ROMEO GIVES JULIET A WELCOMING KISS WHICH PROMPTS THE FOLLOWING
WORDS FROM THE FRIAR.

| FRIAR LAURENCE | FRIAR LAURENCE |
|---|---|
| Romeo will thank you, my daughter, for both of us. | Romeo shall thank thee, daughter, for us both. |

JULIET RETURNS ROMEO'S KISS.

| JULIET | JULIET |
|---|---|
| And I thank him from both of us, or his thanks would be too much. | As much to him, else is his thanks too much. |

| ROMEO | ROMEO |
|---|---|
| Ah, Juliet, if your joy is as great as mine, and your skill at voicing it greater, then let your breath sweeten the air, and the rich music of your tongue fill the room with the happiness you can imagine us sharing together in this sweet encounter. | Ah, Juliet, if the measure of thy joy Be heaped like mine, and that thy skill be more To blazon it, then sweeten with thy breath This neighbour air, and let rich music's tongue Unfold the imagined happiness that both Receive in either by this dear encounter. |

*Note: 'Blazon', proclaim publicly, derived from coats of arms emblazoned on family shields to show publicly your status.*

## JULIET

Reality is richer in matter than in words, it boasts of its substance by its very existence, not by clever wording. Those who can count their wealth are mere beggars, my true love has grown to such excess, I could not possibly count even half my wealth of happiness.

## JULIET

Conceit, more rich in matter than in words,
Brags of his substance, not of ornament.
They are but beggars that can count their worth;
But my true love is grown to such excess
I cannot sum up half my sum of wealth.

> Note: Original texts said "I cannot sum up sum of half my wealth", but modern editions have altered this to the more sensical line above.

## FRIAR LAURENCE

Come, come with me, we will do this quickly.
*Forgive me, but you two should not stay alone*
*Until Holy Church combines two into one.*

## FRIAR LAURENCE

Come, come with me, and we will make short work;
*For, by your leaves, you shall not stay alone*
*Till Holy Church incorporate two in one.*

> Note: 'Incorporate two in one' is from a passage in the Bible, Mathew, 15,5. "For this cause shall a man leave father and mother, and shall cleave to his wife; and they twain shall be one flesh."

> This is the end of Act II. It is worth noting that pausing between acts did not begin until theatre moved under cover in Shakespeare's later life when it became necessary to trim the candles, and there were no hard rules for scene changes. Before Shakespeare's time, plays followed the three rules of drama, the 'unities', derived from Aristotle's 'Poetics', which stated that dramas should take place in a single day, in one place, and have only one plot. Shakespeare would never have written his great works had he followed this ruling.

# ACT III

UNHAPPY CIRCUMSTANCE

# ACT III

## ACT III SCENE I

### THE STREETS OF VERONA. MONDAY AFTERNOON.

IT IS AN HOUR AFTER ROMEO'S SECRET MARRIAGE TO JULIET.

A HOT SUMMER'S AFTERNOON IN TOWN.

MERCUTIO WITH BENVOLIO AND OTHER MEMBERS OF THE MONTAGUE
STAFF (POSSIBLY ABRAHAM AND BALTHASAR FROM THE FIRST SCENE) ARE
IDLY PASSING TIME IN THE STREET.

MERCUTIO IS NOT A MONTAGUE, HE IS A RELATIVE OF PRINCE ESCALUS.

**BENVOLIO**

I beg you, Mercutio, let's go home. The day is hot and there are Capulets about. If we meet any we'll get into a fight for sure. This heat gets everyone's blood boiling.

**MERCUTIO**

Benvolio, you are like one of those fellows who enters a tavern and places his sword on the table saying, 'God permitting, I'll have no need for you!' Then after two drinks draws his sword on the man who draws the beer without good reason.

Note: 'Drawer' – man who draws beer - to 'pull' a measure of beer into a glass using a hand pump. Still in use today in British pubs, where beer is drawn straight from the barrel

**BENVOLIO**

Am I really like such a fellow?

**MERCUTIO**

Come, come. You are as hot headed in your state as any man in Italy; quickly provoked to be angry, and just as quickly angry enough to be provoked.

**BENVOLIO**

I pray thee, good Mercutio, let's retire.
The day is hot, the Capels are abroad,
And if we meet we shall not 'scape a brawl,
For now, these hot days, is the mad blood stirring.

**MERCUTIO**

Thou art like one of these fellows that, when he enters the confines of a tavern, claps me his sword upon the table and says `God send me no need of thee!' and by the operation of the second cup draws him on the drawer, when indeed there is no need.

**BENVOLIO**

Am I like such a fellow?

**MERCUTIO**

Come, come, thou art as hot a Jack in thy mood as any in Italy;
and as soon moved to be moody, and as soon moody to be moved.

BENVOLIO
To what?

MERCUTIO
'To'? Were there two like you, there would soon be none for they would kill each other.
You? - Why, you would quarrel with a man who has one more hair or one less hair in his beard than you have. You would quarrel with a man for cracking nuts for no other reason than you have hazel eyes. What eye but yours could find such a quarrel? Your head is as full of quarrels as an egg is full of yolk, even though your head has been beaten into an omelette from so much quarrelling. You quarrelled with a man for coughing in the street because he woke up your dog who lay sleeping in the sun. Didn't you fall out with that tailor because he was wearing his new jacket before Easter? And with another man for tying his new shoes with old laces? And yet you tell me off for quarrelling!

BENVOLIO
And what to?

MERCUTIO
Nay, an there were two such we should have none shortly, for one would kill the other. Thou? - why, thou wilt quarrel with a man that hath a hair more or a hair less in his beard than thou hast. Thou wilt quarrel with a man for cracking nuts, having no other reason but because thou hast hazel eyes. What eye but such an eye would spy out such a quarrel? Thy head is as full of quarrels as an egg is full of meat, and yet thy head hath been beaten as addle as an egg for quarrelling. Thou hast quarrelled with a man for coughing in the street, because he hath wakened thy dog that hath lain asleep in the sun. Didst thou not fall out with a tailor for wearing his new doublet before Easter; with another for tying his new shoes with old riband? And yet thou wilt tutor me from quarrelling!

*Note: Hazel is a common brown eye colour, named after the hazel nut.*

BENVOLIO
And if I were so quick to quarrel as you, any man investing in my life would lose everything within the hour.

MERCUTIO
Investing in your life? How foolish!

BENVOLIO
An I were so apt to quarrel as thou art, any man should buy the fee simple of my life for an hour and a quarter.

MERCUTIO
The fee simple! O simple!

*Note: 'Fee Simple' means possessing outright ownership by purchase.*

TYBALT, PETRUCCIO AND OTHERS FROM THE RIVAL CAPULET HOUSEHOLD
COME WALKING DOWN THE STREET LOOKING FOR TROUBLE.

BENVOLIO
By heavens above, here come some Capulets.

BENVOLIO
By my head, here comes the Capulets.

MERCUTIO
By hell below, I couldn't care less.

MERCUTIO
By my heel, I care not.

TYBALT SPOTS THE MONTAGUES AND HEADS FOR THEM.

TYBALT
(*to his fellow Capulets*) Stay close behind me, I'll speak with them.
(*to the Montagues, sneering*) Good afternoon, gentlemen, a word with one of you.

TYBALT
Follow me close, for I will speak to them. Gentlemen, good e'en; a word with one of you.

MERCUTIO RISES TO THE BAIT.

MERCUTIO
Only one word with one of us? You could add to it, Tybalt. Make it a word and a blow.

MERCUTIO
And but one word with one of us? Couple it with something, make it a word and a blow.

Note: 'Blow' here means to hit or strike someone, from a common phrase 'a word and a blow'.

TYBALT
You will find me more than up to that, sir, if you give me good reason.

TYBALT
You shall find me apt enough to that, sir, an you will give me occasion.

MERCUTIO
Could you not find good reason without my giving it?

MERCUTIO
Could you not take some occasion without giving?

TYBALT
Mercutio, you consort with Romeo.

TYBALT
Mercutio, thou consortest with Romeo.

MERCUTIO
'Concert'? What do you think we are, musicians? Perhaps you wish to compare us to street buskers, believe me you will hear nothing from us but discord.

MERCUTIO
Consort! What, dost thou make us minstrels? An thou make minstrels of us, look to hear nothing but discords.

Note: Consort means to associate with or accompany, it also has the lesser used meaning of a group of musicians, which Mercutio picks up on. The word concert was used here as it is better known to a modern audience.

MERCUTIO INDICATES HIS SWORD.

### MERCUTIO (CONT'D)
My sword is my fiddlestick. That should make you dance. 'Concert' indeed!

### MERCUTIO
Here's my fiddlestick; here's that shall make you dance. Zounds, consort!

> Note: 'Zounds' was a mild curse, corrupted from the words, 'God's wounds' (that Jesus received when he was crucified). There were many exclamations which had a religious source, some still in use today. As swearing was not allowed on stage, minor curses were used in their place.

### BENVOLIO
It is too public here, Mercutio. Either take this somewhere more private and calmly argue your grievance or leave. Everyone is looking at us.

### BENVOLIO
We talk here in the public haunt of men; Either withdraw unto some private place, Or reason coldly of your grievances, Or else depart. Here all eyes gaze on us.

> Note: Some modern texts replace 'Or reason' with 'And reason', which makes more sense, believing the first 'or' to be an accidental copy of the one below.

### MERCUTIO
Men's eyes were made to look. Let them look. I will not budge from here for any man, that I won't.

### MERCUTIO
Men's eyes were made to look, and let them gaze. I will not budge for no man's pleasure, I

---

ROMEO ARRIVES CHEERILY.

---

### TYBALT
Well peace be with you, sir, here comes my man now.

### TYBALT
Well, peace be with you, sir; here comes my man.

### MERCUTIO
I'll be damned, sir, if Romeo is a servant of yours. Indeed, the only time he'd follow you would be to a duel, in that sense you may call him 'your man', (*sarcastically*) your highness.

### MERCUTIO
But I'll be hanged, sir, if he wear your livery. Marry, go before to field, he'll be your follower. Your worship in that sense may call him ` man'.

### TYBALT
(*angry*) Romeo, the *hate* I have for you is such that I have only this to say; you sir, are a villain!

### TYBALT
Romeo, the love I bear thee can afford No better term than this: thou art a villain.

### ROMEO
Tybalt, the reason that I have to *love* you excuses me from returning your rage. And in reply to your greeting; I am not a villain, so goodbye. I see you do not know the real me.

### ROMEO
Tybalt, the reason that I have to love thee Doth much excuse the appertaining rage To such a greeting. Villain am I none; Therefore farewell. I see thou know'st me not.

ROMEO TURNS TO LEAVE.

TYBALT DRAWS HIS SWORD.

| TYBALT | TYBALT |
|---|---|
| Boy, this will not excuse the hurt you have caused me. Face me and draw your sword! | Boy, this shall not excuse the injuries That thou hast done me; therefore turn and draw. |

> Note: 'Boy' is an insulting term, suggesting he is not a man, as opposed to the usage for one of the staff.

| ROMEO | ROMEO |
|---|---|
| (*still calm*) I swear I've never hurt you, in fact I *love* you more than you could imagine - until you discover the reason for my *love*. And so, good Capulet - a name I now respect as dearly as my own - be satisfied with that. | I do protest I never injured thee, But love thee better than thou canst devise Till thou shalt know the reason of my love. And so, good Capulet, which name I tender As dearly as mine own, be satisfied. |

> Note: The repeated use of the word 'love' in the exchange above. In the earliest text Tybalt said 'hate' first instead of love, which would make sense of Romeo following this up with the opposite word 'love'. Most texts now use the word 'love', though 'hate' has been used here for the translation as it emphasises the change in dynamics caused by Romeo secretly marrying Juliet.

| MERCUTIO | MERCUTIO |
|---|---|
| So calm, so dishonourable, what a vile submission! The threat of a strike wins the day! | O calm, dishonourable, vile submission! Alla stoccata carries it away! |

> Note: 'Alla stoccata' is an Italian fencing term, literally meaning, 'to the strike'. It is used to start a duel or as a challenge. Mercutio has wrongly assumed Romeo will not fight because he is a coward.

MERCUTIO DRAWS HIS SWORD AND FACES TYBALT.

| MERCUTIO (CONT'D) | MERCUTIO |
|---|---|
| Tybalt, you rat catcher, come, will you walk with me? | Tybalt, you rat catcher, will you walk? |

> Note: Again a reference to Tibalt, the King of Cats in folklore.

TYBALT

What argument do you have with me, Mercutio?

TYBALT

What wouldst thou have with me?

MERCUTIO

Good King of Cats, nothing more than one of your nine lives, which I mean to take right now. And depending on your behaviour to me afterwards, I may just beat the other eight out of you as well. Will you pluck your sword out of its scabbard by its ears? Be quick or mine will be about your ears before yours is out

MERCUTIO

Good King of Cats, nothing but one of your nine lives. That I mean to make bold withal, and, as you shall use me hereafter, dry-beat the rest of the eight. Will you pluck your sword out of his pilcher by the ears? Make haste, lest mine be about your ears ere it be out.

> Note: 'Dry-beat' - to beat all the moisture out of something.
>
> 'Pilcher' does not exist as a word. 'Pilch' does, which is a leather garment. Some scholars think this may have been a printer's error for 'pilch, sir'.

TYBALT RAISES HIS SWORD.

TYBALT

I am more than ready for you!

TYBALT

I am for you.

ROMEO

Calm down, Mercutio, put your sword away.

ROMEO

Gentle Mercutio, put thy rapier up.

MERCUTIO

(to Tybalt) Come, sir, let's see your fancy moves!

MERCUTIO

Come sir, your passado.

> Note: Passado is a forward thrust, one foot advanced. For fancy moves, see notes in Act 2 Scene 4 on pretentious duelling language.

MERCUTIO AND TYBALT BRANDISH SWORDS, THRUSTING AT EACH OTHER.

ROMEO DRAWS HIS SWORD.

ROMEO

Draw your sword, Benvolio. Help me part them. Gentlemen, this outrage in public is shameful. Tybalt! Mercutio! The Prince has expressly banned fighting on the streets of Verona.

Stop, Tybalt! Please, Mercutio!

ROMEO

Draw, Benvolio; beat down their weapons. Gentlemen, for shame, forbear this outrage. Tybalt, Mercutio, the prince expressly hath Forbid this bandying in Verona streets. Hold, Tybalt! Good Mercutio!

ROMEO CHARGES BETWEEN TYBALT AND MERCUTIO TO PREVENT THEM
FIGHTING. TYBALT MAKES A LUNGE UNDER ROMEO'S ARM, WHICH HIS BODY
PREVENTS MERCUTIO FROM SEEING AND AVOIDING.

THE BLOW RUNS THROUGH MERCUTIO, WHO COLLAPSES ON THE GROUND.

TYBALT TURNS AND FLEES, FOLLOWED BY HIS FELLOW CAPULETS.

MERCUTIO

I am hit. A curse on both your families! I am finished. Is he gone? And not a mark on him?

BENVOLIO

What, are you hurt, Mercutio?

MERCUTIO

Yes, yes, a scratch, a scratch, but it's enough. Where is my man?

MERCUTIO

I am hurt.

A plague a' both your houses! I am sped. Is he gone, and hath nothing?

BENVOLIO

What, art thou hurt?

MERCUTIO

Ay, ay, a scratch, a scratch. Marry, 'tis enough. Where is my page?

HIS PAGE STEPS FORWARD.

Note: Again Mercutio refers to Tybalt as a cat by saying he received a scratch.

MERCUTIO

(to boy) Quickly, you bastard, fetch a doctor.

MERCUTIO

Go, villain, fetch a surgeon.

Note: 'Villain' here is used as a term of familiarity from someone who is angry at himself or his plight. It also had an additional meaning then of a rustic person.

THE PAGE RUNS OFF.

ROMEO KNEELS TO TEND TO MERCUTIO.

ROMEO

Courage man. It's can't be that bad.

ROMEO

Courage, man; the hurt cannot be much.

MERCUTIO

No, it's not as deep as a well, or as wide as a church door, but it's enough. It'll do. Ask for me tomorrow and you will find a grave man. I am finished for this world. A curse on both your families. Streuth! That dog, that rat, that mouse, that cat! To scratch a man to death! A conceited rogue, a cheat, pretending to fight by the rules!
(*angry*) Why the devil did you have to come between us, Romeo? I was hit under your arm.

MERCUTIO

No, 'tis not so deep as a well, nor so wide as a church door; but 'tis enough, 'twill serve. Ask for me tomorrow and you shall find me a grave man. I am peppered, I warrant, for this world. A plague a' both your houses! Zounds, a dog, a rat, a mouse, a cat, to scratch a man to death! A braggart, a rogue, a villain, that fights by the book of arithmetic! Why the devil came you between us? I was hurt under your arm.

> Note: 'Peppered' in this usage means to inflict severe punishment or suffering.
>
> 'Fights by the book of arithmetic' – fights by whatever means puts the odds in his favour, (striking under Romeo's arm), as opposed to fighting by the rules of combat.

ROMEO

I thought it was for the best.

ROMEO

I thought all for the best.

MERCUTIO

Help me into a house, Benvolio, or I'll pass out. A curse on both your families! They have made worms' meat out of me. I'm done for, finished. (*groans*) Damn your families!

MERCUTIO

Help me into some house, Benvolio, Or I shall faint. A plague a' both your houses! They have made worms' meat of me. I have it, and soundly too. Your houses!

> Note: The earliest text, acknowledged as inaccurate, said, 'A pox on both your houses'. All subsequent texts say 'plague'.  See note at end of scene.

MERCUTIO IS CARRIED AWAY BY BENVOLIO AND OTHERS.

ROMEO

(*aside*) This good man, the Prince's kinsman, my good friend, has been mortally wounded because of me. My reputation is stained with Tybalt's lies. Tybalt - my cousin for the last hour!
Oh, sweet Juliet, your beauty has weakened me and softened my fighting spirit.

ROMEO

This gentleman, the prince's near ally, My very friend, hath got this mortal hurt In my behalf; my reputation stained With Tybalt's slander - Tybalt, that an hour Hath been my cousin. O sweet Juliet, Thy beauty hath made me effeminate, And in my temper softened valour's steel.

> Note: 'Temper' – anger, nature, and also hardening a steel sword by tempering.

BENVOLIO

Oh Romeo, Romeo, brave Mercutio is dead! His gallant spirit that walked the earth so short a time has shunned this earth and ascended above the clouds.

ROMEO

*More days will for today's dark fate succumb.*
*To end, what further woes are yet to come.*

BENVOLIO

O Romeo, Romeo, brave Mercutio is dead!
That gallant spirit hath aspired the clouds,
Which too untimely here did scorn the earth.

ROMEO

*This day's black fate on more days doth depend;*
*This but begins the woe others must end.*

TYBALT RETURNS, STRIDING PURPOSEFULLY.

BENVOLIO

Here comes the mad Tybalt again.

ROMEO

Still alive! Come to gloat in triumph at slaying Mercutio! Let my leniency join him in heaven, my fury will guide me now!

BENVOLIO

Here comes the furious Tybalt back again.

ROMEO

Alive, in triumph! And Mercutio slain?
Away to heaven, respective lenity,
And fire-eyed fury be my conduct now!

Note: Some editions say 'again' instead of 'alive'.

ROMEO DRAWS HIS SWORD.

ROMEO (CONT'D)

(*shouts*) Tybalt! Take back what you called me before – 'a villain' - for Mercutio's soul is only a little way above our heads, waiting for yours to keep him company. Either you, or I, or both of us will be joining him.

ROMEO

Now, Tybalt, take the `villain' back again
That late thou gav'st me, for Mercutio's soul
Is but a little way above our heads,
Staying for thine to keep him company.
Either thou or I, or both, must go with him.

TYBALT DRAWS HIS SWORD.

TYBALT

You wretched boy. You came here with him, you shall leave with him.

ROMEO

My sword will decide that.

TYBALT

Thou, wretched boy, that didst consort him here,
Shalt with him hence.

ROMEO

This shall determine that.

TYBALT AND ROMEO FIGHT.

TYBALT IS FATALLY STRUCK. HE FALLS AND DIES.

BENVOLIO

Romeo, be gone, run!  People are coming and Tybalt is dead! Don't just stand there. Prince Escalus will condemn you to death if you are caught. Now! Go! Quickly!

BENVOLIO

Romeo, away, be gone! The citizens are up, and Tybalt slain. Stand not amazed; the prince will doom thee death If thou art taken. Hence! Be gone, away!

ROMEO DOESN'T MOVE.

ROMEO

Oh, I am fate's foolish plaything.

ROMEO

O, I am fortune's fool!

BENVOLIO

Why do you stay here?

BENVOLIO

Why dost thou stay?

ROMEO COMES TO HIS SENSES AND FLEES.

TOWNSFOLK WHO HAD HEARD THAT MERCUTIO HAD BEEN SLAIN RUSH IN.

CITIZEN 1

The man that killed Mercutio, which way did he go?

CITIZEN 1

Which way ran he that killed Mercutio?

CITIZEN 2

Tybalt, the murderer, where did he run?

CITIZEN 2

Tybalt, that murderer, which way ran he?

BENVOLIO

That's Tybalt. Lying there.

BENVOLIO

There lies that Tybalt.

CITIZEN 1

(*to Tybalt*) Get up, sir, come with me. *In the name of the Prince, you will obey!*

CITIZEN 1

Up, sir, go with me. *I charge thee in the prince's name, obey.*

TYBALT DOESN'T RESPOND. HE IS DEAD. A COMIC LINE.

A CROWD GATHERS AT THE COMMOTION, FOLLOWED BY PRINCE ESCALUS, OLD MONTAGUE, OLD CAPULET AND THEIR FAMILIES.

PRINCE ESCALUS

*Where are the villains who started this fray?*

PRINCE

*Where are the vile beginners of this fray?*

127

**BENVOLIO**

*Oh, noble Prince, I can explain it all;*
*The ill-fated events of this fatal brawl.*
*Tybalt lies there, killed by young Romeo,*
*Who killed your kinsman, brave Mercutio.*

**BENVOLIO**

*O noble prince, I can discover all*
*The unlucky manage of this fatal brawl.*
*There lies the man, slain by young Romeo,*
*That slew thy kinsman, brave Mercutio.*

---

THE CROWD QUIETENS. LADY CAPULET RUSHES TO TYBALT'S BODY.

---

**LADY CAPULET**

*Tybalt! My nephew! Oh, my brother's child!*
*Oh Prince! Oh kinsman! Husband! Oh, blood*
*  has been spilled*
*Of my dear nephew! Prince, if your word is*
*  true,*
*For the killing of ours kill that Montague!*
Oh, nephew, my nephew!

**LADY CAPULET**

*Tybalt, my cousin! O, my brother's child!*
*O prince! O cousin! Husband! O, the blood is spilled*
*Of my dear kinsman! Prince, as thou art true,*
*For blood of ours shed blood of Montague.*
*O cousin, cousin!*

**PRINCE ESCALUS**

*Benvolio, who started this bloody affray?*

**PRINCE**

*Benvolio, who began this bloody fray?*

**BENVOLIO**

*Tybalt, now here dead, whom Romeo did slay.*
Romeo spoke fairly to him, bade him rethink how petty the quarrel was, and reminded him it would displease your good self. He urged Tybalt calmly, with measured voice, and the most humble of manners. But Tybalt would not hear of peace, instead he raised his piercing steel blade to bold Mercutio's breast, who also heated, retaliated, raising his sword and with warlike scorn he beat cold death aside with one hand and struck back at Tybalt with the other, who with dexterity evaded it. Romeo cried out. 'Stop, friends! Friends part!' and before he'd finished his words his agile arm beat down their deadly blades and he rushed between them. Tybalt lashed out cruelly beneath Romeo's arm and in one deadly hit, Tybalt took the life of brave Mercutio.

**BENVOLIO**

*Tybalt, here slain, whom Romeo's hand did slay.*
Romeo, that spoke him fair, bid him bethink
How nice the quarrel was, and urged withal
Your high displeasure. All this, uttered
With gentle breath, calm look, knees humbly
  bowed,
Could not take truce with the unruly spleen
Of Tybalt deaf to peace, but that he tilts
With piercing steel at bold Mercutio's breast,
Who, all as hot, turns deadly point to point,
And, with a martial scorn, with one hand beats
Cold death aside, and with the other sends
It back to Tybalt, whose dexterity
Retorts it. Romeo he cries aloud
` Hold friends! Friends part!' and swifter than his
  tongue
His agile arm beats down their fatal points,
And 'twixt them rushes; underneath whose arm
An envious thrust from Tybalt hit the life
Of stout Mercutio,

---

THE CROWD GASP.

---

### BENVOLIO (CONT'D)

Then Tybalt fled. A little later he came back and found Romeo, who only then had thought of revenge. They were at each other like lightning and before I could part them, the bold Tybalt was struck down dead.

*And as he fell down, Romeo turned and fled.*
*That's the truth, or let Benvolio be dead.*

### LADY CAPULET

*He's also a Montague, and in proof*
*Affection makes him lie; distort the truth.*
*Some twenty at least fought in this dark strife,*
*All twenty of those to take just one life.*
*I beg for justice, which you, Prince, must give;*
*Romeo killed Tybalt, Romeo must not live.*

### PRINCE ESCALUS

*Romeo killed him, he killed Mercutio.*
*Who'll pay the price his dear life is owed?*

### OLD MONTAGUE

*Not Romeo, Prince, he was Mercutio's friend.*
*His fault is in doing what the law should end,*
*The life of Tybalt.*

### PRINCE ESCALUS

          *And for that offence*
*I do exile him from this place at once.*
*I've personal interest in your heart's*
   *proceeding,*
*From your bloody brawls, my kin lies a-*
   *bleeding.*
*I'll punish you all with such a large fine*
*You'll all pay the price for this loss of mine.*

THE CAPULETS AND MONTAGUES PROTEST LOUDLY.

### PRINCE ESCALUS (CONT'D)

*I'll not hear your pleading nor your excuses.*
*Your tears and prayers won't pay for abuses.*
*I'll hear no more. Let Romeo leave fast,*
*Or if he is found that hour is his last.*
*Remove this body, attend to my will.*
*Mercy for murder, pardons those who kill.*

---

BENVOLIO

and then Tybalt fled;
But by and by comes back to Romeo,
Who had but newly entertained revenge,
And to't they go like lightning, for ere I
Could draw to part them was stout Tybalt slain;
*And as he fell did Romeo turn and fly.*
*This is the truth, or let Benvolio die.*

LADY CAPULET

*He is a kinsman to the Montague;*
*Affection makes him false, he speaks not true.*
*Some twenty of them fought in this black strife,*
*And all those twenty could but kill one life.*
*I beg for justice, which thou, prince, must give;*
*Romeo slew Tybalt, Romeo must not live.*

PRINCE

*Romeo slew him, he slew Mercutio:*
*Who now the price of his dear blood doth owe?*

MONTAGUE

*Not Romeo, prince; he was Mercutio's friend;*
*His fault concludes but what the law should end,*
*The life of Tybalt.*

PRINCE

          *And for that offence*
*Immediately we do exile him hence.*
*I have an interest in your hearts' proceeding;*
*My blood for your rude brawls doth lie a-bleeding;*
*But I'll amerce you with so strong a fine*
*That you shall all repent the loss of mine.*

PRINCE

*I will be deaf to pleading and excuses;*
*Nor tears nor prayers shall purchase out abuses;*
*Therefore use none. Let Romeo hence in haste,*
*Else, when he is found, that hour is his last.*
*Bear hence this body, and attend our will.*
*Mercy but murders, pardoning those that kill.*

*Note: 'A plague on both your houses'. The earliest text in 1597, written from memory by actors and now acknowledged as inaccuarate, used 'pox' in place of 'plague'. Plague is the accepted term now.*

*Shakespeare mentions the plague and the pox frequently. Both were rife back then with no cure from antibiotics. Both were horrible diseases which caused death and terrible suffering. Shakespeare himself lost many friends and also his son to the bubonic plague. Theatres were closed from 1592-93 to help stop the spread of the disease. This would have had a severe financial impact on Shakespeare, occurring during the run of his Henry VI plays.*

*These were not the only serious health risks, during Shakespeare's life London was the worst place to be in England. Bubonic plague which devastated Europe, small pox, which Queen Elizabeth suffered from, resulting in her losing all her hair and wearing heavy white make up to disguise the scars on her face, and syphilis, which was passed on through sexual activity, then believed to have been brought back from the Americas by Columbus himself. Interestingly, medical science has recently come up with evidence to support this theory after skeletal analysis of Columbus and his crew.*

*Also rife were the deadly diseases, typhus, spread by body lice among those who didn't bathe, and malaria, spread by mosquitoes from the marshy areas of the River Thames.*

*In 1616 a major epidemic of typhus erupted. There is belief among some scholars that this may have been what killed Shakespeare.*

*You were lucky to survive above the age of thirty-five in London.*

# ACT III SCENE II

## JULIET'S CHAMBER. MONDAY EARLY EVENING.

JULIET IS IN HER CHAMBER, GAZING OUT OF THE WINDOW.

IT IS THREE HOURS AFTER HER WEDDING, TWO HOURS AFTER THE FIGHT.

**JULIET**

(*aside*) Speed up, Apollo, drive your fiery footed steeds, and pull the sun towards your lodgings below the horizon. A horseman such as Phaethon could whip them towards the west and bring the cloud of night in no time. Close your thick curtain of darkness, love-making night, so that eyes may close, and Romeo can leap into my arms unheard and unseen. Lovers can make love by the radiant light of their own passion, and if love is blind then it is best suited to the night. Come innocent night, you sombre black-suited matron, teach me how to lose the game but win the match for our unblemished innocence.

**JULIET**

Gallop apace, you fiery-footed steeds,
Towards Phoebus' lodging. Such a waggoner
As Phaethon would whip you to the west,
And bring in cloudy night immediately.
Spread thy close curtain, love-performing night,
That runaways' eyes may wink, and Romeo
Leap to these arms, untalked-of and unseen.
Lovers can see to do their amorous rites
By their own beauties; or, if love be blind,
It best agrees with night. Come, civil night,
Thou sober-suited matron all in black,
And learn me how to lose a winning match
Played for a pair of stainless maidenhoods.

> Note: Apollo, also known as Phoebus, is the greek sun god. Helios pulled the sun across the sky daily. His son, Phaethon, drove his father's solar chariot for a day but could not control the immortal steeds ('runaways') which pulled it. Zeus killed Phaethon with a thunderbolt to save the earth from destruction.

JULIET BLUSHES AT THE THOUGHT OF WINNING THE GAME BY LOSING HER VIRGINITY.

**JULIET (CONT'D)**

Conceal this wanton blood rising in my cheeks with your black cloak till my confidence grows to see this as just a natural act of true love.
Hurry night, hurry Romeo, bring your light to the darkness. Let it shine on the wings of the night whiter than fresh snow on a raven's back.

**JULIET**

Hood my unmanned blood, bating in my cheeks,
With thy black mantle, till strange love grown
  bold
Think true love acted simple modesty.
Come, night; come, Romeo; come, thou day in
  night;
For thou wilt lie upon the wings of night
Whiter than new snow upon a raven's back.

*Note: 'Hood' was the blindfold used in falconry for untamed ('unmanned') hawks to stop them beating ('bating' – from where we get the expression 'bated breath' – heart beating wildly) their wings in panic when being handled by humans. It is a clever metaphor for her hiding her blushes and nervousness of inexperience for the forthcoming loss of her virginity.*

JULIET (CONT'D)

Come, gentle night, come, loving, dark-browed night, bring me my Romeo, and when he dies take him and cut him into little stars. He will make the heavens so bright that the whole world will see and fall in love with the night, and no longer worship the garish sun.

JULIET

Come, gentle night; come, loving black-browed night,
Give me my Romeo; and, when I shall die,
Take him and cut him out in little stars,
And he will make the face of heaven so fine
That all the world will be in love with night
And pay no worship to the garish sun.

*Note: Some editors change the line "When I shall die" to When he shall die", it makes more sense to say 'he'.*

JULIET (CONT'D)

Oh, I have paid the price for the house of love, but I do not yet possess it, and though I too am sold, I have not yet been enjoyed by the owner. This day is as long as the night before Christmas is to an impatient child that has presents but may not open them. Oh, here comes my Nurse.

JULIET

O, I have bought the mansion of a love,
But not possessed it; and, though I am sold,
Not yet enjoyed. So tedious is this day
As is the night before some festival
To an impatient child that hath new robes
And may not wear them. O, here comes my Nurse.

NURSE ENTERS WRINGING HER HANDS, CARRYING A ROPE LADDER.

JULIET (CONT'D)

And she brings news, and any mouth uttering Romeo's name sounds like heaven to me.
(*to Nurse*) Now, Nurse, what news do you have? What have you got there? The ropes Romeo asked you to fetch?

JULIET

And she brings news; and every tongue that speaks
But Romeo's name speaks heavenly eloquence.
Now, Nurse, what news? What hast thou there?
The cords that Romeo bid thee fetch?

NURSE PUTS DOWN THE ROPE LADDER, VISIBLY UPSET.

NURSE
(*upset*) Yes, yes, the rope ladder.

NURSE
Ay, ay, the cords.

JULIET
Dear me, what news do you have? Why do you wring your hands?

JULIET
Ay me, what news? Why dost thou wring thy hands?

NURSE BURSTS INTO TEARS.

**NURSE**
(*weeping*) Alas, alas, he's dead, he's dead, he's dead! We are undone, my lady, we are undone. Wretched day! He's gone, he's killed, he's dead!

**NURSE**
Ah welladay! He's dead, he's dead, he's dead! We are undone, lady, we are undone. Alack the day! He's gone, he's killed, he's dead.

*Note: 'Welladay' is a corruption of the middle English 'wa la wa', it means 'oh, woe' or 'alas'.*

**JULIET**
Can heaven be so cruel?

**JULIET**
Can heaven be so envious?

**NURSE**
Romeo can, heaven can't. Oh, Romeo, Romeo! Who would ever have thought it? Romeo!

**NURSE**
Romeo can,
Though heaven cannot. O Romeo, Romeo!
Who ever would have thought it? Romeo!

**JULIET**
What kind of devil are you that torments me like this? This is torture from hell itself. Has Romeo killed himself? Say anything but 'aye', for that one small vowel 'I' would be more damaging than the death bringing 'eye' of a basilisk.
*I can't be 'I' if the answer is 'Aye',*
*For his 'eyes' shut forever if you answer 'Aye'.*
*If he's been killed say 'Aye', if not, say 'No'.*
*One word determines my joy or my woe.*

**JULIET**
What devil art thou that dost torment me thus?
This torture should be roared in dismal hell.
Hath Romeo slain himself? Say thou but `Ay'
And that bare vowel `I' shall poison more
Than the death-darting eye of cockatrice.
*I am not I if there be such an `I',*
*Or those eyes shut that makes thee answer `Ay'.*
*If he be slain say `Ay', or if not, `No';*
*Brief sounds determine of my weal or woe.*

*Note: Cockatrice, or Basilisk, a mythical creature which killed anyone just by looking at them. It had the body of a dragon and the head of a cockerel.*

**NURSE**
'I' saw the wound, 'I' saw it with my own 'eyes', God bless his soul…

**NURSE**
I saw the wound, I saw it with mine eyes -
God save the mark!

NURSE CLASPS HER HANDS TO HER CHEST.

| NURSE (CONT'D) | NURSE |
|---|---|
| ...here on his manly chest. A pitiful sight, a bloody pitiful corpse - pale, pale as ashes, all covered in blood, all gore and blood. I near fainted at the sight. | - here on his manly breast: A piteous corse, a bloody piteous corse; Pale, pale as ashes, all bedaubed in blood, All in gore-blood. I swounded at the sight. |

> Note: 'God save the mark'. This was a common saying midwives would say to any child born with a birth mark to avert evil as a mark was seen as an evil omen. Save the mark from evil. A similar saying was, 'God bless the mark'.
>
> 'Swounded' which some texts update to 'swooned'. It is possibly a corruption of the two words 'swoon', and the exclamation 'swounds', which was considered a soft swear word, short for 'God's wounds', meaning the wounds Jesus received on the cross. Shakespeare often has Nurse saying words incorrectly, for comedic effect and to portray her character of a woman who pretended she was educated but got her words wrong.

JULIET IS NOW DISTRAUGHT. SHE BELIEVES ROMEO IS DEAD.

| JULIET | JULIET |
|---|---|
| (*distraught*) My heart is breaking, my poor empty heart, breaking this instant! My eyes imprisoned, never to look upon freedom again. Vile earth take my earthly body, end life here and now, to share one final miserable bed with you and Romeo! | O break, my heart - poor bankrupt, break at once! To prison, eyes, ne'er look on liberty; Vile earth, to earth resign, end motion here; And thou and Romeo press one heavy bier! |

> Note: 'Bier' is the wooden frame a body or coffin is carried on.

| NURSE | NURSE |
|---|---|
| Oh, Tybalt, Tybalt! The best friend I had! Oh, noble Tybalt, honest gentleman. To think I should ever live to see you dead! | O Tybalt, Tybalt, the best friend I had! O courteous Tybalt, honest gentleman, That ever I should live to see thee dead! |

JULIET IS CONFUSED AT NURSE'S RAMBLINGS.

| JULIET | JULIET |
|---|---|
| What storm is this that blows so much confusion? Is Romeo slain, and is Tybalt dead? My dear cousin and my dearer husband? *If so then sound dreadful trumpet of doom, For what point is living if these two are gone?* | What storm is this that blows so contrary? Is Romeo slaughtered and is Tybalt dead? My dearest cousin, and my dearer lord? *Then, dreadful trumpet, sound the general doom; For who is living if those two are gone?* |

NURSE

Tybalt is gone, and Romeo is banished.
Romeo, who killed him - he is banished.

NURSE

Tybalt is gone and Romeo banished.
Romeo, that killed him, he is banished.

> Note: Shakespeare wrote the word 'banished' to be pronounced as three syllables;
> Ban-is-shed. It is repeated many times.

JULIET

(*frantic to understand*) Oh, God! Did Romeo shed Tybalt's blood?

JULIET

O God, did Romeo's hand shed Tybalt's blood?

NURSE

He did, he did, rue the day! He did.

NURSE

It did, it did, alas the day! It did.

JULIET'S FONDNESS FOR ROMEO TURNS TO LOATHING.

JULIET

(*now hateful of Romeo*) Oh the heart of a snake, hidden behind the face of an Angel. What beast ever appeared so charming? A beautiful devil, an angelic fiend! A raven with dove's feathers, a wolf in sheep's clothing! Evil so divine! Just the opposite of your just appearance. A saintly sinner, an honourable villain!
Oh, divine nature, what were you doing in hell when you enclosed the spirit of a fiend in the mortal paradise of such sweet flesh. Was there ever a book containing such vile matter so attractively bound? Oh, that deceit should live in such a gorgeous palace!

JULIET

O serpent heart, hid with a flow'ring face!
Did ever dragon keep so fair a cave?
Beautiful tyrant, fiend angelical,
Dove-feathered raven, wolvish-ravening lamb,
Despised substance of divinest show!
Just opposite to what thou justly seem'st,
A damned saint, an honourable villain!
O nature, what hadst thou to do in hell
When thou didst bower the spirit of a fiend
In mortal paradise of such sweet flesh?
Was ever book containing such vile matter
So fairly bound? O, that deceit should dwell
In such a gorgeous palace!

> Note: 'A book so fairly bound' refers back to Juliet's mother's earlier words.

NURSE

There's no trust, no faith, no honesty in men. They're all liars before God. All wicked deceivers and cheats, all of them. Where's Peter? I need a strong drink. This grief, this misery, this sadness makes me weary. Shame on Romeo!

NURSE

There's no trust,
No faith, no honesty in men; all perjured,
All forsworn, all naught, all dissemblers.
Ah, where's my man? Give me some aqua vitae.
These griefs, these woes, these sorrows make me old.
Shame come to Romeo!

JULIET NOW CHANGES TO DEFENDING ROMEO.

JULIET

May your tongue come out in blisters for wishing such a thing! He was not born to be shamed, upon his brow shame itself is ashamed to sit, rather, it is a throne where honour may be crowned king above all else. Oh, how beastly I was to scold him.

NURSE

You would defend the man who killed your cousin?

JULIET

Should I speak ill of the man who is my husband?
(*speaking as if to her absent husband*) Ah, my poor husband, who else would defend your name if even I, your wife of only three hours, has destroyed it? But why, villain, did you kill my cousin?

JULIET

Blistered be thy tongue
For such a wish! He was not born to shame.
Upon his brow shame is ashamed to sit,
For 'tis a throne where honour may be crowned
Sole monarch of the universal earth.
O what a beast was I to chide at him!

NURSE

Will you speak well of him that killed your cousin?

JULIET

Shall I speak ill of him that is my husband?
Ah, poor my lord, what tongue shall smooth thy name
When I, thy three-hours wife, have mangled it?
But wherefore, villain, didst thou kill my cousin?

JULIET SEARCHES FOR WAYS TO DEFEND ROMEO.

JULIET (CONT'D)

Because my villainous cousin would have killed my husband. Back foolish tears, back where you came from. They belong to sadness, I should be rejoicing.
My husband is alive, Tybalt would have killed him. Tybalt is dead, he would have killed my husband. This is good, so why then am I weeping? Because a word, worse than Tybalt's death, kills me. I would gladly forget it, but oh, it prays on my mind, like a damned guilty act upon the mind of a sinner!
"Tybalt is dead, Romeo is *banished*". That '*banished*', that one word '*banished*' is worse than ten thousand slain Tybalts.

JULIET

That villain cousin would have killed my husband.
Back, foolish tears, back to your native spring;
Your tributary drops belong to woe,
Which you, mistaking, offer up to joy.
My husband lives, that Tybalt would have slain;
And Tybalt's dead, that would have slain my husband.
All this is comfort; wherefore weep I then?
Some word there was, worser than Tybalt's death,
That murdered me. I would forget it fain,
But O it presses to my memory
Like damned guilty deeds to sinners' minds.
`Tybalt is dead, and Romeo banished.'
That `banished', that one word `banished'
Hath slain ten thousand Tybalts.

JULIET BREAKS DOWN IN TEARS AGAIN.

### JULIET (CONT'D)

Tybalt's death would have been sad enough if it had ended there. But if bad news attracts more bad news, then why, when she said 'Tybalt is dead' could she have not followed it with 'your father' or 'your Mother' or even both, which at least I know I will have to face one day? But to follow 'Tybalt is dead' with 'Romeo is banished'. To just say that word is like saying Father, Mother, Tybalt, Romeo, Juliet are all slain, all dead. 'Romeo is banished'. There is no end, no limit, no measure to the depth of the death and despair implied in that word. No words could describe such misery.

Where is my Mother and Father, Nurse?

### NURSE

Weeping and wailing over Tybalt's body. Do you want to join them? I will take you there.

### JULIET

*Do they wash his wounds with tears? Mine*
*    shall be spent*
*When theirs are long dry, for Romeo's*
*    banishment.*
*Take away these ropes. Poor ropes, you are*
*    denied,*
*Both of us are, for Romeo is exiled..*
*He sent you as a pathway here to my bed,*
*But I, still a maiden, will here die widowed.*
*Come ropes, come Nurse, to my sad wedding*
*    bed,*
*And death, not Romeo, take my maidenhead.*

### JULIET

> Tybalt's death
Was woe enough, if it had ended there;
Or if sour woe delights in fellowship
And needly will be ranked with other griefs,
Why followed not, when she said `Tybalt's dead',
Thy father or thy mother, nay, or both,
Which modern lamentation might have moved?
But with a rearward following Tybalt's death,
`Romeo is banished' - to speak that word
Is father, mother, Tybalt, Romeo, Juliet,
All slain, all dead. `Romeo is banished',
There is no end, no limit, measure, bound,
In that word's death; no words can that woe
    sound.
Where is my father and my mother, Nurse?

### NURSE

Weeping and wailing over Tybalt's corse.
Will you go to them? I will bring you thither.

### JULIET

*Wash they his wounds with tears? Mine shall be spent*
*When theirs are dry, for Romeo's banishment.*
*Take up those cords. Poor ropes, you are beguiled,*
*Both you and I, for Romeo is exiled.*
*He made you for a highway to my bed,*
*But I, a maid, die maiden-widowed.*
*Come, cords, come, Nurse; I'll to my wedding bed,*
*And death, not Romeo, take my maidenhead!*

---

*Note: Maidenhead means virginity.*

---

NURSE PICKS UP THE ROPE LADDER.

NURSE

Hurry to your bedroom, I'll find Romeo to
comfort you. I know where he is.
*Listen, your Romeo will be here tonight.*
*I'll go to him hid where the Friar does dwell.*

NURSE

Hie to your chamber; I'll find Romeo
To comfort you. I wot well where he is.
*Hark ye, your Romeo will be here at night.*
*I'll to him; he is hid at Laurence' cell.*

JULIET TAKES A RING FROM HER FINGER AND PASSES IT TO NURSE.

JULIET

*Oh, find him! Give this ring to my true knight,*
*Tell him to come here for his last farewell.*

JULIET

*O find him! Give this ring to my true knight,*
*And bid him come to take his last farewell.*

# ACT III  SCENE III

## FRIAR LAURENCE'S QUARTERS.  MONDAY EVENING.

ROMEO IS HIDING OUT IN THE FRIAR'S QUARTERS.

FRIAR LAURENCE RETURNS TO GIVE ROMEO NEWS OF HIS FATE.

**FRIAR LAURENCE**

Romeo, come out, come out, you poor fearful man. Trouble is attracted to you it seems, you are married to misfortune.

FRIAR LAURENCE

Romeo, come forth, come forth, thou fearful man.

Affliction is enamoured of thy parts,

And thou art wedded to calamity.

ROMEO EMERGES FROM HIDING.

**ROMEO**

Father, is there any news? Has the Prince passed sentence on me? What new sorrows await my acquaintance?

ROMEO

Father, what news? What is the prince's doom?

What sorrow craves acquaintance at my hand

That I yet know not?

**FRIAR LAURENCE**

My dear son, I fear you are becoming too familiar with such unpleasant company. I bring news of the Prince's judgment.

FRIAR LAURENCE

Too familiar

Is my dear son with such sour company.

I bring thee tidings of the prince's doom.

**ROMEO**

What less than doomsday can the Prince's doom be for me?

ROMEO

What less than doomsday is the prince's doom?

*Note: 'Doomsday' means the day of death, and 'doom' means a terrible fate.*

**FRIAR LAURENCE**

A lesser judgment was issued from his lips. Not your death, but your banishment.

FRIAR LAURENCE

A gentler judgement vanished from his lips:

Not body's death, but body's banishment.

*Note: No one is quite sure why Shakespeare used the word 'vanished' here. Some scholars believe it was a copyist's error, but an alternative could be that it is the word banished with one letter change. Wordplay.*

ROMEO

What! Banishment! Have mercy on me, say 'death'. Exile holds more fear for me, much more than death. Don't say 'banishment'.

FRIAR LAURENCE

With immediate effect you are banished from Verona. But have patience, the world is broad and wide.

ROMEO

There is no world for me outside Verona's walls, except for torment, torture and hell itself. Banished from here is banished from the world, and exile from the world is death. 'Banished' is death under a different name. By calling death 'banished' you cut off my head with a golden axe and smile at the stroke that murders me.

ROMEO

Ha, banishment! Be merciful, say ' death';
For exile hath more terror in his look,
Much more than death. Do not say 'banishment'.

FRIAR LAURENCE

Hence from Verona art thou banished.
Be patient, for the world is broad and wide.

ROMEO

There is no world without Verona walls
But purgatory, torture, hell itself.
Hence banished is banished from the world,
And world's exile is death. Then ' banished'
Is death mistermed. Calling death ' banished'
Thou cutt'st my head off with a golden axe,
And smil'st upon the stroke that murders me.

> Note: The earliest text had 'banishment is death...' Later texts wrote this as 'banished is death...', possibly because the previous two lines said the word 'banished' three times, so this kept the consistency. Both mean the same thing and in current texts either word can be found depending on the publisher.
>
> By saying 'golden axe' he is using the metaphor that it may appear to be the kinder, more gentle option but the result is just the same as if with an axe made of iron. You still kill me while smiling at how kind you have been to me.

FRIAR LAURENCE

Oh, damnable sin! Oh, what rude ungratefulness! For your deed the law demands death, but the kind Prince, taking a sympathetic view of your part, has brushed aside the law, and turned that black word 'death' to banishment. This is a rare, kind mercy and you refuse to see it.

FRIAR LAURENCE

O deadly sin! O rude unthankfulness!
Thy fault our law calls death, but the kind prince,
Taking thy part, hath rushed aside the law
And turned that black word death to
  banishment.
This is dear mercy and thou seest it not.

> Note: 'Rushed aside' may have been a printer's error for 'brushed aside'.

ROMEO

It is torture, not mercy. Heaven is here where Juliet lives, and every cat, dog, little mouse, every worthless creature can live here in heaven and gaze at her, but Romeo can not. The flies have more value in life, more honour and more opportunities at courtship than Romeo. They may touch the white wonder of dear Juliet's hand, and steal immortal heaven from her lips, which in pure and virginal modesty, still blush when they touch together, thinking their own kisses a sin. The flies are free to do this, but I am banished, from this I must fly. And you say that exile is not death?

ROMEO

'Tis torture and not mercy. Heaven is here,
Where Juliet lives, and every cat and dog
And little mouse, every unworthy thing,
Live here in heaven and may look on her;
But Romeo may not. More validity,
More honourable state, more courtship lives
In carrion flies than Romeo. They may seize
On the white wonder of dear Juliet's hand,
And steal immortal blessing from her lips,
Who, even in pure and vestal modesty
Still blush, as thinking their own kisses sin;
But Romeo may not, he is banished.
Flies may do this, but I from this must fly;
They are free men, but I am banished.
And sayst thou yet that exile is not death?

---

ROMEO IS NOW BECOMING OVERLY DRAMATIC.

---

ROMEO (CONT'D)

Have you no poison ready, no razor sharp knife, no sudden means of death – though none are so mean a death as 'banishment'? 'Banished'? Oh Father, the damned use that word in hell to much howling. How could you have the heart, as a divine, God fearing, sin absolver, and, you say, my 'friend', to tear my soul apart with the word 'banished'?

ROMEO

Hadst thou no poison mixed, no sharp-ground knife,
No sudden mean of death, though ne'er so mean,
But `banished' to kill me? `Banished'!
O Friar, the damned use that word in hell;
Howling attends it: how hast thou the heart,
Being a divine, a ghostly confessor,
A sin-absolver, and my friend professed,
To mangle me with that word `banished'?

FRIAR LAURENCE

You foolish man, listen to me a minute.

FRIAR LAURENCE

Thou fond mad man, hear me a little speak.

ROMEO

Listen to you speak again of banishment?

ROMEO

O, thou wilt speak again of banishment.

FRIAR LAURENCE

I can give you armour to face that word, courage in the face of adversity, philosophy to comfort you, even though you are banished.

FRIAR LAURENCE

I'll give thee armour to keep off that word;
Adversity's sweet milk, philosophy,
To comfort thee, though thou art banished.

| | |
|---|---|
| **ROMEO**<br>Still you say that word 'banished'! Forget your philosophy! Unless philosophy can create a Juliet, move a town, reverse a Prince's judgment, it is of no help. It's useless. Say no more. | **ROMEO**<br>Yet ' banished'! Hang up philosophy!<br>Unless philosophy can make a Juliet,<br>Displant a town, reverse a prince's doom,<br>It helps not, it prevails not. Talk no more. |
| **FRIAR LAURENCE**<br>Oh, I see then that madmen have no ears. | **FRIAR LAURENCE**<br>O, then I see that madmen have no ears. |
| **ROMEO**<br>Why would they need to, when wise men have no eyes? | **ROMEO**<br>How should they, when that wise men have no eyes? |

Note: Romeo suggests it is obvious by just looking to see the state he is in.

| | |
|---|---|
| **FRIAR LAURENCE**<br>Let me at least discuss your predicament with you. | **FRIAR LAURENCE**<br>Let me dispute with thee of thy estate. |
| **ROMEO**<br>You couldn't begin to understand how I feel with your vows of celibacy. If you were my age, if you loved Juliet, if you had only been married an hour and had murdered Tybalt, if you were in love as I am, and you were banished like me, then you could discuss my predicament. Then you might tear out your hair and fall to the ground in despair as I do… | **ROMEO**<br>Thou canst not speak of that thou dost not feel.<br>Wert thou as young as I, Juliet thy love,<br>An hour but married, Tybalt murdered,<br>Doting like me, and like me banished,<br>Then mightst thou speak, then mightst thou tear thy hair<br>And fall upon the ground, as I do now, |

ROMEO THROWS HIMSELF TO THE GROUND.

| | |
|---|---|
| **ROMEO (CONT'D)**<br>…ready to be measured for my grave. | **ROMEO**<br>Taking the measure of an unmade grave. |

KNOCKING AT THE DOOR.

| | |
|---|---|
| **FRIAR LAURENCE**<br>Get up, someone's knocking. Goodness, Romeo, hide yourself. | **FRIAR LAURENCE**<br>Arise, one knocks. Good Romeo, hide thyself. |
| **ROMEO**<br>I will not, unless the breath of my heartsick groans enshroud me in mist, hiding me from prying eyes. | **ROMEO**<br>Not I, unless the breath of heartsick groans,<br>Mist-like, infold me from the search of eyes. |

MORE KNOCKING AT THE DOOR.

**FRIAR LAURENCE**
Goodness, how they knock!
(*to door*) Who's there?
(*to Romeo*) Romeo, get up, you will be caught!

**FRIAR LAURENCE**
Hark how they knock! - Who's there? - Romeo, arise;
Thou wilt be taken.

MORE KNOCKING AT THE DOOR. ROMEO DOES NOT GET UP.

**FRIAR LAURENCE (CONT'D)**
(*to door*) Wait a moment!
(*to Romeo*) Stand up! Run to my study!
(*to door*) One moment!
(*to Romeo*) Goodness me, what stupidity is this?

**FRIAR LAURENCE**
Stay awhile! - Stand up;
Run to my study. - By and by! - God's will,
What simpleness is this?

KNOCKING AT THE DOOR, MORE URGENT.

**FRIAR LAURENCE (CONT'D)**
(*to door*) I'm coming, I'm coming! Who knocks so loudly? Who is it, what do you want?

**FRIAR LAURENCE**
I come, I come.
Who knocks so hard? Whence come you, what's your will?

**NURSE**
(*exterior*) Let me in and I'll tell you. I come from Lady Juliet.

**NURSE**
[*Within.*] Let me come in, and you shall know my errand.
I come from Lady Juliet.

FRIAR LAURENCE OPENS THE DOOR.

**FRIAR LAURENCE**
You are welcome then.

**FRIAR LAURENCE**
Welcome then.

NURSE WALKS IN.

**NURSE**
Oh, Holy Friar! Oh, tell me, Holy Father, where's my lady's husband, where's Romeo?

**NURSE**
O holy Friar! O tell me, holy Friar,
Where is my lady's lord, where's Romeo?

**FRIAR LAURENCE**
There on the ground, drunk with his own tears.

**FRIAR LAURENCE**
There on the ground, with his own tears made drunk.

NURSE

Oh, he is just as my mistress, just as she is. Oh, grieving in sympathy! A pitiful predicament! She lies just the same, blubbering and weeping, weeping and blubbering.

(*to Romeo*) Stand up, stand up! Stand, and be a man! For Juliet's sake, for her sake, rise and stand! Why should you fall into so deep an Ohhhhhh? (*a long, overly dramatic sigh of woe and despair - the type associated with the back of the hand on the forehead and the head thrown back*)

NURSE

O, he is even in my mistress' case, Just in her case! O woeful sympathy, Piteous predicament! Even so lies she, Blubbering and weeping, weeping and blubbering.

Stand up, stand up. Stand, an you be a man. For Juliet's sake, for her sake, rise and stand. Why should you fall into so deep an O?

---

Note: Some editions split the above lines from nurse between her and the Friar

'O' is the archaic way of spelling 'Oh'. As it was written as a capital letter the word 'oh' was emphasised - a drawn out exclamation of woe and despair.

---

ROMEO LIFTS HIMSELF FROM THE FLOOR TO STOP NURSE MOCKING HIM.

ROMEO

Nurse!

ROMEO

Nurse!

NURSE

Ah sir, ah sir, it all won't matter when we're dead.

NURSE

Ah sir, ah sir, death's the end of all.

---

Note: Nurse's words of comfort hit wide of the mark, but are prophetic.

---

ROMEO

(*pitifully*) Have you spoken to Juliet? How is she? Does she think me a common killer, especially now I've tarnished the joy of our early days with blood so close to hers? Where is she? And how is she? And what does my concealed wife say about our now cancelled love?

ROMEO

Spak'st thou of Juliet? How is it with her? Doth not she think me an old murderer Now I have stained the childhood of our joy With blood removed but little from her own? Where is she? And how doth she? And what says My concealed lady to our cancelled love?

NURSE

Oh, she says nothing, sir. She just weeps and weeps, and then falls on her bed, and then gets up again, crying out for Tybalt, and then for Romeo, and then falls down again.

NURSE

O, she says nothing, sir, but weeps and weeps, And now falls on her bed, and then starts up, And Tybalt calls, and then on Romeo cries, And then down falls again.

ROMEO

It's as if with deadly aim that name had been shot from a gun and murdered her, just as that name's curséd hand murdered her cousin.

ROMEO

As if that name,
Shot from the deadly level of a gun,
Did murder her; as that name's cursed hand
Murdered her kinsman.

---

ROMEO DRAWS HIS DAGGER.

---

ROMEO (CONT'D)

Oh, tell me Father, tell me, in what vile part of my body my name lies? Tell me so that I may plunder it from my hateful body.

ROMEO

O tell me, Friar, tell me
In what vile part of this anatomy
Doth my name lodge? Tell me that I may sack
The hateful mansion.

---

NURSE GRABS THE DAGGER AWAY FROM ROMEO.

---

FRIAR LAURENCE

Pull yourself together, Romeo! Are you a man? Your body suggests you are, but your tears are not manly, and your wild acts suggest the unruly fury of an animal. An uncontrolled woman dressed as a man, a vile unnatural beast.

FRIAR LAURENCE

Hold thy desp'rate hand.
Art thou a man? Thy form cries out thou art.
Thy tears are womanish; thy wild acts denote
The unreasonable fury of a beast.
Unseemly woman in a seeming man,
And ill-beseeming beast in seeming both!

> Note: Back then women were looked on as the weak, feeble sex, despite having a powerful Queen for many years in Elizabeth I.

FRIAR LAURENCE (CONT'D)

You amaze me. By my order of St. Francis, I thought you were better tempered and more controlled. So you killed Tybalt? Will you kill yourself? And in doing so slay the lady who lives for you, by committing this damnable sin against yourself? You may wish you hadn't been born, but heaven and earth combined with your body at birth. All three would be lost to you at once. Dear, dear, you shame your body, your love, and your intelligence. Like a rich man you have assets in abundance, but you put none of them to the good use expected from one with your body, your love, and your brain.

FRIAR LAURENCE

Thou hast amazed me. By my holy order,
I thought thy disposition better tempered.
Hast thou slain Tybalt? Wilt thou slay thyself,
And slay thy lady that in thy life lives,
By doing damned hate upon thyself?
Why rail'st thou on thy birth, the heaven and
  earth?
Since birth and heaven and earth, all three, do
  meet
In thee at once; which thou at once wouldst lose.
Fie, fie, thou sham'st thy shape, thy love, thy wit,
Which, like a usurer, abound'st in all,
And usest none in that true use indeed
Which should bedeck thy shape, thy love, thy wit.

> Note: Suicide was considered a damnable sin. God gave you life only he should take it.

### FRIAR LAURENCE (CONT'D)

'**Your**' noble body is just a hollow waxwork dummy, lacking the substance and courage of a noble man.

'**Your**' dear vows of love so recently sworn, just hollow perjury, killing the love which you vowed to cherish.

'**Your**' brain, the embellishment of your body and love, just leads them both astray. Like gunpowder in an untrained soldier's hand it is set afire by ignorance, and you are destroyed by that which should have defended you.

### FRIAR LAURENCE

Thy noble shape is but a form of wax,
Digressing from the valour of a man;
Thy dear love sworn but hollow perjury,
Killing that love which thou hast vowed to
  cherish;
Thy wit, that ornament to shape and love,
Misshapen in the conduct of them both,
Like powder in a skilless soldier's flask
Is set afire by thine own ignorance,
And thou dismembered with thine own defence.

---

ROMEO MAKES A CHURLISH FACE WHICH ANGERS THE FRIAR.

### FRIAR LAURENCE (CONT'D)

What? Pull yourself together man! Your Juliet is alive, for whose sake you wished yourself dead - for that you should be happy. Tybalt would have killed you, but you killed Tybalt - for that you should be happy. The law, which threatened death, has favoured you, and turned it to exile - for that you should be happy.

A shower of blessings has befallen you, happiness courts you in her kindness, but like a misbehaved, sullen child, you pout at your good fortune and your love. Take heed, take good heed, such people die lonely and miserable.

### FRIAR LAURENCE

What, rouse thee, man! Thy Juliet is alive,
For whose dear sake thou wast but lately dead -
There art thou happy. Tybalt would kill thee,
But thou slew'st Tybalt - there art thou happy.
The law that threatened death becomes thy
  friend,
And turns it to exile - there art thou happy.

A pack of blessings light upon thy back,
Happiness courts thee in her best array,
But like a misbehaved and sullen wench
Thou pout'st upon thy fortune and thy love.
Take heed, take heed, for such die miserable.

---

THE FRIAR WALKS TO THE DOOR PLACING HIS HAND ON THE HANDLE AS IF USHERING THEM OUT.

#### FRIAR LAURENCE (CONT'D)

Go, go to your love as was arranged. Climb to her chamber and comfort her. But be careful you do not stay past nightfall when the gates to Verona are shut and a guard is posted, for then you could not leave for Mantua, which is where you shall live until we can find the right time to announce your marriage, reconcile your families, beg the pardon of the Prince, and call you back with two million times more joy than when you left in such wretchedness.

#### FRIAR LAURENCE

Go, get thee to thy love as was decreed; Ascend her chamber. Hence, and comfort her; But look thou stay not till the Watch be set, For then thou canst not pass to Mantua, Where thou shalt live till we can find a time To blaze your marriage, reconcile your friends, Beg pardon of the prince, and call thee back With twenty hundred thousand times more joy Than thou went'st forth in lamentation.

THE FRIAR TURNS TO NURSE, NOW HIS LECTURE IS OVER.

*Note: "Stay not till the watch be set", Romeo will do the opposite and leave at dawn. The 'watch' is the night watchmen (city guards), not a wrist watch.*

#### FRIAR LAURENCE (CONT'D)

Go ahead, Nurse. Give my regards to your lady, and tell her to hasten her family to bed, which, with such heavy sorrow is the best place for them. Romeo is coming.

#### NURSE

Oh Lord, I could have stayed here all night listening to your wise words. Oh, what education does for you!
(*to Romeo bawdily*) My lord, I'll tell my lady you will come.

#### ROMEO

Do that, and ask my love to be ready to scold me.

#### FRIAR LAURENCE

Go before, Nurse. Commend me to thy lady, And bid her hasten all the house to bed, Which heavy sorrow makes them apt unto. Romeo is coming.

#### NURSE

O Lord, I could have stayed here all the night To hear good counsel. O, what learning is! My lord, I'll tell my lady you will come.

#### ROMEO

Do so, and bid my sweet prepare to chide.

*Note: Chide him (tell him off) for killing Tybalt right after their marriage and ruining their chances of living a happy married life together. He is acknowledging his guilt in advance and saying he is not going to be making up silly excuses for his behaviour.*

NURSE MAKES TO LEAVE THEN STOPS, REMEMBERING SOMETHING,
RUMMAGING IN HER POCKETS.

NURSE

Oh, here, sir, a ring she asked me to give you, sir. Hurry, don't delay, it's getting late.

NURSE

Here, sir, a ring she bid me give you, sir. Hie you, make haste, for it grows very late.

---

ROMEO TAKES THE RING, MUCH CHEERED NOW.

THE NURSE LEAVES HURRIEDLY.

---

ROMEO

How well my spirits are revived by this.

ROMEO

How well my comfort is revived by this.

FRIAR LAURENCE

Go now, Romeo; good night. And remember your fate depends upon you either being gone before the night guards are posted, or leaving the city by daybreak in disguise. Stay awhile in Mantua. I'll find your servant, and through him update you from time to time with any developments here in Verona.

Give me your hand. It is late. Farewell. Good night.

FRIAR LAURENCE

Go hence; good night. And here stands all your state:
Either be gone before the Watch be set,
Or by the break of day disguised from hence.
Sojourn in Mantua; I'll find out your man,
And he shall signify from time to time
Every good hap to you that chances here.
Give me thy hand. 'Tis late; farewell. Good night.

---

THEY SHAKE HANDS, UNBEKNOWNST TO BOTH THIS IS A FINAL FAREWELL.

---

ROMEO

*A joy greater than joy calls out to me,*
*It is a grief so brief to part with thee.*
Farewell.

ROMEO

*But that a joy past joy calls out on me,*
*It were a grief so brief to part with thee.*
Farewell.

# ACT III SCENE IV

## A ROOM IN CAPULET'S HOUSE. LATE MONDAY EVENING.

OLD CAPULET IS TALKING WITH LADY CAPULET AND COUNT PARIS.

### OLD CAPULET

Because of these unfortunate events, Paris, we have not had time to press our daughter on the matter. You must understand, she loved her cousin Tybalt dearly, as did I. (*sighs*) Oh well, we were all born to die. It's very late. She'll not come down tonight. I assure you, if not for your presence, I too would have been in bed an hour ago.

### CAPULET

Things have fall'n out, sir, so unluckily
That we have had no time to move our daughter.
Look you, she loved her kinsman Tybalt dearly,
And so did I. Well, we were born to die.
'Tis very late, she'll not come down tonight.
I promise you, but for your company
I would have been abed an hour ago.

### COUNT PARIS

These times of woe are not times to woo. Goodnight, Madam Capulet, give my fondest regards to your daughter.

### PARIS

These times of woe afford no times to woo.
Madam, good night; commend me to your
   daughter

### LADY CAPULET

I will, and I will know her mind by early tomorrow. Tonight she shuts herself away with her grief.

### LADY CAPULET

I will, and know her mind early tomorrow.
Tonight she's mewed up to her heaviness.

*Note: 'Mewed' has nothing to do with cats, it is yet another hawking term. A mew is a place or a cage where a trained hawk is placed alone to moult (also called mew) its feathers. From this we get the term 'mews' for a row of converted dwellings designed for stabling horses. The first mews in this sense was the Hawk Mews royal stables at Charing Cross in London.*

### OLD CAPULET

Count Paris, before you leave, I'll make the bold offer of my child's hand. I think she will obey my wishes. No - more than that - I'm 'sure' she will.
- Wife, go to her before you go to bed. Tell her about the love of my future son, Paris, and mark my words - tell her that next Wednesday... But wait, what day is it now?

### CAPULET

Sir Paris, I will make a desperate tender
Of my child's love. I think she will be ruled
In all respects by me; nay, more, I doubt it not.
Wife, go you to her ere you go to bed;
Acquaint her here of my son Paris' love,
And bid her, mark you me, on Wednesday next -
But soft, what day is this?

COUNT PARIS
Monday, my lord.

PARIS
Monday, my lord.

OLD CAPULET
Monday! Hmm! Well, Wednesday is too soon then. Let's make it Thursday.
(*to Lady Capulet*) On Thursday, tell her, she will marry this noble count. Can you have everything ready by then? Do you think it's too hasty? We'll not have a large do - just a couple of friends. With my nephew, Tybalt, so recently slain it may be thought we were lacking in respect if we had too big a celebration. So we'll have maybe half a dozen friends and that'll be the end of it.
(*to Paris*) So what do you say to Thursday, Count Paris?

CAPULET
Monday! Ha ha! Well, Wednesday is too soon;
A Thursday let it be. A Thursday, tell her,
She shall be married to this noble earl.
Will you be ready? Do you like this haste?
We'll keep no great ado - a friend or two;
For, hark you, Tybalt being slain so late,
It may be thought we held him carelessly,
Being our kinsman, if we revel much.
Therefore we'll have some half a dozen friends,
And there an end. But what say you to Thursday?

Note: A 'friend or two' has rapidly grown into 'half a dozen' (six). Old Capulet is keen to marry off his daughter to Paris as he is a relative of the Prince. It would be good for his status and place him higher in ranking than Old Montague. Later he will hire twenty cooks, no small celebration!

For some reason, Capulet calls Paris an earl, an English title.

COUNT PARIS
My lord, I wish Thursday were tomorrow.

PARIS
My lord, I would that Thursday were tomorrow.

OLD CAPULET
Well, on your way then. On Thursday it is.
(*to wife*) Go to Juliet before you go to bed, dear wife, prepare her for her wedding day.

CAPULET
Well, get you gone. A Thursday be it then.
[*To Lady Capulet*] Go you to Juliet ere you go to bed;
Prepare her, wife, against this wedding day.

PARIS TURNS AND LEAVES.

OLD CAPULET (CONT'D)
(*to Paris*) Farewell, my lord.
(*calls*) Boy! A light for my bed!
(*to Paris*) Good grief, it is so late that we'll soon be calling it early. Goodnight.

CAPULET
Farewell, my lord.
Light to my chamber, ho!
Afore me, it is so very late that we
May call it early by and by. Good night.

*Note: There may be a problem in the text in this last speech. Paris apparently leaves saying no goodbyes. However, Capulet says goodbye twice and it is not apparent who he is talking to in the final goodnight. It may make more sense if the first farewell is spoken by Paris, especially as he says 'my Lord', a title one would be expected to use for a future father-in-law and a title he had just used in his previous line. Then as he leaves, Capulet replies with his 'Goodnight'. If we follow it as written, saying good night twice to Paris and Paris not saying a single word in reply is strange, but it can be made to work, and is every day in productions.*

*Trivia: In the days before electricity, homes were lit by naked flames. Servants would carry a candelabra of lit candles to light the way between rooms. The master would call for 'a light'. As Old King Cole did in the nursery rhyme.*

# ACT III SCENE V

## JULIET'S BEDCHAMBER. TUESDAY DAWN.

THE NEW LOVERS, ROMEO AND JULIET, STAND ON THE BALCONY OF JULIET'S
BEDROOM AS THE DAWN CHORUS SLOWLY BEGINS.

### JULIET

Do you have to go? It is not nearly daybreak yet. It was the nightingale, not the lark, that pierced your fearful ear. She sings every night from the pomegranate tree. Believe me, love, it was the nightingale.

### JULIET

Wilt thou be gone? It is not yet near day.
It was the nightingale, and not the lark,
That pierced the fearful hollow of thine ear.
Nightly she sings on yon pomegranate tree.
Believe me, love, it was the nightingale.

> Note: It is likely Shakespeare knew that only male nightingales sing, he is referring to Ovid's 'Metamorphoses', where Philomela, the mythical daughter of King Pandion of Athens, was turned into a nightingale to escape her sad plight and gave it its sad song. Many poets and authors were influenced by the story of Philomela including the poet, Keats, and she appears again singing a lullaby in 'A Midsummer Night's Dream'.
>
> The pomegranate tree was not native to England, it came from the Middle East where the nightingale frequented the pomegranate groves and famously sang loudly from them. First introduced into Europe via Italy by the Romans.

### ROMEO

It was the lark, herald of the morning, not the nightingale. Look, my love, cruel streaks of light pierce the clouds on the eastern horizon, the stars are burnt out and the joyful day stands on tiptoe behind the misty mountain tops. I must go and live, or stay and die.

### ROMEO

It was the lark, the herald of the morn,
No nightingale. Look, love, what envious streaks
Do lace the severing clouds in yonder east.
Night's candles are burnt out, and jocund day
Stands tiptoe on the misty mountain tops.
I must be gone and live, or stay and die.

### JULIET

That light is not daylight, I swear it. It is a meteor exhaled by the sun and sent as a torch bearer to light your way to Mantua. Therefore stay a while, you need not leave yet.

### JULIET

Yon light is not daylight, I know it, I.
It is some meteor that the sun exhales
To be to thee this night a torch-bearer
And light thee on thy way to Mantua.
Therefore stay yet; thou need'st not to be gone.

ROMEO

Let me be arrested, let me be put to death.
I will be content if you want it that way.
I'll say the grey light is not the morning's
eye, but the pale reflection of the moon's
face, and it's not the lark whose song rings
out from the heavens so high above our
heads.
*My wish to stay's more than my will to go.*
*Come, welcome death! Juliet wishes it so.*
*Don't you, my love? Let's talk, it's not yet day.*

ROMEO

Let me be ta'en, let me be put to death;
I am content so thou wilt have it so.
I'll say yon grey is not the morning's eye,
'Tis but the pale reflex of Cynthia's brow;
Nor that is not the lark, whose notes do beat
The vaulty heaven so high above our heads.
*I have more care to stay than will to go.*
*Come death, and welcome! Juliet wills it so.*
*How is't, my soul? Let's talk; it is not day.*

> Note: Cynthia was another name for Diana, goddess of the moon, chastity, and
> hunting, depicted in art as dressed in white, carrying a bow (shaped like a crescent
> moon), and often with the crescent moon just above or on her head. Some scholars
> think the word 'brow' should be 'bow', others that as the moon is just above her
> head her brow would reflect ('reflex') the moon.

ROMEO LEADS JULIET BACK INTO THE ROOM. JULIET'S BRAVADO LEAVES
HER. ROMEO HAS CALLED HER BLUFF. SHE STOPS HIM.

JULIET

*It is, it is! Quick, be gone, on your way!*
It is the lark that sings so out of tune, with
strained harsh discords and shrill notes.
Some say the lark makes sweet music, this
is not so, for she divides us. Legend says
the lark and the loathsome toad
exchanged eyes. Oh, now I wish they had
exchanged voices too,
*That voice it tears us from each others arms,*
*Chasing you away, with the hunter's alarm.*
*Oh, go now! Lighter and lighter it grows.*

JULIET

*It is, it is. Hie hence, be gone, away!*
It is the lark that sings so out of tune,
Straining harsh discords and unpleasing sharps.
Some say the lark makes sweet division;
This doth not so, for she divideth us.
Some say the lark and loathed toad change eyes;
O now I would they had changed voices too,
*Since arm from arm that voice doth us affray,*
*Hunting thee hence with `hunt's-up' to the day.*
*O now be gone! More light and light it grows.*

> Note: 'Harsh discords' are notes which clash, and 'unpleasing sharps' are high
> notes painfully out of tune. 'Sweet division' – division is a way of singing a note
> with a trill, a wordplay on dividing the pair.
>
> Folklore says the ugly toad has beautiful eyes, whereas the beautiful lark has ugly
> eyes, therefore they must have swapped eyes.
>
> 'Hunt's up' – As the dawn chorus of birdsong was the hunter's early morning
> alarm call, any song intended to wake or stir someone in the morning was called a
> 'hunt's up'.

ROMEO

*Light and lighter, dark and darker our woes.*

ROMEO

*More light and light: more dark and dark our woes.*

QUIET KNOCKS ON JULIET'S DOOR.

NURSE
(*quietly from outside the door*) Madam!

NURSE
(*off*) Madam!

JULIET
Nurse?

JULIET
Nurse?

NURSE
(*quietly from outside the door*) Your mother is on her way to your room.
*It is daybreak, be careful, and look out.*

NURSE
(*off*) Your lady mother is coming to your chamber.
*The day is broke; be wary, look about.*

THE NURSE SCAMPERS OFF.

JULIET LOOKS SADLY AT THE WINDOW.

JULIET
*Let daylight in, let light of my life out.*

JULIET
*Then, window, let day in and let life out.*

ROMEO WALKS OUT ONTO THE BALCONY.

ROMEO
*Farewell, farewell! One kiss, and I'll descend.*

ROMEO
*Farewell, farewell! One kiss, and I'll descend.*

THEY KISS AND HE STARTS TO DESCEND THE ROPE LADDER.

JULIET
(*calling down to him*)
*Gone so soon, my lord, lover, husband, friend?*

JULIET
*Art thou gone so, love, lord, ay husband, friend,*

ROMEO PAUSES AT THE FOOT OF THE LADDER AND LOOKS UP AT JULIET.

JULIET (CONT'D)
I must hear from you every day by the hour, for every minute apart will seem like many days. By this reckoning I will have aged many years before I behold my Romeo again.

JULIET
I must hear from thee every day in the hour,
For in a minute there are many days.
O, by this count I shall be much in years
Ere I again behold my Romeo.

ROMEO
(*from below*) Farewell!
*I will not miss an opportunity*
*To send my greetings and my love to thee.*

ROMEO
Farewell!
*I will omit no opportunity*
*That may convey my greetings, love, to thee.*

| | |
|---|---|
| **JULIET** | JULIET |
| Oh, do you think we shall ever meet again? | O think'st thou we shall ever meet again? |
| **ROMEO** | ROMEO |
| Of that I have no doubt, and all these sorrows will serve to add sweet content to our reminisces in times to come. | I doubt it not, and all these woes shall serve For sweet discourses in our times to come. |
| **JULIET** | JULIET |
| Oh God, I had a terrible premonition! I imagined I saw you, now you are so low down, as one sees the dead in the bottom of a tomb. Either my eyesight fails me, or you look pale. | O God, I have an ill-divining soul! Methinks I see thee, now thou art so low, As one dead in the bottom of a tomb. Either my eyesight fails, or thou look'st pale. |
| **ROMEO** | ROMEO |
| *Believe me, love, in my eyes so do you.* *This sorrow drains our blood. Adieu, adieu!* | *And trust me, love, in my eye so do you.* *Dry sorrow drinks our blood. Adieu, adieu!* |

ROMEO BLOWS JULIET A KISS AND SCAMPERS AWAY ACROSS THE GROUNDS.

GENTLE KNOCKING ON JULIET'S DOOR. JULIET RETURNS TO HER
BEDCHAMBER CLOSING THE BALCONY DOOR QUIETLY BEHIND HER.

SHE SEES HER LOVER CLIMB THE GARDEN WALL AND DISAPPEAR FROM VIEW.

| | |
|---|---|
| **JULIET** | JULIET |
| (*aside*) Oh, fortune, fortune, men call you fickle. If you are so fickle, what would you need with someone like Romeo who has great faith? Be fickle, fortune, for then I hope, you will not keep him long, but send him back to me. | O fortune, fortune, all men call thee fickle; If thou art fickle, what dost thou with him That is renowned for faith? Be fickle, fortune, For then I hope thou wilt not keep him long, But send him back. |

LADY CAPULET KNOCKS AGAIN LOUDER AND SPEAKS OUTSIDE THE DOOR.

| | |
|---|---|
| **LADY CAPULET** | LADY CAPULET |
| (*outside*) Hello, Juliet! Are you up? | Ho, daughter! Are you up? |
| **JULIET** | JULIET |
| (*buying time*) Who is it calling me? | Who is't that calls? |

JULIET QUICKLY REARRANGES HER ROOM FOR INCRIMINATING EVIDENCE.

JULIET (CONT'D)

(*aside*) It is my mother. Is she late going to bed or early rising? What on earth causes her to come so early?

JULIET

It is my lady mother.
Is she not down so late, or up so early?
What unaccustomed cause procures her hither?

---

JULIET THROWS HERSELF ON HER BED IN GRIEF
HIDING HER HEAD IN THE PILLOW SOBBING,

LADY CAPULET ENTERS THE ROOM.

---

LADY CAPULET

What is the meaning of this, Juliet?

LADY CAPULET

Why, how now Juliet?

JULIET

(*sobbing*) Mother, I am not well.

JULIET

Madam, I am not well.

---

LADY CAPULET ASSUMES JULIET IS GRIEVING FOR HER COUSIN, TYBALT,
WHO ROMEO KILLED THE DAY BEFORE. HER MOTHER OF COURSE KNOWS
NOTHING OF THE WEDDING TO ROMEO OR THEIR STOLEN NIGHT OF PASSION
SHE ALMOST STUMBLED ACROSS.

THIS GIVES JULIET THE PERFECT COVER FOR HER EMOTION,
ALTHOUGH TO HER MOTHER IT SEEMS EXCESSIVE.

---

LADY CAPULET

Still weeping for your cousin's death? Trying to wash him from his grave with tears? Even if you could, you could not bring him back to life. So be done with your crying. Grief in moderation shows your love, but too much shows a lack of wits.

LADY CAPULET

Evermore weeping for your cousin's death?
What, wilt thou wash him from his grave with tears?
And if thou couldst, thou couldst not make him live;
Therefore have done. Some grief shows much of love,
But much of grief shows still some want of wit.

JULIET

Oh, let me weep for such deep feelings of loss.

JULIET

Yet let me weep for such a feeling loss.

LADY CAPULET

Then you weep for your feelings of loss, not for your friend.

LADY CAPULET

So shall you feel the loss, but not the friend
Which you weep for.

JULIET

I feel the loss so much, I have no choice but to forever weep for my friend.

JULIET

Feeling so the loss,
I cannot choose but ever weep the friend.

---

JULIET OF COURSE MEANS ROMEO, BUT SHE CANNOT LET HER MOTHER
KNOW THE TRUTH.

LADY CAPULET
Well, my girl, remember you weep not so much for his death but that the villain who killed him still lives.

JULIET
What villain, mother?

LADY CAPULET
That villain, Romeo.

JULIET
A villain who is now many miles apart. God pardon him! I do, with all my heart. Even though no man makes my heart grieve as much as him.

LADY CAPULET
Well, girl, thou weep'st not so much for his death As that the villain lives which slaughtered him.

JULIET
What villain, madam?

LADY CAPULET
That same villain, Romeo.

JULIET
[Aside.] Villain and he be many miles asunder. [Aloud.] God pardon him! I do, with all my heart; And yet no man like he doth grieve my heart.

---

> Note: The 'aside' direction was added in the 18<sup>th</sup> century by Hamner and copied by subsequent publications, but it is now commonly thought that this should be spoken aloud as it is ambiguous in a similar manner to her other lines. It was removed for the translation.

---

LADY CAPULET
That is because the treacherous murderer lives.

JULIET
Yes, mother, away from the reach of my hands. I wish that I alone might avenge my cousin's death.

LADY CAPULET
We will have vengeance, don't you fear. Now stop crying. I'll send message to someone in Mantua, where that banished fugitive now lives, who will give him such a potion that he will soon be keeping Tybalt company. And then I hope you will be satisfied.

LADY CAPULET
That is because the traitor murderer lives.

JULIET
Ay, madam, from the reach of these my hands. Would none but I might venge my cousin's death.

LADY CAPULET
We will have vengeance for it, fear thou not. Then weep no more. I'll send to one in Mantua, Where that same banished runagate doth live, Shall give him such an unaccustomed dram That he shall soon keep Tybalt company; And then, I hope, thou wilt be satisfied.

JULIET

Indeed, I shall never be satisfied with Romeo till I behold him – dead – is my poor heart, it's so upset for a relative. Mother, if you can find a man to deliver the poison, I would mix it so that Romeo would fall into a quiet sleep upon receiving it. Oh, how my heart hates to hear his name when I cannot come to him, to wreak the love I felt for my cousin, upon the body of the one who slaughtered him!

JULIET

Indeed I never shall be satisfied
With Romeo till I behold him, dead,
Is my poor heart so for a kinsman vexed.
Madam, if you could find out but a man
To bear a poison, I would temper it
That Romeo should, upon receipt thereof,
Soon sleep in quiet. O how my heart abhors
To hear him named, and cannot come to him
To wreak the love I bore [for] my cousin
Upon his body that hath slaughtered him!

Note: 'To wreak the love I bore my cousin' is a word short. The word 'for' has been added here to the original text, other editors have chosen their own words to add or left it as is.

LADY CAPULET

You mix the potion and I'll find such a man. But now I'll tell you some joyful news, daughter.

LADY CAPULET

Find thou the means, and I'll find such a man.
But now I'll tell thee joyful tidings, girl.

JULIET

Joy would be most welcome in such a needy time. What is it, pray tell me, mother?

JULIET

And joy comes well in such a needy time.
What are they, beseech your ladyship?

LADY CAPULET

Well... you have a considerate father, child. One, who to spare you from your unhappiness, has arranged a surprise day of joy. It was a surprise even to me.

LADY CAPULET

Well, well, thou hast a careful father, child;
One who, to put thee from thy heaviness,
Hath sorted out a sudden day of joy
That thou expects not, nor I looked not for.

JULIET

A day well timed, mother. What day is planned?

JULIET

Madam, in happy time, what day is that?

LADY CAPULET

Well, my child, early Thursday morning, the gallant, young and noble gentleman, Count Paris, at St. Peter's Church shall happily make you a joyful bride.

LADY CAPULET

Marry, my child, early next Thursday morn
The gallant, young, and noble gentleman,
The County Paris, at Saint Peter's Church
Shall happily make thee there a joyful bride.

JULIET IS STUNNED AT THIS UNEXPECTED ANNOUNCEMENT.

JULIET

(*shocked*) By St. Peters Church and St. Peter too, he will not make me a joyful bride! I am amazed at this rush, that I must be wed before the man who wishes to be my husband has even come to court me. Mother, I pray you tell my lord and father that I will not marry yet. And when I do, I swear it shall be to Romeo - whom you know I hate - rather than to Count Paris. Good news indeed! (*she cries*)

JULIET

Now, by Saint Peter's Church, and Peter too, He shall not make me there a joyful bride. I wonder at this haste, that I must wed Ere he that should be husband comes to woo. I pray you, tell my lord and father, madam, I will not marry yet; and when I do, I swear It shall be Romeo, whom you know I hate, Rather than Paris. These are news indeed!

---

JULIET WEEPS SORROWFULLY AGAIN.

THE VOICES OF OLD CAPULET AND NURSE ARE HEARD APPROACHING.

---

LADY CAPULET

Here comes your father. You can tell him yourself, and see how he takes it from your lips.

LADY CAPULET

Here comes your father; tell him so yourself, And see how he will take it at your hands.

---

OLD CAPULET AND NURSE COME INTO THE ROOM.

JULIET BURIES HER HEAD INTO THE PILLOW SOBBING.

---

OLD CAPULET

Ah, Juliet. When the sun sets, the dew soaks the earth, but for the sunset of my brother's son, Tybalt, it pours down. What have we here, a fountain, girl? Still crying? Showering tears forever more?

CAPULET

When the sun sets the earth doth drizzle dew, But for the sunset of my brother's son It rains downright. How now! A conduit, girl? What, still in tears? Evermore showering?

---

JULIET CONTINUES WEEPING FACE DOWN ON HER BED.

---

OLD CAPULET (CONT'D)

You are like a boat, and a sea, and a wind, all in one little body, because your eyes, which I'll call the sea, still ebb and flow with tears and your body is the boat sailing in this salty flood. The winds are your sighs, raging with your tears, and your tears raging with them. Without a sudden calm they'll capsize your storm-tossed body.

CAPULET

In one little body Thou counterfeit'st a bark, a sea, a wind; For still thy eyes, which I may call the sea, Do ebb and flow with tears; the bark thy body is, Sailing in this salt flood; the winds thy sighs, Who, raging with thy tears, and they with them, Without a sudden calm, will overset Thy tempest-tossed body.

Note: Original texts had 'earth doth drizzle'. Most later editions have ammended this to 'air doth drizzle' as it makes better sense of the sentence.

The speech is nautical, suggesting Juliet's tears will cause a flood. 'Sudden calm' is when the wind suddenly stops and leaves a sailing ship becalmed, unable to move. 'Bark' is a boat, from the word 'barque', which is a sailing ship.

---

OLD CAPULET TURNS TO HIS WIFE.

---

### OLD CAPULET (CONT'D)
What will we do, wife? Have you told her our plans?

### LADY CAPULET
Yes, sir. She thanks you, but she will have none of it. I wish the foolish girl were married to her grave.

### OLD CAPULET
Calm down, explain yourself, wife. What do you mean she will have none of it? She doesn't thank us? Is she not pleased? Does she not count her blessings, unworthy girl as she is, that we have arranged so worthy a gentleman to be her bridegroom?

### JULIET
I am not pleased that you have, but I am grateful that you have. I can never be pleased with what I hate, but I am still thankful to hate something which was done out of love.

### CAPULET
How now, wife!
Have you delivered to her our decree?

### LADY CAPULET
Ay sir; but she will none, she gives you thanks.
I would the fool were married to her grave.

### CAPULET
Soft; take me with you, take me with you, wife.
How will she none? Doth she not give us thanks?
Is she not proud? Doth she not count her blest,
Unworthy as she is, that we have wrought
So worthy a gentleman to be her bride?

### JULIET
Not proud you have, but thankful that you have.
Proud can I never be of what I hate,
But thankful even for hate that is meant love.

---

OLD CAPULET BECOMES ANGRY.

---

OLD CAPULET

(*angry*) What, what, what, what! Splitting hairs? What's this? 'Pleased' - and 'I thank you' – and 'I thank you not' - and 'not pleased'? Worthless girl, you. Don't thank me with no thanks, or not pleased to be pleased. You will get your pretty little body ready by next Thursday to go with Count Paris to St. Peter's Church, or I will drag you there on a sled! Take that sick look off your face, immature fool, sullen faced brat!

CAPULET

How how how how, chopped logic! What is this? `Proud' and `I thank you' and `I thank you not'; And yet `not proud'? Mistress minion, you, Thank me no thankings nor proud me no prouds, But fettle your fine joints 'gainst Thursday next To go with Paris to Saint Peter's Church, Or I will drag thee on a hurdle thither. Out, you green-sickness carrion! Out, you baggage, You tallow-face!

> Note: A 'hurdle' was a wooden frame used to drag prisoners to the gallows to be hung.
>
> 'Green-sickness' was mentioned earlier in Act 2 Scene 2'. Then Romeo was referring to the false belief that the cause (now known to be chlorosis, or iron deficiency) in young women was due to lack of sexual activity. It was also believed to cause hysteria in adolescent girls.
>
> 'Carrion' is the decaying flesh of dead animals, and 'baggage' meant a disagreeable woman. In Britain it now has been shortened to 'bag' and more commonly used in derogatory expressions to a woman such as 'silly old bag', though its use is in decline now. 'Tallow-face' is pale like a candle.

IT APPEARS OLD CAPULET IS ABOUT TO STRIKE JULIET IN ANGER.

LADY CAPULET RESTRAINS HIM.

LADY CAPULET

Calm down, husband! Have you lost your senses?

LADY CAPULET

Fie, fie! What, are you mad?

JULIET FALLS TO HER KNEES BEFORE HER FATHER.

JULIET

Good father, I beg you on bended knees, please hear me out, let me speak.

JULIET

Good father, I beseech you on my knees, Hear me with patience but to speak a word.

> Note: The meaning is 'to speak but (just) a word'. Get a word in edgeways.

OLD CAPULET BRUSHES HER AWAY WITH A SWEEP OF HIS HAND.

| OLD CAPULET | CAPULET |
|---|---|
| Hang you, young hussy, disobedient wretch! I'm telling you – be at the church on Thursday or never look me in the face again. | Hang thee, young baggage, disobedient wretch! I tell thee what - get thee to church a Thursday, Or never after look me in the face. |

---

JULIET MAKES TO SAY SOMETHING IN HER DEFENCE.

---

JULIET

But...

| OLD CAPULET | CAPULET |
|---|---|
| Silence! Do not say a word, do not answer me back or you will feel my hand. | Speak not, reply not, do not answer me; My fingers itch. - |

> Note: His fingers itch (crave) to strike Juliet. From Capulet's words, Juliet tried to say something. An extra line was added in tranlation to show this.

---

OLD CAPULET TURNS TO HIS WIFE.

---

| OLD CAPULET (CONT'D) | CAPULET |
|---|---|
| Wife, we thought ourselves blessed that God had given us this, our only child, but I now see this one is one too many, and that we were cursed in having her. Away with her, worthless girl! | Wife, we scarce thought us blessed That God had lent us but this only child; But now I see this one is one too much, And that we have a curse in having her. Out on her, hilding! |

> Note: The original text said 'sent us', some later editions prefer 'lent us'.
>
> 'Hilding' is a worthless, despicable person.

| NURSE | NURSE |
|---|---|
| God in heaven, bless her! You are at fault, sir, to scold her so. | God in heaven bless her! You are to blame, my lord, to rate her so. |

> Note: Of course, Nurse is the only one who knows the real reason behind Juliet's grief, and how she cannot be married again, but she is unable to reveal the truth and it is not her place to criticise the master of the household.

| OLD CAPULET | CAPULET |
|---|---|
| And how is that, Lady Know-it-all? Hold your tongue, smart-arse. Go chatter with your gossips, get out! | And why, my Lady Wisdom? Hold your tongue, Good Prudence; smatter with your gossips, go! |

| NURSE | NURSE |
|---|---|
| I mean no disrespect... | I speak no treason. |

| | |
|---|---|
| OLD CAPULET | CAPULET |
| Oh, God in heaven! | O, God 'i'good e'en! |
| NURSE | NURSE |
| Can't a person speak? | May not one speak? |
| OLD CAPULET | CAPULET |
| Shut up, you mumbling fool! Go preach your 'wisdom' over a gossip's table, we don't need it here. | Peace, you mumbling fool! Utter your gravity o'er a gossip's bowl; For here we need it not. |
| LADY CAPULET | LADY CAPULET |
| You are too hot in the head. | You are too hot. |
| OLD CAPULET | CAPULET |
| (in reply to his wife) Good God, it makes me mad! Day and night, night and day, work and play, alone and in company, my one care has been to find her a match. And now, having provided a gentleman of noble parentage, a good income, young and well brought up - stuffed, as they say, with the honourable qualities, and as good a combination as could be wished in any man - only to have a wretched, whimpering fool, a whining doll, who, when fortune offers the perfect marriage answers; 'I'll not wed, I cannot love, I'm too young, I do beg your pardon'! | God's bread, it makes me mad! Day, night, work, play, Alone, in company, still my care hath been To have her matched; and having now provided A gentleman of noble parentage, Of fair demesnes, youthful, and nobly trained, Stuffed, as they say, with honourable parts, Proportioned as one's thought would wish a man; And then to have a wretched puling fool, A whining mammet, in her fortune's tender, To answer 'I'll not wed, I cannot love, I am too young, I pray you pardon me'! |

Note: 'Demesnes' means land, estate, property. It rhymes with 'domain'.

OLD CAPULET DIRECTS HIS ATTENTIONS ANGRILY TOWARDS JULIET.

| | |
|---|---|
| OLD CAPULET (CONT'D) | CAPULET |
| If you will not marry, I'll pardon you alright! Go graze with the cattle, you'll not live in this house with me. | But, an you will not wed, I'll pardon you! Graze where you will, you shall not house with me. |

OLD CAPULET PACES BACK AND FORTH ANGRILY.

OLD CAPULET (CONT'D)

Look on it, think on it. I am not in the habit of joking. Thursday is near. With hand on your heart, consider whether you are part of my family. If you are, then I'll give you away to my friend, if you are not, then hang, beg, starve, die in the streets, for, by my soul, I'll never acknowledge your existence, nor shall anything of mine ever be yours. Believe me, think about it carefully.

CAPULET

Look to't, think on't; I do not use to jest.
Thursday is near. Lay hand on heart; advise.
An you be mine, I'll give you to my friend;
An you be not, hang, beg, starve, die in the streets,
For, by my soul, I'll ne'er acknowledge thee,
Nor what is mine shall never do thee good.
Trust to't, bethink you,

---

OLD CAPULET REACHES THE DOOR.

OLD CAPULET (CONT'D)

I'll not change my mind!

CAPULET

I'll not be forsworn.

---

OLD CAPULET STORMS OUT, SLAMMING THE DOOR.

JULIET

(in despair) Is there no pity sitting up in the heavens that sees into the depths of my grief? Oh, my sweet mother, don't cast me away! Delay this marriage for a month, a week even. If you don't, then make my bridal bed in that dark tomb where Tybalt lies.

JULIET

Is there no pity sitting in the clouds
That sees into the bottom of my grief?
O, sweet my mother, cast me not away!
Delay this marriage for a month, a week;
Or, if you do not, make the bridal bed
In that dim monument where Tybalt lies.

---

AN OMINOUS PREMONITION.

LADY CAPULET

Don't talk to me, I'll not speak on your behalf. Do as you will...

LADY CAPULET

Talk not to me, for I'll not speak a word.
Do as thou wilt,

---

LADY CAPULET OPENS THE DOOR AND PAUSES.

LADY CAPULET

...for I am done with you!

LADY CAPULET

...for I have done with thee.

---

LADY CAPULET LEAVES, ALSO SLAMMING THE DOOR IN A HUFF.

NOW ONLY JULIET AND NURSE REMAIN IN THE ROOM.

JULIET

Oh God!

Oh nurse, how can this be prevented? My husband is on earth, my marriage vows in heaven. How will I be able to marry again here on earth, unless my husband returns his vows from heaven by leaving this earth? Help me, what should I do?

JULIET

O God! O Nurse, how shall this be prevented?
My husband is on earth, my faith in heaven;
How shall that faith return again to earth,
Unless that husband send it me from heaven
By leaving earth? Comfort me, counsel me.

---

NURSE WRINGS HER HANDS HELPLESSLY.

---

JULIET (CONT'D)

Alack, alas, that heaven should practice such cunning schemes upon so gentle a subject as myself!

JULIET

Alack, alack that heaven should practise stratagems
Upon so soft a subject as myself!

---

JULIET THROWS HERSELF UPON HER NURSE.

---

JULIET (CONT'D)

Have you nothing to say? Have you no words to cheer me? I need some comfort and support, Nurse.

JULIET

What sayst thou? Hast thou not a word of joy?
Some comfort, Nurse.

---

NURSE THINKS FOR A MOMENT, THEN COMES UP WITH AN IDEA WHICH MAY
HELP REPAIR THE DAMAGE SHE WAS PARTY TO, SAVING HER OWN SKIN BY
TELLING JULIET TO COMMIT BIGAMY.

---

NURSE

I believe I have... listen to this...

Romeo is banished, and it's a safe bet he would never dare come back to assert his claim on you. Even if he did, it could only be in secret. So, as things stand now, I think it best if you married the count. Oh, he's a lovely gentleman! Romeo's a dirty rag compared to him. An eagle, madam, has not so green, so quick, so fair an eye as Paris has. Curse my heart if I'm wrong, but I think you'd be happier in this second match, it's much better than your first. Even if it isn't, your first husband is dead - or as good as if he were living here and you were unable to have use of him.

NURSE

Faith, here it is: Romeo
Is banished, and all the world to nothing
That he dares ne'er come back to challenge you,
Or, if he do, it needs must be by stealth.
Then, since the case so stands as now it doth,
I think it best you married with the County.
O, he's a lovely gentleman;
Romeo's a dishclout to him. An eagle, madam,
Hath not so green, so quick, so fair an eye
As Paris hath. Beshrew my very heart,
I think you are happy in this second match,
For it excels your first; or, if it did not,
Your first is dead, or 'twere as good he were
As living here and you no use of him.

| JULIET | JULIET |
|---|---|
| You speak from your heart? | Speak'st thou from thy heart? |

| NURSE | NURSE |
|---|---|
| And from my soul too, or a curse on them both. | And from my soul too, else beshrew them both. |

> Note: 'Beshrew' was a dated word even in Shakespeare's time, it means to curse or invoke evil upon. Its origin is from middle English (1150 – 1470).

| JULIET | JULIET |
|---|---|
| Amen to that! | Amen! |

> Note: Amen means 'I agree' in Latin. Commonly used in prayer. Juliet is rudely agreeing to a curse on Nurse.

| NURSE | NURSE |
|---|---|
| What? | What? |

JULIET NOW PRETENDS SHE WASN'T BEING RUDE AND THAT SHE HAS NOW COME AROUND TO HER FATHER'S WAY OF THINKING TO BUY HERSELF TIME.

| JULIET | JULIET |
|---|---|
| Well, you have been a great comfort to me. Go, and tell my mother that having displeased my father, I have left for Father Laurence's quarters to confess my sins and be absolved. | Well, thou hast comforted me marvellous much. Go in, and tell my lady I am gone, Having displeased my father, to Laurence' cell To make confession and to be absolved. |

| NURSE | NURSE |
|---|---|
| That I will, this is a sensible choice. | Marry, I will; and this is wisely done. |

A RELIEVED NURSE HURRIES OUT, LEAVING JULIET ALONE.

| JULIET | JULIET |
|---|---|
| (aside) Wicked old woman! Oh, wicked devil! Is it more of a sin to wish me be untrue to my marriage vows, or to run down my love with that same tongue with which she has praised him as beyond comparison so many thousand times? Be gone advisor! From this moment on, my secrets will never be shared with you again. I'll go to the Friar to ask his advice, if all else fails, I still have the power to take my own life. | Ancient damnation! O most wicked fiend! Is it more sin to wish me thus forsworn, Or to dispraise my lord with that same tongue Which she hath praised him with above compare So many thousand times? Go, counsellor; Thou and my bosom henceforth shall be twain. I'll to the Friar, to know his remedy. If all else fail, myself have power to die. |

ANOTHER OMINOUS PREMONITION OF JULIET'S.

*Note: Committing suicide was considered a terrible sin against God. Only God had the power to create life and take it away. Doing so would commit your soul to eternal damnation in Hell. Something truly feared and believed in Shakespeare's time.*

.

# ACT IV

CELEBRATION TURNS TO TRAGEDY

# ACT IV

## ACT IV SCENE I

### FRIAR LAURENCE'S QUARTERS. TUESDAY MORNING.

COUNT PARIS AND FRIAR LAWRENCE ARE TOGETHER TALKING IN HIS QUARTERS
WITHIN THE MONASTERY.

**FRIAR LAURENCE**
On Thursday, Count Paris? This is very hasty.

**COUNT PARIS**
My father, Old Capulet, wishes it so, and I have no desire to lessen his haste.

**FRIAR LAURENCE**
You say you do not know the lady's feelings on this. This is highly irregular. I don't like it.

---

**FRIAR LAURENCE**
On Thursday, sir? The time is very short.

**PARIS**
My father, Capulet will have it so,
And I am nothing slow to slack his haste.

**FRIAR LAURENCE**
You say you do not know the lady's mind.
Uneven is the course; I like it not.

---

THE FRIAR IS WORRIED. HE MARRIED JULIET TO ROMEO THE DAY BEFORE.

**COUNT PARIS**
She has not stopped crying over Tybalt's death, therefore I have talked little of love. The goddess of love, Venus, does not smile upon a house of tears. Now, sir, her father considers it unhealthy that she is so overcome by sorrow, and in his wisdom hastens our marriage to stem her flood of tears - made worse by dwelling alone in her misery - by putting her in the company of people again. Now you know the reason for this haste.

**FRIAR LAURENCE**
(*aside*) If only I didn't know the reason it should be slowed.

---

**PARIS**
Immoderately she weeps for Tybalt's death,
And therefore have I little talked of love;
For Venus smiles not in a house of tears.
Now, sir, her father counts it dangerous
That she do give her sorrow so much sway,
And in his wisdom hastes our marriage
To stop the inundation of her tears,
Which, too much minded by herself alone,
May be put from her by society.
Now do you know the reason of this haste.

**FRIAR LAURENCE**
[*Aside.*] I would I knew not why it should be slowed.

FRIAR LAWRENCE NOTICES JULIET APPROACHING WITH SOME RELIEF.

FRIAR LAURENCE (CONT'D)
(*normal*) Look, sir, here comes the lady herself toward my quarters.

FRIAR LAURENCE
- Look, sir, here comes the lady toward my cell.

JULIET ENTERS, SURPRISED TO FIND PARIS THERE.

COUNT PARIS
I am happy to meet you, my lady, and my wife!

PARIS
Happily met, my lady and my wife.

JULIET
You may say that, sir, when I may be a wife.

JULIET
That may be, sir, when I may be a wife.

COUNT PARIS
That 'may be' will be, my love, next Thursday.

PARIS
That ' may be' must be, love, on Thursday next.

JULIET RECITES AN OLD SAYING IN REPLY.

JULIET
What will be, will be.

JULIET
What must be, shall be.

FRIAR LAURENCE
That's for certain.

FRIAR LAURENCE
That's a certain text.

COUNT PARIS
Have you come to confession with the Friar?

PARIS
Come you to make confession to this father?

JULIET
To answer that, I would be confessing to you.

JULIET
To answer that, I should confess to you.

COUNT PARIS
Do not deny to him that you love me.

PARIS
Do not deny to him that you love me.

JULIET
I will confess to you that I love him.

JULIET
I will confess to you that I love him.

> Note: Juliet is playing with words, she of course means she loves Romeo but suggests she means Father Laurence.

COUNT PARIS
So will you confess, I am sure, that you love me.

PARIS
So will ye, I am sure, that you love me.

171

JULIET

If I do so, it will be of more value said behind your back than to 'your' face.

JULIET

If I do so, it will be of more price Being spoke behind your back than to your face.

Note: This starts a passage of banter between the two of 'your face', 'my face' etc.

COUNT PARIS

Poor soul, 'your' face is spoilt with tears.

PARIS

Poor soul, thy face is much abused with tears.

JULIET

The tears win small victory by that, 'my' face was bad enough before their addition.

JULIET

The tears have got small victory by that, For it was bad enough before their spite.

COUNT PARIS

You wrong 'your' face more than the tears with that statement.

PARIS

Thou wrong'st it more than tears with that report.

JULIET

That is no lie, sir, which is a truth, and what I said, I said to 'my' face.

JULIET

That is no slander, sir, which is a truth; And what I spake, I spake it to my face.

Note: It is possible Juliet is implying that she is being two faced, and of course refering back to something having more value when said behind a person's back.

COUNT PARIS

'Your' face is mine now, and you have insulted it.

PARIS

Thy face is mine, and thou hast slandered it.

JULIET

That may be so, for it is not my own.

JULIET

It may be so, for it is not mine own.

Note: As she belongs to Romeo through marriage.

JULIET TURNS TO FRIAR LAURENCE.

JULIET (CONT'D)

Are you free now, holy Father, or shall I come back at evening mass?

JULIET

Are you at leisure, holy father, now, Or shall I come to you at evening mass?

Note: Evening mass was a church service Verona was noted for as it was banned by Pope Pious V but continued on at only a few churches.

FRIAR LAURENCE

I am free now to perform my duties, my sorrowful daughter.

FRIAR LAURENCE

My leisure serves me, pensive daughter, now.

FRIAR LAURENCE TURNS TO COUNT PARIS.

**FRIAR LAURENCE (CONT'D)**
My lord, we must be left alone now.

FRIAR LAURENCE
My lord, we must entreat the time alone.

**COUNT PARIS**
God forbid that I should disturb your holy devotion!

PARIS
God shield I should disturb devotion!

COUNT PARIS TAKES JULIET BY THE HAND.

**COUNT PARIS (CONT'D)**
Juliet, early Thursday, I will come to wake you, till then, adieu, and take this holy kiss.

PARIS
Juliet, on Thursday early will I rouse ye;
Till then, adieu; and keep this holy kiss.

COUNT PARIS KISSES JULIET'S HAND THEN TURNS AND LEAVES.

**JULIET**
Oh Father, shut the door! And when you have done so, come weep with me. I am beyond hope, beyond cure, beyond help!

JULIET
O, shut the door, and when thou hast done so
Come weep with me -past hope, past cure, past help!

FRIAR LAURENCE WALKS TO THE DOOR.

CHECKING IT IS CLEAR OUTSIDE HE CLOSES IT AND RETURNS TO JULIET.

**FRIAR LAURENCE**
Oh Juliet, I already know what grieves you. It is beyond the limits of my comprehension. I have heard you must be married to Paris on Thursday, and it seems nothing can delay it.

FRIAR LAURENCE
O Juliet, I already know thy grief;
It strains me past the compass of my wits.
I hear thou must, and nothing may prorogue it,
On Thursday next be married to this County.

**JULIET**
Don't tell me, Father, that you know of this, unless you can tell me how I may prevent it. If with all your wisdom you can offer no help, then just call my intention wise, and with this dagger I'll resolve it here and now.

JULIET
Tell me not, Friar, that thou hear'st of this,
Unless thou tell me how I may prevent it.
If in thy wisdom thou canst give no help,
Do thou but call my resolution wise,
And with this knife I'll help it presently.

JULIET PULLS OUT A DAGGER CONCEALED WITHIN HER CLOTHING.

> *Notes: Knives were carried by women in Shakespeare's time, to cut and eat food and protect themselves. To the audience it would have seemed nothing out of the ordinary and not deemed to be carried for premeditated self-harm.*

### JULIET (CONT'D)

God joined my heart with Romeo's, you joined our hands. And before my heart is forcefully joined with another, this hand - sealed by you with Romeo's - shall be the seal to a very different contract. In treacherous revolt this hand shall slay my faithful heart and my marriage.

### JULIET

God joined my heart and Romeo's, thou our hands;
And ere this hand, by thee to Romeo's sealed,
Shall be the label to another deed,
Or my true heart with treacherous revolt
Turn to another, this shall slay them both.

> *Notes: Labels were attached to official documents, they were stamped with a 'seal'. A seal is made by dripping hot wax onto the parchment and then an impression is made in the molten wax with an official stamp.*

JULIET PLACES THE KNIFE AGAINST HER CHEST.

### JULIET (CONT'D)

So, from your long years of experience, give me some advice. Be warned, if the authority of your years and your holy training cannot bring about an honourable solution, this bloody knife shall be judge and jury over myself and my desperate plight. Don't take too long to speak, I long to die, especially if your speech offers no remedy.

### JULIET

Therefore, out of thy long-experienced time,
Give me some present counsel, or, behold,
'Twixt my extremes and me this bloody knife
Shall play the umpire, arbitrating that
Which the commission of thy years and art
Could to no issue of true honour bring.
Be not so long to speak; I long to die
If what thou speak'st speak not of remedy.

FRIAR LAURENCE PLACES HIS HAND ON THE KNIFE.

### FRIAR LAURENCE

Wait, my daughter, I can see some ray of hope, but it requires an action as desperate in execution as the one we are desperate to prevent.

### FRIAR LAURENCE

Hold; daughter, I do spy a kind of hope
Which craves as desperate an execution
As that is desperate which we would prevent.

> *Note: Wordplay on 'execution' – to carry out something or to kill someone.*

JULIET LOWERS THE HAND WITH A LOOK OF DESPERATE HOPE.

#### FRIAR LAURENCE (CONT'D)

If you have the strength of will to kill yourself rather than marry Count Paris, then it is likely you would undertake something *'like'* death to drive away this unfortunate situation. You desire death itself to escape from disgrace, so, if you have the courage, I'll give you the remedy.

#### JULIET

Oh, ask me to jump from the battlements of any tower, or walk in a den of thieves rather than marry Paris. Ask me to lay in a snake pit, chain me up with wild bears, or lock me nightly in a mausoleum among the rattling bones, stinking flesh, and yellow jawless skulls of the dead. Or ask me to enter a newly dug grave and lay with a dead man in his coffin - things that, just to speak about, have made me tremble - and I would do them without fear or hesitation, to be able to live as a faithful wife to my sweet love.

#### FRIAR LAURENCE

If, rather than to marry County Paris,
Thou hast the strength of will to slay thyself,
Then is it likely thou wilt undertake
A thing like death to chide away this shame,
That cop'st with death himself to 'scape from it;
And, if thou dar'st, I'll give thee remedy.

#### JULIET

O, bid me leap, rather than marry Paris,
From off the battlements of any tower,
Or walk in thievish ways, or bid me lurk
Where serpents are; chain me with roaring bears,
Or hide me nightly in a charnel-house
O'ercovered quite with dead men's rattling bones,
With reeky shanks and yellow chapless skulls;
Or bid me go into a new-made grave
And hide me with a dead man in his shroud -
Things that, to hear them told, have made me
    tremble -
And I will do it without fear or doubt,
To live an unstained wife to my sweet love.

---

FRIAR LAURENCE RETRIEVES A VIAL FROM A CLOSET AS HE SPEAKS IN REPLY TO
THE PROPHETIC WORDS OF JULIET.

---

#### FRIAR LAURENCE

Wait then. Go home, be cheery, give your consent to marry Paris. Tomorrow is Wednesday. Tomorrow night, make sure you sleep alone, do not let your nurse stay with you in your bed chamber. Take this vial, and when you are in bed, drink the contents of it. The cold liquid will run its course through your veins. Your pulse will stop, no warmth and no breath will be apparent to show you live.

#### FRIAR LAURENCE

Hold, then; go home, be merry, give consent
To marry Paris. Wednesday is tomorrow;
Tomorrow night look that thou lie alone,
Let not the Nurse lie with thee in thy chamber.
Take thou this vial, being then in bed,
And this distilling liquor drink thou off;
When presently through all thy veins shall run
A cold and drowsy humour, for no pulse
Shall keep his native progress, but surcease:
No warmth, no breath, shall testify thou liv'st;

---

*Trivia: The word 'surcease' is not derived from the same source as 'cease', though they are similar in usage. The 'cease' ending was added to the Old French word 'sursis' (which meant delay or refrain) due to it's similar meaning. 'Cease' is derived from the Middle English word of 'cessare', meaning to yield.*

| FRIAR LAURENCE (CONT'D) | FRIAR LAURENCE |
|---|---|
| The rosy colour will drain from your lips and cheeks, your eyes will shut, just like death when it shuts out life. You will be paralysed, and each limb, stiff, stark and cold, will appear like death. In this temporary state of death you will lie for forty-two hours, and then awake as if from a pleasant sleep. Now, when the bridegroom comes in the morning to collect you, you will be there dead. | No warmth, no breath, shall testify thou liv'st; The roses in thy lips and cheeks shall fade To wanny ashes, thy eyes' windows fall Like death, when he shuts up the day of life. Each part, deprived of supple government, Shall stiff and stark and cold appear, like death; And in this borrowed likeness of shrunk death Thou shalt continue two and forty hours, And then awake as from a pleasant sleep. Now, when the bridegroom in the morning comes To rouse thee from thy bed, there art thou dead. |

*Note: For accuracy, forty-two hours should have been fifty-two. If she took the potion when going to bed, forty-two hours later would have been late afternoon at best. Romeo arrived late at night and Juliet had still not awoken.*

JULIET SHUDDERS APPREHENSIVELY.

| FRIAR LAURENCE (CONT'D) | FRIAR LAURENCE |
|---|---|
| Then, as is customary, you will be dressed in your finest clothes, and borne uncovered to the ancient vault where the Capulet family lie. In the meantime, in preparation for your awakening, I will send letter to Romeo so that he knows of our plans. He shall come straight here, and he and I will watch your waking. That very night Romeo will take you to Mantua, and this will free you from your embarrassing predicament, providing no sudden change of heart or cowardly fear prevents you from carrying it out. | Then, as the manner of our country is, In thy best robes, uncovered on the bier, Thou shalt be borne to that same ancient vault Where all the kindred of the Capulets lie. In the meantime, against thou shalt awake, Shall Romeo by my letters know our drift, And hither shall he come; and he and I Will watch thy waking, and that very night Shall Romeo bear thee hence to Mantua. And this shall free thee from this present shame, If no inconstant toy nor womanish fear Abate thy valour in the acting it. |

*Note: 'Bier' is the wooden frame used to carry a body to its final resting place Although coffins were in use then, Shakespeare has Juliet and Tybalt buried in a new type of tomb known as 'shroud tombs'. A midwife would wash the body and wrap it in a sheet (a shroud), the body being interred in the tomb with no coffin. A second type of tomb introduced at the same time was for wealthy women who died in childbirth. The woman was clothed (usually in night clothes as if sleeping) and unshrouded. Juliet's tomb seems to be a combination of both as she was clothed in her finery and unshrouded. This was also common practise in Italy and was how Brooke described the burial in his poem that Shakespeare borrowed from.*

*'Inconstant toy' means 'Capricious whim'. Copied from Brooke's poem.*

JULIET

Oh, give me, give me! Don't speak to me of fear!

JULIET

Give me, give me! O, tell not me of fear!

---

FRIAR LAURENCE HANDS THE VIAL TO JULIET.

FRIAR LAURENCE

Here. You must leave. Be strong and successful in your resolve. I'll send a friar with speed

*To Mantua, for Romeo my letter to serve.*

FRIAR LAURENCE

Hold; get you gone. Be strong and prosperous In this resolve. I'll send a friar with speed *To Mantua with my letters to thy lord.*

---

JULIET LOOKS AT THE VIAL FRIAR LAURENCE HAD HANDED HER.

JULIET

*Love give me strength, strength give me the nerve.*

JULIET

*Love give me strength, and strength shall help afford.*

---

JULIET SECRETES THE VIAL SAFELY IN HER POCKET AND WALKS TO THE DOOR.

JULIET (CONT'D)

Farewell, dear Father.

JULIET

Farewell, dear father!

---

JULIET LEAVES, CLOSING THE DOOR BEHIND HER.

---

*Note: Rhyming couplet to signify the end of the scene.*

---

# ACT IV SCENE II

## CAPULET'S HOUSE. TUESDAY EVENING.

A HALL IN CAPULET'S HOUSE. OLD CAPULET IS GIVING ORDERS TO THE STAFF.

LADY CAPULET AND NURSE ARE ALSO PRESENT.

OLD CAPULET FOLDS A SHEET OF NOTEPAPER AND HANDS IT TO A SERVANT.

*Note: Lady Capulet is referred to as being present, but she seems to not hear her husband talking of changing the wedding day.*

| OLD CAPULET | CAPULET |
|---|---|
| Invite all the guests on this list. | So many guests invite as here are writ. |

THE SERVANT EXITS WITH THE LIST.

| OLD CAPULET | CAPULET |
|---|---|
| And you man, go hire me twenty master chefs. | Sirrah, go hire me twenty cunning cooks. |

*Note: Master chefs in Shakespeare's day were among the highest paid professions. So not only is the figure of twenty absurd, it is also extremely extravagent. 'Cunning cooks' was a term for a top chef and could be said with various inflections for comedy or disgust at the trade.*

| PETER | SERVANT |
|---|---|
| I assure you, you will have no bad ones, sir. I will make sure they pass the finger licking test myself. | You shall have none ill, sir, for I'll try if they can lick their fingers. |

| OLD CAPULET | CAPULET |
|---|---|
| What! Why test them for that? | How! Canst thou try them so? |

| SERVANT | SERVANT |
|---|---|
| Because, sir, 'tis a bad cook who cannot lick his own fingers. Therefore, if he cannot lick his fingers, he will not be present. | Marry sir, 'tis an ill cook that cannot lick his own fingers; therefore he that cannot lick his fingers goes not with me. |

*Note: Taken from an old rhyme: "As the old cocke crowes so doeth the chick. A bad cooke that cannot his owne fingers lick." Meaning either his fingers were dirty or he did not like the taste of his own food.*

| OLD CAPULET | CAPULET |
|---|---|
| (*laughing*) Be gone with you! | Go, be gone. |

| OLD CAPULET (CONT'D) | CAPULET |
|---|---|
| We will be ill prepared at such short notice. Nurse, has my daughter gone to see Father Lawrence? | We shall be much unfurnished for this time. What, is my daughter gone to Friar Laurence? |

| NURSE | NURSE |
|---|---|
| Aye, absolutely. | Ay, forsooth. |

Note: Forsooth was another dated word used by nurse. The audience will have recognised it as an old-fashioned word, used in affected (pretentious) speech, such as someone trying to sound educated or posh who obviously wasn't. It means 'in truth' and is now only used ironically.

| OLD CAPULET | CAPULET |
|---|---|
| Well, with some luck he may talk some sense into her. The ungrateful, self-willed hussy she is. | Well, he may chance to do some good on her. A peevish self-willed harlotry it is. |

Note: Capulet refers to Juliet in a derogatory manner by calling her 'it'.

JULIET ENTERS LOOKING HAPPIER THAN EARLIER.

| NURSE | NURSE |
|---|---|
| Look, here she comes now from confession with a cheerful look. | See where she comes from shrift with merry look. |

| OLD CAPULET | CAPULET |
|---|---|
| (*mocking*) Well, here she is, my headstrong child! Where have you been wandering? | How now, my headstrong! Where have you been gadding? |

| JULIET | JULIET |
|---|---|
| A place where I have learnt to repent the sin of my disobedience to you and your orders, and I am persuaded by holy Father Laurence to fall to my knees and beg your forgiveness. | Where I have learnt me to repent the sin Of disobedient opposition To you and your behests; and am enjoined By holy Laurence to fall prostrate here, To beg your pardon. |

JULIET DROPS TO HER KNEES BEFORE HER FATHER.

| JULIET (CONT'D) | JULIET |
|---|---|
| Forgive me, father, I beg you! From this moment I will obey your every command. | Pardon, I beseech you! Henceforward I am ever ruled by you. |

OLD CAPULET IS OVERJOYED TO HEAR THIS.

| OLD CAPULET | CAPULET |
|---|---|
| Send for Count Paris! Go tell him the news. I will have this wedding knot tied up tomorrow morning! | Send for the County; go tell him of this. I'll have this knot knit up tomorrow morning. |

JULIET IS STUNNED, TAKEN COMPLETELY BY SURPRISE. SHE MANAGES TO
COMPOSE HERSELF TO AVOID SUSPICION AND BUY TIME TO THINK.

| JULIET | JULIET |
|---|---|
| I met the young Count at Father Laurence's quarters and gave him what love I thought befitting, without overstepping the bounds of decency. | I met the youthful lord at Laurence' cell, And gave him what becomed love I might, Not stepping o'er the bounds of modesty. |
| OLD CAPULET | CAPULET |
| I am glad to hear this. This is good news. Stand up child. | Why, I am glad on't; this is well. Stand up. |

OLD CAPULET HELPS JULIET TO HER FEET.

| OLD CAPULET (CONT'D) | CAPULET |
|---|---|
| This is as it should be. | This is as't should be. |

OLD CAPULET BECKONS TO A SERVANT.

| OLD CAPULET (CONT'D) | CAPULET |
|---|---|
| I must speak with the Count. Yes indeed. (to Servant) Go man, fetch him here. | Let me see the County; Ay, marry, go, I say, and fetch him hither. |

THE SERVANT LEAVES.

| OLD CAPULET (CONT'D) | CAPULET |
|---|---|
| (to his family) Before God, our whole city is much indebted to the holy Father. | Now, afore God, this reverend holy Friar, All our whole city is much bound to him. |

## Act IV Scene II – Capulet's House – Tuesday Evening

IF LADY CAPULET ENTERED AT THIS POINT IT WOULD MAKE HER SURPRISE MORE
UNDERSTANDABLE, AS SHE WOULD NOT HAVE HEARD HER HUSBAND'S
PREVIOUS WORDS ON CHANGING THE DAY OF THE WEDDING.

| | |
|---|---|
| **JULIET**<br>Nurse, will you come with me to my room, to help me choose something befitting to wear for tomorrow. | **JULIET**<br>Nurse, will you go with me into my closet, To help me sort such needful ornaments As you think fit to furnish me tomorrow? |
| **LADY CAPULET**<br>No, it's not till Thursday. There is plenty of time for that. | **LADY CAPULET**<br>No, not till Thursday; there is time enough. |
| **OLD CAPULET**<br>Go nurse, go with her. We're going to church tomorrow. | **CAPULET**<br>Go, Nurse, go with her. We'll to church tomorrow. |

JULIET EXITS WITH NURSE.

LADY CAPULET IS SHOCKED.

| | |
|---|---|
| **LADY CAPULET**<br>We will not be prepared in time, we'll be short of provisions, and it's almost night already. | **LADY CAPULET**<br>We shall be short in our provision; 'Tis now near night. |
| **OLD CAPULET**<br>Hush, I will get to it, everything will be ready, I assure you, my love. Go to Juliet, help dress her up in her finery. I will not go to bed tonight. Leave it to me. I will be housewife this once.<br>(*loud to servants*) Servants!<br>(*pauses and no reply*) They are all gone. Well, I'll walk to Count Paris myself and prepare him for tomorrow. My heart is wonderfully light since this wayward girl has seen sense. | **CAPULET**<br>Tush, I will stir about; And all things shall be well, I warrant thee, wife. Go thou to Juliet, help to deck up her. I'll not to bed tonight; let me alone; I'll play the housewife for this once. What ho! They are all forth; well, I will walk myself To County Paris to prepare up him Against tomorrow. My heart is wondrous light Since this same wayward girl is so reclaimed. |

*Note: 'Reclaimed' is another falconry term. To bring a bird back to obedience using whoops and whistles after it has been distracted.*

# ACT IV SCENE III

## JULIET'S BEDCHAMBER. TUESDAY NIGHT.

JULIET AND NURSE PREPARE CLOTHES IN JULIET'S BEDROOM FOR THE WEDDING
THE NEXT DAY. THE BED HAS CURTAINS AROUND IT - A FOUR POSTER BED.

**JULIET**

Yes, these clothes are best. But, kind Nurse, please leave me to myself tonight. I will need to say many prayers to move the heavens to smile on my predicament, which you know full well is unholy and sinful.

**JULIET**

Ay, those attires are best; but, gentle Nurse,
I pray thee leave me to myself tonight,
For I have need of many orisons
To move the heavens to smile upon my state,
Which, well thou know'st, is cross and full of sin.

*Note: Orisons are prayers. From the Latin 'orare', to pray.*

LADY CAPULET ENTERS THE ROOM.

**LADY CAPULET**

What, are you busy getting ready? Do you need my help?

**LADY CAPULET**

What, are you busy, ho? Need you my help?

**JULIET**

No, mother. We have already chosen what is best suited for the ceremony tomorrow. So please, let me be alone now, and let the Nurse sit up with you tonight, for I am sure you have your hands full with all this sudden upheaval.

**JULIET**

No, madam, we have culled such necessaries
As are behoveful for our state tomorrow.
So please you, let me now be left alone,
And let the Nurse this night sit up with you,
For I am sure you have your hands full all
In this so sudden business.

**LADY CAPULET**

Good night. Get to bed and rest.
(*bawdy*) You will need it.

**LADY CAPULET**

Good night;
Get thee to bed and rest, for thou hast need.

**JULIET**

Farewell!

**JULIET**

Farewell!

LADY CAPULET LEAVES, USHERING NURSE OUT OF THE ROOM.

JULIET (CONT'D)

(aside) God knows when we will meet again. I feel a cold shiver of fear running through my veins that almost freezes the life out of me. I'll call them back to comfort me.

(calls) Nurse!

JULIET

God knows when we shall meet again.
I have a faint cold fear thrills through my veins
That almost freezes up the heat of life;
I'll call them back again to comfort me.
Nurse!

JULIET PAUSES, WAITING FOR A REPLY. NONE COMES.

JULIET (CONT'D)

What good would she be here? For this dismal scene I must act alone.
The vial...

JULIET

What should she do here?
My dismal scene I needs must act alone.
Come, vial.

Note: Shakespeare writes, 'act alone'. He frequently uses stage and acting terms, he famously says 'all the world's a stage' in 'As You Like It'.

JULIET PRODUCES THE VIAL OF POTION FRIAR LAURENCE HAD GIVEN HER.

SHE HESITATES, HOLDING IT UP, LOOKING AT IT.

JULIET (CONT'D)

What if this mixture does not work at all? Will I be married tomorrow morning after all?

JULIET

What if this mixture do not work at all?
Shall I be married, then, tomorrow morning?

JULIET OPENS A DRAWER AND REMOVES A DAGGER FROM IT.

JULIET (CONT'D)

No, no! This dagger will prevent it. Lay down here beside me.

JULIET

No, no! This shall forbid it. Lie thou there.

JULIET PLACES THE DAGGER BESIDE THE BED.

JULIET (CONT'D)

What if it is poison that the Friar has deviously provided to kill me, in case he is dishonoured by this marriage because he had already married me to Romeo? I fear it is. And yet again, perhaps it is not, for he has always proven to be a devout holy man.

JULIET

What if it be a poison which the Friar
Subtly hath ministered to have me dead,
Lest in this marriage he should be dishonoured
Because he married me before to Romeo?
I fear it is. And yet methinks it should not,
For he hath still been tried a holy man.

JULIET RAISES THE POTION TO DRINK IT, THEN HESITATES.

| JULIET (CONT'D) | JULIET |
|---|---|
| What if I am laid out in the tomb, and I wake before Romeo arrives to save me? What a terrifying thought! Will I not be suffocated in the vault, whose foul mouth breathes in no fresh air, and die of asphyxiation before my Romeo comes? Or, if I live, what about the horrible thoughts of death and darkness together with the terror of the place? It is a mausoleum, an ancient receptacle filled with the bones of all my ancestors, buried there for many hundreds of years. Where bloody Tybalt, so recently dead, lies rotting in his shroud. The place where they say, at a certain hour of the night spirits walk abroad. | I will not entertain so bad a thought. How if, when I am laid into the tomb, I wake before the time that Romeo Come to redeem me? There's a fearful point! Shall I not then be stifled in the vault, To whose foul mouth no healthsome air breathes in, And there die strangled ere my Romeo comes? Or, if I live, is it not very like The horrible conceit of death and night, Together with the terror of the place - As in a vault, an ancient receptacle Where for this many hundred years the bones Of all my buried ancestors are packed; Where bloody Tybalt, yet but green in earth, Lies fest'ring in his shroud; where, as they say, At some hours in the night spirits resort - |
| Oh no, oh no, what if I wake too early? With the loathsome smells, and shrieks like mandrakes being torn from the earth, that upon hearing, living mortals are driven to madness – Oh, if I wake, shall I not be driven out of my mind, imprisoned with all these hideous terrors, and like a mad man play with my forefathers bones, and drag the mangled Tybalt from his shroud, and in this madness, use my grandfather's bone as a club and dash out my desperate brains? | Alack, alack, is it not like that I, So early waking -what with loathsome smells, And shrieks like mandrakes torn out of the earth, That living mortals, hearing them, run mad – O, if I wake, shall I not be distraught, Environed with all these hideous fears, And madly play with my forefathers' joints, And pluck the mangled Tybalt from his shroud, And, in this rage, with some great kinsman's bone, As with a club, dash out my desp'rate brains? |
| (*becoming hysterical*) Oh, look! I think I see Tybalt's ghost, searching for Romeo who impaled his body upon the point of his sword! Stop, Tybalt, stop! Oh, Romeo, Romeo, Romeo! Here is my drink, I drink it for you! | O look, methinks I see my cousin's ghost Seeking out Romeo that did spit his body Upon a rapier's point! Stay, Tybalt, stay! Romeo, Romeo, Romeo! Here's drink - I drink to thee! |

JULIET DRINKS THE POTION AND LAYS ON THE BED BEHIND ITS CLOSED CURTAINS.

# ACT IV  SCENE IV

## A HALL IN THE CAPULET HOUSEHOLD. LATE TUESDAY NIGHT.

SHAKESPEARE INCLUDED THIS SCENE TO ADD SOME LIGHT RELIEF TO FOLLOW THE PREVIOUS DRAMATIC SCENE AND ADD A TIME GAP.

THE STAFF HAVE BEEN ROUSED AND ARE ALL BUSY MAKING PREPARATIONS FOR THE UNEXPECTED BIG EVENT THE NEXT DAY.

A DISTANT BELL CHIMES THREE TIMES.

LADY CAPULET IS IN THE HALL WITH A LIST IN HER HAND LOOKING STRESSED. NURSE WALKS IN WITH A BASKET OF FRESHLY PICKED PRODUCE.

> Note: On stage, Juliet's bed would have been pushed to the back of the stage and left there, visible to the audience. The actors would come on and act out this scene as if the bed wasn't there. Then at the end of the scene they would all leave the stage, ready for Nurse to come on to wake Juliet.

**LADY CAPULET**
Nurse, wait. Take these keys and fetch more spices.

**NURSE**
They need these dates and quinces in the kitchen, m'lady.

LADY CAPULET
Hold, take these keys and fetch more spices, Nurse.

NURSE
They call for dates and quinces in the pastry.

OLD CAPULET ENTERS THE ROOM WEARING AN APRON TO PROTECT HIS CLOTHES. SOMETHING NEVER SEEN IN THE 16TH CENTURY ON A MAN.

**OLD CAPULET**
Come on, hurry, hurry, hurry! The second cock has crowed, the town bell has rung. It's three o'clock. Make sure there are plenty of meat pies, dear Angelica, and spare no cost.

CAPULET
Come, stir, stir, stir! The second cock hath crowed,
The curfew bell hath rung, 'tis three o'clock.
Look to the baked meats, good Angelica.
Spare not for cost.

> Note: If Nurse is Angelica (as is assumed), Old Capulet is in a very good mood. The day before he was calling her names for siding with Juliet. Perhaps that is why in her next line, Nurse is so open and candid to her master. Servants knew their place back then.
>
> A curfew bell was rung to cover over all fires in summer at 9pm not 3am. This allowed heat with no flame, preventing fire from unattended fireplaces in wood built houses. Seventy years later would be the Great Fire of London, 1666.

185

NURSE
Get out, you are meddling in woman's work. Go to bed! Goodness, you'll be ill tomorrow for staying up watching the night pass.

NURSE
Go, you cot-quean, go
Get you to bed. Faith, you'll be sick tomorrow
For this night's watching.

OLD CAPULET
No, not a bit. Why, I have watched a night through before now for a lesser cause, and never been ill.

CAPULET
No, not a whit. What, I have watched ere now
All night for lesser cause, and ne'er been sick.

LADY CAPULET
Yes, chasing young ladies in your day.

LADY CAPULET
Ay, you have been a mouse-hunt in your time;

---

LADY CAPULET STARTS TO LEAVE THE ROOM.

---

LADY CAPULET (CONT'D)
But now I watch you, to stop your watching.

LADY CAPULET
But I will watch you from such watching now.

---

OLD CAPULET CALLS AFTER HER.

---

OLD CAPULET
Jealous woman, a jealous wife!

CAPULET
A jealous-hood, a jealous-hood!

---

AS LADY CAPULET EXITS WITH NURSE, THREE SERVANTS ENTER CARRYING MEAT ON SPITS, LOGS AND BASKETS. THEY LOOK INCREDULOUS AT CAPULET'S APRON BUT SAY NOTHING, PRETENDING NOT TO NOTICE.

OLD CAPULET CALLS TO THE SERVANT WITH A BASKET.

---

OLD CAPULET (CONT'D)
Wait man, what have you there?

CAPULET
Now fellow, What is there?

PETER
Things for the cook, sir. I don't know what though.

1ST SERVANT
Things for the cook, sir, but I know not what.

OLD CAPULET
Well hurry, man, hurry!

CAPULET
Make haste, make haste.

---

THE SERVANT LEAVES.

OLD CAPULET TURNS HIS ATTENTION ON THE SERVANT CARRYING LOGS.

---

OLD CAPULET (CONT'D)
And you man, fetch drier logs. Call Peter, he'll show you where they are.

CAPULET
Sirrah, fetch drier logs.
Call Peter, he will show thee where they are.

#### 2ND SERVANT

My wooden head will lead me to the logs, sir, and save troubling Peter.

#### OLD CAPULET

Ha ha, well said. A comic bastard, ha ha. So you are a blockhead.

#### 2ND SERVANT

I have a head, sir, that will find out logs,
And never trouble Peter for the matter.

#### CAPULET

Mass, and well said; a merry whoreson, ha!
Thou shalt be loggerhead.

THE SERVANTS LEAVE. CAPULET NOTICES THAT IT IS NOW GETTING LIGHT.

> *Note: In England during summer it gets light around 4am, but not in Italy. Shakespeare was writing for an English audience most of whom would never travel abroad.*

#### OLD CAPULET (CONT'D)

Good grief! It's day. Count Paris will be arriving at any moment with his musicians, or so he said.

#### CAPULET

Good faith, 'tis day!
The County will be here with music straight,
For so he said he would.

THE SOUND OF MUSICIANS CAN BE HEARD IN THE DISTANCE.

OLD CAPULET HEARS IT AND PANICS.

#### OLD CAPULET (CONT'D)

I hear him coming. Nurse! Wife! Where are you? Nurse! Quickly!

#### CAPULET

I hear him near.
Nurse! Wife! What ho! What, Nurse, I say!

NURSE ENTERS IN A RUSH, BEFORE SHE CAN SPEAK, OLD CAPULET BARKS OUT HIS ORDERS.

#### OLD CAPULET (CONT'D)

Go and wake Juliet. Go dress her in her finery. I'll go and talk with Paris. Quickly, hurry, hurry! The bridegroom is here already. Hurry, I say.

#### CAPULET

Go waken Juliet, go and trim her up;
I'll go and chat with Paris. Hie, make haste,
Make haste; the bridegroom he is come already.
Make haste, I say.

# ACT IV  SCENE V

## JULIET'S BEDCHAMBER. WEDNESDAY MORNING.

JULIET IS LYING ON HER BED BEHIND CLOSED CURTAINS.

NURSE KNOCKS ON THE DOOR TO JULIET'S BEDCHAMBER AND CALLS TO
ROUSE JULIET FOR HER WEDDING.

| NURSE | NURSE |
|---|---|
| Mistress!... Young Miss!... Juliet!... Fast asleep I'll bet. | Mistress! What, mistress! Juliet! Fast, I warrant her, she. |

THE NURSE ENTERS THE ROOM AND BUSTLES ABOUT.

THE CURTAINS AROUND THE BED ARE STILL CLOSED.

| NURSE (CONT'D) | NURSE |
|---|---|
| Come on lamb! My Lady! Goodness me, you lazybones! Wake up, love! Madam! Sweetheart! Come on, bride! What, not a word? Getting your full pennyworth of sleep now, eh? Sleep for a week then... (*bawdy*) for tonight, I warrant, Count Paris, is <u>set up</u> for the night and you shall get little rest. God forgive me; the things I say! | Why, lamb! Why, lady! Fie, you slug-a-bed! Why, love, I say! Madam! Sweetheart! Why, bride! What, not a word? You take your pennyworths now, Sleep for a week; for the next night, I warrant, The County Paris hath set up his rest That you shall rest but little. God forgive me! |

NURSE CHUCKLES AND CROSSES HERSELF.

---

Note: 'Set up his rest' was a term used in an Italian card game called Primero, which became very popular in 16th Century England. It was played for money, the closest game these days being poker. To 'set up your rest' was to make a final wager which, if lost, would put you out of the game. It does not translate well, especially the wordplay on 'rest'. It is like saying 'all in' in poker.

---

| NURSE (CONT'D) | NURSE |
|---|---|
| Heavens above! How sound asleep she is! I must wake her. | Marry, and amen. How sound is she asleep! I needs must wake her. |

NURSE CALLS MORE URGENTLY.

NURSE (CONT'D)
Madam... Madam... Madam!
That's right, let the Count catch you in bed, <u>he'll wake you up with a surprise all right!</u> Is that not so?

NURSE
Madam, madam, madam!
Ay, let the County take you in your bed;
He'll fright you up, i'faith. Will it not be?

> Note: "Will it not be?' is ambiguous, it could mean, 'is that not so?', or it could mean, 'will you not wake up?'.

NURSE OPENS THE CURTAINS AROUND THE BED.

JULIET LIES ON THE BED FULLY CLOTHED BUT APPEARS TO BE STILL ASLEEP.

NURSE (CONT'D)
What, you are dressed? Did you lay down and fall asleep in your clothes? I must wake you.

NURSE
What, dressed, and in your clothes, and down again!
I must needs wake you.

NURSE BECOMES CONCERNED, CALLING LOUDER AND TRYING TO SHAKE JULIET AWAKE.

NURSE (CONT'D)
Lady! Lady! Lady!

NURSE
Lady! Lady! Lady!

NURSE FEARS THE WORST AND CALLS OUT FOR HELP IN A PANIC.

NURSE (CONT'D)
Oh no! Help, help! My lady's dead! Oh, rue the day I was born!
Some brandy! Help! My lord! My lady!

NURSE
Alas, alas! Help, help, my lady's dead!
O welladay that ever I was born!
Some aqua-vitae, ho! My lord! My lady!

LADY CAPULET RUSHES IN.

LADY CAPULET
What is all the noise!

LADY CAPULET
What noise is here?

NURSE
Oh, mournful day!

NURSE
O lamentable day!

LADY CAPULET
Whatever's the matter?

LADY CAPULET
What is the matter?

NURSE
Look, look! Oh, tragic day!

NURSE
Look, look! O heavy day!

---

LADY CAPULET SEES JULIET'S LIFELESS BODY.

**LADY CAPULET**
Oh no, oh no! My child, my only life! Wake up, look at me, or I will die with you! Help, help! Call for help!

**LADY CAPULET**
O me, O me! My child, my only life, Revive, look up, or I will die with thee! Help, help! Call help!

---

OLD CAPULET RUSHES IN AT THE COMMOTION AND SEES JULIET LYING FULLY CLOTHED ON HER BED AND ASSUMES SHE IS EITHER ASLEEP OR BEING A TYPICALLY AWKWARD TEENAGER.

---

**OLD CAPULET**
This is shameful, get Juliet up. Her bridegroom is here.

**CAPULET**
For shame, bring Juliet forth; her lord is come.

**NURSE**
She's dead, deceased. She's dead, rue the day!

**NURSE**
She's dead, deceased. She's dead, alack the day!

**LADY CAPULET**
Rue the day! She's dead. she's dead, she's dead!

**LADY CAPULET**
Alack the day! She's dead, she's dead, she's dead!

**OLD CAPULET**
Ha! Let me see her...

**CAPULET**
Ha, let me see her.

---

OLD CAPULET THINKS THEY ARE OVER-REACTING AND CHECKS JULIET.

---

**OLD CAPULET (CONT'D)**
Oh God! She's cold... there's no pulse... and her limbs are stiff. Life and these lips are long parted. Death lies on her, like an untimely frost upon the sweetest flower in the field.

**CAPULET**
Out, alas, she's cold!
Her blood is settled and her joints are stiff;
Life and these lips have long been separated.
Death lies on her like an untimely frost
Upon the sweetest flower of all the field.

**NURSE**
Oh, tragic day!

**NURSE**
O lamentable day!

**LADY CAPULET**
Oh, pitiful time!

**LADY CAPULET**
O woeful time!

---

THE SOUND OF MINSTRELS PLAYING MUSIC CAN BE HEARD APPROACHING IN THE DISTANCE.

---

OLD CAPULET

Death has taken her away to make me wail, tying up my tongue, I cannot speak.

CAPULET

Death, that hath ta'en her hence to make me wail,
Ties up my tongue and will not let me speak.

> Note: Despite Old Capulet saying he is speechless he has a lot more to say.

FRIAR LAURENCE ENTERS THE ROOM. HE HAD OF COURSE BEEN EXPECTING THIS TO HAPPEN, THOUGH HE CARRIES OUT THE PRETENCE OF IGNORANCE. THE FRIAR IS ACCOMPANIED BY COUNT PARIS AND MUSICIANS.

FRIAR LAURENCE

Come, is the bride ready to go to church?

FRIAR LAURENCE

Come, is the bride ready to go to church?

OLD CAPULET

Ready to go, but never to return, Father. (*to Paris*) Oh, my son, Paris, the night before your wedding day and death has lain with your wife. There she lies, the flower she was, deflowered by him. Death is my son-in-law, death is my heir. He has married my daughter. I will die and leave him everything. My life's belongings, all belong to death.

CAPULET

Ready to go, but never to return.
O son, the night before thy wedding day
Hath death lain with thy wife. There she lies,
Flower as she was, deflowered by him.
Death is my son-in-law, death is my heir;
My daughter he hath wedded. I will die,
And leave him all. Life, living, all is death's.

> Note: 'Deflowered' – lost her virginity.  Death has taken her virginity, not her husband. 'Lain with your wife' is a euphemism for having sex with your wife. He will leave his possessions to death because Juliet is his only heir.

COUNT PARIS

I have been so longing to see this morning, and then it brings me a sight like this?

PARIS

Have I thought long to see this morning's face,
And doth it give me such a sight as this?

LADY CAPULET

Accursed, unhappy, wretched, hateful day! The most miserable hour that time ever saw in the eternal toil of his endeavours! Just one, poor one, one poor loving child. Just one thing to give me happiness and delight, and cruel death has snatched it from me!

LADY CAPULET

Accursed, unhappy, wretched, hateful day!
Most miserable hour that e'er time saw
In lasting labour of his pilgrimage!
But one, poor one, one poor and loving child,
But one thing to rejoice and solace in,
And cruel death hath catched it from my sight!

LADY CAPULET WAS OVERLY DRAMATIC, NOW EVERYONE FOLLOWS SUIT. THIS ABSURD SHOW OF GRIEF WAS INCLUDED FOR COMIC EFFECT BECAUSE THE AUDIENCE KNOWS JULIET IS NOT DEAD.

### NURSE

Oh, misery! Oh, wretched, wretched, wretched day! Most sorrowful day! The most miserable day that I have ever, ever known! Oh, what a day, what a day, what a day! Oh, hateful day! Never was there such a black day as this! Oh, woeful day, oh, woeful day!

### COUNT PARIS

Cheated, divorced, wronged, spited, slain! Death at his most detestable has cheated me. By cruel, cruel death I am undone! Oh, my love! Oh, my life! - No longer my love in life, but my love in death!

### OLD CAPULET

Insulted, afflicted, hated, martyred, killed! Merciless time, why did you choose now to murder, to murder our celebration? Oh, child, oh, child! A part of me, but now my parted child. You are dead - alas, my child is dead, and with my child my happiness is buried!

---

### NURSE

O woe! O woeful, woeful, woeful day. Most lamentable day, most woeful day That ever, ever, I did yet behold! O day! O day! O day! O hateful day! Never was seen so black a day as this! O woeful day, O woeful day!

### PARIS

Beguiled, divorced, wronged, spited, slain! Most detestable death, by thee beguiled, By cruel cruel thee quite overthrown! O love! O life! - not life, but love in death!

### CAPULET

Despised, distressed, hated, martyred, killed! Uncomfortable time, why cam'st thou now To murder, murder our solemnity? O child, O child! - my soul and not my child! Dead art thou - alack, my child is dead, And with my child my joys are buried.

---

FRIAR LAURENCE STEPS IN AS THE VOICE OF REASON.

---

### FRIAR LAURENCE

Peace! Stop this shameful talk! The cure to this chaos lies not in these chaotic outbursts! Heaven and yourselves shared a part in creating this beautiful young girl, now heaven has all of her. Both heaven and Juliet are the better for it. Your part in her, her body, you could not keep from death, but heaven keeps its part, her soul, in eternal life. Your greatest desire was to better her through marriage: to advance her was your idea of heaven. And now you weep, upon seeing she *is* advanced above the clouds, as high as heaven itself?

### FRIAR LAURENCE

Peace, ho, for shame! Confusion's cure lives not In these confusions. Heaven and yourself Had part in this fair maid; now heaven hath all, And all the better is it for the maid. Your part in her you could not keep from death, But heaven keeps his part in eternal life. The most you sought was her promotion, For 'twas your heaven she should be advanced; And weep ye now, seeing she is advanced Above the clouds, as high as heaven itself?

---

FRIAR LAURENCE HAS TURNED THE SITUATION AROUND TO MAKE THEM ALL
FEEL GUILTY FOR JULIET'S DEATH AND FOR THEIR BEHAVIOUR.

FRIAR LAURENCE (CONT'D)

*Oh, you love your child poorly, this must cease,*
*You act like madmen, seeing she's at peace.*
*She's not well married that lives married long,*
*But she's best married that dies married*
*young.*

FRIAR LAURENCE

*O, in this love you love your child so ill*
*That you run mad, seeing that she is well.*
*She's not well married that lives married long,*
*But she's best married that dies married young.*

---

FRIAR LAURENCE IS NERVOUSLY AWARE OF THE PREDICAMENT HE HAS
PLACED JULIET IN. HE HURRIES THEM UP.

---

FRIAR LAURENCE (CONT'D)

Now, dry your tears. Put your bouquets of rosemary on this sweet body, and, as is customary, dress her in her finery and carry her to the church.
*For though our foolish nature bids us woe,*
*Our tears should be for joy and not sorrow.*

FRIAR LAURENCE

Dry up your tears, and stick your rosemary
On this fair corse, and, as the custom is,
All in her best array bear her to church;
*For though fond nature bids us all lament,*
*Yet nature's tears are reason's merriment.*

> Note: Rosemary herb is for remembrance, common in funerals. Friar Laurence tells them their tears should be tears of joy as Juliet is now in Heaven with God.

OLD CAPULET

All the festive items we prepared for a happy marriage must now be used for a sad funeral. Our musicians will be the mournful church bells, our wedding banquet now a sad burial feast, our solemn hymns now sullen dirges, our bridal bouquets now wreaths for a buried corpse. Everything has been turned upside down.

CAPULET

All things that we ordained festival
Turn from their office to black funeral:
Our instruments to melancholy bells,
Our wedding cheer to a sad burial feast,
Our solemn hymns to sullen dirges change,
Our bridal flowers serve for a buried corse,
And all things change them to the contrary.

FRIAR LAURENCE

Sir, go and get ready, and Madam, go with him. And Count Paris, sir, you go too. Everyone prepare to follow this innocent, sweet corpse to her grave.
*The heavens frown upon you for your sin,*
*Anger them no more with acts against them.*

FRIAR LAURENCE

Sir, go you in; and, madam, go with him;
And go, Sir Paris. Everyone prepare
To follow this fair corse unto her grave.
*The heavens do lour upon you for some ill;*
*Move them no more by crossing their high will.*

> Note: This is the second time 'Lour' has been used in the play. It means a frown on a person, or a dark and threatening look to a sky. It's similar to the word 'glower' which is more common in usage today.

THEY PLACE FLOWERS ON JULIET'S BODY AND CLOSE THE BED CURTAINS.

THEY ALL FILE OUT EXCEPT NURSE AND THE MUSICIANS.

1ST MUSICIAN
Goodness, we should pack up our instruments and leave.

NURSE
My good, honest fellows, yes, pack up, pack up! You can see this is a pitiful case.

1ST MUSICIAN
Faith, we may put up our pipes and be gone.

NURSE
Honest good fellows, ah, put up, put up; For well you know this is a pitiful case.

NURSE LEAVES THE ROOM, SOBBING.

THE SECOND MUSICIAN POINTS TO HIS DELAPIDATED INSTRUMENT CASE.

1ST MUSICIAN
Yes, by my soul, this 'case' does need amending.

1ST MUSICIAN
Ay, by my troth, the case may be amended.

THE HEAD SERVANT, PETER (CLOWN), ENTERS THE ROOM.

PETER
Musicians, oh musicians, play 'Heart's Ease'. 'Heart's Ease'! Oh, to give me the will to live, play 'Heart's Ease'.

1ST MUSICIAN
Why 'Heart's Ease'?

PETER
Musicians, O musicians, `Heart's ease', `Heart's ease'! O, an you will have me live, play `Heart's ease'.

1ST MUSICIAN
Why `Heart's ease'?

Note: 'Heart's Ease' was a jolly ballad, entirely inappropriate for a funeral.

PETER
Oh musicians, because the very heart of me is playing 'Heavy Heart'. Oh, play me a cheerful dirge to comfort me.

PETER
O musicians, because my heart itself plays `My heart is full of woe'. O, play me some merry dump to comfort me.

Note: Cheerful and dirge are two complete opposites in music, happy and sad.

1ST MUSICIAN
Not a dirge, not us! This is no time to play.

PETER
You will not then?

1ST MUSICIAN
No.

1ST MUSICIAN
Not a dump, we. 'Tis no time to play now.

PETER
You will not then?

1ST MUSICIAN
No.

PETER
Then I will pay you soundly.

1ST MUSICIAN
What will you pay us?

PETER
Not money, upon my word, but an insult, you useless busker.

PETER
I will then give it you soundly.

1ST MUSICIAN
What will you give us?

PETER
No money, on my faith, but the gleek. I will give you the minstrel.

PETER MAKES A RUDE GESTURE. THE 1ST MUSICIAN IS TAKEN ABACK.

*Note: Gleek was a jesting insult and also a popular card game in Shakespeare's time. Calling a musician a minstrel was a deliberate insult, no more than a street busker. In return the Musician reminds Peter he is a mere servant.*

1ST MUSICIAN
And you are the servant from hell.

1ST MUSICIAN
Then will I give you the serving-creature.

PETER PULLS OUT A DAGGER.

PETER
Then I will lay the 'servant from hell's' dagger about your head. I will bear no crotchety behaviour, I'll 'doh' you, I'll 're' you, do you note 'me'?

PETER
Then will I lay the serving-creature's dagger on your pate. I will carry no crotchets. I'll re you, I'll fa you, do you note me?

*Note: To lay a dagger on your pate is like pistol whipping someone instead of shooting them. It suggests they are not worthy of fighting or killing – or in this case, stabbing.*

*As he says 're you' he imitates knocking a man about one side of the head with his dagger, as he says 'fa you', the other side.*

*Crotchet is a musical note, crotchety means irritable. Doh, re, and me are pitches of musical notes, used in the translation as they are more familiar to us in this pattern. 'Note me' puns on a musical note and taking notice, paying attention.*

*Important note: Shakespeare often introduces characters irrelevant to the plot as comedic interludes, to contrast the drama that has gone before. He doesn't have them tell jokes (though often a comedic actor would introduce his own topical jokes between lines). He instead has them use wordplay and innuendo - to show off his writing ability as much as to amuse the audience. As was once said, if Shakespeare had intended us to laugh he would have written a joke. He didn't. Notable interludes in Shakespeare's works include the musicians after Juliet's false death, the grave diggers in Hamlet, the Porter in Macbeth, and the Clown in Othello. Peter was originally played by the famous comedian of the time, Will Kemp.*

| | |
|---|---|
| **1ST MUSICIAN**<br>If you 'doh - re - me' us, then *you* note *us*! | 1ST MUSICIAN<br>An you re us and fa us, you note us. |
| **2ND MUSICIAN**<br>Pray sir, put away your dagger and show some wits. | 2ND MUSICIAN<br>Pray you, put up your dagger and put out your wit. |

PETER BRANDISHES HIS DAGGER ANGRILY.

| | |
|---|---|
| PETER<br>You shall see my wit! I will pummel you with an iron wit, before I put away my iron dagger. Answer me this then, like men. | PETER<br>Then have at you with my wit! I will dry-beat you with an iron wit, and put up my iron dagger. Answer me like men. |

PETER RECITES A RHYME.

| | |
|---|---|
| PETER (CONT'D)<br>*'When woeful grief, the heart does wound,*<br>*And sadness dire, the mind oppress,*<br>*Then music with her silver sound'* –<br>(*he stops the rhyme*) Why 'silver sound'? Why 'music with her silver sound'? | PETER<br>*"When griping griefs the heart doth wound,*<br>*And doleful dumps the mind oppress,*<br>*Then music with her silver sound"* –<br>Why `silver sound'? Why `music with her silver sound'? |

PETER SNEERS AT THE MUSICIANS.

| | |
|---|---|
| PETER<br>What do you think, Simon **'Catgut'**? | PETER<br>What say you, Simon Catling? |

*Note: Catgut refers to the material violin strings were made of, i.e. intestines of sheep, known as 'catgut'. Catling was a small lute with catgut strings, and also another name for the catgut string itself.*

| | |
|---|---|
| **1ST MUSICIAN**<br>Perhaps, sir, because silver has a sweet sound. | 1ST MUSICIAN<br>Marry, sir, because silver hath a sweet sound. |
| PETER<br>Clever. What do you think Hugh **'Fiddler'**? | PETER<br>Prates. What say you, Hugh Rebeck? |

*Note: Rebec is an ancient fiddle (violin) with three strings.*

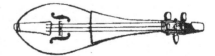

### 2ND MUSICIAN

I'd say 'silver sound' because musicians make sound for silver.

### 2ND MUSICIAN

I say `silver sound' because musicians sound for silver.

> Note: 'For silver' – for money. An old term still in use today is 'cross my palm with silver', meaning put a silver coin in my hand, as opposed to a cheaper copper coin or a more expensive gold coin.

### PETER

Clever too! What do you think James **'Plucker'**?

### PETER

Prates too. What say you, James Soundpost?

> Note: A sound post is a wooden post inside the body of a stringed instrument which serves as a structural support that also transfers sound from the top plate to the back plate altering the tone of the instrument by changing the vibrational modes of the plates. The sound post is sometimes referred to as the âme, a French word meaning "soul". It is not commonly known so 'plucker' was used.

### 3RD MUSICIAN

Streuth, I don't know what to say.

### 3RD MUSICIAN

Faith, I know not what to say.

### PETER

Oh, I beg your pardon! You're the singer aren't you? Then I will sing it for you. It is *'music with her silver sound'* because musicians get no gold for making a sound.

### PETER

O, I cry you mercy, you are the singer. I will say for you. It is `music with her silver sound' because musicians have no gold for sounding.

---

PETER SINGS AS HE LEAVES THE ROOM.

---

### PETER (CONT'D)

*'Then music with her silver sound*
*With speedy help does lend redress'.*

### PETER

*"Then music with her silver sound*
*With speedy help doth lend redress."*

---

EXIT PETER.

---

### 1ST MUSICIAN

What an insolent man that servant is!

### 1ST MUSICIAN

What a pestilent knave is this same!

### 2ND MUSICIAN

Hang him, the moron! Come, we'll wait in here for the mourners, and some dinner.

### 2ND MUSICIAN

Hang him, Jack! Come, we'll in here tarry for the mourners, and stay dinner.

*Note: They'll wait so they can be paid for playing for a funeral, instead of a wedding, and get fed along with it. Dinner is the main meal of the day, in England it was often a midday meal followed by afternoon tea and evening supper, though it is now generally called lunch (short for luncheon) if taken midday. Although much relaxed now, once the meal routine in England was, breakfast first thing, a morning break for 'elevenses' at eleven am, dinner at midday, afternoon tea at three, high tea at six, then a light supper later in the evening. Musicians famously 'sang for their supper'.*

*Trivia: 'Jack' was a name often used derogatorily (as nurse did earlier in Act II Scene IV) and another term for a knave (as it also is in playing cards). It was derived from the name 'John' but came to be a general term for any man, e.g. Jack of all trades, lumberjack, steeplejack, I'm alright, Jack, etc. It is common in other languages too, we get the word 'Zany' from the same source. In 16th Century Italian theatre, the servants acting as clowns in the Commedia Dell'arte were typically called 'Zani', a common shortened term for Giovanni (Italian for John).*

# ACT V

A TRAGIC END TO A TRAGIC TALE

# ACT V

## ACT V SCENE I

### A STREET IN MANTUA. LATE WEDNESDAY.

NEXT DAY IN MANTUA, ROMEO IS UNAWARE OF RECENT EVENTS.

ROMEO

If I am to believe my dream, even though it seems too good to be true, good news is at hand. My heart sits lightly in my chest, and all day an unaccustomed spirit lifts me above the ground so cheerful are my thoughts.

I dreamt my lady came and found me dead - a strange dream, that allows a dead man to think! - and she breathed so much life into me with kisses on my lips that I was revived and felt like an Emperor.

Oh yes! How sweet love must be when possessed, if dreams of love are so rich in joy!

ROMEO

If I may trust the flattering truth of sleep,
My dreams presage some joyful news at hand.
My bosom's lord sits lightly in his throne,
And all this day an unaccustomed spirit
Lifts me above the ground with cheerful
   thoughts.
I dreamt my lady came and found me dead -
Strange dream that gives a dead man leave to
   think! -
And breathed such life with kisses in my lips
That I revived, and was an emperor.
Ah me, how sweet is love itself possessed,
When but love's shadows are so rich in joy!

> Note: 'Flattering truth' has led to many arguments into the contradiction in terms of truth and dreaming. The earliest publication of Romeo – known to be inaccurate – has 'flattering eye' which some editions adopt as it makes more sense. This line links to Romeo saying in Act II, Scene II, "I am afraid, being in night, all this is but a dream, too flattering sweet to be substantial".

BALTHASAR, ROMEO'S SERVING MAN, ARRIVES AT SPEED.

ROMEO (CONT'D)

News from Verona! How are things, Balthasar? Have you brought me a letter from Father Laurence? How is my mother? Is my father well? How is my Juliet? I'll ask that again, for everything is well if she is well.

ROMEO

News from Verona! How now, Balthasar,
Dost thou not bring me letters from the Friar?
How doth my lady? Is my father well?
How doth my Juliet? That I ask again,
For nothing can be ill if she be well.

BALTHASAR

Then she is well, and everything is well. Her body lies in the Capulet burial vault, and her immortal soul now lives with the angels. I saw her laid to rest in her family's tomb and immediately took a swift horse to tell you.

BALTHASAR

Then she is well, and nothing can be ill. Her body sleeps in Capels' monument, And her immortal part with angels lives. I saw her laid low in her kindred's vault, And presently took post to tell it you.

> Note: 'Post horse' was the swiftest horse, used for delivering mail. Fast horses were kept at staging 'posts' to be exchanged for an exhausted one.
>
> "Capels' monument" is taken direct from Brooke's poem where Capel and Capulet were both used to refer to the Capulets.

ROMEO LOOKS STUNNED.

BALTHASAR (CONT'D)

Oh, pardon me for bringing such bad news, sir, but you left me the duty of keeping you informed.

BALTHASAR

O, pardon me for bringing these ill news, Since you did leave it for my office, sir.

ROMEO

Can it really be so?

ROMEO

Is it e'en so?

ROMEO LOOKS UP TO THE HEAVENS AND SPEAKS ANGRILY.

ROMEO (CONT'D)

Then I defy you, fate!

ROMEO

Then I defy you, stars!

> Note: Some versions had "deny you". Both mean he refuses to believe in fate or what is written in the stars anymore, he will be master of his own destiny.

ROMEO TURNS TO HIS MAN.

ROMEO (CONT'D)

You know where I am staying, get me pen and paper and hire fast horses. I will leave tonight.

ROMEO

Thou knowest my lodging. Get me ink and paper, And hire posthorses; I will hence tonight.

> Note: Post horses were specially chosen for their speed, strength and stamina for delivering mail. From this we get the phrase 'post-haste', meaning with great speed, the word then being written on urgent letters.

**BALTHASAR**

I beg you, sir, have patience. You look pale and upset. I fear some wild actions on your part.

**ROMEO**

Tush! Your fears are mistaken. Leave me and do what I asked of you. Have you no letter for me from Father Laurence?

**BALTHASAR**

No, my good lord.

**ROMEO**

No matter. Now go and hire those horses. I'll be with you shortly.

**BALTHASAR**

I do beseech you, sir, have patience;
Your looks are pale and wild and do import
Some misadventure.

**ROMEO**

Tush, thou art deceived.
Leave me, and do the thing I bid thee do.
Hast thou no letters to me from the Friar?

**BALTHASAR**

No, my good lord.

**ROMEO**

No matter. Get thee gone,
And hire those horses. I'll be with thee straight.

---

BALTHASAR LEAVES HURRIEDLY.

---

**ROMEO (CONT'D)**

(*aside*) Well, Juliet, I will <u>lie with you</u> tonight. I must think of a way. Oh, how swiftly dark deeds enter the thoughts of desperate men!

**ROMEO**

Well, Juliet, I will lie with thee tonight.
Let's see for means. O mischief, thou art swift
To enter in the thoughts of desperate men!

> Note: 'Lie with' meant have sex with, which added emphasis to the fact he could never lie with her in that way again, only in death.

---

ROMEO COMES UP WITH AN IDEA.

---

**ROMEO (CONT'D)**

I remember a chemist who lives around here, I noticed him earlier. A scruffy man, with large eyebrows, collecting herbs for his medicines.

**ROMEO**

I do remember an apothecary,
And hereabouts a' dwells, which late I noted
In tattered weeds, with overwhelming brows,
Culling of simples.

---

ROMEO STARTS WALKING DETERMINEDLY.

---

ROMEO (CONT'D)

A poor looking man, his miserable existence had worn him down to skin and bones. In his bare shop, hung a tortoise shell, a stuffed alligator, and the dried skins of deformed fish. On the shelves a wretched collection of empty boxes, green earthenware pots, bottles, musty plant seeds, bits of old twine, and old perfumed rose petal cakes, thinly scattered to make some form of a display. Seeing this poverty, I thought to myself; 'If ever a man needed a poison in a hurry, here is a wretched creature who would sell it to him', even though the sale of it carries the death sentence in Mantua. Oh, this very thought anticipated my need, and this needy man must sell it to me.

ROMEO

Meagre were his looks,
Sharp misery had worn him to the bones,
And in his needy shop a tortoise hung,
An alligator stuffed, and other skins
Of ill-shaped fishes; and about his shelves
A beggarly account of empty boxes,
Green earthen pots, bladders, and musty seeds,
Remnants of packthread, and old cakes of roses,
Were thinly scattered to make up a show.
Noting this penury, to myself I said
'An if a man did need a poison now,
Whose sale is present death in Mantua,
Here lives a caitiff wretch would sell it him'.
O, this same thought did but forerun my need,
And this same needy man must sell it me.

> Note: Caitiff means cowardly, despicable. Weeds are clothes.

ROMEO REACHES THE APOTHECARY.

ROMEO (CONT'D)

As I remember, this should be the house.

ROMEO

As I remember, this should be the house.

ROMEO FINDS IT IS CLOSED.

ROMEO (CONT'D)

Being a holiday, the poor man's shop is shut.

ROMEO

Being holiday, the beggar's shop is shut.

ROMEO KNOCKS ON THE DOOR AND CALLS LOUDLY.

ROMEO (CONT'D)

Hello! Chemist!

ROMEO

What ho! Apothecary!

FINALLY THE APOTHECARY RESPONDS FROM INSIDE THE SHOP.

APOTHECARY

(off) Who calls so loudly?

APOTHECARY

Who calls so loud?

ROMEO

Come here, man.

ROMEO

Come hither, man.

THE APOTHECARY COMES TO THE DOOR.

ROMEO (CONT'D)
I can see you are a poor man. Here...

ROMEO
I see that thou art poor.

ROMEO PRODUCES A BAG OF COINS AND SHOWS THE MAN.

ROMEO (CONT'D)
... here are forty gold coins. Let me have a measure of poison, a fast acting one that will travel quickly through the veins so a life-weary taker will fall down dead and the body be expelled of breath as violently and speedily as the powder fired from the bowels of a canon.

ROMEO
Hold, there is forty ducats; let me have
A dram of poison, such soon-speeding gear
As will disperse itself through all the veins,
That the life-weary taker may fall dead,
And that the trunk may be discharged of breath
As violently as hasty powder fired
Doth hurry from the fatal cannon's womb.

> Note: Ducats were gold coins common across Europe to be used as universal currency. Each country had their own design(s) but the value was the same and each would bear the inscription 'Sit tibi, Christe, datus Quem tu regis iste Ducatus', meaning, 'Lord, let this duchy, which you rule, be dedicated to you'.
>
> A dram was a small measure of liquid, now only used in reference to Scottish whisky, 'A wee dram of whisky'. It was one eighth of a fluid ounce or 3.5ml.

APOTHECARY
Such deadly drugs I do have. But Mantua's law is the death penalty to any man who sells them.

APOTHECARY
Such mortal drugs I have, but Mantua's law
Is death to any he that utters them.

> Note: 'Utters' here does not mean 'speaks', it means to put out.

ROMEO
Your life is so bare and wretched, and yet you fear death? Starvation shows in your face, need and hunger show in your eyes. The contempt of the world and the hardships of begging hang heavy on your back. The world is not your friend, nor is the world's law. The world has no law to make you rich, so don't be poor, overcome it and take this money.

ROMEO
Art thou so bare and full of wretchedness,
And fear'st to die? Famine is in thy cheeks,
Need and oppression starveth in thy eyes,
Contempt and beggary hangs upon thy back,
The world is not thy friend, nor the world's law.
The world affords no law to make thee rich;
Then be not poor, but break it, and take this.

ROMEO JIGGLES THE MONEY BAG.

APOTHECARY

My poverty, not my conscience, accepts.

ROMEO

I pay your poverty, not your conscience.

APOTHECARY

My poverty, but not my will, consents.

ROMEO

I pay thy poverty and not thy will.

THE APOTHECARY GOES INTO THE SHOP FOR A WHILE MIXING THE
REQUIRED POTION, THEN RETURNS TO THE DOOR, LOOKING UP AND DOWN
THE STREET, HE REPLIES SURREPTITIOUSLY.

APOTHECARY

Mix this with any other liquid and drink it. It is strong enough to 'dispatch' twenty men instantly.

APOTHECARY

Put this in any liquid thing you will,
And drink it off, and if you had the strength
Of twenty men it would dispatch you straight.

Note: He uses 'dispatch' as a euphemism for 'kill'.

ROMEO

Here is your gold - a worse poison to men's souls, responsible for more murder in this loathsome world than these mixtures you are forbidden to sell. I sell you poison. You have sold me none.

ROMEO

There is thy gold, worse poison to men's souls,
Doing more murder in this loathsome world
Than these poor compounds that thou mayst not sell.
I sell thee poison, thou hast sold me none.

ROMEO AND THE APOTHECARY EXCHANGE GOODS.

ROMEO (CONT'D)

Farewell, buy food, and put some flesh on your bones.

ROMEO

Farewell, buy food, and get thyself in the flesh.

ROMEO LOOKS AT THE VIAL GIVEN TO HIM.

ROMEO (CONT'D)

*(aside) Come tonic, not poison,  and go with*
*    me*
*To Juliet's grave, for there I must use thee.*

ROMEO

*Come cordial, and not poison, go with me*
*To Juliet's grave, for there must I use thee.*

ROMEO TURNS AND LEAVES.

THE APOTHECARY WATCHES HIM WALK AWAY.

# ACT V SCENE II

## FRIAR LAURENCE'S QUARTERS. LATER WEDNESDAY.

FRIAR LAURENCE IS IN HIS QUARTERS.

FRIAR JOHN RUSHES IN.

**FRIAR JOHN**
Holy Franciscan Father, Brother Laurence, hello!

**FRIAR JOHN**
Holy Franciscan Friar! Brother, ho!

WITHOUT TURNING, FRIAR LAURENCE RECOGNISES THE VOICE.

**FRIAR LAURENCE**
That sounds like the voice of Friar John.

**FRIAR LAURENCE**
This same should be the voice of Friar John.

FRIAR LAURENCE STANDS AND GREETS FRIAR JOHN WARMLY.

**FRIAR LAURENCE (CONT'D)**
Welcome back from Mantua. What does Romeo say? Or if he wrote a reply, give me his letter.

**FRIAR LAURENCE**
Welcome from Mantua! What says Romeo?
Or, if his mind be writ, give me his letter.

FRIAR JOHN LOOKS ANXIOUS.

**FRIAR JOHN**
I sought a fellow Franciscan monk to accompany me who was in the city visiting the sick. Upon finding him, the health officers in town, suspecting we'd both been in a house where the plague was rife, sealed up the doors and put us in quarantine. I couldn't get to Mantua.

**FRIAR JOHN**
Going to find a barefoot brother out,
One of our order, to associate me
Here in this city visiting the sick,
And finding him, the searchers of the town,
Suspecting that we both were in a house
Where the infectious pestilence did reign,
Sealed up the doors and would not let us forth,
So that my speed to Mantua there was stayed.

> Note: The plague was rife during Shakespeare's time. Theatres were closed for periods to help stop the spread of it, Shakespeare lost family and friends to it. It was a subject close to his heart he often referred to.

NOW IT IS FRIAR LAURENCE'S TURN TO LOOK ANXIOUS.

**FRIAR LAURENCE**

Who carried my letter to Romeo then?

**FRIAR JOHN**

I could not send it - here it is - nor could I get a messenger to return it to you, so fearful were they of infection.

**FRIAR LAURENCE**

Who bare my letter, then, to Romeo?

**FRIAR JOHN**

I could not send it, here it is again,
Nor get a messenger to bring it thee,
So fearful were they of infection.

---

*FRIAR LAURENCE IS WORRIED.*

---

**FRIAR LAURENCE**

What dreadful misfortune! By my holy order, that letter was not trivial, it contained instructions of great importance, and the failure to act on them may have grave consequences. Friar John, go quickly. Get me a crow-bar and bring it straight to my quarters.

**FRIAR JOHN**

Brother, I'll bring one straight to you.

**FRIAR LAURENCE**

Unhappy fortune! By my brotherhood,
The letter was not nice, but full of charge
Of dear import, and the neglecting it
May do much danger. Friar John, go hence;
Get me an iron crow and bring it straight
Unto my cell.

**FRIAR JOHN**

Brother, I'll go and bring it thee.

---

*FRIAR JOHN LEAVES.*

---

**FRIAR LAURENCE**

I must go to the tomb alone. Juliet will wake within the next three hours. She'll be very angry with me that Romeo has not been informed of events. I'll send another letter to Mantua,
*I'll keep her here till Romeo has come.*
*Poor living corpse, closed in a dead man's tomb!*

FRIAR LAURENCE

Now must I to the monument alone.
Within this three hours will fair Juliet wake;
She will beshrew me much that Romeo
Hath had no notice of these accidents.
But I will write again to Mantua,
*And keep her at my cell till Romeo come.*
*Poor living corse, closed in a dead man's tomb!*

# ACT V  SCENE III

## Graveyard of the Capulet's Tomb.  Wednesday night.

> *Note: There is speculation about which graveyard in Verona Shakespeare based his story on. You can even go and see the tomb she was laid in - according to the Verona tourist board that is. What is certain is that Shakespeare based his story on various sources, not from personal experience or from factual history. Even if the story has some element of truth it had become so distorted through the various versions handed down that it must be treated as a work of fiction.*

### COUNT PARIS

Give me your torch, boy. Go, keep a look out from a distance. On second thoughts, extinguish it first in case anyone sees. Lay with your ear to the ground under the yew tree there, and listen for the footsteps of anyone approaching. The soil is loose and soft from digging graves, you will hear them coming.  If you do, whistle to me. Give me those flowers. Go. Do as I told you.

### PARIS

Give me thy torch, boy. Hence, and stand aloof.
Yet put it out, for I would not be seen.
Under yond yew trees lay thee all along,
Holding thy ear close to the hollow ground;
So shall no foot upon the churchyard tread,
Being loose, unfirm, with digging up of graves,
But thou shalt hear it. Whistle then to me
As signal that thou hear'st something approach.
Give me those flowers. Do as I bid thee; go.

The Servant extinguishes the torch and hands the flowers to Count Paris who then leaves the Servant alone in darkness.

### SERVANT TO PARIS

(*aside*) I'm almost afraid to wait here alone in the graveyard, but I'll try to be brave.

### PAGE

[*Aside.*] I am almost afraid to stand alone
Here in the churchyard. Yet I will adventure.

The Servant lays his ear to the ground as Count Paris scatters flowers around the closed tomb where Juliet now lies.

### COUNT PARIS

*Sweet flower, with flowers your bridal bed I've*
*    strewn,*
*How sad your cover is of dust and stones!*
*Which every night I'll wash with sweet*
*    perfume,*
*Or failing that, with tears from all my moans.*
*My vigil for you, I shall nightly keep*
*By your grave with flowers and to weep.*

### PARIS

*Sweet flower, with flowers thy bridal bed I strew -*
*O woe, thy canopy is dust and stones! -*
*Which with sweet water nightly I will dew;*
*Or, wanting that, with tears distilled by moans.*
*The obsequies that I for thee will keep*
*Nightly shall be to strew thy grave and weep.*

> Note: It is not clear why Paris's visit should be in secret, especially as it is so soon after the funeral earlier that day. This visit may be purely a vehicle for him to have a confrontation with Romeo.

IN THE DISTANCE HIS SERVANT WHISTLES A WARNING.

### COUNT PARIS (CONT'D)

My boy warns me that someone's coming.
*What damnéd person this way tonight fares*
*To foil my rituals and my true love's prayers?*
What, and with a torch? I'll hide in the darkness awhile.

### PARIS

The boy gives warning something doth approach.
*What cursed foot wanders this way tonight*
*To cross my obsequies and true love's rite?*
What, with a torch? Muffle me, night, awhile.

PARIS RETIRES INTO THE DARKNESS TO OBSERVE.

ROMEO AND BALTHASAR ARRIVE AT THE TOMB WITH A TORCH, A PICKAXE
AND A CROWBAR.

### ROMEO

Give me that pickaxe and the crow-bar. Wait, take this letter. Make sure you deliver it to my father early tomorrow morning. Give me the torch. Upon your life, whatever you see or hear, I order you to stay away and do not interrupt me from what I came to do.

### ROMEO

Give me that mattock and the wrenching iron. Hold, take this letter; early in the morning See thou deliver it to my lord and father. Give me the light. Upon thy life I charge thee, Whate'er thou hear'st or seest, stand all aloof And do not interrupt me in my course.

BALTHASAR PASSES THE ITEMS TO ROMEO AND TAKES THE LETTER.

ROMEO (CONT'D)

The reason I'm descending into this bed of death is partly to gaze upon my lady's face, but mainly to take from her dead finger a precious ring, it is of the greatest importance I have this ring. Now, be gone. But if curiosity should get the better of you and you return to spy on me, by heaven, I will tear you limb from limb, and scatter your remains round this limb hungry graveyard. The late hour and my intentions make me wild and savage, fiercer and more raging than a pack of hungry tigers or a roaring sea.

ROMEO

Why I descend into this bed of death
Is partly to behold my lady's face,
But chiefly to take thence from her dead finger
A precious ring, a ring that I must use
In dear employment. Therefore hence, be gone;
But if thou jealous dost return to pry
In what I further shall intend to do,
By heaven, I will tear thee joint by joint,
And strew this hungry churchyard with thy limbs.
The time and my intents are savage-wild,
More fierce and more inexorable far
Than empty tigers or the roaring sea.

---

BALTHASAR IS FEARFUL OF ROMEO'S INTENTIONS AND HIS RAGE.

---

BALTHASAR

I shall go, sir, and not trouble you.

BALTHASAR

I will be gone, sir, and not trouble ye.

ROMEO

And in doing so you show me real friendship. Take this purse, live well and be prosperous, and farewell, my good fellow, Balthasar.

ROMEO

So shalt thou show me friendship. Take thou that.
Live and be prosperous; and farewell, good fellow.

---

ROMEO PASSES A PURSE OF MONEY.

BALTHASAR LEAVES. WHEN HE IS A SAFE DISTANCE AWAY HIS CONCERN GETS
THE BETTER OF HIM AND HE CONCEALS HIMSELF TO OBSERVE.

---

BALTHASAR

*(aside)*
*All the same, myself, I'll hide hereabout,*
*His looks I fear, and his intent I doubt.*

BALTHASAR

*[Aside.]*
*For all this same, I'll hide me hereabout;*
*His looks I fear, and his intents I doubt.*

---

ROMEO STARTS FORCING OPEN THE TOMB WITH THE TOOLS THEY HAD
BROUGHT, CURSING AS HE WORKS.

---

ROMEO

You detestable stomach, you belly full of death, gorged with the sweetest morsel on this earth, my Juliet. I will force your rotten jaws open, and to spite you I will cram you full of more food.

ROMEO

Thou detestable maw, thou womb of death,
Gorged with the dearest morsel of the earth,
Thus I enforce thy rotten jaws to open,
And in despite I'll cram thee with more food.

ROMEO MANAGES TO FORCE THE TOMB OPEN.

COUNT PARIS OBSERVES ALL THIS FROM HIS PLACE OF CONCEALMENT.

| COUNT PARIS | PARIS |
|---|---|
| (*aside*) It is that banished, 'high and mighty' Montague, the one who murdered my beloved's cousin - the grief of which caused my fair maiden's death – <br> *And now here he comes to do some vile harm* <br> *To the dead bodies. I have to stop him.* | This is that banished haughty Montague <br> That murdered my love's cousin - with which grief <br> It is supposed the fair creature died - <br> *And here is come to do some villainous shame* <br> *To the dead bodies. I will apprehend him.* |

COUNT PARIS APPROACHES ROMEO, DRAWING HIS SWORD.

| COUNT PARIS | PARIS |
|---|---|
| Stop your evil act, vile Montague! Can vengeance be pursued after death? <br> *Condemned, exiled villain, hereby do I* <br> *Arrest you, come with me, for you must die.* | Stop thy unhallowed toil, vile Montague! <br> Can vengeance be pursued further than death? <br> Condemned villain, I do apprehend thee. <br> Obey, and go with me, for thou must die. |
| ROMEO | ROMEO |
| I must indeed, that's why I came here. My good young man, do not challenge a desperate man. Flee, leave me. Think of these dead bodies, let them frighten you away. I beg you, youth, do not place another sin upon my head by forcing me to fight. Oh, go! By heaven, I wish you less harm than I do myself, for I have come here armed against myself. <br> *Be gone, stay alive, and hereafter say* <br> *A madman's mercy made you run away.* | I must indeed, and therefore came I hither. <br> Good gentle youth, tempt not a desp'rate man; <br> Fly hence and leave me. Think upon these gone; <br> Let them affright thee. I beseech thee, youth, <br> Put not another sin upon my head <br> By urging me to fury. O be gone! <br> By heaven, I love thee better than myself, <br> For I come hither armed against myself. <br> *Stay not, be gone; live, and hereafter say* <br> *A madman's mercy bid thee run away.* |

> Note: Here Romeo calls Paris a 'youth' twice. This may suggest he was that much older than Paris. He may also have been trying to show affection, as in his next speech he calls Paris, 'boy', which is an insult.

| COUNT PARIS | PARIS |
|---|---|
| I'll not listen to your pleading, I apprehend you for the criminal you are here and now. | I do defy thy conjuration, <br> And apprehend thee for a felon here. |

> Note: 'Conjuration' normally means a magic incantation or casting of a spell. A lesser usage of it was in the act of pleading for something earnestly, often on bended knee, which is the usage here.

ROMEO

Why do you provoke me? Then have it your way, boy!

ROMEO

Wilt thou provoke me? Then have at thee, boy!

---

ROMEO DRAWS HIS SWORD AND THEY FIGHT.

THE SERVANT TO PARIS SEES THIS FROM A DISTANCE.

---

SERVANT TO PARIS

Oh Lord, they're fighting! I must go and call the guards.

PAGE

O Lord, they fight! I will go call the Watch.

Note: In the 16<sup>th</sup> Century both England and Italy used privately funded watchmen as peace keepers and firemen. Equivalent to calling for the police today.

---

HE RUNS OFF TO GET HELP.

COUNT PARIS IS STRUCK A FATAL BLOW AND HE FALLS.

---

COUNT PARIS

Oh, I'm finished! If you have any mercy, open the tomb, lay me beside... Juliet.

PARIS

O, I am slain! If thou be merciful, Open the tomb, lay me with Juliet.

---

COUNT PARIS DIES. ROMEO LOOKS ON CONFUSED.

---

ROMEO

Out of respect I will. Let me see your face.

ROMEO

In faith I will. Let me peruse this face.

---

ROMEO TAKES THE TORCH TO EXAMINE HIS FOE.

---

ROMEO (CONT'D)

Mercutio's cousin, Count Paris! What did my servant say, when my storm-tossed mind was distracted as we rode here? I think he told me Paris was to marry Juliet. Did he say it? Or did I dream it? Or is it rage at hearing 'him' talk of Juliet that makes me think this?

ROMEO

Mercutio's kinsman, noble County Paris! What said my man when my betossed soul Did not attend him as we rode? I think He told me Paris should have married Juliet. Said he not so? Or did I dream it so? Or am I mad, hearing him talk of Juliet, To think it was so?

---

ROMEO OPENS THE GATE TO THE TOMB.

---

ROMEO (CONT'D)

Oh well, let me take your hand, a hand joined with mine in bitter misfortune.

ROMEO

O, give me thy hand, One writ with me in sour misfortune's book.

ROMEO LIFTS PARIS AND CARRIES HIM INSIDE THE TOMB.

| ROMEO (CONT'D) | ROMEO |
|---|---|
| I'll bury you in a glorious grave. A grave? Oh no! A beacon, my slaughtered young man. For here lies Juliet, and her beauty makes this vault like a king's banqueting hall, full of light. | I'll bury thee in a triumphant grave. A grave? O no! A lantern, slaughtered youth, For here lies Juliet, and her beauty makes This vault a feasting presence full of light. |

> Note: Romeo now calls him 'youth' again. No longer the disrespectful, 'boy'.
>
> A lantern was originally a turret with windows all the way around to both let in daylight and be visible from a distance when lit at night. Today we know it as a light that is hand carried which emits light all around.

ROMEO PLACES THE BODY OF PARIS NEXT TO JULIET.

| ROMEO (CONT'D) | ROMEO |
|---|---|
| Death, lie down here, buried by a dead man. | Death, lie thou there, by a dead man interred. |

NOW AGAIN WITH HIS JULIET, ROMEO FINDS AN INNER PEACE AT THE
THOUGHT OF SPENDING AN ETERNITY WITH HER.

| ROMEO (CONT'D) | ROMEO |
|---|---|
| Often men at the point of death feel elation! What nurses call a lightning before death. | How oft when men are at the point of death Have they been merry! Which their keepers call A lightning before death. |

> Note: There is a medically recognised phenomenon of a 'lightening', or clearing of the mental state in the hours before death, particularly in those delirious.

ROMEO LOOKS AT THE DARK VAULT.

| ROMEO (CONT'D) | ROMEO |
|---|---|
| Oh, how can I call this dark place a lightning? Oh, my love, my wife! Death, that has sucked the sweetness from your breath has no power over your beauty. You are not beaten yet, beauty still reigns in your crimson lips and cheeks, death's pale victory flag has yet to be raised there. | O how may I Call this a lightning? O my love! My wife! Death that hath sucked the honey of thy breath Hath had no power yet upon thy beauty. Thou art not conquered; beauty's ensign yet Is crimson in thy lips and in thy cheeks, And death's pale flag is not advanced there. |

---

ROMEO SEES THE BODY OF TYBALT.

---

ROMEO (CONT'D)

Tybalt, do you lie there wrapped in your bloody shroud? Oh, what greater favour can I do you, than with the hand that ended your young life, end the life of the one who was your enemy? Forgive me, cousin.

ROMEO

Tybalt, liest thou there in thy bloody sheet?
O, what more favour can I do to thee
Than with that hand that cut thy youth in twain
To sunder his that was thine enemy?
Forgive me, cousin.

Note: 'Cousin' meant any relative, which Romeo and Tybalt were by Romeo's marriage to Juliet.

---

HE LOOKS AT JULIET LYING THERE SO PEACEFULLY.

---

ROMEO (CONT'D)

Ah, dear Juliet, why do you still look so beautiful? Is it because death, though lacking physical presence, is amorous? And that bodiless, horrible monster keeps you in the dark here to be his mistress? To prevent that I will stay here with you forever, never again to leave this dismal palace of eternal night. I will remain here, right here, with worms for chambermaids. Right here I will set up my everlasting resting place and shake from this world-weary body the burden of ill-fated stars. Eyes, take your last look.

ROMEO

Ah, dear Juliet,
Why art thou yet so fair? Shall I believe
That unsubstantial death is amorous,
And that the lean abhorred monster keeps
Thee here in dark to be his paramour?
For fear of that I still will stay with thee,
And never from this palace of dim night
Depart again. Here, here will I remain
With worms that are thy chambermaids. O, here
Will I set up my everlasting rest
And shake the yoke of inauspicious stars
From this world-wearied flesh. Eyes, look your last;

Note: 'Set up my rest' - once again the popular expression from the card game 'Primero' meaning to make a final stand, to gamble everything.

---

ROMEO HUGS JULIET.

---

ROMEO (CONT'D)

Arms, take your last embrace. And lips, oh, you doors of life-giving breath, seal with an innocent kiss our eternal bond in all consuming death!

ROMEO

Arms, take your last embrace; And lips, O you
The doors of breath, seal with a righteous kiss
A dateless bargain to engrossing death.

---

HE KISSES JULIET AND TAKES OUT THE VIAL OF POISON.

---

| ROMEO (CONT'D) | ROMEO |
|---|---|
| Come, bitter conductor, come unsavoury guide, you desperate pilot, and now, this instant, run my seasick, weary body onto the dashing rocks! Here's to my love! | Come, bitter conduct, come, unsavoury guide, Thou desperate pilot, now at once run on The dashing rocks thy seasick weary bark! Here's to my love! |

> Note: Bark means boat. A pilot would guide a boat into a harbour which the ship's captain was not familiar with to avoid it running aground or hitting rocks. The 'bitter conductor' is a reference to Charon, the ferryman of Hades in Greek mythology, who carries souls of the newly deceased across the rivers Styx and Acheron that divide the world of the living from the world of the dead. In this case, Romeo is hoping the pilot guides his boat onto the rocks, thereby killing him and putting his soul with Juliet.

ROMEO OPENS THE VIAL AND DRINKS IT.

HE STRUGGLES FOR BREATH TO SPEAK.

| ROMEO (CONT'D) | ROMEO |
|---|---|
| Oh, chemist, you were right. Your poison is quick! So with a kiss I die. | O true apothecary, Thy drugs are quick! Thus with a kiss I die. |

ROMEO KISSES JULIET AND DIES.

OUTSIDE, FRIAR LAURENCE NEARS THE TOMB CARRYING A LANTERN, A CROWBAR AND A SPADE.

| FRIAR LAURENCE | FRIAR LAURENCE |
|---|---|
| St. Francis be my speedy protector! How often have my old feet stumbled over graves tonight! | Saint Francis be my speed! How oft tonight Have my old feet stumbled at graves! |

> Note: Stumbling was seen as a bad omen. If he hadn't stumbled he may have reached Romeo in time to save him. It was also said that if you stumbled as soon as you left home it was a sign of bad luck to follow.

BALTHASAR SEES THE FRIAR AND APPROACHES HIM, SURPRISING HIM.

| FRIAR LAURENCE (CONT'D) | FRIAR LAURENCE |
|---|---|
| Who's there? | Who's there? |

| BALTHASAR | BALTHASAR |
|---|---|
| Balthasar, a friend, one who knows you well. | Here's one a friend, and one that knows you well. |

### FRIAR LAURENCE

A blessing be upon you then! Tell me, my friend, why is a torch vainly lending its light to grubs and eyeless skulls over there? If I'm not mistaken it glows in the Capulet's tomb.

### FRIAR LAURENCE

Bliss be upon you. Tell me, good my friend, What torch is yond that vainly lends his light To grubs and eyeless skulls? As I discern, It burneth in the Capels' monument.

### BALTHASAR

It does, holy father, my master is there, one you are fond of.

### BALTHASAR

It doth so, holy sir, and there's my master, One that you love.

### FRIAR LAURENCE

Who is that?

### FRIAR LAURENCE

Who is it?

### BALTHASAR

Romeo.

### BALTHASAR

Romeo.

### FRIAR LAURENCE

How long has he been there?

### FRIAR LAURENCE

How long hath he been there?

### BALTHASAR

At least half an hour.

### BALTHASAR

Full half an hour.

### FRIAR LAURENCE

Come with me to the tomb.

### FRIAR LAURENCE

Go with me to the vault.

### BALTHASAR

I daren't, sir. My master thinks I have gone and he threatened me with death if I returned to see what his intentions were.

### BALTHASAR

I dare not, sir.
My master knows not but I am gone hence,
And fearfully did menace me with death
If I did stay to look on his intents.

### FRIAR LAURENCE

Stay here then. I'll go alone. I am afraid, very afraid something terrible has happened.

### FRIAR LAURENCE

Stay then, I'll go alone. Fear comes upon me;
O, much I fear some ill unthrifty thing.

### BALTHASAR

As I slept under this yew tree, I dreamt my master had a fight with someone, and my master killed him.

### BALTHASAR

As I did sleep under this yew tree here
I dreamt my master and another fought,
And that my master slew him.

### FRIAR LAURENCE

Romeo!

### FRIAR LAURENCE

Romeo!

---

FRIAR LAURENCE HOBBLES SPEEDILY TO THE TOMB.

FRIAR LAURENCE (CONT'D)

Oh no, oh no, what are these bloodstains at the entrance to the tomb? What is the meaning of these abandoned, bloodied swords, laying stained in this place of peace?

FRIAR LAURENCE

Alack, alack, what blood is this which stains
The stony entrance of this sepulchre?
What mean these masterless and gory swords
To lie discoloured by this place of peace?

FRIAR LAURENCE ENTERS THE TOMB.

HE SEES ROMEO LYING DEAD.

FRIAR LAURENCE (CONT'D)

Romeo! Oh, so pale! Who else? What, Paris too? And soaked in blood? Oh, what unholy hour is responsible for this desperate twist of fate.
The lady stirs.

FRIAR LAURENCE

Romeo! O, pale! Who else? What, Paris too?
And steeped in blood? Ah, what an unkind hour
Is guilty of this lamentable chance!
The lady stirs.

JULIET STARTS COMING ROUND.

SHE SEES THE FRIAR STANDING THERE BY HIS TORCHLIGHT.

JULIET

Oh, Father, my comfort and strength! Where is my husband? I remember this was the place I was to awaken, and here I am. But where is my Romeo?

JULIET

O comfortable Friar, where is my lord?
I do remember well where I should be,
And there I am. Where is my Romeo?

THEY HEAR A NOISE IN THE DISTANCE.

FRIAR LAURENCE

I hear a noise, Lady, come quickly from this nest of death, disease and eternal sleep. A power greater than we can challenge has thwarted our plans. Come, come away. Your husband, your true love, lies beside you dead, and Paris too. Come, I'll hide you in a sisterhood of holy nuns. Quickly, do not question me, for the guards are coming. Come, now, dearest Juliet, I daren't stay any longer.

FRIAR LAURENCE

I hear some noise. Lady, come from that nest
Of death, contagion, and unnatural sleep.
A greater power than we can contradict
Hath thwarted our intents. Come, come away;
Thy husband in thy bosom there lies dead,
And Paris too. Come, I'll dispose of thee
Among a sisterhood of holy nuns.
Stay not to question, for the Watch is coming.
Come, go, good Juliet; I dare no longer stay.

JULIET

You go, get away. I'll not leave.

JULIET

Go, get thee hence, for I will not away.

---

FRIAR LAURENCE HESITATES THEN TURNS AND HURRIES AWAY.

JULIET LOOKS AROUND TRYING TO UNDERSTAND WHAT HAS HAPPENED.

| JULIET (CONT'D) | JULIET |
|---|---|
| What's this? A vial, clasped in my true love's hand? | What's here? A cup, closed in my true love's hand? |

JULIET SNIFFS THE VIAL.

Note: The Chemist told Romeo to mix liquid with the poison. We must assume Romeo had mixed it before.

| JULIET (CONT'D) | JULIET |
|---|---|
| Poison, I see now, it brought about his untimely end. Oh, selfish man! You have drunk it all and left no welcoming drop for me to follow you. I will kiss your lips. Hopefully some poison still lingers on them to kill me with a restorative and restore me to you. | Poison, I see, hath been his timeless end. O churl, drunk all and left no friendly drop To help me after? I will kiss thy lips; Haply some poison yet doth hang on them To make me die with a restorative. |

SHE KISSES ROMEO TENDERLY.

| JULIET (CONT'D) | JULIET |
|---|---|
| Your lips are still warm. | Thy lips are warm. |

SHE HEARS VOICES IN THE DISTANCE.

| 1ST GUARD | 1ST WATCHMAN |
|---|---|
| (off) Lead on, boy. Which way? | [Within.] Lead, boy. Which way? |

| JULIET | JULIET |
|---|---|
| Oh, noise? I must be quick. | Yea, noise? Then I'll be brief. |

JULIET SEES ROMEO'S DAGGER.

| JULIET (CONT'D) | JULIET |
|---|---|
| Oh, Romeo, thank goodness, your dagger! | O happy dagger. |

JULIET DRAWS ROMEO'S DAGGER.

| JULIET (CONT'D) | JULIET |
|---|---|
| My body will be your sheath, | This is thy sheath. |

JULIET STABS HERSELF.

| JULIET (CONT'D) | JULIET |
|---|---|
| Rust there in me, and let me die. | There rust, and let me die. |

*Note: Some editions say 'Rest in me'. Rust seems the most appropriate as it suggests the knife will be there a long time in just one word.*

JULIET DIES, FALLING ACROSS THE BODY OF ROMEO.

THE SERVANT OF COUNT PARIS AND GUARDS ARRIVE.

| SERVANT TO PARIS | PAGE |
|---|---|
| This is the place. There, where the torch burns. | This is the place; there, where the torch doth burn. |

| 1ST GUARD | 1ST WATCHMAN |
|---|---|
| The ground is covered in blood. Search the graveyard. You men, go, arrest whoever you find. | The ground is bloody; search about the churchyard.<br>Go, some of you: whoe'er you find, attach. |

SOME OF THE GUARDS RUN OFF.

THE 1ST GUARD ENTERS THE TOMB FOLLOWED BY OTHER GUARDS.

| 1ST GUARD (CONT'D) | 1ST WATCHMAN |
|---|---|
| What a dreadful sight! The Count lies here slain! And Juliet bleeding, (*he feels for a pulse*) warm, and newly killed... but she has been buried two days, and Romeo lays here too! Go, tell the Prince. Run and tell the Capulets, and the Montagues. You others search around here. | Pitiful sight! Here lies the County slain;<br>And Juliet, bleeding, warm, and newly dead,<br>Who here hath lain this two days buried.<br>Go, tell the prince, run to the Capulets,<br>Raise up the Montagues. Some others search |

*Note: It's unclear why he should not mention Romeo. He calls for both the Capulets and the Montagues to be woken, and the Prince who is the relative of Paris. Romeo has been included in the translation for clarity.*

MORE GUARDS RUN OFF.

| 1ST GUARD (CONT'D) | 1ST WATCHMAN |
|---|---|
| We can see the ground where these pitiful bodies lie, but the true grounds for their actions we won't know until we've examined the evidence. | We see the ground whereon these woes do lie,<br>But the true ground of all these piteous woes<br>We cannot without circumstance decry. |

---

*Note: The 1ˢᵗ Guard has punned the word "ground".*

---

GUARDS RE-ENTER WITH BALTHASAR.

| | |
|---|---|
| **2ND GUARD**<br>Here's Romeo's errand boy. We found him hiding in the graveyard. | **2ND WATCHMAN**<br>Here's Romeo's man. We found him in the churchyard. |
| **1ST GUARD**<br>Hold him securely until the Prince gets here. | **1ST WATCHMAN**<br>Hold him in safety till the prince come hither. |

---

MORE GUARDS RE-ENTER WITH FRIAR LAURENCE.

| | |
|---|---|
| **3RD GUARD**<br>Here's a holy man, he trembles, sighs and weeps. We took this crow-bar and spade from him as he was coming out the side entrance of the graveyard. | **3RD WATCHMAN**<br>Here is a friar that trembles, sighs, and weeps. We took this mattock and this spade from him As he was coming from this churchyard's side. |
| **1ST GUARD**<br>Very suspicious! Hold the holy man too. | **1ST WATCHMAN**<br>A great suspicion; stay the friar too. |

---

PRINCE ESCALUS ARRIVES WITH ATTENDANTS.

| | |
|---|---|
| **PRINCE ESCALUS**<br>What terrible thing has happened that we have been disturbed from our rest so early? | **PRINCE**<br>What misadventure is so early up, That calls our person from our morning rest? |

---

OLD CAPULET AND LADY CAPULET RUSH IN WITH SERVANTS.

| | |
|---|---|
| **OLD CAPULET**<br>What is it that everyone is shouting about so loudly? | **CAPULET**<br>What should it be that is so shrieked abroad? |
| **LADY CAPULET**<br>Oh, the people in the street cry 'Romeo', or 'Juliet', and others cry 'Paris', and they all run shouting towards our family tomb. | **LADY CAPULET**<br>O, the people in the street cry `Romeo', Some `Juliet', and some `Paris', and all run With open outcry toward our monument. |
| **PRINCE ESCALUS**<br>What has so shocked everyone that they disturb our ears? | **PRINCE**<br>What fear is this which startles in our ears? |

1ˢᵀ GUARD

Your highness, here lies the Count Paris, slain, and Romeo dead, and Juliet who died the other day, still warm and newly killed.

PRINCE ESCALUS

Search, investigate, find out how this foul murder came about.

1ˢᵀ GUARD

Here is a holy man, and the errand boy of the slaughtered Romeo, with tools on them suitable for opening these dead men's tombs.

OLD CAPULET

Oh heavens! Oh wife, see how our daughter bleeds! The dagger is misplaced, for look, its place in the back of that Montague is empty, instead it is wrongly sheathed in my daughter's bosom.

1ˢᵀ WATCHMAN

Sovereign, here lies the County Paris slain, And Romeo dead, and Juliet, dead before, Warm and new killed.

PRINCE

Search, seek, and know how this foul murder comes.

1ˢᵀ WATCHMAN

Here is a friar, and slaughtered Romeo's man, With instruments upon them fit to open These dead men's tombs.

CAPULET

O heavens! O wife, look how our daughter bleeds!
This dagger hath mista'en, for lo, his house Is empty on the back of Montague, And it missheathed in my daughter's bosom.

> Note: Some editions use "is sheathed" instead of "missheathed".

LADY CAPULET

Oh my! This sight of death is like a bell summoning me to an early grave.

LADY CAPULET

O me! This sight of death is as a bell That warns my old age to a sepulchre.

---

OLD MONTAGUE ARRIVES WITH SERVANTS.

---

PRINCE ESCALUS

Come in, Montague. You've been woken up early to see your son and heir early down to sleep.

PRINCE

Come, Montague, for thou art early up To see thy son and heir more early down.

> Note: Word play on early and up and down.

OLD MONTAGUE

Alas, your Highness, my wife died tonight. The grief of my son's exile took her last breath. What further sorrow awaits my aged body?

MONTAGUE

Alas, my liege, my wife is dead tonight; Grief of my son's exile hath stopped her breath. What further woe conspires against mine age?

PRINCE ESCALUS

Look, and you shall see.

PRINCE

Look, and thou shalt see.

OLD MONTAGUE RUSHES TO ROMEO'S DEAD BODY.

### OLD MONTAGUE
Oh, ignorant boy, what manners is this to push in front of your father to the grave?

### MONTAGUE
O thou untaught! What manners is in this,
To press before thy father to a grave?

### PRINCE ESCALUS
Stop these cries of anguish for now, till we can clear up the uncertainties, find their cause, their reason, and the true sequence of events. Then I'll lead you in your mourning, and possibly to your death too. For now be strong, let patience rule us in this misfortune. Bring the suspicious parties forward.

### PRINCE
Seal up the mouth of outrage for a while,
Till we can clear these ambiguities
And know their spring, their head, their true
   descent;
And then will I be general of your woes,
And lead you even to death. Meantime forbear,
And let mischance be slave to patience.
Bring forth the parties of suspicion.

> Note: Prince Escalus plays on the image of a stream, with spring, head and descent (flow of water).

### FRIAR LAURENCE
I am the key suspect. Although least able to do harm I am most suspected, as the time and place of this dreadful murder weigh heavily against me. Here I stand, both to accuse and excuse myself. I myself being both judge and jury.

### FRIAR LAURENCE
I am the greatest, able to do least,
Yet most suspected, as the time and place
Doth make against me, of this direful murder;
And here I stand, both to impeach and purge
Myself condemned and myself excused.

### PRINCE ESCALUS
Then tell us at once all you know about this.

### PRINCE
Then say at once what thou dost know in this.

### FRIAR LAURENCE
I will be brief, because the short time I have left on this earth is not so long as this sad tale. Romeo, who lies there dead, was the husband of Juliet, and she, also there dead, was Romeo's faithful wife. I married them, and their secret wedding day was also Tybalt's last. His untimely death banished the newly-wed bridegroom from this city. It was for him, and not Tybalt, that Juliet pined.

### FRIAR LAURENCE
I will be brief, for my short date of breath
Is not so long as is a tedious tale.
Romeo, there dead, was husband to that Juliet;
And she, there dead, that Romeo's faithful wife.
I married them; and their stol'n marriage day
Was Tybalt's doomsday, whose untimely death
Banished the new-made bridegroom from this
   city;
For whom, and not for Tybalt, Juliet pined.

FRIAR LAURENCE TURNS TO OLD CAPULET ACCUSINGLY.

### FRIAR LAURENCE (CONT'D)

You, Capulet, to remove the sea of grief from her, promised, by force, her hand in marriage to Count Paris. She then came to me, and with wild looks asked me to devise some way to save her from this second marriage or she would kill herself there and then in my quarters. Then I gave her, as I am trained in medicine, a sleeping potion, which took effect as I had intended, for it brought upon her the appearance of death. Meanwhile, I wrote to Romeo telling him to be here on this dire night - as this was the time the potions power would cease - to help take her from her temporary grave.

### FRIAR LAURENCE

You, to remove that siege of grief from her,
Betrothed and would have married her perforce
To County Paris. Then comes she to me,
And with wild looks bid me devise some mean
To rid her from this second marriage,
Or in my cell there would she kill herself.
Then gave I her - so tutored by my art -
A sleeping potion, which so took effect
As I intended, for it wrought on her
The form of death. Meantime I writ to Romeo
That he should hither come as this dire night
To help to take her from her borrowed grave,
Being the time the potion's force should cease.

---

GASPS FROM EVERYONE.

---

### FRIAR LAURENCE (CONT'D)

But, Friar John, who carried my letter, was accidently held up and last night returned my letter to me. Then all alone, at the pre-arranged hour of her waking, I came to take her from her family vault, meaning to keep her secretly at my quarters until I could notify Romeo. But when I arrived some minutes before the time of her awakening, I found noble Paris and faithful Romeo laying here in untimely death. She awoke, and I pleaded with her to come with me and suffer this work of heaven with patience. But then a noise outside scared me away, and she, too distressed to follow, would not go with me, but, as it seems, took her own life. As to the marriage, her Nurse is privy to the secret. This is what I know, and if any of this misfortune is my fault, then let my old life be sacrificed before it's due time, by the punishment of the severest law.

### FRIAR LAURENCE

But he which bore my letter, Friar John,
Was stayed by accident, and yesternight
Returned my letter back. Then all alone
At the prefixed hour of her waking
Came I to take her from her kindred's vault,
Meaning to keep her closely at my cell
Till I conveniently could send to Romeo.
But when I came, some minute ere the time
Of her awakening, here untimely lay
The noble Paris and true Romeo dead.
She wakes; and I entreated her come forth
And bear this work of heaven with patience;
But then a noise did scare me from the tomb,
And she, too desperate, would not go with me,
But, as it seems, did violence on herself.
All this I know, and to the marriage
Her Nurse is privy; and if aught in this
Miscarried by my fault, let my old life
Be sacrificed some hour before his time
Unto the rigour of severest law.

PRINCE ESCALUS

Despite all this, we have always known you as a devout holy man. Where's Romeo's errand boy? What does he have to say?

PRINCE

We still have known thee for a holy man. Where's Romeo's man? What can he say to this?

---

BALTHASAR STEPS FORWARD.

---

BALTHASAR

I brought my master news of Juliet's death, and then in great haste he came from Mantua to this place, to this tomb. He asked me to give this letter to his father early tomorrow, and as he entered the tomb he threatened me with death if I did not go and leave him there undisturbed.

BALTHASAR

I brought my master news of Juliet's death,
And then in post he came from Mantua
To this same place, to this same monument.
This letter he early bid me give his father,
And threatened me with death, going in the vault,
If I departed not and left him there.

PRINCE ESCALUS

Give me the letter, I'll read it. Where is the Count's boy who notified the guards?

PRINCE

Give me the letter, I will look on it.
Where is the County's page that raised the Watch?

---

THE SERVANT STEPS FORWARD.

---

PRINCE ESCALUS (CONT'D)

Boy, what was your master doing in this place?

PRINCE

Sirrah, what made your master in this place?

SERVANT TO PARIS

He came to lay flowers on his lady's grave, and he ordered me to stand guard, which I did. Then someone came with a torch to open the tomb, and at once my master challenged him. Then I ran away and called the guards.

PAGE

He came with flowers to strew his lady's grave,
And bid me stand aloof, and so I did.
Anon comes one with light to ope the tomb,
And by and by my master drew on him;
And then I ran away to call the Watch.

---

PRINCE ESCALUS READS THE LETTER.

---

PRINCE ESCALUS

This letter confirms the holy Father's words... the course of their love... the news of her death... And here he writes that he bought some poison from a destitute chemist, and with it he came to the tomb to die and lie with Juliet.

PRINCE

This letter doth make good the Friar's words, Their course of love, the tidings of her death; And here he writes that he did buy a poison Of a poor 'pothecary, and therewithal Came to this vault to die and lie with Juliet.

PRINCE ESCALUS LOOKS ACCUSINGLY AT THOSE GATHERED.

PRINCE ESCALUS (CONT'D)

Where are these enemies, Capulet and Montague?

PRINCE

Where be these enemies? Capulet, Montague,

CAPULET AND MONTAGUE STEP FORWARD. ESCALUS ADDRESSES THEM.

PRINCE ESCALUS (CONT'D)

See how great your hatred is, that the heavens see fit to punish you by means of killing the sole joys in your life by love. And I, for turning a blind eye to your squabbles, have lost two relatives. We are all punished.

PRINCE

See what a scourge is laid upon your hate, That heaven finds means to kill your joys with love; And I, for winking at your discords too, Have lost a brace of kinsmen. All are punished.

CAPULET TURNS TO MONTAGUE.

OLD CAPULET

Oh, brother Montague, give me your hand in friendship. This is my daughter's wedding gift. I can ask for nothing more.

CAPULET

O brother Montague, give me thy hand. This is my daughter's jointure, for no more Can I demand.

OLD MONTAGUE

But I can give you more, Capulet. I will build a statue of her in solid gold, and all the while Verona stands,
*There'll be no statue of higher worth set*
*Than the one of true, faithful Juliet.*

MONTAGUE

But I can give thee more,
For I will raise her statue in pure gold,
That whiles Verona by that name is known,
*There shall no figure at such rate be set*
*As that of true and faithful Juliet.*

OLD CAPULET

*As grand shall stand Romeo's by his lady's*
  *side,*
*Poor victims both of our family feud.*

CAPULET

*As rich shall Romeo's by his lady's lie,*
*Poor sacrifices of our enmity.*

PRINCE ESCALUS

*A sad gloomy peace this morning it brings,*
*The sun out of sorrow will close its eyes*
*Go now, for more talks of these wretched*
*    things.*
*Some shall be pardoned and some I'll chastise,*
*For never was a tale of greater woe*
*Than this of Juliet and her Romeo.*

PRINCE

*A glooming peace this morning with it brings;*
*The sun for sorrow will not show his head.*
*Go hence, to have more talk of these sad things.*
*Some shall be pardoned, and some punished;*
*For never was a story of more woe*
*Than this of Juliet and her Romeo.*

# THE END

Made in the USA
Coppell, TX
08 April 2021